THE PARIS CORRESPONDENT

THE
PARIS
CORRESPONDENT

Alan S. Cowell

OVERLOOK DUCKWORTH
NEW YORK • LONDON

This edition first published in paperback in the United States and the UK in 2013 by
Overlook Duckworth, Peter Mayer Publishers, Inc.

NEW YORK:
141 Wooster Street
New York, NY 10012
www.overlookpress.com
For bulk and special sales, please contact sales@overlookny.com,
or write us at the above address

LONDON:
Gerald Duckworth & Co. Ltd.
30 Calvin Street
London E1 6NW
info@duckworth-publishers.co.uk
www.ducknet.co.uk

Copyright © 2011 by Alan S. Cowell

Cataloging-in-Publication Data is available from the Library of Congress

Book design and type formatting by Bernard Schleifer
Manufactured in the United States of America

2 4 6 8 10 9 7 5 3 1

ISBN 978-1-4683-0062-8 (US)
ISBN 978-0-7156-4148-4 (UK)

*To the memory of
Gérard de Nerval*

AUTHOR'S NOTE

This work of fiction makes no secret of its debt to Reynolds Packard's novel, *The Kansas City Milkman*, republished many decades ago as *Dateline Paris*—a study of journalism, love and liquor in a turbulent era of war and mischief.

As the Internet propels the news business into uncharted territory, my book is a tribute to Packard's—in the parlance of the trade, a nulede with updates.

WHAT DID BOGART SAY?

"We'll always have Paris."

Everyone had Paris, *their* Paris.

Maybe that was why people like Joe Shelby fetched up here, scouring the sidewalks for second chances, new starts; heading into the oldest trap of all in a city where everyone had a dream, a chimera, a star-struck, eternal nanosecond when the world fell away and you balanced on the slender axis of love, adrift in a galaxy of endless possibilities.

Paris was like one big, romantic harbor of lost souls just waiting to be reunited with their peripatetic owners.

One night in Paris, the song said, is like a year in any other place.

One night in Paris . . .

Of course, it was all hooey.

People have written long, abstruse essays to explain that the Eiffel Tower is not simply a chunk of iron beams and rivets but a statement, a conundrum, a point of reference, both viewed and viewpoint, integral to the skyline yet a platform from which to observe the same vista.

It soars. It endures, like Paris itself—the bridges, Notre Dame, the river, the artists of Montmartre, the lewd fare of the Pigalle, the sphinxlike riddles of a city where your heart soars or splinters, where you seek your literary tryst with Baudelaire and Balzac and Nerval and resynchronize your mental and emotional clock to decades, centuries gone by and start scribbling rambling sentences like this one in expensive purpose-bought notebooks made famous by great writers.

Then, just as you think you will recover some vital essence mislaid in the bustle of youth, you bump into a pickpocket on the

Métro. And you discover that what really disappeared was your Amex card.

Maybe, as his universe shattered and reformed into unfamiliar constellations, Joe Shelby was looking for some kind of Truth, some guiding star—*l'Étoile.*

And maybe, of course, I should have recognized the warning signs and steered clear.

What else did Bogart say?

"Of all the gin joints, in all the towns, in all the world, he walked into mine."

Or something like that.

Part One

WARILY, WATCHFULLY, POINT ON PATROL IN HOSTILE TERRAIN, JOE Shelby surveyed the newsroom of the *Paris Star*—the stained carpeting and exposed air-conditioner ducts; the battered, battleship-gray paintwork of his new professional home, his Valhalla.

He walked with a cane made of ebony, its handle fashioned of yellowing ivory from some distant age when laws did nothing to protect the elephant. His gait seemed slightly lopsided, crabbed. The years had whittled him, made him skinnier, in the spindleshank manner of aging rock stars. His hallmark black linen jacket hung slightly from his shoulders. I couldn't help thinking that, when our backs were turned, our enemies (and there were ever more of them) would draw sniggering comparisons to Jack Lemmon and Walter Matthau, somewhere between *The Front Page* and *Grumpy Old Men*, dinosaurs let loose for a final lumber around the news paddock they had once galloped as stallions.

When they joked about endangered species, they wouldn't be talking about the creature that provided the handle on Shelby's cane.

In the old print days, I had edited his telexed dispatches as they winged in from N'Djamena and Kinshasa, Beirut and Grozny. There had been times when I took dictation from him over the phone from Gaza or Soweto or Saigon to the background drumbeat of gunfire. As he declaimed his stories, using his peculiar phonetic orthography, you could almost smell the cordite and hear the boom-boom. "No, you dummy, *P* for Peter, *H* for Harry, *U* for Uncle . . . the girl's name was Phúc . . ."

Now, at the perilous, uncharted intersection of the digital, Internet, warp-speed web era and our own middle years, we had been assigned to run Nonstop News, a distant outpost of the *Graphic,* a font of news for its website and sometimes its hallowed pages, a digital acolyte for New York and the *Paris Star.* We worked the hours when the mother ship in New York was dark, straddling the razor edge, the front line, the first, crepuscular flush of the digital dawn. Our unit—the Nonstop News Desk, usually abbreviated to NND—was located in Paris to take advantage of the time zone six hours ahead of New York. Our mission was to keep the websites of both papers up to speed, even as Gotham City snoozed in fitful slumber.

If you looked at the site at 2 a.m. or 5 a.m. on the eastern seaboard of America, you would see the telltale marks of our presence—tiny, spidery notations in red that denoted our updating and reworking and rejiggering of the news as it happened: three minutes ago, posted 03.33 a.m., updated one minute ago, NEWS ALERT.

Just like in the old wire service days, we would bat out ledes and bulletins, snaps and urgents.

Whambo-zambo-zippo.

I was not sure if either of us—let alone our employers—understood fully what we were getting ourselves into.

"Hello, sweetheart, gimme rewrite."

"Clancy! Ed Clancy! Jesus!"

Shelby looked me up and down as if I had failed to pass muster at some inscrutable parade, then took my outstretched hand and shook it, stooping from his great shambling height to grab me in a bear hug. For all his uncertain health, he was still a powerful guy. I found myself looking up at those familiar, aquiline features once likened (by himself, primarily) to Hollywood's best—the long crooked nose and hooded eyes offset now by the dark concentric rings of tired flesh below them. The onetime mop of curly brown hair had turned pan-scrub gray, verging on silver. The tropical suns of Africa, Asia, and the Middle East had tanned his skin to a texture of cracked leather and a hue of bleached gold.

He eased himself in behind a steel desk, propping his cane

against a chipped and slightly unsteady file cabinet. I had somehow prevented the cost-cutters of the IT staff from confiscating his desktop computer when they learned he owned a laptop, but by way of compensation, they had removed the printer that went with the desktop. I would not, in fact, have been surprised to find them measuring his workspace to see if it could be trimmed to size, like undertakers eyeing a sickly patient for a cut-price coffin and a pauper's grave.

"So how's this going to work?"

"I ping you."

"You ping me? You—*ping*—me?"

He repeated the words slowly and with puzzlement, as if trying to decipher an obscure and difficult text.

"Ping. Instant messaging. I write a message over there"—I gestured to my desk across the early-morning newsroom, becalmed before the deadline panic that would overtake it later—"and I press a button and it pops up here."

"Couldn't you just call? Or walk over?"

"No. These days, we ping."

"Ping?"

"It's the sound it makes when it lands. Ping."

"And I Pong?"

"Okay, okay, ha, ha. So I ping you and say, 'Riots in Mongolia. Five dead.'"

He was about to light a cigarette before I stopped him: company policy, French law, universal edict. Smoking bad, longevity good.

"And I do what? Call their next of kin? Jump on a plane? Hold the front page?"

"You call the Mongolia bureau and say, 'Five dead?'"

"Do you we have a Mongolia bureau?"

"No."

"So I call . . . ?"

"Beijing. Hong Kong. Someplace in Asia."

"So how do you know there are five dead in Mongolia riots?"

"I read the news wires."

"So I call up someplace in Asia where they also read the wires and may indeed already have determined that the rioting in Ulan Bator has been inconsequential, and I say, 'Five dead in Mongolia. Gimme three hundred.'"

"No. You say, 'Is this true and who says so and who can I quote?'"

"And then I ping you?"

"No. You give me three hundred and then you ping me and then I put it on the web."

"Whambo-zambo."

"Whambo-zambo."

"Do you remember the days—" he began.

"Don't go there," I muttered, almost begging.

"—when we were *real* journalists?"

"Are there really riots in Mongolia?"

"Actually, no. But there are flash floods in Kyrgyzstan." Even to my own ears, I sounded overeager. "Near the American base."

"You don't say. Do we care?"

"We care."

"Because?"

"Because news is nonstop. An actuality loop. Because the goat must be fed."

"Who's that?"

A predatory flicker stirred in Shelby's baleful green eyes—a warning sign I recalled from the old days when he and the Africa rat pack transited Paris from Nairobi en route to N'Djamena and raised hell at La Coupole and the George Cinq.

I followed his gaze across the deserted newsroom to the copy-desk, where the powers-that-be always insisted that an editor start early to turn around the columns and the artsy stuff.

"That," I said, "is the executive editor's squeeze. Rumored squeeze, maybe I should say. Gloria Beeching."

"You know, I believe I met her someplace—Bucharest. East Berlin. Sarajevo. The Wall."

He was already sucking in his gut and dripping Visine eye drops to banish the early-morning bloodshot.

As surreptitiously as was possible in a large and empty space, I looked across at her, trying to see her through Shelby's eyes. The Gloria I encountered most days was part of the ambience of the newsroom. But seeing her now through Shelby's eyes, she made quite an impression: my thesaurus of tired metaphors came up with swan-from-cygnet, butterfly-from-chrysalis—that kind of thing. She sat straight-backed, her luxuriant chestnut curls tied up in a loose bun that showed off the pale curve of her neck. Her posture accentuated the lines of her torso. She glanced in my direction, but her hazel eyes fell on Shelby. She smiled. I grimaced.

"How many 'don't go theres' do I have to spell out for you?"

"Whambo-zambo," he said enthusiastically. "Ping-Pong."

On Day One of operations at Nonstop News–Paris Outpost (the Paree OP, as Shelby liked to call it from his time covering the Marines), Marcel Duffie, the executive editor of the *Star*, rolled in fashionably late—just to remind everyone else that the hours of toil allocated to the hoi polloi did not apply to him. He was a short, pudgy man, with slightly bulging dark eyes and a smear of black hair across his shiny, cue ball skull. His hands were unusually pale and small, and they reminded me of the claws of a vole, designed to scrabble through dirt toward invisible light. It was unwise, though, to underestimate Marcel Duffie. As a practitioner of the political maneuver, the deft jab of the stiletto, he was peerless. He harvested snippets of information the way a good quartermaster stores ammo for the big battle, the overwhelming barrage, the shock and awe. The only door he left open to his enemies was the exit.

Duffie did not like intrusions into his scheme of things, and Shelby was the worst kind of interloper, which made me his accomplice, his abettor.

Usually, his first port of call was the copy desk on those days when Gloria Beeching had been assigned the early shift, sitting rapt in front of her screen, arching her back with artful languor as she crossed *i*'s and dotted *t*'s in the silence of computerized editing.

In newsrooms of yore—and still on period-movie sets—there had been the rattle of typewriter keys and the ring of a bell as the carriage reached the end of its travel and was slammed back to start a new line with the abrupt ferocity of a train wreck. There had been muttered curses and vicious metal spikes skewering palimpsests of discarded copy paper and service messages. There had been ashtrays and clerks scurrying hither and thither, pneumatic tubes whizzing metal containers stuffed with folded pieces of paper from copyeditors to typesetters in the Linotype room. There had been the loud chorus of news arriving on long-forgotten machines as the world trembled on the brink of history.

Snap—coup in Nigeria! Bulletin—Saigon falls!

Modern newsrooms were quiet as the grave, a particularly apt simile for our industry. We communed in the dark interstices of cyberspace. We could announce World War Three in a whisper. (In a way, as it turned out, we did.)

I kept an old metal spike on my desk just to remind myself that the *Star* had once been a buzzy, paper-strewn place where you breathed ink and felt the floor rumble under your feet when the presses started to roll, like a quake-zone aftershock.

But Duffie was not perambulating down memory lane because he was not really old enough—or perhaps he was just too smart—to have acquired a history to call his own. In any event, he had other things on his mind, as he invariably did when he approached Gloria Beeching. Ostensibly, his route led to the water cooler, but as he passed her, he glanced toward her and, as if synchronized by nature's oldest chronograph, she paused in her editing and stretched, her eyes roaming around the newsroom until their glances crossed—a coded, silent semaphore so swift that you'd have missed the moment if you weren't on the lookout for it.

On Day One of NND, he got halfway toward the copydesk, strolling with the nonchalance of a boulevardier confident that his faithful paramour waited at the next pavement café. And then he came to a confused halt.

Gloria was not alone.

Abandoning his cane, Shelby had sidled over to remind her that they met in Bucharest or Berlin or Bangui or wherever. He had clipped his new *Star* credential onto the loop of 'Nam-era webbing around his neck that carried his smorgasbord of identities, some of them slightly, even ludicrously, out of date—NYPD, ISFOR, KFOR, ISAF, IDF, INA, NATO, NYG—some no more than faded hiero-glyphics in Cyrillic script, Arabic, Hebrew, Pashto, Mandarin, Hindi.

"Your best is on your chest," I heard her murmur, curling her fingers through his bandolier of laminated photo IDs and tugging him gently toward her.

Emboldened, he was regaling her with war stories that seemed to be having the desired effect of making her laugh.

"So the second pigeon carried a message saying, 'This bird is accompanying the bird that's got the story.' And that's what got them so confused in Bulawayo. Because the bird with the story had headed out to Botswana!"

I had heard Shelby's punch lines a thousand times. They never got any better but he spun his yarns with such feeling that most people laughed just to humor him. Gloria Beeching seemed genuinely amused. Marcel Duffie did not seem to get the joke at all.

"Shelby!" He grunted at me as he retreated past my door to his big corner office. "Always was an asshole."

"But now he's our asshole," I said, sounding helpful, I thought.

"If he survives here a month, it'll be a month too long."

"And I guess you'll make it your business to make sure he doesn't."

"Count on it, Clancy. Him and you both. Jeez. This place needs some new blood. Wasn't there something with him about a leave of absence, therapy, stress disorder? Breakdown? Burnout?"

"Not to my knowledge," I said.

At that moment, I was almost telling the truth.

Across the newsroom, Gloria Beeching chuckled merrily as Shelby pirated someone else's anecdote to tell her: "And if your mom asks what you do for a living in Paris, honey, don't tell her you work for a newspaper. Tell her you play the piano in a whorehouse."

CHAPTER TWO

LOOKING BACK, IT MAY WELL BE THAT THE SEEDS OF OUR SUBSEQUENT travails were sown in what came to be known to a very narrow circle of initiates as the Argentine Soy Vote Affair.

For me, I guess, it was a warning signal that, whatever had happened to Shelby between his last assignment as a freewheeling war correspondent and his arrival in Paris, something had changed, perhaps in his perception of reality, or maybe just in his relationship with the truth.

The *Star* newsroom was like any other community of individuals, jostling for advantage, kudos, power. But Shelby had spent too much time alone, or with just a few friendly colleagues, roaming the front lines and the bush hotels and the five-star, end-of-story retreats, to have become embroiled in the battles that enliven newsrooms from Houston to Hong Kong. Looking at him, I sometimes thought of an exquisite beast astray from the cover of its native habitat, blinking into the light, threatened but naïvely indifferent to the gathering predators, the snares, the line of hunters awaiting the beaters' advance.

And other times I just thought of him as an old hack who should have known better.

The Argentine Soy Vote Affair began on the far side of the globe. In Buenos Aires, the Argentine Senate was debating whether to lower taxes on exports of soya beans. Big deal, I guess, would be most people's reaction, but the vote was crucial to the survival of a government that had won influential backing in Washington. The time difference was not in our favor. B.A. was six hours behind us, and the interminable senatorial debate was unfolding in the middle of the Argentine night.

The *Graphic*'s South America correspondent, for reasons that remain opaque, was in Rio—nice place, wrong country—and had anyhow gone to bed exhausted. We were relying on a stringer called Rosaria to call in when the vote came through: If the soy measure was approved, the government survived. If it was voted down, the government fell.

Finally, the phone rang.

Shelby grunted.

"You sure, Rosaria?"

There was a pause while he scribbled figures on a yellow legal pad: 305–304.

"So the soy law was rejected."

He scribbled again.

"And the government falls."

He listened.

"You were there in the Senate? You counted? You sure?"

While they were talking, I was scanning the news agency wires. They had nothing. I checked other websites.

"Looks like we got a scoop here," I said.

"Who the hell is Rosaria?"

"Stringer. Solid."

"Whambo-zambo," he said as his tanned, slender fingers began to dance across the keyboard of his computer terminal.

"What you writing this in?"

"Personal basket. Private queue. Just till we get confo from the wires. Then I'll shift it over to some other queue to post. Ping-Pong."

He wrote on. Hit buttons. Pressed Save.

"Checked dummy tags?"

"What?"

"Dummy tags. In the editing program. There's a command: Clean Up Dummy Tags."

"What the hell are dummy tags?"

"Damned if I know. Something technical, beyond knowing. Like phantom pings."

"Phantom pings? Did you just say phantom pings?"

"Yeah. When your computer makes a sound like an incoming instant message—ping!—but there's nothing there."

"Whatever next?"

Shelby tapped a key.

"Well, whatever they are, the dummy tag pings are all cleaned up."

I leaned over his shoulder, clicked onto the *Graphic* website, and got something of a surprise. A major, unpleasant surprise. The kind that gives you a churning in your stomach when you know something has gone very wrong and will come back to bite you in the ass, injecting pure venom with no known antidote.

In faraway New York, the overnight web producer had been busy. There was Shelby's story: Buenos Aires dateline, double byline, Rosaria and Shelby.

And the headline: "Government Falls on Soy Vote."

Except that it didn't.

The news wires tipped us first.

By a narrow margin of 305–304 votes, the Argentine Senate approved controversial legislation on soya export tariffs, averting a government collapse.   —Reuters

Argentine government wins key ballot.   —The Associated Press

The phone rang and I heard Shelby speaking to Rosaria.

"What do you mean you got it the wrong way round?"

Then I had a question. "How did it get posted if it was in your personal basket?" I asked Shelby. "That is technologically impossible."

"Oh, shit," he said, looking at his screen. "I guess it was in the wrong queue."

"You guess? We are leading the *Graphic* website with a totally one-hundred-eighty-degree-wrong story, and you guess?"

"Must have been the dummy tags."

On the keyboard, his magic fingers were whirring again, and his voice was pitched so low that I thought he was talking to himself.

"Take a smoke break, Ed. I mean, if you don't want to have to say you knew anything about this, take a smoke break. You dummy. Dummy tags! Phantom pings! Phantom votes!"

I took the elevator down to the exit level.

It was one of those mornings when the Parisians linger in the sunlight over their cigarettes. All along the street outside the Star's offices, knots of wage slaves congregated on sidewalks washed clean each morning by men with brooms made of twigs whose long use had curved them to resemble the Grim Reaper's scythe—ominous portents after the Argentine soy vote debacle.

Even after all my time in Paris, it still amazed me that, just after dawn, some mysterious system of valves and stopcocks pumped water from the Seine into the gutters, flushing cigarette butts and other detritus into the sewers below. I imagined this noisome flow pouring along cobbled tunnels beneath the streets we strolled every day, ignorant of what ran below, debouching at some stage into the great river, seeding it with nicotine-stained filters and shreds of unburned, biodegradable tobacco. It was a thought that rarely distracted me from drawing the deep, hasty drags of the committed nicotine addict in hurried respite from the smoke-free zones of modern humanity, then flipping the used and exhausted butt into those selfsame gutters, sure in the knowledge that, come morning, every trace of my carcinogenic indulgence would be flushed away and later churned and shredded by the propellers of the *bateaux-mouches* with their cargoes of tourists rubbernecking at Notre Dame.

At sidewalk level, there had been a time when the pages of the *Paris Star* were displayed in a series of glass showcases whose maintenance was entrusted to a salaried French worker with full pension rights. Now, though, that display—and the employee—had been replaced by a single flat-screen electronic display showing the home page of the *Graphic* website. I stared at it balefully. Despite all the evidence from the news agencies—and from our own correspondent—the page still blared our headline: "Government Falls on Soy Vote."

I saw my professional life flash before my eyes—the triumphs and setbacks, the victories that had lofted me to the masthead. I remembered the great moments when I had seen my work rewarded in six-column headlines: the bombing of the Marine barracks in Beirut, 9/11, the liberation of Kabul, the fall of Baghdad. The politicians had come and gone and, like the Vicar of Bray, I had escorted them in and out with headlines of appropriate hoopla and solemnity—Bush out, Clinton in; Clinton out, Bush in; Bush out, Obama in. Yeltsin, Putin, Blair and Chirac and Schroeder. I had survived them all.

Until this.

I imagined driving home to my beautiful wife to explain that the cardboard box of mementos under my arm was all that remained of my years before journalism's mast—from cabin boy to almost-skipper—braving wild oceans of words and headlines; skirting shoals of deceit, reefs of untruth. I thought of the averted looks I would almost intercept as I stowed my old metal spike alongside my coffee mug and framed awards and made my final departure from the newsroom, with more than a few metaphorical equivalents lodged between my shoulder blades.

Someone would say, So who gets his slot on the masthead? But there would be no wake for Ed Clancy.

It was the kind of mindless, inconceivably stupid error that ruined lives, honed the daggers of a thousand Brutuses. Even if I was not dragged before my accusers that day, my mistake would haunt me, a high-speed virus gnawing at my professional flesh. I glanced again at the website. A telltale flicker told me that, somewhere along its quivering neural pathways, through servers and coaxial cables and satellite downloads, it was being updated, perpetuating my shame.

I glanced back at the website. The headline had changed.

"Argentine Recount. Soy Vote, Government in Balance."

I blinked. There had been no recount—that much I knew. But then the site flickered again. A new headline emerged, signaled by a small, boastful line in red: "Updated 30 seconds ago."

"Argentine Government Survives Soy Challenge."

I noticed that the byline had changed, too. Only Rosaria's name was now associated with this rapid-fire sequence of flare and invention.

As I marveled, Marcel Duffie strolled by and peered briefly at the story dominating the *Graphic* website.

"Fast work on the recount," he said with something of an inscrutable glance in my direction. He made no attempt to disguise the sneer in his voice.

"Whambo-zambo," I said.

When I lit another cigarette with the old flint-driven, liquid-fuelled lighter Shelby had once sent me from Saigon or Mogadishu or someplace, it took an effort to disguise the tremor in my finger-tips.

"Zippo-zappo."

CHAPTER THREE

LONG BEFORE HE JOINED THE *GRAPHIC*, SHELBY SUBSISTED ON freelance assignments and stand-in shifts on the news wires for Amalgamated and United out of Saigon, one of those footloose kids who worked their passage to Indochina just to hear the sound of real gunfire and befriend the grunts—Homer Bigart style—as they patrolled the paddy fields far from home. When the Khmer Rouge and the Viet Cong triumphed, he had been among the valiant few who clung on to the last, watching the tanks ("*T* for Tommy, *A* for Apple . . .") break through the palace gates as the choppers plucked America's finest from the rooftops.

Then, like many of them, he moved on to the Middle East and Africa, relishing, craving the call from Paris or New York that would propel him on his travels. How do you feel about Sarajevo, the top editor would say, and the old hands would pretend to be blasé— another day, another story. But in the young hearts beating beneath the scarred carapace of a thousand bylines, they were the spry dogs they had always been, unleashed once more to hunt down their newsy prey, freed from mundane restraints of behavior or cost, sanc-tified by the magic litany of boarding passes, check-ins, passport control, security, and, in the old days, the first-class or business lounge (now considered an affront to the gods of financial rectitude but, then, common enough).

No matter how often the order came—and sometimes when it did not—the urge took them to be on the road without paying, to go to war on someone else's ticket. Risking your life was price tag enough without the tedium of receipts and accountancy. They sniffed the wind for tales to tell and scoops to break in Ouagadougou or

Babylon, Lamu or Leningrad (as it was in those days of difficult visas and KGB hoodlums). Flying out, Shelby used to say when he waxed his most lyrical, you shed the shackles of need and duty that hemmed in most of the human race; you floated free on a wave of adrenaline and credit card platinum.

And anyone who denied it, he liked to say, just had not been there.

He boasted that he was the last of his kind to have sent dispatches by carrier pigeon—a title he was likely to retain as long as a newer generation of foreign correspondents relied on satellite phones to call in from the more outlandish places. He was happy to be spoken of as old-school: outlandish, hard-charging, but never knowingly wrong; never bearing false testimony from the arenas of humanity's depravity.

I am, he liked to say, the shitholes man. I go to places the others won't.

He put it about that his father had met his mother in the First Class cabin of a Pan Am red-eye from L.A. to Sydney, Australia, in the early days of intercontinental flights. But there was a persistent rumor—too good to dismiss out of hand—that Shelby was the unacknowledged, undocumented product of a brief liaison between a French starlet called Jenny Colon and Don Shelby, the legendary reporter who ran the Paris slot at the old and now defunct Interpress wire service in the late 1940s. Shelby the Elder was still talked about in reverential tones by a certain generation of reporters—those who managed to keep one foot out of the grave. In the annals of his rise and fall, reference was always made to the trilby hat punctured by two neat bullet holes that he inherited (some said stole) from his mentor, Clay Brewster, having done the same with Brewster's wife. But the subject of Joe Shelby's provenance was taboo, even among those, like me, who had spent long hours with him in the confessional booths of bars across the city.

He spoke with a hybrid accent, American at its heart but suffused with affectations of English, pepperings of "old boy" and "dear fellow" and, like Gatsby, "old sport."

His legends went before him and lingered long after: the time the Saigon bureau chief gave him $4,000 to finance a ten-day swing through Southeast Asia and he spent it all in twenty-four hours without ever leaving the city; the time a companion discovered him in flagrante delicto in Zimbabwe and he drove a friend's Aston Martin across a lawn and into another friend's front parlor to provide an alibi whose logic he could not later recall.

When I first heard he was taking the NND job, I wondered whether they had chosen the right guy.

The web wanted news hot and fresh—the poetry would come later. The first break might even be clunky, shaped by the blacksmith's hammer rather than the jeweler's filigree.

But like all reporters—in their own eyes, at least—Shelby considered his compositional style no less literary than Tolstoy's, his poetry no less lyrical than Byron's, his words as fluid and evocative as those of any Nobel laureate. Touch his opening paragraphs—his ledes, in the idiom of his trade—and you defiled his soul. Even I— his most lenient, longest-suffering editor—did not escape the diamond glint of his narrowed eyes, the hardening of his voice to a menacing growl if I questioned the deployment of his periods and commas, verbs and adjectives, without circumspection and respect. The web, the digital era, the constant tinkering and updating of "content"—all this was anathema to him.

Maybe I was jaundiced, biased. We agreed on a lot of things, Shelby and I. And we agreed to differ on a whole lot more. But you never forgot the Great Divide. The *Graphic* placed its correspondents on pedestals, like minor gods. But editors like me had observed their entrances and exits a hundred times, watched their trajectories soar and fizzle. If they were the gods, we were the High Priests: we knew how frail those pedestals were, like the egos they supported, and we knew just how easily those mortal plinths could be sundered at the whim of higher divinities.

We had different takes, too, on the most basic of approaches to life's challenges. Shelby and his ilk favored the doomed charge into the jaws of battle, the grand gesture, the devil-may-care, live-now-pay-later exuberance of the premodern foreign correspondent.

But over the years, I had learned that, most times, you could achieve more by waiting until the fog of war had cleared before you made your move, nailed your colors to whatever mast you chose—and then only if it was absolutely necessary.

Okay. I had my share of critics. Sometimes I got it wrong biding my time. But more often patience paid off.

If Shelby was a chronicler, I was an observer.

If Shelby played by the rules of history's *grandes batailles*—the Charge of the Light Brigade, for instance—my game was chess. For me, the endgame was all.

Even as one of the dwindling few who had survived to count Shelby as a friend, I couldn't altogether blame Duffie for his ambivalent attitude to the new arrival in his newsroom.

It was one thing to be buddies across a thousand miles of bad phone connections, or to carouse with him on a transit halt, knowing that, the next morning, the passport control officers at Charles de Gaulle would scrutinize his bleary visage and wish him well—and good riddance—on his way out of France on the Air Afrique flight to Chad or Cameroon or Senegal. But it was quite another to find yourself locked into the journalistic equivalent of a lifer's shared cell.

When you met up with him, it was as if he was beckoning you to join him on the far side of some *Alice in Wonderland* portal that led to a world where everything changed gear, changed perspective; as if he was luring you to enter Narnia or Oz and not be too surprised about what you might encounter. You could almost feel yourself decoupling from your familiar coordinates, drifting free.

You could not know Shelby well without recalling W. B. Yeats and those lines about the center not holding. Or Shakespeare's cries of havoc and slipped dogs.

So why now? Why me?

One minute his byline was attached to datelines in Lebanon, Yemen, Egypt. The next—hey presto!—he was ambling into the down-at-heel newsroom of the *Star*, conjured out of nowhere, one more mystery to be unraveled.

Shelby had not been forced to come to Paris. He could have chosen anyplace where the broadband networks and time zones allowed
him to do the job.

But he had chosen Paris, my Paris. I started to understand how
the French felt in 1940.

And there was another thing.

Only a few weeks before his arrival, I had heard rumors that
Faria Duclos, the *grand amour* of Shelby's life, had been taken to see
medical specialists in Paris because of some unspecified malady.
There was talk that Gibson Dullar, Shelby's archrival—both professionally and personally—was finagling his way into a top job on the
Graphic, eyeing promotion at Shelby's expense. My source for all
this was Elvire Récamier, war photographer extraordinaire, who
never left the battlefront while there was still blood to be sniffed in
the gutters, mayhem to feed her hunger for the Great Image to match
those of Capa and Leroy and Demulder. She was petite, dark, skinny. A snapshot of her working undercover in Tehran showed her
almond eyes, framed by a niqab, twinkling with impiety, exuding
mischief.

"I will not run for these bast-a-a-a-rds," she had famously
remarked in Beirut when she came under a withering hail of fire that
sent other photographers and reporters scampering for whatever
cover they could find. She was as indestructible as she was inventive,
as rigorous with her celluloid (and later digital) images as she was
cavalier with the facts of her after-hours gossip. It was said she could
not pass through airport security without the shrapnel lodged in her
body triggering alarms.

I lapped up every word of her stories and measured my belief in
them in the low percentiles. But I never ignored the possibility of a
nuclear truth: What more could you ask of an inveterate theorist of
conspiracies, an elfin aficionado of human foibles?

Elvire Récamier's speculative angst about the arrival of the old
crew dovetailed with my own. You could sense galaxies shifting, tec-
tonic plates groaning: too many coincidences, too many people mov-

ing simultaneously into the frame. A drama scripted in far-flung combat zones was teetering toward an oft-postponed finale on the cobbled avenues and teeming boulevards of Paris.

My Paris.

"What a pair, Gib Dullar and Joe Shelby," she began as we sat together one spring evening, sipping drinks at a café near her loft in the Marais in what might have been the overture before the main show began.

"You know they were once the best of friends. Brothers. Oh, yes. You laugh, but it is true. They were both kids. They were both Romeos. They both liked the boom-boom in any way—on the battlefield, in the bedroom. They loved the fighting. They loved being first. And that was fine until they both loved the same woman.

"I will tell you a story." She settled in for the narrative, rearranging her cigarettes and lighter and a dewy glass of Kir Royal, aligned with one side of a triangular yellow ashtray marked "Ricard" as if she was seeking some kind of geometric order to banish the loose ends that history always leaves as its inconvenient bequest. Or perhaps, I caught myself thinking, she was marshaling her recollections to ensure they matched previous accounts she might have offered to other people. As my mother used to say—and she should know, I'm afraid to say—liars need good memories.

"Way back. In the old days—in Vietnam, Cambodia—I met a young man called Gibson Dullar and I was a young woman myself and there was some fire between us, more than a spark I believed, until one day another young man called Joseph Shelby arrived on the scene with my friend Faria Duclos and I could see where the spark really belonged. Dullar burned for her. With his big eyes, he followed her like a puppy. Always wanting to wag his tail for her!"

I detected an edge of bitterness.

"Then I began to notice that my *amour*, Gibson, was not there so often anymore. He was not going to the same battles as I was. And when you saw his stories on the *agences* you saw they were from the same places as Faria's images. So I figured I'd play a game.

If Faria was not everywhere I was, then maybe Joe Shelby would be where I was. So I—what do you say?—tipped my hat to him. And you know—*entre nous*, Clancy—there were some moments, after some *bataille*, when it had been very dangerous, when you were just glad to be alive that maybe it might have gone somewhere in some hotel or at some OP. But Joe Shelby was not stupid. He figured out my game and Dullar's. It was love—*L majuscule*, capital L."

She sighed, placed her lighter below her cigarette pack as if drawing a line, took a sip of Kir Royal.

I waited. Traffic hooted. Police sirens blared. Waiters sneered. This was Paris, after all, though the slightly misty look in Elvire's eyes suggested she was thousands of miles to the east, in the Mekong Delta or someplace, decades adrift.

"Bah," she exclaimed with that peculiar plosive exhalation the French do so well, as if concluding an inner debate she had not shared with anybody. "So Joe Shelby made his plan. He asked around to find out where she was and where Dullar was. And presto! What does he discover? Well, *bien sûr*: treachery afoot. They were together at some military base in the boonies. You could imagine how it would be. After the patrols with the Marines, the bullets, the ambushes. Alone together with all their adrenaline pumping. Their hearts full, their bodies alive with the fire. Shelby knew there was not much time left to beat his rival to Faria's door. So to speak. It was not easy to get to where she and Dullar were. It was late in the evening. There was a curfew. You could only get to the base on one road, and at night, it was Charlie's road. That is what the Americans called the Viet Cong: Charlie. Charlie was everywhere. He had every ditch and turning covered. Every village. Every rice paddy. But as Shelby thought about Dullar and Duclos, together, beyond reach, he took a couple of pipes."

"Pipes?"

"Opium, of course. Do not look so shocked. Anyhow, Shelby believed he had no time left. Somehow he knew that if he left the two of them alone, it would be *le grand* boom-boom and he would lose her. My plan was to make him angry at her so he would come to me. Instead it made him fall in love with her when he saw some other

lion in the pride. In *Afrique*, they say 'two bulls in the kraal.' Two
bulls in Faria's kraal. So it was a mess. Joe came to me at the
Caravelle and said goodbye. *Adieu,* he said. Not *au revoir* or anything like that. *Adieu.* Farewell. Curtain. You say 'curtain'?"

"Curtains."

"Okay. Curtains. The *grand geste.* He had borrowed a big
motorbike from another hack and he gave me an envelope to pay for
it if he did not get back or anything happened to it. He called his
friends in the American staff and asked them to radio ahead that he
was coming. They told him he was crazy but he set off anyhow."

She was smiling now, a big, happy, nostalgic smile as if Shelby's
act of folly had reaffirmed the essence of the human condition.

"Well, you can imagine. One crazy round-eye on a big Honda
motorbike zooming between the rice paddies."

She said "zoom" as if the word contained far more o's than the
usual English spelling. Her eyes were like dark, hypnotic pools and I
found myself drawn to their vortex in a manner that might be considered unseemly for a married man. She ran the pink tip of her
tongue around the scarlet bud of her lips, pursed to deliver the next
chapter of this drama. Looking at her, I could see that Faria Duclos
must have exerted an awesome magnetism to draw Shelby into the
perils of Charlie's night and away from the exotic enticements of
Elvire Récamier.

"The VC had radios, too," she continued, slightly breathlessly,
"and every time he slowed down there was a new ambush, so he did
not slow down anymore. Just zoomed"—*zooooomed*—"with his
typewriter in a rucksack on his back. That is the story that went
around, anyhow. Go figure. How many people stole that story and
said it was them, with the tracer bullets red and green like fireflies,
like comets in the night. *Vroom, vroom!* Imagine. The night. The
mist on the paddy fields. The motor screaming. The bullets
whistling."

Elvire told a good yarn, and I had the feeling that I was not the
first to be regaled with it. And maybe not the first to muse on its
veracity. When the old-timers in our line got together to recall the
efforts they exerted to excavate truth's kernel from life's obfuscation,

you could be sure that no two versions of any recognizable event would coincide completely: everyone reached the front line first; everyone ducked the same bullets, smuggled themselves exclusively onto the same evidently elastic cargo plane to reach the same rebel bridgehead on some indistinct African river, interviewed the same reclusive dictator next to a cage full of prowling leopards.

I sipped at my double Jameson, allowing my mind to stray back to the youngblood Shelby had been when I first met him—all cock and rib, as they used to say. I knew from the stories he had filed from tight spots that he had gotten into many such locations, usually, later on, with Faria Duclos. (Unlike some—and I am thinking mainly of Gibson Dullar—he never lied about his datelines.) So Elvire Récamier's account had a certain plausibility. I found myself conjuring an image of the young knight-errant bent over the chromed handlebars of his giant mechanical steed, twisting the throttle to squeeze every last drop of power out of the howling engine, locks flattened by the wind, slicing through a night filled with insects and bullets.

Elvire's eyes had narrowed, and she fell briefly silent, transposed to the bitter night when a man risked all to spurn her for another.

"So, thank God, because he has called ahead, when he gets to the American base, the grunts at the gate behind their sandbags know that something crazy is going on but of course they are not going to open up to just anybody. It could be a bomber. A crazy. So Shelby slows right down and the Marines shine their light on him and see he is American and the VC see the lights and they see Shelby and they open fire and Shelby starts the motorbike again but a bullet hits the tire and it skids and slides and he falls off and gets up and runs toward the base with his rucksack and by now the Marines are shooting at Charlie and there is World War Three. So inside the base Faria Duclos is there with her camera doing low-light shots of Marines under fire and Gibson Dullar is there with his notebook, ducking down for cover. Someone's bullets hit the motorbike again and its gasoline tank explodes so there is a big blaze—*whoooomph* —and all Faria can see through her range finder is this one running figure coming through the gates. A silhouette against the flames. And then, because the VC have given away their position, the Americans

call in support from the air and there is napalm. *Whoooosh!* Do you
like the smell of napalm, Ed?"

"I never smelled it."

"But like in the movie, the smell of victory?"

She was teasing me, the way field types tease the home desk, the
way they imply, if you weren't there, you can't know. (Though real
warriors always say their trade is 90 percent crushing boredom, 10
percent terror.)

"So what happened then?" I injected a world-weariness into my
voice as if listening to a child offering a particularly inventive tale of
the dog eating the homework.

"So Faria is thinking: *Merde*, a pretty good image. A fighting
retreat by a lonely soldier. The lost warrior returns. Napalm. Fire.
Tracer bullets. Marines on rock and roll. The noise is terrible. Fifty-
caliber machine guns. Mortars. Outgoing. Incoming. RPGs. Booom
fucking booom! Later, Faria told me all this. She laughed. It was her
favorite story to put me in my place. Because then she realizes it is
not a soldier or someone. It is Joe Shelby!"

Elvire reached the crescendo with a gusto that defied all skepticism.

"So Joe comes through the gate and the battle dies down and the
Marines call him many names for being so crazy. But no one was
killed—on their side. And plenty of VC maybe got fried. And no one
cared about the motorbike although it cost Shelby a thousand dollars, which was mega-bucks in those days. So there they all are,
Shelby and Duclos and of course Dullar, all in that tent where Dullar
figured he would be alone with Duclos and get over his leg. And
Shelby takes the rucksack off his back and inside, wrapped in an air-
mail edition of the *New York Graphic*, is a single red rose he has
brought from Saigon. His old party trick—the single red rose. And—
this is the best part—when he looks at his typewriter, stuck in the
middle of it is a bullet! A freaking bullet that would have cut his
spine if it had not been stuck in the typewriter. So the pen is mightier
than the sword after all! But of course, when Faria saw that, she
knew her heart must be with the man who had driven through the
killing fields with a rose in his rucksack and a bullet in his typewriter
to save her from his rival. For many years she kept the bullet on a

leather string around her neck. And Gibson Dullar has never, ever forgiven Joe Shelby. And I have never forgiven him for doing that for Faria Duclos and not for me! But you know the worst thing?"

"What was that?"

"The worst thing was that they moved Dullar into a different tent, away from the two lovebirds. And that night, Charlie attacked again and a tracer round set his tent on fire and he burned."

"Burned?"

"On his arms. His chest. He needed skin grafts for months. And that really is what he never forgave Shelby for. Fire!"

"And now?"

She paused and looked out at the evening traffic clogging the Rue Réaumur, the trendy young kids with their laptop bags hurrying along the sidewalks. I wondered if an IBM ThinkPad would stop a bullet as efficiently as an Olivetti Lettera or a Hermes Baby.

"Well, maybe now is not so different," she said.

"How so?"

"Shelby is coming to Paris. Duclos is coming back. Dullar is hovering."

"Hardly bright young things, though, Elvire."

"Well, neither are you," she said sharply.

"You still love him! I'll be damned." I was not sure whether I meant Shelby or Dullar, or whether I was just out for a little devilry.

"Still? Love? You Anglo-Saxons are always so simplistic. Love! Trust! Apple pie and mother! You forget that love is pain. Froufrou is not free. When you hurt the ones who love you, when you spurn and neglect them, they want payback before they will love again, if they will ever love again. For you Americans, love just happens. Wham-bam. Thank you. Short story. End of story. Soap opera. For us French, it is the whole five acts—do you say the whole nine yards?—the drama of life, the *grand amour*. It is not over until the lady sings. And this lady has many songs left to sing. You better believe it, Ed Clancy. You will see. Shelby better believe. In my work I capture the decisive moment. I know how to wait patiently until it comes. And then I act. But my memory is long, longer than you think. Elvire Récamier does not forget the sins of the past."

I figured it was the Kir Royal talking because the Elvire Récamier I had come to include in my collection of characters was a woman of deep, abiding, and ultimately benevolent passions, a warm heart in a tough-guy shell. But there was something else woven in there, a legacy of 'Nam—enduring love yearning for release from old hurts.

I made a mental note to squirrel away that kernel of emotional intelligence: the wise man knows when silence is the best counsel—another big difference between me and Shelby.

She placed a cigarette between her lips and did not move until I flicked my Zippo to light it.

After a long smoky pause, with gradually slowing inhalations and exhalations, she continued: "You know she is very ill. After everything, all the boom-boom, the pipes of opium and all the other stuff, her nerves are curtain. In a wheelchair. And Shelby is not so good either. So maybe this is Dullar's last chance to do something. Who knows? One night in Paris . . ."

I completed the line for her: ". . . may be your last."

CHAPTER FOUR

IT HAD NOT BEEN MY FIRST OR LAST NIGHT IN PARIS BY ANY MEANS.
I was a lifer, one of those expatriates from Hoboken, New Jersey,
or Missoula, Montana, who stay too long and have no home to go
back to in the USA and fall for the myth that Paris is the new New
York; that the French like the Yanks because Lafayette preferred
them to the British in 1776, because we liberated them from the
Germans; that somehow we own Paris because we have shared so
much of its history and slept with so many of its women, just as their
men have cavorted with so many of ours.

I counted my time at the *Star* in decades and dated my adventures to the days when the dollar ruled and there were no farmed
oysters on sale in the off-season and writers really did hang out at Le
Dôme waiting for the ghost of Hemingway or Miller to settle on
their slumped shoulders and whisper inspiration into their jaded
ears.

I was the honeyed voice calling on unreliable phone lines to foreign correspondents in Rangoon or Rio to cajole and flatter them
into filing early, promising that I would not change their deathless
prose so long as they made their deadlines and thus enabled me to
put the pages to bed in time to climb into my buzzy red open-top
Alfa Romeo sports car and head out around the Étoile, bouncing
along the cobbles of the Champs-Élysées, down the Rue des Saints-
Pères, toward the bars of Saint-Germain-des-Prés.

Shelby and I traced our memories to the golden age when you
could eat truffles and drink wine and still have cash in your pocket to
take a special friend to Claridge's in London for the weekend. I had
been promoted early and had clung to the masthead ever since, even

as the boisterous tides and treacherous eddies of layoffs rose about me, raising up and then dumping a host of top editors. My favorite among them all was a man who filled his morning coffee mug with cognac, never read the paper, and was known as Two-Jackets Johnson because he always kept a sport coat draped over his office chair to give the impression of proximity to the coalface while he wore a second jacket in some distant brasserie, bar, or *boîte*. (The operative jacket was distinguished by a fresh-cut carnation in the buttonhole—a signal known only to the few who would never betray him.)

With just one jacket, no buttonhole, and the cognac reserved (mostly) for after hours, I had survived them all.

But these days, the barbarians were at the gate.

The divine beast of Print to which we had bowed throughout our professional lives, to which we had made our offerings of articles and news and all too transient prose, was expiring. If we had imagined that our words alone could sustain it, we were wrong. Deprived of the advertising lifeblood they craved, newspapers were foundering. Like misguided skippers on the bridges of so many stricken vessels, newsmen and newswomen were going down with the ships on which they had once sailed the kindly oceans of expense-account lunches, five-star hotels, and mortal peril.

It was the end of the era that spooled back to the presses of Gutenberg and Caxton.

Print—that great, gorgeous, messy alchemy of ink and hot type and whirring reels of paper and working stiffs in stained coveralls—was expiring but not quite finished. Its digital heir, the Internet, with its rapid-fire news and needle-sharp technology, was already muscling in, even though, like some itinerant prodigal, some down-at-heel pretender, it could not pay its way. But the days were long gone when those huge newspaper ads from Bloomingdale's and Saks Fifth Avenue financed all our free lunches.

Maybe it was easier for the big boys, the *New York Times* and the *Wall Street Journal*, with their deep pockets and long lines of credit. But we had always been number three, the little kid brother scrambling to keep up, trying to do the same job with a fifth of the bureaus, a quarter of the ads, and half the circulation. Of course, we punched above our weight. We moved quick and nimble. We were hungry to bring the giants down a peg or two. We had our scoops and knockouts. But financially, we had no backup; no passing benefactor; no generous, kind family to sustain us—only the cruel mistress of the marketplace.

There were moments when I almost sympathized with Marcel Duffie—almost. If you thought about it rationally, he had a point. We needed ads to finance the way we had always run things. But the ads weren't there anymore. While we were looking the other way, a whole new generation had arisen, believing that the Internet somehow suspended the first rule of business, that you get what you pay for. These days, with their tablets and smartphones and laptops, everyone seemed to believe news was free; that it didn't cost money to send Shelby & Co. hurtling across the planet to feed at humanity's latest kill, to pay people like me to process the news. But the irreducible core was simple: news comes with a serious price. And whatever the citizen journalists with their cell phone cameras might tell you, that price is worth paying.

If you want an objective take on what happens in Afghanistan or Gaza or Cairo or Moscow or Paris, you can't rely on governments and their flacks and spin doctors to tell you. Tweets can be pretty useful—like signposts on a faint trail, pointing to the right direction, marking the way through the jungles of official obfuscation and the competing lies of war. But in 140 characters they can't cover the whole story—or explain who's telling it. Anonymous blogs don't share their sources, their biases. They might be for real. They might just be rants—or plants. Unpalatable though it might seem, you are stuck with the Shelbys and the Clancys to filter out the dross. And if you are Marcel Duffie, or someone like him, you have to make the judgment calls and decide what's better—free lunches and business-class tickets for Joe Shelby, or saving enough money to keep on doing what you do best and sending your reporters to cover the news, even if they may no longer do so from those favored old watering holes. Part of me believed the economies were designed—like curative surgery—to permit the greater organism to survive. Part of me wanted desperately to believe that, when the cuts were done, it would all turn out to have been a beneficial exercise—like a regime of cold baths, small salads, and long runs to make a better person of you.

Then there were the other arguments—the idealists who figured citizen reporters on their cellphones, calling in the news from Tehran to Tuscaloosa, would take up the slack when what they scornfully called the mainstream media collapsed. But who would they call the news in to? Who would keep these breathless messengers honest?

And there had been the occasional bright light, the occasional visionary who believed reports of the death of print had been much exaggerated. People like to quote the example of a big-time Manhattan executive who upped sticks while still in his 50s and headed back out to Minneapolis to rescue *The Star Tribune*. Sure, he got there after the all-too-familiar cycles of decline—layoffs, cost-cutting, private equity firms loading the title with debt, even bankruptcy. But then people started buying paper again. Circulation crept up. Profits, too. The media pundits in New York began to pay attention: was this the template?

But a big part of me saw it in a different light altogether. Newspapers were dying the death of a thousand cuts. They started off like Shelby—bighearted and slightly crazy—and they ended up like Duffie—small and mean-spirited. So many titles had already disappeared from the newsstands, replaced by websites or not at all. It was the common wisdom that the Internet would take over where newspapers failed as humanity's mirror, reflecting back the best and the worst, from war zones to concert halls.

And it would perform that function with much greater efficiency. On the web, there were no forests to chop down to make the pulp to make the paper to print the word because there were no printers or paper, only infinite gigavistas stretching to a Big Brother future where the web snared us all 24-7.

And there was another monster out there: the conflation of news and "content."

News was what really sold newspapers. News was what the reader wanted—hard fact, history's dawn, truth you could base a judgment on. But when newspapers perished it was because people like Duffie figured that the creation of "content" to separate the ads—in the paper or on the web—was a mechanical process that could be achieved without people like Shelby. Or me.

No news was very bad news indeed.

So, in this penurious interregnum, until someone worked out how to make the Internet pay, the auditors roamed the *Star's* gloomy corridors with their clipboards, paring here, trimming there, never quite leaving blood in the corridors, but always nipping and tucking at their twitching victim.

The masthead—the power league of editorial status—shrank as overpaid bosses took monstrous buyouts and were not replaced. With magisterial authority, accountants who had never ventured far from their calculators issued all-points bulletins to those in the quake zones and riots and trenches: each taxi ride must be accounted for individually and only if no public transport is available in your part of the coup-stricken capital; meals with sources (takeout preferred) will not be reimbursed beyond $10; when in war zones please rotate the use of bulletproof vests, helmets, gas masks and suits for use in times of chemical, biological, radiation, and nuclear hazard; the company encourages the purchase of low-budget camping equipment (one-person tents only!) as a substitute for hotel accommodation.

Titanic-style, we plowed the oceans toward our tryst with the iceberg of history that was the World Wide Web.

No truffles now. Brown bag trumped a la carte.

No Claridge's.

No mistresses—for me, at least.

Over the years I had moved my center of operations from the downtown bustle to the sticks. I had traded the Alfa Romeo for a Jeep and switched my investments, just in time, from stock on the markets to bloodstock. With Shelby, in the old days, I had stolen a few horses. Now I owned a few on a spread outside Paris where Marie-Claire Risen, my first—and hopefully last—wife, ran the equestrian business and waited, so far as I knew, to welcome me home with a modest tipple and an immodest embrace.

The last thing I needed was Shelby on the old rampage, whambo-zambo, with the editor's squeeze—or anyone else's for that matter.

In the end, my loyalty to him came under immense and potentially ruinous strain, but in those early days, it was boundless.

CHAPTER FIVE

AFTER THE ARGENTINE SOY VOTE RECOUNT—A SCOOP CONDEMNED
to eternal exclusivity—Shelby and I resolved to hit the town. I called
home to say I would be late, held up on business. But not really to
my surprise, Marie-Claire registered some opposition to this bold act
of boyish exclusivism and said that—*au contraire*—she would drive
into town to join us and we would meet in Saint-Germain.

"No. Seriously. It's business. With Shelby. I wouldn't want you
to waste your time."

"Where are you meeting?"

"Deux Magots."

"Flore is better."

And that was that.

She was far more tutored in the nuances of upscale Paris than I.
But whatever the venue, I was not relishing the idea of introducing
her to Joe Shelby.

For one thing, I had foolishly regaled Marie-Claire with a selection of the more colorful Shelby stories that sprang to mind when I
learned he would be assigned to Paris. Of course, I had maintained
a judicious silence about the most outrageous, three-or-four-in-a-
bed anecdotes that seemed to swirl around Shelby like some lewd
miasma, not necessarily related to fact. But I should have known
that it was unwise to recount too many old hack tales without the
risk of being perceived as a past, or potential, player in those
chortling, late-night sagas of hotel rooms and rebel encampments.
Every denial on my part would be taken perversely as a confirmation, no matter how hard I tried to distance myself from Shelby's
possibly fictional misdeeds.

It was not I who had dictated eight hundred words of copy from a Thai massage parlor without interrupting the business at hand; it was not I who had lost his shoes beside a hotel swimming pool in the Congo while distracted by submarine romance involving a Wagnerian Lufthansa stewardess. But had I told those Shelby stories to my stern and beloved bride, she would immediately have suspected my complicity and direct participation—guilt by projection.

Another reason for my less-than-enthusiastic anticipation of our *apéritif à trois* was that, in my experience, it was never wise to lionize a friend or colleague. Build up someone's reputation as an adventurer, a lover, or, worst of all, a swordsman—to use that old, politically incorrect, and all-too-Freudian expression—and there was every chance that his renown and prowess would be taken as a challenge.

Either way, I had not been married to Marie-Claire for long enough to claim total familiarity with her likely responses to every situation. (She was not the kind of person who would ever permit such a boast about her, in any event.) Neither did I, at that point, sense that she saw the future in quite the same exclusive, Darby-and-Joan terms that I secretly yearned for. Even as I assented to her choice of venue, I was trying to recall exactly what I had told her about Shelby that I might regret.

In his long career, Shelby had moved from one grand establishment to another, entertaining with ambassadorial regularity and commitment, never omitting his closest friends from a long list of those to be invited to cocktails, catered dinners, and rambunctious barbeque parties in Bangkok or London or Johannesburg. Early on, he had converted a ramshackle ruin in New Delhi into a luxurious palace, with staff to tend to his every need and those of his guests. His tennis courts and pools, snuggled behind razor-wired walls in various third-world hellholes, enjoyed near-mythical status as social venues where the parties and the misbehavior never seemed to end.

But not once did he shirk coverage of the most unpleasant events. Not once, he liked to claim, had he missed a deadline—although it

had sometimes been a close-run race against the clock and the atten-
tions of the eager companions who shared his taste for war zones.
Not once did he withdraw the pledge to his friends that his house was
their house, a communal approach that they sometimes extended to
his nearest and dearest: in his younger days, Shelby lived in constant
suspension between loyalty and lust.

When he looked for his spiritual forebears, he scoured hack history and alighted on legends like Reynolds Packard of United, who
had once dedicated a book to "my wife's lovers—in friendship and
appreciation." Yet as I knew and Elvire Récamier knew, there was
one constant in Shelby's life, one love who really counted—and all
the rest was window-dressing.

Thankfully, I had assured Marie-Claire of that.

Shelby belonged to a generation at the *Graphic* that had basked
in glory at the height of print's prosperity, lived in style, worked hard
and spent hard.

He was, perhaps, the last of the "receipt lost" generation before
the Auks of the Abacus took over his universe.

But then the Angel of Austerity arrived. No longer would reloca-
tion budgets be open-ended. No longer would financial comptrollers
be hoodwinked by requests from reporters in Hong Kong for permission to transport "just my old junk"—only to find themselves paying the freight costs for huge wooden vessels built to ply the South
China Sea. There was a loophole, however, and with his move to
Paris, Shelby found it and quite literally drove through it in style.

The wrinkle lay in his discovery that, while the movement of
household goods and furniture between assignments was subjected
to ever-closer restrictions, "office equipment" was covered by a
separate budget over which no one seemed to have claimed oversight. Soon after his arrival in Paris, thus, a truck arrived containing what the manifest indicated to be the appurtenances of some
mythical bureau of far more opulent proportions than Shelby's
new accommodations at the *Star*.

Shelby boasted the kind of kit that Henry Morton Stanley or

Evelyn Waugh's *Boot of the Beast* might have chosen for an expedition to explore Abyssinia, or find the source of the Nile, or locate Dr. Livingstone himself.

On its own, the Zodiac fifteen-foot inflatable boat might not have drawn comment, neatly wrapped as its components were in heavy-duty blue plastic pouches, each the size of a large suitcase or a small portmanteau. But there was no mistaking the long shaft and scuffed propeller of the 50-horsepower Mercury outboard that came with it, or the boat hook, or the paddles of polished marine ply and the spare tanks for gasoline. (I wondered if, in some old, archived expense account, there was a claim to be reimbursed for "riverboat to reach pygmy warriors (receipt lost).") Then there were the trophies: a twenty-pound tiger fish from Zimbabwe, mounted on varnished teak, as if turning to attack, locked forever in a snarl of razor-sharp teeth; the petrified jaws of a prowling shark caught off Mombasa when it swallowed a tuna on the end of Shelby's deep-sea fishing line; the massive head of a Colorado black bear, shot by Shelby as he lay injured from a fall in a ravine high in the Rockies. There was much more, all piling up in a vacant storeroom once used for pens and notebooks before the newspaper stopped supplying them to reporters: a batch of antique cane angling poles in dented aluminum tubes; a Picasso ceramic, mounted and framed in glass; an antique Blickensderfer 7 typewriter; a supposedly decommissioned AK-47 assault rifle with a folding metal stock and a suspiciously live-looking clip of 7.62 mm (intermediate) ammunition ("office ornamentation," Shelby called it); a long coffin-size box with no clear markings or purpose, listed on the manifest as "press clippings" but in fact containing a collection of silk carpets from Beirut and Baghdad and Tehran purchased cannily as a hedge against abrupt cash-flow restrictions; a large samovar in working order; a hookah that smelled suspiciously of illicit substances; several aluminum Halliburton suitcases festooned with baggage labels from the Nile Hilton in Cairo, the Mount Nelson in Cape Town, the Beirut Commodore, and Raffles in Singapore; a large Impressionist painting of water lilies at Giverny, retrieved from the ruins of a post-coup presidential mansion in Bangui, which Shelby always insisted was "just a cheap copy."

Most people missed the unloading of the pièce de résistance, but I didn't.

I happened to glance out my first-floor window to see how much more was left to be unloaded from the truck parked on the street below. The workers had rigged two long steel ramps to the rear of their vehicle and, with infinite caution, rolled out a long, low crate that seemed to have wheels. A shipper's label on the side identified whatever was inside as "File Cabinets/Misc."

The crate was big enough, I figured, to house enough file cabinets and miscellaneous items for an average-size law firm. But it remained a mystery why such contents would require wheels—particularly aluminum wheels with complex spokes and low-profile tires.

Once it was safely unloaded, the workers jimmied away the wooden walls of the crate to reveal its true contents, and the mystery was solved, only, perhaps, to be replaced by another puzzle: How on earth, in these days of draconian oversight by gimlet-eyed accountants, who could spot lunch-with-mistress disguised as lunch-with-source at a thousand paces, could Shelby have had the chutzpah to believe he could get away with this crude piece of legerdemain by some dubious shipping agency in some distant and equally dubious port?

From the crate emerged a pristine two-seater Jaguar XKR sports car in polished silver, packed in white Styrofoam chips for all the world as if it were a Christmas present delivered in a seasonal snowfall. I sprinted down to street level to admire its sleek lines.

Shelby supervised the unloading with a look on his craggy features that blended concern for the paint job and the fussiness of a mother hen tending her brood. Even before the chips had been cleared away, he had folded himself with surprising nimbleness into the pale leather of the driver's seat and turned the key, listening rhapsodically to the sound of the four-liter, 400-horsepower V8 engine burbling into life.

Shelby's most recent assignment before Paris had been in his beloved Lebanon, and I made a mental note to prize out of him at some stage the story of how he acquired a Jaguar sports car in a perennial war zone—and exported it in one piece.

"Well, hop aboard, Clancy, me bucko," he said, blipping the throttle as I slid into the passenger seat.

If I had been more observant, I would have spent less time examining the gauges and gearshift and more time wondering why, even as we drove off, Shelby loaded the glove box with two scuffed leather volumes, both written by the French poet Gérard de Nerval, which I had seen many times on his desk.

One was the famed collection of sonnets called *Les Chimères*.

The other was *Aurélia*, the poet's account of his descent into madness.

I was no great expert on nineteenth-century French poets, but I knew that Nerval had been a pretty confused sort of character. For a start, his name was not Nerval; it was Labrunie. So he had faked his own roots to disguise humdrum origins: in the post-revolutionary times France was going through, I guess he figured "de Nerval" had more of a doomed aristocratic ring to it. He spent plenty of time, on and off, under psychiatric care and plenty of time, too, in mourning for a mother who died far away while he was young. Not being a literary type, I couldn't vouch for his poetry (my skills were limited to turning tortured stringer copy into legible news), but it seemed to me that Nerval, or Labrunie, was something of a fruitcake. In his late forties, midway through the nineteenth century, Nerval hanged himself. It was rumored that he used a silk ribbon that he believed had once been part of the Queen of Sheba's waistband. They found his body hanging from the railings in the Rue de la Vieille-Lanterne. Before his death, it was said, he had used that same ribbon as a leash to take his pet lobster for walks through the Tuileries and Luxembourg gardens. Finally, the poet had found his place in the French national memory secured and sign posted by a slender marble column bearing his name across the way from Honoré de Balzac's grave in the Père-Lachaise cemetery over in the Twentieth— the same vast expanse of tombs and mausoleums that offered a final resting place to a more recent icon of despair, Jim Morrison.

"Watch out for the lobsters," I called out above the rumble of the Jaguar's engine.

"They're on order," he shouted back. "And the silk ribbon."

With a minimal amount of fiddling, the roof folded itself back and we drove off, leaving a shower of white chips in our wake as the removals crew offered a round of spontaneous applause and huzzahs and effortlessly Gallic shrugs.

Now, after the soy vote fiasco, Shelby and I headed out once more in the convertible Jaguar, rippling along the cobbles of the Avenue de la Grande Armée.

"Follow the star," he told me.

"Star?"

"What?"

"You said, 'Follow the star.'"

"Star. *L'Étoile.*" Shelby waved expansively at the Arc de Triomphe with its star-burst of avenues leading off from the central runway-scale circle around it. The French call it L'Étoile, but I had the feeling that he had been thinking of some other stellar being.

"You wouldn't always have done that."

"Done what?"

"The soya bean rowback. Should have been a correction. Straight up. Honest. Goddamn it. Have you forgotten what the word "honest" means? H for Harry, O for Orange, N for Nuts . . ."

Shelby peered at me, narrowing his lizard eyes. We were on the Champs-Élysées now, dodging and weaving through the traffic, then cruising alongside the wide sidewalk with its cafés and movie houses and boutiques. The car—and its raffish, devil-may-care driver—drew significant looks from women across the generations. Most men tended to focus on the eighteen-inch alloy wheels and the torpedo phallus of the louvered hood.

"Rowback?" he said.

"You know what I mean."

"An existential point."

"I still say you wouldn't have done it. Not in the print days. Jeez. Sometimes back then I thought you were a poet."

"'And all that is left in me is an obstinate writer of prose,' as the man said."

"Man? What man?"

"'I composed my first poems out of the enthusiasm of youth.'"
He turned to me with a lupine smile. "'The second ones were written out of love,'" he said, lowering his voice to a tremulous basso
profundo, pronouncing the word "*lerv*." "'The last ones,'" he went
on, "'out of despair.' Unquote. Gérard de Nerval."

He laughed uproariously. I had no idea what he was talking about.

Despite appearances to the contrary, despite the parties and the
revels, Shelby had always taken his trade seriously. Even in the most
taxing of circumstances—there was that rumored episode in a cage-
dancing bar in Phuket, for instance—he had been able to establish
communications with his editors to iron out blunders. Corrections,
printed in that prissy style so familiar to newspaper readers ("An
article in Monday's edition referred erroneously to Ouagadougou as
the capital of Upper Volta. The country is now called Burkina
Faso.") provoked in him days of shamed regret. Errors haunted him.
A misspelled name that survived the shock waves of editing made
him squirm.

Worse still was the double whammy when a correction contained
an error that demanded its own correction, as if the fixes had begun
to procreate like some virus. The more abstruse the mistake, the
worse it seemed; the more persnickety to the casual observer, the
more heinous the crime.

"Listen," he said, "if readers figure we can't spell their names
properly, how the hell can we expect them to believe us when we
unravel the mysteries of the cosmos?"

Verbatim, Shelby could recite corrections he harvested from his
own newspaper and others with the zeal of a true collector.

An article on Friday about a National Aeronautics and Space
Administration report on warmer temperatures in the past decade
misidentified the agency that oversees the National Climatic Data
Center, and a correction in this space on Wednesday reversed two
words in that agency's name in some editions. The National Oceanic

and Atmospheric Administration (not "Atmospheric and Oceanic") has jurisdiction over the data center; NASA does not manage it.
—*The New York Times*

A reference to the Indian foreign minister misstated her gender.
—*The New York Graphic*

"This way be dragons," Shelby would intone when he launched onto the theme of the Correction as Curse, a sin so venal that no amount of prayer and penance could expunge it. In religion, you could go to the priest, bend the knee, whisper your admissions of hanky-panky, misbehavior, slap, tickle, and tears.

"Forgive me, father . . ."

And, duly titillated, the cleric would apportion the appropriate dose of atonement. But not in print. Print fixed your error for all the world to snicker at. Forever. Religions might forgive, but in newspapers, sins were archived. The worst two words in Shelby's professional vocabulary were "Correction appended."

Carelessness was no excuse. Readers and editors would never, ever forgive the whambo-zambo blooper that might crop up in the heat of any reporter's compositional passion.

An article describing Wayne Rooney's soccer career described incorrectly a recent change of heart about playing for Manchester United. His new readiness to play for the team represents a 180-degree turn, not a 360-degree turn.
—*The Paris Star*

Ho, ho, ho—you could hear them chortling forever more.

Even the flimflam of travel articles was not safe from human carelessness and the mandatory abasement that came in its wake. Shelby's catalog of truly humiliating climb-downs included one that he recited with mournful incredulity, as if it could—and would—happen to anyone guilty of even the most momentary lapse of concentration.

The cover article on June 19 about Places to Go misidentified the civil war that kept safari camps closed for a decade. The war was in

Zimbabwe, not Zambia. The article also misstated the length of time of a train trip between Cape Town and Pretoria and misidentified the type of train used. The trip is by overnight sleeper train, not by a bullet train, and the trip usually takes 28 hours, not one hour. And the article referred incorrectly to the area of Africa in which a beach and an island are located. Diani beach and the island of Lamu are on the Indian Ocean coast of eastern Kenya, not the north which is the landlocked border with Ethiopia. —*The Paris Star*

Facts, Shelby used to say in the old print days, are the warp and weft of our business. Get the facts right and the poetry would follow. "But never bend the *verifiable* facts," he said. "And note please that I am referring exclusively to the *verifiable* truth."

His digital debut seemed to contradict all his adages. Suddenly speed trumped accuracy; get the words up on the web and the facts would follow.

As a driver, if not skilled to Formula One standards, Shelby was certainly enthusiastic and fearless, maneuvering the powerful Jaguar with deft assurance and utter disregard for the buzzing hordes of small Citroëns and boxy Smart cars that hovered around him like swarms of summer insects. The V8 engine rumbled and howled, as if warming up for the Le Mans sport car race, circa 1980. The cream-colored leather upholstery smelled new and luxurious.

"Listen up, Clancy." Shelby said, as if explaining an obvious point to a slow child. He could really be irritating. "It's a question of being right at the time. It's a question of how long is 'now.' In the paper days, 'now' lasted twenty-four hours, from one day's paper to the next. You had to be right for twenty-four hours. And if you were right for twenty-four hours, chances were you could be right for a lot longer. Now it's warp-time, nano-time. You are right—or wrong—in a space of time so brief it hardly exists before it moves on. Time is subdivided, chopped into the merest slivers. Chopped sliver—I like that. Time as chopped sliver. If you are 'wrong'—he took his hands briefly off the custom wood-rimmed steering wheel to imitate quotation marks, a gesture I find irritating at the best of times and even more so heading into the Place de la Concorde at something over the legal speed-limit—"you are wrong so briefly that your error is diluted. Within seconds you are right. There is no time to confess because your sin is too brief to be noted. Your wrongness is preserved nowhere. There is no record of error, no evidence, no members of the jury except maybe in some geeky parallel universe. Wrongness is relative—Einstein."

I thought of Marcel Duffie and imagined him prowling that parallel universe where the web was infinitely transparent with all its errors preserved in cyber-aspic for all time to be inspected and recalled to life as expediency dictated.

"Bull," I said, but he wasn't listening.

"Paper! Ink!" He embarked on a victory lap of the Place de la Concorde to expand on his theme. "They give our words weight, permanence. An organic life, maybe decaying, but decay that lasts decades, centuries. Look at this."

With one hand, he waved the small leather volume of his beloved poet while, with the other, he piloted the Jaguar around the obelisk at the center of the Concorde, the squeal of the tires punctuating his words.

"When this was written and published, they had barely built the Arc de Triomphe. No one had even dreamed of the Eiffel Tower. And yet here's the self-same text , worn only by human touch, legible, living, surviving in a way that its author has not, immortal. Imagine the eyes that have read it, the hearts that have soared, the tears that have poured onto its pages. All that history, all those people, their pain, their joy, all of it is here, now, in this single volume. Sure, cyberspace is infinite in time, eternal. But it is ephemeral, a whole universe in servers and computers, and whatever we do within that galaxy does not even constitute a planet, just an asteroid, a stray meteorite. Our words on the screen have the appearance of weight but no physical being. They exist and don't exist simultaneously. As soon as we end our shift, the next bunch of hacks starts to dismantle everything we have done. In newspapers, our work lasted twenty-four hours. Then, as the Brits say, it wrapped the next day's fish and chips. And those twenty-four hours fed our egos, made us think that what we did was the first draft of history. But you can't wrap anything in the web. Across the pond, in their time zone, we are just the night shift, the moles who leave piles of stuff on the lawns to be cleaned up the next morning; the Draculas who suck the blood out of the news, then scurry back into our sarcophagi as daylight comes. We are nocturnal beasts, like hippos, who come out to feed in the dark hours when our bosses are sleeping and shit all over the riverbank. Then, come first light, we slide back under the surface, and all they hear from us is a distant bark of disgruntlement from across the waters."

He offered the appropriate imitation of a hippopotamus as we anchored briefly at a traffic light on the Place de la Concorde, startling a passing cyclist who wobbled on her Vélib rental bike.

"*Excusez-moi, mademoiselle,*" Shelby said with flirtatious contrition.

"*Je vous en prie,*" she said, smiling forgiveness.

Age shall not weary them . . .

We drove on, crossing the Seine at the Assemblée Nationale, throwing an oblique left into the Boulevard Saint-Germain, where the rich folks lived. Shelby was heading toward the see-and-be-seen zone of Brasserie Lipp and Les Deux Magots. With these wheels, he would find effortless, illegal parking outside any number of fancy establishments.

"Now you listen to me, Shelby." I think my tone surprised him. Like a lot of his kind, he had lived so long in a world free of restraint that he was not used to being talked back to. "What you have said is bullshit. And you know it. What we do now plays by the same rules we have always played by—the rules *you* have always played by, especially. You've risked your life—and other people's—plenty of times to get at what you told your readers, your editors, was the truth. Let that slip now and the vultures will be circling, I promise. You won't know it till it happens. Then all those little mistakes, those lapses you think disappear into cyberspace, those errors—they will turn around and bite you in the ass. It'll be like you've stumbled into a tank of piranhas, and no one will throw you a lifeline."

He had taken his hands for the steering wheel again to cover his ears and mutter something that sounded like "blah-di-blah-di-blah."

"Your metaphors really suck," he said.

"Listen," I said. "You and I have one single stock in trade: We get it right. We break stories. We publish them."

"That's three," he said.

"Three what?"

"Stocks in trade."

"I'm serious, Shelby. Whether it's one or three, the reality is the same. The only way we can defend ourselves against an early buyout is to keep on getting things right. To resist all the pressures. To tell them to cool it when they want us to post unconfirmed news." I was tempted to tell him about the deadline Marcel Duffie had invented for us—a month, tops, before he initiated some doomsday scenario.

The mere mention of the word "buyout" made him shudder and switch lanes inadvertently in the mighty Jaguar, waving a vaguely lewd gesture in response to a chorus of blaring horns and protesting tires. I gripped the dash and plowed on.

"You just don't seem to realize how many people would like to see you go down because you are who you are—and me with you. But I'm not ready for that. So don't you fuck up. No more soy votes. No more recounts. Right?"

"Whimpo-whampo," he said. "Jesus, Clancy. What happened to your sense of humor?"

As instructed by Marie-Claire, we took seats at Café de Flore, the rival to Les Deux Magots made famous by Jean-Paul Sartre and Simone de Beauvoir. Shelby insisted on positioning himself on the outside terrace where he could keep watch on his beloved wheels, although I knew that the Paris smart set favored the first-floor salon indoors to set itself apart from the hoi polloi who could not be expected to know any better.

Shelby ordered a scotch, and I took a glass of Sancerre, keen to pace myself—especially at these prices, far beyond the modest pocketbook of an editor at the *Star*. He gazed out at the Boulevard

Saint-Germain with its humming traffic. The Jaguar had found a prized mooring alongside the sidewalk, and strollers turned their heads to see who might cavort on such exotic wheels.

"So, do you feel soiled, used?" he said, almost sneering. "Did you lose your cherry in the great Argentine soy vote scandal, Ed Clancy?"

"If you put it that way, no. If you mean, did I have more faith in the great Joe Shelby, then the answer is sure, I did."

A mud-spattered SUV had drawn to a halt alongside the Jaguar, reversing, nimbly for its size, to squeeze into a gap between Shelby's car and a late-model Porsche. The rear of the SUV was equipped with the kind of chunky tow hitch people use to pull trailers and horse boxes, and its solid, phallic curve was within centimeters of the Jaguar's pristine paintwork when the pilot of the SUV brought it to a halt. The driver's door swung open and a tall red-haired woman— the kind people always stop to look at—stepped down onto the side-walk, tossing the keys to one of the many *voituriers* who had sud-denly materialized to offer their assistance in parking the car. The woman strode toward us, smiling.

"Shelby, meet Marie-Claire Risen. Marie-Claire—Joe Shelby."

I offered the introductions with a sinking heart.

"*Enchanté*," Shelby said in surprisingly fluent French, raising my wife's hand for one of those air kisses I thought had disappeared with the Austro-Hungarian Empire.

"How gallant," she said.

Fuck you, Joe Shelby, I thought.

CHAPTER SIX

MARIE-CLAIRE TURNED FROM JOE SHELBY AND GAVE ME A HUG.

"What chivalrous friends you have," she said.

Shelby preened.

"Up to a point."

She gave me an odd, surprised look and squeezed my hand.

"So, Joe," she said, "welcome to Paris. What do you think of our capital city?"

"It's all true," Shelby said. "The light. The poets. The palaces. The elegance." He paused almost imperceptibly to shift the stress onto what he was about to say. "The beautiful women."

He narrowed his eyes slightly, and I found myself thinking, I don't believe this. But, of course, I did. Marie-Claire was very beautiful, even in her most casual moments. Leaving the stud farm to meet us, she seemed to have spent no time at all changing clothes and she was still dressed in her horsey kit: beige riding breeches with high black boots polished to a deep luster, fawn cashmere sweater, Hermès silk scarf in muted countryside tones, a quilted green Barbour jacket tossed casually over her shoulders. When she shucked it off to drape it over one of those tiny wicker-backed bistro chairs, the sweater stretched across the outline of her breasts.

Indisputably, she matched Shelby's description—and then some.

If she had been carrying her riding crop, half the male population cruising the boulevard would have lined up to be disciplined.

"Don't be fooled," she told Shelby. "Those beautiful women

may look like kittens on the outside, but they are tigers inside."

Shelby did a passable imitation of a feline growl, and she laughed. I did not.

"How was your day?" I said, taking her hand, turning it to show off the wedding band and chunky sparkler that had cost me a slice of my pension.

The waiter was hovering and she ordered a Perrier. Shelby renewed our rounds.

"So what brings you to Paris, Joe?" Marie-Claire went on. "I feel as if I know you already. My husband has been dining out on Joe Shelby stories for years."

"Only the good ones, I hope."

"Just the true ones, Joe," I interjected.

"No, really. I mean it." She was not to be distracted from her line of questioning. "People come to Paris for many reasons, most of them wrong. And when Paris lets them down, they are disappointed."

"I hope I won't be disappointed," Shelby said.

"Joe has a lot of friends in Paris, don't you, Joe? Lady friends, I mean." It was meant as a low blow, but it broke the first rule: Never talk up your buddies in front of your spouse.

"Aha!" Marie-Claire said lightly, with a charming smile. "So it is romance. *Toujours l'amour, n'est-ce pas, Edward?*"

"Edward!" Shelby exclaimed. "I guess I had never figured there was an Edward in there. I always had you down as an Ed. Plain and simple. Mister Ed."

Marie-Claire looked sharply between us.

"Well, I guess there are some lady friends. One at least. But I'm told she is in a wheelchair now and does not have too long to go. So I guess it's not so much *amour* as *adieu*."

She laid her hand on Shelby's arm.

"But I am so sorry," she said. "Edward had not told me."

"Well, I don't like to wear my heart on my sleeve."

The only place you would wear your heart, if you had one, I found myself thinking, would be in your pants. Or in someone else's.

Shelby had brought his Nerval with him and she tapped the cover of *Les Chimères* without opening it.

"Well, I guess we can do without *le Soleil noir de la Mélancolie* here," she said, half schoolmarm, half joking. I guessed she was quoting directly from one of the poems.

"You know him? You've read Nerval! My God, fantastic!"

"Mr. Shelby, I am French. For me to have read Gérard de Nerval is about as unusual as an American reading Walt Whitman. So where were you before Paris?"

"Middle East. Africa. Asia. You name it, I guess. I never counted the datelines."

He glanced at me and I glowered back with a look that said, Oh, yes, you did, you asshole. At least till the number of countries reached a hundred. Like your other conquests.

I just hoped we'd end the evening without the pigeon story.

"So where was home?" Marie-Claire asked.

"Home! Home for a day we used to say. Some hotel room, some bar. Someplace or another."

Jesus!

"And where was most recent?"

"Beirut, Lebanon."

"Of course, the license plate," she said, gesturing toward the car she had come close to remodeling with the tow hitch of her SUV.

"You noticed, huh?"

"Well, it stands out a bit. The XKR is a pretty rare beast in these parts—you know the princes and the sheikhs go more for Ferraris and Rolls."

I could not tell if that was supposed to be a bit of a put-down, but Shelby did not really notice it if it was.

"Like a fine pedigree stallion," he said. "The XKR is a thoroughbred. Last in a line of development, every little glitch ironed out. Beautiful lines." He paused again to smile at Marie-Claire. "Power under the hood."

"So how did you get it here?" she asked with an innocence I knew to be feigned.

"The car? Right. Well, it's an interesting story. A long story."

"Why not cut it short?" I heard myself saying.

"That's your job, Edward," he said very quickly and tartly.

"You're the editor. I just tell the stories. You do the cutting."

"Now, boys," Marie-Claire said in the tone she normally reserved for rambunctious stable lads.

"Okay, okay, out of line. Sorry. Ed, really. *Il miglior fabbro*, that's Ed. The great craftsman. Eliot's dedication to Ezra Pound in *The Waste Land*, 1923."

"1922," she corrected him. "But the epithet underestimates *mon mari*. So much more than a craftsman."

Now it was my turn to preen.

"The car?" she reminded him.

"Right, right. The car. In the Bekaa Valley. Do you really want to hear this?"

He raised his glass, looked at it quizzically, and lowered it again.

"The Bekaa. Lebanon."

He looked at us as if he was trying to remember who or where we were—or who he was.

"The car," I said. "You were telling us how you got the Jag."

"Of course. Funny old yarn. Long story short, for Ed's sake. Well. It all came down to a shooting match."

"Shooting match? My God. I thought you were a reporter, not a gunslinger," Marie-Claire said.

"Both! You better believe it." Shelby pointed a long and knuckly index finger at each of us, flicking his thumbs as if cocking the hammer on matched revolvers. One hand seemed to droop slightly, which kind of spoiled the Wyatt Earp impression. I put it down to whatever his illness was.

"Well. Like I said. Bekaa Valley. What do you expect? Gun central. You remember Bashir? Bashir Fares?"

The name was vaguely familiar from those half-told stories about warlords and spooks that were never quite confirmed enough to print. Shelby was in full flow.

"So Bashir came up to me in the restaurant near the old ruins at Anjar, where they serve the grilled trout, and he and his goons were practicing pistol-shooting with nine-mills aiming at a cigarette pinned upright on a chair back at twenty paces. Bashir was one tough hombre. Minister's son. Top intelligence officer."

Marie-Claire broke in. "He did a lot of the bad stuff at Hama—personally. Heroin. Car bombs. Remind me to tell you the full story sometime. If they ever got him to the Hague . . . but go on. Sorry for the interruption."

Where did she know this stuff from?

"That's the guy," Shelby continued, looking at Marie-Claire with a new respect. "Bad hat. Known him for years. He always thought he was numero uno, and I guess I had had too much arrack to resist. 'Wanna play?' he said. 'Hundred bucks a shot. Winner takes all.' So I said, 'Sure.' Now I was with a bunch of guys—farewell party from Lebanon and they'd thrown me a lunch in the Bekaa. Some friends! Right on the Syrian border with Israeli drones cruising around overhead. And you remember old Dmitri, the famous snapper? Well, he took me to one side and said, 'Whatever you do, Joe, don't hit the cigarette.' And I said, 'Shit, Dmitri, I just put a hundred on the spot.' And he said, 'How much is your life worth?'"

The waiter refreshed our drinks and set down dainty little dishes of nuts and pretzels, and Shelby scrunched a mouthful before continuing. I had a feeling that strangers at adjacent tables had quieted their own conversations to listen in. He seemed to like the audience.

"Now you know how I am these days. Cane. Crip. Fucked. Pardon me, Marie-Claire. Delete expletives. Sorry. So I figured, What the hell? What is my life worth? Not a lot."

Marie-Claire made to dispute the point, as Shelby evidently had scripted her to, but he silenced her with his wilting hand.

"No, no. Just facts. The quacks all say you can't kick this thing. You're only going to get worse. I mean, how much worse can it be? Anyhow. Back to the Bekaa. So I said, 'Okay, Bashir, hand me the shooter.' I guess I figured a hundred bucks would be cheaper than a trip to the old Swiss clinic."

He broke off and laughed with a bitterness I took to be feigned. But it was the first time I had heard him acknowledge his illness, let alone permit a peek into the prognosis. I wondered if he and Faria Duclos shared the same ailment along with everything else they had in common.

"Well, it was looking like no contest. I was none too steady on the old pins what with the cane and a few glasses of arrack under my belt. And I could see Dmitri out of the corner of my eye doing that finger-across-the-throat thing they take pretty seriously out in the Bekaa. So Bashir whips out a platinum-plated nine-mill, barely draws a bead, and fires—*pouf*—and that's one less Marlboro for the world's nicotine police to worry about. 'Still want to play,' he says? 'Sure,' I said. And now this is the weird thing. I propped myself up with one hand on the cane and aimed with the other and I actually tried to miss. But when I pulled the trigger—bingo! I'm right on target. I've hit the freaking cigarette and Bashir is looking pretty pissed. And his goons are kind of sniggering that a stupid old crip with a stick is shooting evens with the boss. So we try again. Same thing happens except this time I was aiming at the goddamn smoke because I figured I'd miss it, but I hit it anyhow."

"What's this got to do with the car, Joe? I thought you said you were cutting a long story short. Spare me the unexpurgated version."

Marie-Claire laughed at my interruption. Shelby did not.

"Patience, Edward, patience," he said. "Some stories just can't be rushed. Isn't that right, Marie-Claire? Some things are worth taking time over, right? Where was I? Okay. So Dmitri and the boys are getting a bit edgy and moving out toward Dmitri's old Subaru, and Bashir is getting more and more pissed and he says, 'You shoot pretty well for a hundred bucks. How about raising the stakes?' 'Like to what?' I said. 'How about your watch?' he says."

Shelby shot his cuff and brandished his scratched steel Rolex.

"I mean this watch. This watch that has been with me since Tehran in '79. This watch keeps the bogeymen away. It's my talisman. So I say, 'Shit, Bashir. This watch means a lot to me. What will you shoot for?' And he looks around and there parked outside the restaurant is a beautiful new XKR Jag. Silver. 'Okay,' he says. 'Your watch. My car.'

"Now this has got a lot of attention and there's a bit of a crowd. 'Best of five,' Bashir says. And I'm in way past the point where you can back out. 'Okay,' I say, 'best of five.' I put my watch on the table. He tells one of his goons to put the Jag keys on the table. And we set up. Five smokes on two chairs. A chalk line to fire from. New ammo fresh out of the box to reload the nine-mills. 'Penalty shootout,' I said. He didn't think that was very funny. And that's not all. His goons are all getting a bit fidgety with their AKs, slipping the safeties on and off. So, round one—*bang!* Shit. Sorry, Marie-Claire. He misses. I hit. Round two: I miss. He hits. Evens. One each and three rounds to go. Round three, we both hit. Round four, the same. Then the final round. I go first. I notice Dmitri going ape. I can't make it obvious to him that I've accepted I'm going to lose my watch and I'm trying to miss without letting it show. So I aim slightly off. But just as I go to pull the trigger, the goddamn Israeli drone overhead fires off a missile, my bad leg does something funny, the gun swings round, and—*bang*—I've hit the cigarette. Like in some kind of circus act."

Shelby paused for effect, his eyes wide in mock amazement. He took a slug of his drink to spin out the story.

"So. There's silence. Total silence. And then suddenly Bashir laughs and holsters the nine-mill. And the heavies laugh and lower their AKs. 'Take the car,' he says. 'It's no good on these roads anyhow.' And he throws me the keys and I put my watch back on and his goons bring round a few Range Rovers and off they all go. 'Take the car . . .' It seemed crazy. And then I figured why: he reckoned the drone was looking for him in the Jag so the next guy to drive it was quite literally toast so he figured he had won either way. Wrong again, as it turned out."

"Is any of this true, Shelby?" I asked.

"Every word," he said. "Just like the Argentine soy vote."

Marie-Claire was giving him a delighted, if somewhat sardonic, round of applause.

I knew she would leave early—she kept equestrian hours, rising in time to supervise the staff for the first misty dawn ride-out on the gallops—so I would need to head back to the office to retrieve my Jeep from the parking garage,

"It has been a pleasure to meet you, Joe. I think that, quite possibly, a lot of what Edward told me about you is probably true."

"In other words, Joe, that you are just an old bullshitter."

"Thank you, Ed," Shelby said, but this time with a smile.

Marie-Claire rose from the table, and whatever physical challenges he might have said he faced, Shelby was on his feet to help her
into her quilted Barbour coat, take her by the shoulders, and lean in
for the double-cheek embrace that can mean as much or as little as
you want.

"Don't be too late," my wife told me. She kissed me square on
the lips. No ambiguity there.

She clambered into her SUV. I noticed that, as she nudged into
the Boulevard Saint-Germain, she permitted the tow hitch to touch
the prow of the XKR—not enough to scar, just enough to make a
kind of contact. Shelby noticed it, too, and looked speculatively at
the big, mud-spattered 4x4 as Marie-Claire pulled into the traffic
with supreme indifference to anyone she might inconvenience.

"What a gal," he said. "You old rogue, Clancy. You netted the
best. And all she got was you—hook, line, and sinker.

"Mind you," Shelby said. "I guess it's not all upside. I mean,
that's a hell of an act to keep up with."

Sometimes he showed glimmers of understanding. Even—heaven
forbid—sensitivity.

But like Charlie in 'Nam, he had a good way of camouflaging it.

CHAPTER SEVEN

MY TIME WITH MARIE-CLAIRE BEGAN AT A PARTY IN A FANCY APART-ment with a view of the Seine, one of those interludes when people congregate in high-ceilinged salons with tall windows and stucco ceilings and silk carpets rolled back from parquet floors, sipping champagne in the languid search for nonintrusive conversation, the defeat of ennui, and, this being Paris, *amour* without commitment—the carnal gratification that consumes the sacrosanct hours between 5 and 7 p.m. when all secrets are kept and all sins are erased.

I was not the man she arrived with. That honor fell to the tall, slender, and exquisitely handsome scion of a noble French line with the baleful, world-weary look and profound facial canyons of true decadence. His hair was a long dark wave streaked with silver at the temples. He had the look of an eagle, accentuated by a prow-like nose and hooded brown eyes. Among the pack of louche artists and boozy journalists I ran with in those days, Freddy de Lusignan—we nicknamed him The Duke—was an object of deep admiration, seeming to prove the impossible proposition that you could indeed fool all the people pretty much all the time.

The Duke lived with no visible, formal employment but enjoyed many invitations and perquisites—borrowed homes and borrowed partners, free access offered without reserve to house parties and yachts. His whereabouts were often uncertain as he progressed between so-and-so's place in Tuscany and what's-his-name's villa in the Engadine. His journeys kept pace with the seasons—sunny summers by the sea at Île de Ré and Saint-Tropez, snowy winters in Courchevel or Gstaad. There was a rumor, which he nurtured with hints and throwaway allusions, that he was working on the definitive, multi-volume chronicle of

Paris to rival *The Alexandria Quartet* in its poetic majesty, or Balzac's *Comédie humaine* in its sweep and gritty detail. But the substance of this eternal work-in-progress was never determined or confirmed, any more than the existence of an agent or publisher or, heaven forbid, a manuscript. All that was vaguely known was that his pre-revolutionary title and its rumored ranking in the *Almanach de Gotha* imparted some particular cachet—the juju of the highborn. People setting up companies paid for the inclusion of his name on their letterhead as if it were a brand to guarantee integrity and connectedness. They turned to him to be introduced to the elite at the Élysée and the Quai d'Orsay, with whom he had maintained contact since his brief spell at the École Nationale d'Adminstration. He liked to call himself a phantom director, but there was nothing spectral about the invoices he sent out when the royalties on his name fell due, handwritten in red ink on heavy embossed paper: they were for real.

Much of what I learned about Marie-Claire came from conversations that began guardedly that night and developed slowly into the kind of dialogue people have when the beginnings of trust have pried open a chink in their natural caution. As her story unfolded, I understood her reticence well since it mirrored my own: there are some things no one likes to admit, secrets that are given up only when the fear of betrayal has given way to hard-earned confidence.

She had spent her childhood in the temporary homes and ever-changing schoolrooms offered to the children of high-ranking French army officers, shunted from one deployment or diplomatic post to another, in Djibouti and N'Djamena, Moscow and Washington, before her father's final teaching job at the military academy in Saint-Cyr offered her the chance to take her place at Sciences Po.

She studied economics, politics and languages—Russian and German among them. Then she did a stint at law school, focusing on mergers and acquisitions. She had been snapped up by a top-three American investment bank that prized her skills in harvesting new European business and demanding tough terms. In her closed, elevated circle, she was highly sought after. A crop of embossed invitations beckoned her to the smarter events on the cocktails-and-canapés circuit, where her father secretly hoped she would meet a dashing French husband to bring him grandchildren and the contentment of having done the right thing by his offspring and seen them happily on their way.

But she disappointed him. A Gallic match proved elusive, despite the sustained efforts of many young and handsome would-be suitors. Instead, she fell for a wiry, chisel-featured American she encountered at a discreet conference designed to bring together the representatives of business and government in the kind of covenant that neither side wishes to advertise. His résumé listed a series of quick military promotions, then a transfer to Special Forces, followed by a fuzzier spell as an attaché of some kind, assigned to embassies in Iraq, Pakistan, and Afghanistan. When she met him, he was, technically, a civilian contractor, heading up a private security company with offices in Washington, Paris, and London.

They made a slightly enigmatic couple, both glamorous in their way—she young and flawlessly fetching; he considerably older, as if his years provided him with some gravitas, some inner core of wisdom that she did not find in younger men. Whatever it was, it did not bring the heir-and-spare brood her father had prayed for.

There were some who said—cynically and, I believe, wrongly— that she married Nick Franjola to further her career, to stretch her contacts into heady new areas of influence, wealth, and power. But in reality, she was simply bowled over, and when I finally brought myself to inquire, she made no secret of that.

Franjola, she said, exuded danger, menace. He had lived among crazy and violent people; he was a buccaneer, an adventurer of the old kind who would disappear into the wilds of the Hindu Kush or the Horn of Africa and emerge, weeks later, scarred and silent.

Yet he had survived his adventures to build a niche at the intersection of diplomacy, politics, and the kind of international mischief that, overnight, turned the presidents of emerging nations into ex-presidents—or, indeed, deceased presidents. He had been running from any kind of marital commitment for years, and when he met her, the considered opinion among their peers was that she was quite a catch and he was one lucky S.O.B. But the cynics figured it wouldn't last: true, their trajectories seemed to intersect with felicitous serendipity, but hers was on the way up. His wasn't.

His work took him too frequently to obscure places on obscure missions from which she was firmly excluded—the Ogaden, Helmand, Waziristan. She could not believe that he was merely the "consultant" that his latest visiting card proclaimed him to be, but he declined to enlighten her as to his true role or employer. Being married to a secret agent was one thing; she suspected his silver-tongued duplicity went further. Much further.

From musty corners of his traveling clothes and hidden pockets in his scuffed canvas tote bags, she began to build a body of evidence that led to only one conclusion. How else could she explain the torn condom wrappers, the Internet orders for Viagra? What other reason could there be for the encrypted area of his PDA that, when deciphered by an inquisitive and technologically savvy spouse, was found to list a tally of exotic female names with phone numbers and addresses in the most unlikely places.

The divorce was speedy and, from her perspective, advantageous, a result of impressive and exhaustive—if surreptitious—research, burrowing through the records of Franjola's declared and undeclared assets. In addition to the formal division of the spoils—the apartments in London and New York, the investment portfolio, the pension, even a share of the gold ingots she had discovered in a safe-deposit box in Liechtenstein—Marie-Claire Risen had Xeroxed his public Rolodex and downloaded a less visible contacts list from his laptop. The catalogue of influence was extensive, almost convincing her that the conspiracy theorists were right and the world was indeed controlled by a secret cabal of wealth and power.

Her trove of new contacts stretched from Foggy Bottom to the Quai d'Orsay, from the boardrooms of Raytheon and BAE to the discreet banking institutions of Zug and Geneva. There were unlisted numbers in there for the doorkeepers who controlled access to Rumsfeld and Cheney, Blair and Putin. She found coded annotations that got calls returned from inscrutable offices along the River Thames at Millbank and Vauxhall, in the forests outside Munich, and, predictably, in Langley, Virginia.

She set up her own consultancy with big-name clients who wanted to penetrate the right circles in Paris and London and New

York without seeing their names all over the newspapers.

Her striking looks did her no harm in her infiltration of the elite. Dressed impeccably by Hermès and Versace, she could talk art, politics, money, or plain dirty in several languages. She knew her Gevrey-Chambertin from her Vosne-Romanée, her Petrus from her Château Margaux. She knew when to listen, when to glitter, when to withdraw discreetly. With high, almost Slavic cheekbones and icy, inscrutable green eyes, she turned heads and ignited envy among women and a desire among alpha males to possess or be possessed by her. But she always insisted—to me, at least—that she achieved far more with flirtation than she might have done with consummation.

Like any military brat, she could be pretty vulgar, too.

On the night I first saw her, she and her aristocrat buddy turned rock and roll into something close to public coitus. They danced, gyrated, twirled, and strutted in lockstep while lesser mortals built a charmed circle around their peacock twists and turns. The party's theme was the sixties, and she wore a miniskirt with a geometric Mary Quant design in black-and-white zigzags and fringed metallic-blonde hair that, in my naivety, I first thought was not a wig. (He had no need of fancy dress: he had spent the era in Saint-Tropez and along the King's Road with Jagger and Clapton in their ruffed shirts and velvet trousers and could not remember a moment of it. But he still had the outfits in his Louis XV wardrobe to prove it. And they still fit his svelte frame.)

There was not a man in the room who was not thinking of how it would be to bed her—or him, for that matter, to judge from the way some glances strayed between the two of them.

Like a belly dancer in a sultan's harem, or a pole dancer in a roadside bar in Texas, she drew strength and audacity from the raw carnal interest of her audience. I found myself waiting for the moment when her nobleman disappeared, presumably to powder his nose, to ambush her.

Like they say, you should be careful what your wish for: if your dreams come true too soon, you start to wonder when some cold dawn will bring them to an abrupt end.

We danced. We talked. We entwined. Something happened that I could not explain then and still find amazing every time I look at her in an unguarded moment and realize that she chose me. I believe both of us were taken by surprise, ambushed by something that old dogs like me know in our hearts cannot possibly exist, at least not for us: love at first sight. But that is, in fact, the only conceivable explanation.

As a halfway-up-or-down-the-masthead editor, producing a small newspaper in Paris, I could not compete with her contacts in power or prestige. I had no glamour or usefulness. I was the kind of saturnine guy you saw in the dark corners at parties when indoor smoking was still allowed, hidden behind the glowing tip of a cigarette, storing impressions, aloof, disengaged, slightly drunk but never smashed. More Bogart than Clooney, I fancied. My dancing involved little more than a vague shuffling at the heels; I dressed in undesigned Levi's and canvas jackets; most times I smelled of horses, whiskey, and nicotine. I told sardonic jokes and kept myself to myself. But I was a different man when Marie-Claire took my hand. I danced with some flamboyance. I sparkled with wit. I was Johnny Depp and Leonardo DiCaprio rolled into one; James Cagney in manner, James Dean in looks. That, at least, is how she made me feel. I could not escape the feeling that, for some reason I could not grasp, she actually liked me. It was an unfamiliar sentiment.

I guess the only downside—one that would come back to haunt me—was the moment when I blundered into a bathroom in search of the john and confronted her and her aristo buddy snorting chemicals from a purpose-made silver tube. Neither of them seemed concerned about being rumbled by a stranger, and they invited me to take a line. But, then as now, I am strictly a juicer, so, like the tabloid reporters in the old days used to say, I made my excuses and left, figuring it was the powder that warped her vision of me, making me seem more than I would always be for her—a ticket into the slow lane, reentry into the gravitational pull of the mundane. That night, recklessly and somewhat mendaciously, I talked up the scope and pedigree of my bloodstock interests. The Duke turned out to be no more than a knight-deterrent to keep unwanted overtures at bay, while she was his cover, his fag hag until he found a boy to go home with.

We snuck away from the party, drove out to the farm in my beat-up Jeep Cherokee, and saddled a pair of feisty three-year-olds to ride across the dewy gallops. She steered her mount away from the manicured meadows with their shrouds of morning mist to plunge along uncharted woodland byways with me in tow, low, springy boughs lashing us, fallen logs demanding unexpected leaps.

Leaps into the unknown.

Across the Rubicon.

She rode with panache, precision, elegance, so different from my Wild West cowboy manners in the saddle. I had to push hard to keep up with her. Her mount seemed transformed, wanting to give its all, just as I did—more than anything I had ever known.

She moved in. I made no objection. She ran the business but kept her own interests ticking over through trusts and surrogates. She turned my modest stable for the prepubescent gymkhana set into a prime stud farm with gleaming white fences imposing geometric symmetry on the greensward.

In the process, she made me feel quite a stud, too.

Of course, we would not have been a couple if we did not have our differences, our divergent perspectives that grew from the beginning and would not go away. I guess the one that really made me uneasy was the cocaine.

Right at the start I asked her to desist, and she said—in a kindly, mild sort of way—no.

We were dining in town at a place on the Rue du Faubourg Saint-Honoré during the boy-meets-girl phase when I misguidedly tried to impress her with my gourmand savoir faire without disclosing the strains on my credit card. I had ordered a Jameson for myself, and she had requested just a Perrier.

That was when I raised the C word.

She took a sip of her water and looked across at me with a clear, level gaze. I remember how the low lights on the table and the candles all seemed to fuse and splinter in the crystal glass of bubbly water so that it looked as if she were illuminated by a saintly halo.

She tapped my glass of Jameson resting on the white linen between us.

"How often do you drink this stuff, Ed?"

"Well, I guess, occasionally?"

"Up a little."

"Well, maybe, regularly."

"Like daily?"

"I guess."

"And what do I say about that?"

"Nothing."

"Well, then?" she said.

I made one last stab at establishing authority.

"But chemicals are different. Addictive. Expensive. Dangerous. Fatal to the septum. The central nervous system. Habit-forming."

She tapped my whiskey glass again.

"Touché," I said.

Marie-Claire reached across the white linen and took my hand.

"Ed, it's lovely to see you so concerned. But don't be. It's occasional. A foible. I promise it won't get in the way. It won't be a habit. But, on principle, my dearest Edward"—she pronounced it "Édouard" in the throaty French way—"you must understand that you cannot make all the rules. You must have trust. *Non?*"

At that point, the sommelier arrived with the Sancerre I had ordered. I sniffed at the proffered sample and pronounced it impeccable.

"And I will trust you, too," she said. "Your nose for news and wine especially."

Round one and many more to her.

But I watched her like a hawk.

I had been doing my job for too long to believe everything I was told, especially when love was invoked to buttress trust.

The truth was it wasn't just the narcotic I feared. Somehow the drug was a symbol of where she had come from and of the fear that she might weary of my terrestrial offerings and seek liftoff once more into the remote galaxies where she had sparkled with such grace and ease when I first met her. Reynolds Packard might have been able to dedicate a book to his wife's lovers. I could not even bear the thought of their existence. The very idea filled me with horror.

CHAPTER EIGHT

AFTER MARIE-CLAIRE DROVE OFF, SHELBY AND I SAUNTERED OVER to Deux Magots.

I gestured to the waiter for a round.

"So what happened to Faria Duclos?" I asked.

He looked at me sharply and lit a cigarette.

"Those things are bad for you."

"Bad for me? How can anything be bad for me, Clancy? What do you think it'll do to me? Make me limp? Screw up my nervous system? Put me on the fast track to the Dignitas clinic in Zurich where they give you the bye-bye shot just after they swipe your credit card, then show you the last exit? I've got all that already, Clancy. I'm screwed whichever way. Look at me. A couple of Marlboros isn't going to make any fucking difference."

The obscenity drew a few offended glances—people have no sense of tolerance anymore.

"So get it cured. If you're sick, see a doctor."

"Boy, have I ever seen doctors. Chinese needle doctors. Belgian voodoo doctors. German mystic doctors. Doctors with fancy rooms in Harley Street. Doctors on the Nile where they boil their needles in kitchen kettles. The Mayo Clinic. Queen Square. Witch doctors. Shamans. Sangomas. Muti men. Hypnotists. Mumbo jumbo merchants. Homeopaths. Osteopaths. Chiropractors. You name it, buddy."

"And?"

"And, more or less, they all say the same thing: we don't know except for one thing."

"And that would be?"

"We can't fix it."

"So the prognosis is?"

"The prognosis is: put your house in order, do whatever you have to do to make whatever peace you need to make with whomever. Because one day, sooner or later, who knows when, those old systems of yours are just going to close down."

"Is that why you came to Paris?"

"Kind of." He was suddenly evasive.

Recalling his story from the Bekaa Valley, I realized that Shelby had not anchored his narrative in time. Old hands always tell cub reporters that their articles must answer the key questions: who, why, how, when, where, and, usually, how much? But Shelby's anecdote had no "when." There were no dates, no chronology. Somehow, the way he told it, the *suggestion* was that he had simply driven his prized Jaguar back to Beirut, shipped it to Paris, and emerged at the *Star* newsroom in one unbroken span of time. But life was not like that. There had been gaps, unexplained lacunae in the narrative. I remembered news items about Bashir Fares that said he had been avoiding the Bekaa Valley for months because of Israeli drones, hiding out in the safer confines of a poolside bar at the Sheraton in Damascus. So that placed Shelby's story much earlier than he seemed to be indicating. And I recalled Marcel Duffie musing about a gap in Shelby's CV. What was that? Rehab? Therapy? Plain old-fashioned R&R?

Shelby was not saying.

"And Faria," I said. "You mentioned her to Marie-Claire. What gives, for Chrissakes?"

"Ah, Faria. 'Nam. Mideast. Africa. And now Paris."

"You know she's here?"

"She's here."

"You saw her?"

He shook his head and then looked up into some middle distance between street level and the rooftops.

"Why not?"

"She didn't ask."

"That doesn't make sense. Maybe she's waiting for you to ask. Maybe she's too sick to ask. Maybe you don't have much time to wait for an invitation. From her of all people."

"Of all people." He laughed when I had not expected him to, a short, barking exclamation without humor. "What did you hear?"

"Just hack stuff. And what's been in the papers. She's quite a celebrity here. They say she has some incurable nerve thing. Lou Gehrig's. ALS. Big league."

When he said nothing, I kept on talking.

"So you know how these things go, right? They cut through the systems until there's nothing left. No speech. No swallowing. No movement."

"I read the goddamn medical journals, Clancy. Sure I know. How would I not know? But she's not that bad, right?"

"I heard she's getting pretty bad. Why don't you go and find out?"

"I told you. She didn't ask."

"She was—is—the love of your life and now you can't even go see her?"

"And let her see me like this?"

"Bullshit, man. This isn't a fashion parade. We could go now, Joe. You really ought to see her. Before it's too late. For both of you. Okay. Maybe you aren't Mr. Universe anymore. And maybe she isn't so good either. But you owe it to each other. You have to talk. You have to take whatever is left."

"So when did you get to be Dr. Therapist, Edward?" He pronounced the word in exaggerated French: *Édouaaard*. "Give me a break. I told you. I'll get to her. When she wants me to."

"You're scared, aren't you?"

I knew I was pushing the limits, but I felt emboldened, as much by the wine as by the sight of Shelby flirting with my wife as if I didn't exist. "You're frightened of looking at her and seeing yourself. The great war correspondent!"

"You don't know what fear is, Ed. Believe me."

I thought he would be angry, but all I detected in his voice was a terrible wistfulness.

"Fear isn't the worst thing, Ed."

"No? So what is?"

"Guilt."

Way back, when Shelby and Duclos had been a number, they had invited me often enough to join them for dinner at Chez l'Ami Jean or La Gitane as they transited Paris to draw breath and decompress from their adventures, stopping off to buy new leather jackets at Dada Cuir in the Eleventh and fripperies at Le Bon Marché in the Seventh. (On one trip to the leather store, Shelby had been particularly taken with a retro-look flier's helmet in brown leather, the kind worn by doomed and dashing young men as they clambered into the cockpits of their Spitfires and P-51 Mustangs. Never to return. Before he could find his wallet, Faria Duclos had produced a bundle of francs—the currency they used here in those days—and presented him with the headgear as a gift.)

In those far-off times, photographers needed to transit the First World to renew their stocks of Tri-X Pan black-and-white film and AA batteries and, sometimes, chemicals for the field darkrooms to process their images in distant places. I knew she stocked up on other substances, too, disguising them from the prying eyes of cops and customs officers in those same containers of 35mm film and sachets of developer and fixer.

Their reasons for choosing me as a companion on their resupply missions were never really clear.

Some couples need a third party as a buffer zone, a neutral space between them, a firebreak. It's a thankless task. Sometimes you are just an impediment, an unwelcome insulator disrupting the current between the poles of electric passion. And other times you are the no-man's-land between combatants whose rages equal their lusts, pounded by incoming fusillades from both sides. And sometimes you become the unwitting ally of one side or the other. You are drawn in, recruited—part spy, part double agent—to pass messages and intelligence between them, gather responses, report back. In my case, Faria Duclos became my control, running me in her unending quest for advantage and sympathy from Shelby.

But, for all the years I had known her, I had never seen her in her true element—caught in the firefights, traversing the killing fields on which she had built her reputation. Together, the three of us—sometimes four if I brought along a companion—had reveled into the small hours. Often as not, I begged off, exhausted, as they boogied till dawn, desperate for one last crazy swerve of freedom on the safety of some dance floor before their flights bore them off to places where people neither drank nor danced. Only died.

Maybe I had been no more than the gooseberry, the perennial spare prick at their non-wedding. But now they needed to make each other whole after all they had been through, needed to dock in the safe harbor of memory from their time together. Because if they did not, their business would be unfinished, and they would die apart and their souls would find no peace. For some reason, I figured I was the only one who could navigate those particular shoals, though what gave me the credentials, I'll never know. I was hardly qualified as a healer of human folly.

Right from the beginning, Paris had been a refuge, a sanctuary, a place where I could invent a little bit of personal truth and live by it. In the Select in Montparnasse or at Harry's no one asked for your CV. Your money was good at the bar and your secrets were your own. Even Shelby, who got as close as anyone, didn't know much about where I came from. The surname was enough: Clancy, Irish, top o' the morning.

If no one asked, there was no one to tell that my parents still lived in Queens and rarely wrote or called except to ask for loans; that, after the first twenty grand didn't get paid back, I never replied to their begging letters; that I had not invited them to my wedding because I was too embarrassed to imagine my scrawny, half-shaven father in his sneakers and Yankees cap and my mother in her bulging Lycra mingling with the glossy set I cultivated in France. They did not even know that Marie-Claire existed, or that we were, in theory, comfortably off with our horses and land. If they ever found that out, they would be at our doorstep with their hands out.

I had not told Marie-Claire the full story, either, preferring to intimate that my folks were somehow shy and incapacitated, unable to undertake long journeys by air. Sure, I said, I'll take you to meet them when we head Stateside. But I knew I never could. Or would. I knew I would never forgive them for sending me to the Catholic boarding school where the Brothers beat you and, if you looked for sympathy at home, you got none. Good Irish American folks were what they had always pretended to be. But when I checked out their genealogy, there was no trace of the Clancys of the Dingle Peninsula from which they claimed descent. There were plenty of other Clancys, of course, but none that came from the nonexistent addresses and unheard-of villages they defined as their roots. It was easy enough to cut loose.

Early on, the newspapering life drew me to it: late hours, raffish colleagues, the promise of the Big Story that would propel me into the Big League. Working sports, I developed a passion for the horse-track, and spent longer than I should have interviewing trainers and jockeys, hanging around yards and winner's enclosures until it became a passion to emulate those proud owners parading their steeds after some victory or other. Perhaps that liking for the thrill and the sweat of the turf came from some kind of Irish roots, as bogus as my parents' ties to the old country turned out to be. But still, I felt a hankering to be some place else, away from whatever frail roots bound me to America.

When I saved enough from lowly work on the sports desk and the police beat, and with my pockets swollen by the occasional win from the tips you only hear about if you spend enough time among the stable-lads and the grooms, I left abruptly and ran away across an ocean to land in France, where I stayed.

I had not been a total recluse. There'd been friends, live-ins, near-misses, train wrecks, but no one I still stayed in touch with. While Shelby and Faria Duclos were circling the globe, I was here, in Paris—my Paris—where the bartenders knew me. I began to think that, in the end, I would grow old with my horses and the tremulous pining for human company would slowly fade away. Then Marie-Claire came along and I guess that's what

finally gave me my diploma in the ways of the heart so familiar
to Shelby and Duclos.

From Vietnam to the Middle East and Africa, theirs had been
one of the great *amours* among the combat junkies they counted as
their friends, their fellow addicts to the debauchery of war, all of
them in thrall to the stillness of the dead, escaping the silver bullet
one more time until the next throw of the dice on some indistinct
front line. Wherever there was conflict and the usual pack of
reporters and photographers arrived in town, Faria Duclos, with her
wild, unkempt black hair and spectral, skinny frame, would be
among the first—but only as long as it took her to get credentialed,
pick up the threads, and divine the dark zone where the others would
not venture but where some instinct told her the images would be at
their most stark and the perils most extreme.

The stories were endless: the time they came upon the genocidal
gangs in Rwanda still going about their ghastly carnage; the time she
confronted the "war vets" of Zimbabwe with only an old Leica camera; the time, outside of Baghdad, when they had been with a patrol
that lost half its men and they fought their way out with them and
there was much talk about whether Shelby had overstepped the
unwritten rules that forbade reporters from carrying, let alone firing,
weapons. Then there was the mystery that neither of them discussed,
even with their closest friends. Somewhere in Africa, on some jaunt
or other, Shelby had met Eva Kimberly, a cool, coiffed, colonial scion
of old white money in black-ruled Africa—the antidote to the pho-
tojournalist's craziness. He had abandoned Duclos, telling her that
he could no longer fly wing on her sorties, protecting her, shielding
her. And she had headed off alone, back into the maelstrom of con-
flicts that sustained her. But that was not by any means the end of
the story.

In Gaza, at a time when Shelby's undiagnosed, stumbling illness
had begun to manifest itself as a serious and likely enduring afflic-
tion, their paths crossed again—not altogether coincidentally but for
all the world to see.

Reunited, they headed out to some flash point in the tumble-down cinder block moonscape of Palestinian misery. Predictably, they ran into trouble between the lines. Lacking his old agility, Shelby was pinned down until she came to his side—his dark angel, supporting him as they limped through withering crossfire to safety. Live television cameras caught the moment, and the war-zone embrace that followed it.

On her television screen in faraway Primrose Hill in London, Eva Kimberly saw it in every last horrifying detail: the hug that became an embrace, the survivors' grin that turned into a lingering kiss.

And yet—and this, the old-timers said, was the mystifying point in the whole saga—having wrenched him from the jaws of death and planted the kiss of life on his unresisting lips, Faria Duclos moved on again, drawn to places he could no longer really go with his walking cane and his inability to scamper away from trouble.

In some ways, none of them literal, Shelby was still running. But how could anyone ever really understand? To most of us, his buddies and partners in crime, it seemed as if everything had been within his reach and yet he had not taken it. His dream had slipped through his fingers.

Maybe he had come to Paris to look for it, only to discover that he did not even know where to begin.

And then, as we sat mulling our destinies at Deux Magots, Gloria Beeching sashayed into view.

She was dressed casually, but with evident attention to the detail of her coiffure and makeup. At the office I had usually seen her in the copyeditor's mandatory uniform of lumpy gray cardigan and shapeless skirt, her sneakers beside her desk after she changed into office brogues, her hair pinned up in a casual tangle. Now she wore low-rise black jeans with a designer icon on the back pocket, a silvery, looped belt, and a white top that accentuated her cleavage, topped by a short black jacket that followed the parabola of her waistline. She had let her hair down in a lustrous dark mane.

"You did say dinner *à deux*, didn't you?" she asked Shelby, inclining her head toward me with a quizzical expression.

Shelby turned to me with a what-can-you-do shrug.

"Maybe another time, Ed," Shelby said.

"Yeah, maybe another time."

As I left, he was launching into another stolen story, telling Gloria Beeching that, in Journalism 101, the only lesson that counted was not among those trotted out by professors at Columbia J-school. It was a nostrum that Reynolds Packard immortalized a half-century earlier in the title of a book.

"When you think of who you are writing for, and who you want to understand your stories, and what language you should use," Shelby was saying, "then there is only one person to keep in mind as you compose: the Kansas City milkman."

"And his wife," Gloria insisted.

She had read old Packard, too.

I couldn't wait to be gone. I wanted to retrieve the Jeep and head back home to Marie-Claire and grab her and say to her, Honey, whatever it is we have together, please don't ever let it go. Because I never, ever will.

But there was one more errand on my must-do list, one more promise that I could not avoid.

CHAPTER NINE

THE CAB FROM SAINT-GERMAIN SKIRTED THE CLOGGED TRAFFIC CIRCLE outside the Wepler seafood place where, when he was not composing his magisterial tributes to abundant sexuality, Henry Miller liked to consort with the hookers who took refuge there from the cold. (His favorite, so the story went, sported a wooden leg).

The neon glare of the world's red-light districts always spreads a miasma of seediness, destroying the last vestige of pretense that the business at hand is anything other than the crude trade in momentary gratification. London's Soho or New York's Eighth Avenue, the Patpong Road in Bangkok, the Reeperbahn in Hamburg, or the De Wallen of Amsterdam—wherever vendors erect their beacons to the lewd commerce that undermines human claims to a higher form of being, they do so in neon: Sex Shop, Peep Show, Girls, Girls, Girls. Or Boys, Boys, Boys. Or Both, Both, Both.

The driver turned south, navigating a grid of streets to reach a narrow canyon of Haussmannian apartment houses staring into one another's tall windows. Most of them had huge, ceremonial carriage gates—memories of an earlier, grander era—with smaller pedestrian entries set into them, controlled by codes punched into a keypad. As I paid off the cab, I noticed the small door open at the address I had been given for Faria Duclos, located between two streetlamps but not fully illuminated by either. There was something vaguely familiar about the person slipping out, some memory that stirred like an indistinct sound you can't identify. Then I was pocketing my change and *la fiche* from the cab fare. (I had asked for a receipt more out of habit than need: no one redeemed my expenses anymore.) The mystery man did not look back.

I fumbled for the piece of paper Elvire Récamier had provided with the coordinates, punched in the requisite four digits, and heard the faint, satisfying click signifying that access had been electronically approved.

The apartment was on the seventh floor, so I figured it would be one of those long, thin places right under the zinc roof, created from the mansards that had once offered rooms to the maids of the rich folks living down below. I squeezed into an elevator the size of a small closet and noticed that, to judge from the available buttons, it went only as far as the sixth. Why make it easy for Monsieur to pay clandestine visits to Mademoiselle? Why give the maids their own easy access when the space taken up by a lift shaft would make an extra room for one more of them? So much for the "*égalité*" part of the national motto. (I had never been too sure about the "*liberté*" and "*fraternité*" bits either in these post-revolutionary days.) The elevator took a long time to wheeze and creak to the apex of its allotted course, as if it were sending a warning on ahead. It delivered me into darkness. I groped for a light switch.

A narrow spiral staircase ran up from the landing on the sixth floor. As I set foot on its metal rungs, I wondered how someone stymied by physical disability would cope. There was no way an invalid in advanced stages of decline would make it alone: somebody must be looking out for her. Above me, I heard, or sensed, an indistinct waft of music. The air carried a familiar trace of marijuana.

The entrance to the apartment was unmarked—no name, no number—and in the absence of a bell push, I knocked vigorously. The music—early Dylan, maybe?—faded away and I heard a faint whirring noise that grew louder.

No footsteps, though. I remember thinking, Why are they are no footsteps? Then I felt foolish for asking myself the question.

Even as she opened the door and peered up at me, she was looking beyond me for someone else who was not there. I hoped that would distract her from my shock at seeing her, but whatever her physical appearance, she still had her wits about her.

"Clancy," she murmured huskily, as if her vocal chords could not stretch to much more than a whisper. It sounded like "*Clonsee.*"

"*Tu es tout seul,*" she said. "*Moi aussi.*"

She was in one of those electric-powered wheelchairs operated by controls on the arms, like the handsets that children use to manipulate radio-steered boats or cars or airplanes. Her legs, always stilt-skinny, fell from her waist like twin strands of dark dried rope. Her signature tight, black jeans hung as loosely as shredded rigging on a ghost ship. She was wearing a black T-shirt and an old leather jacket in the same color—one of those Dada Cuir trophies of the Shelby days. Hanging around her neck, outside her T-shirt, a mangled piece of lead hung from a worn leather thong. The bullet. Shelby's Vietnam bullet. Even indoors, she wore a wide-brimmed straw hat, tilted to hide a side of her face.

I wondered if she had dressed like that because she expected *him* to knock at the door instead of me, in his own matching outfit, like they were headed to some macabre costume party, transporting them both back across time to the days when they ruled the world and each other.

She reversed the wheelchair jerkily along a corridor with uneven wood-tile floors, then spun around to enter a long, low loft with the kind of casement windows that moviemakers choose to frame the vistas of lovelorn poets in their garrets. From the seventh floor, looking south at the city, she had a great view—all the way to Saint-Sulpice on the left and to the Eiffel Tower on the right. The tower was sparkling, as it did every hour, to waste electricity and remind people what city they are in. Looking uphill to the north, I thought I could just see a single red spar from the Moulin Rouge.

The walls, even where they sloped inward under the eaves of the building, were filled with prints of her most famous photographs, all in black-and-white: the dead-eyed marine in Hue; the murdered white family in Zimbabwe, their bodies mimicking the broken dolls in the arms of the savaged children; the Palestinian man in Gaza cradling a dead infant; the Israeli soldier with prayer shawl and machine gun. There were moonscapes from Fallujah;

improbable images of the broken jigsaws of quake zones in Pakistan and Haiti; the tilted, holed minarets of south Lebanon— the stage sets of the drama she sought out and passed on to a remote world, as if to shake its complacency. Most of her photographs had been taken at close quarters with a wide-angle lens, capturing in shocking intimacy a helpless victimhood that had gone far beyond self-regard or self-pity. Blank eyes gazed from Balkan prison camps, Afghan compounds, sandbagged revetments—an unremitting gallery of pain and loss. At a vernissage, they might have drawn comment for their uniform horror; as interior decoration, they made you shiver, as if all the depravity she had ever seen had come full circle, enfolding her.

"So. He did not come." She was always one to get straight to the point. "I guess I cannot blame him."

Below the brim of her hat, someone had drawn her long hair back and tied it in a loose bun. Once it had been a lustrous black. Now it was thin, shot with gray, defying any effort to disguise the advancing years. In her most vibrant days she had liked to wisecrack about how her slender frame made her "a smaller target for the bad guys." Now she was downright gaunt, as if the flesh and musculature had retreated wholesale from her bones, leaving her skin to hang from them. A thin plastic pipe looped from an oxygen tank on the back of her wheelchair to feed her nostrils. Her lips were pale—gray lines drawn in papyrus. But the eyes held me, deep, black, glowing with light, as if to say, Look into me, into these eyes; *this* is me, not the body you see; in here is the real me, like so many years ago when we were young. I was reminded of a time I drove by a prison and, at one barred window out of a hundred, saw a single inmate staring out at a world that had locked him in and thrown away the key.

"Do not be shocked, Clancy. You get used to it." She smiled, and I noticed that her teeth had been whitened, almost jaunty against the pallor.

"Faria," I said.

"For God's sake, Clancy. Control yourself," she said in a mockstern whisper.

I wiped my eyes.

"You really know how to make a girl feel good."

Faria Duclos had started her working career as a model, traveling from a small town in Normandy to Paris, where she hit the big time on the catwalks and magazine covers. But she had always been fascinated not so much by images of herself as by the cameras that made them. So she bought one: a Leica, long predating the digital era with its mechanical shutter and split image focusing. On a fashion shoot in Jordan, she had witnessed a street battle and photographed it from the level and the perspective of the combatants. The result earned her sales around the world. Her pictures were labeled exclusive. She left the catwalk for the battlefield. On a shelf in her apartment the old Leica—an M2—held pride of place in a glass display case. But if the work on her walls was designed as a retrospective, it also had the unmistakable feel of a valedictory, a farewell.

She nodded toward a dark, antique dresser where a bottle of Talisker—Shelby's favorite—stood unopened. Next to it, a bouquet of expensive red roses was still wrapped in florists' cellophane.

"Help yourself," she said.

I did, tearing at the heavy lead foil to open the bottle and pouring a solid jolt of its peaty, smoky, fiery contents.

I took her bony hand and squeezed it. She tried to reciprocate the gesture, but her fingers barely moved, as if the brain had sent out a signal that was just too faint for what was left of the organism to hear. The backs of her hand were channeled into the skeletal ravines caused by muscle loss—"guttering," neurologists like to call it, though not in front of patients who might think the term too cavalier. I guessed it had been a long time since she had been able to raise a Leica or press a shutter. Or walk through passport control in a strange country. Or talk her way through a roadblock. Or dodge bullets.

"Tell me, Faria."

"There is not a lot to tell," she said. "You must laugh in the face of danger."

The expression was one Shelby used to mock a colleague who

adopted that motto too frequently, usually from the safety of a bar. It took me a moment to realize that the grimace agitating her spectral features was supposed to reflect her old, wry merriment at the folly of her trade and its practitioners.

I leaned forward to catch her words. That was when I noticed the catheter bag catching her urine. She intercepted my glance and lowered her eyes. Look at me now, she seemed to be saying in this dialogue without words. Look at what has become of me.

"My night nurse will be here soon, and he will chase you away, so I will try to be quick. Quick. Ha! I do not do quick anymore." She was offering her imitation of laughter again and I laughed with her, though I felt more like kneeling in homage. When she spoke of her prospects, she was so matter-of-fact that, at first, you did not realize she was talking about herself. I guess she had been so close to the end for so long that nothing really surprised her anymore.

"They say it will not be long. Maybe weeks. Days. Who knows? Shelby is in Paris?"

"He is here."

"He is sick?"

"He walks with a cane."

"It should be a crutch. He always had a crutch. Me, or Eva, or Elvire. I would like to see him."

"I will tell him."

"No. Do not tell him. He must come of his own free will. When he is ready."

"But if . . ." My sentence tailed off.

While I spoke she had been wrestling with her unresponsive arms to produce the stub end of a reefer from the folds of her clothing.

"Cigarette me." It was an old joke and I smiled.

I took the roach and placed it between her lips, where her own hands would not reach. I flicked my lighter and she took a shallow drag, then another and a third before she signaled to me to remove it.

"Medicinal," she said. "But do not tell the *médecin*! You were saying, Ed Clancy. 'But if' what? If I die before he gets here? If I die without telling him I forgive him, that I would have taken him back anytime if he had only asked? That I would have nursed him if I were not broken? Is that what you wanted to ask me? Would that be true? Maybe he thinks I hate him. Maybe a little bit I do. Maybe he thinks I am sick because of him and the places we went. Maybe he is right. Funny that we both are fucked up." In her Édith Piaf whisper it sounded like "ferked up." She knew her accent gave her a free pass on English obscenities.

"Maybe it is possible to love and hate at once. Maybe, now, we will never, ever know. Maybe it was for me to look for him, and up to him to look for me. For him to know and me to find out. Or vice versa."

She fell back against the worn padding of her wheelchair. Her speech had exhausted her.

"He will come. I will make him come."

"He will come if he wants to," she said. "Only then."

"You might not recognize him."

"Impossible."

"He's older . . ."

"We are all older, Clancy. Especially you." Her laughter rustled again like a zephyr crossing dry leaves.

"But I know what he would say to you."

"You always did think you knew too much about other people, Edward." She pronounced my name the way Marie-Claire did. There was an accusatory tone to her voice, but then it softened. "Do not say anything Shelby would not."

"I know what he would say." I was beginning to sound defensive. "And I know what he would like to say and could not."

"A riddle?"

"He thinks you do not want to see him."

"But, Clancy, you know I do. And what would he say when he came to visit?"

"He would say . . ." I stopped to rephrase my words and took a deep breath as I prepared my little speech. "Look, you guys have your secrets. No question. And I know there's something about all this that no one will tell me. But this is the thing, Faria. Whether Shelby said it or not, you would know from his eyes and his hand in yours that he still loves you more than anyone on the planet."

She looked at me, and I thought she would weep. Like I was doing.

But instead, she smiled and said, "And how does he know that there is no one else who loves me just as much?"

I thought of the mystery man leaving the building. I thought of the roses next to Shelby's unopened whiskey bottle.

"I guess that was the question you never answered for him," I said.

"No, no. Clancy. Do not be cruel. Not now. Not to me, to this sick old woman I have become. This crone who dares not look in the mirror. I know what people say. They say when I went back on the road, after he started getting sick, it was because I could not love him in that condition. But the truth was, I wanted to set him free to decide for himself what he wanted to become of us."

I refilled my whiskey—three fingers, no ice—in a big, chunky tumbler. She gestured to her stash and I rolled another joint for her, lighting it and letting her puff on it. When she tried to inhale too deeply, she coughed and her eyes watered.

"Quick, before the night nurse. One more toke," she said.

The conversation drifted. I talked about Elvire and her stories from 'Nam, the desperate motorcycle ride, the bullet in the typewriter (she gestured to her makeshift necklace), the rose in the backpack, and Gibson Dullar hovering, back then. Way back.

"I do not remember Gibson Dullar being there," she said, suddenly haughty and distant. For a second I thought her eyes flickered toward the unwrapped roses.

I heard the door open and close behind me.

A man who did not look like a night nurse entered the apartment. He had an honest, open face and curly blond hair. He wore an expensive tweed sport coat, a blue cotton shirt open at the neck, and freshly pressed Levi's. He was much younger than Faria or I. His eyes matched his shirt and shone like a puppy's when she looked at him.

"Ivar," he said, holding out a hand to me in introduction.

"This is the famous Shelby?" he said, turning to Faria, slightly bemused, as if the image he had did not at all match the person he found rising from her side to greet him.

She did her laugh-wheeze whisper again. Dry as old leaves.

"Clancy. Shelby's sidekick," she said. The story of my life in three words.

"Ivar Bild," he said. "From Sweden."

"I would never have guessed."

"Ivar is my agent in Scandinavia," she said. The look between them told me he was—or had been, or wanted to be—much more than that.

I assumed it was he who had brushed back her hair, dressed her in her old combat clothes, prepared her public face, even as his own love consumed him. Maybe it was he, too, who rolled her joints, changed her oxygen bottles, switched the catheter bag and emptied its contents into the john. He struck me as being one of those men with older women who have the gift of seeing beyond age; who cherish the secret, bedside photograph we all keep hidden, like a portrait of Dorian Gray in reverse, preserving eternal youth. I wondered if he was the man I had seen leaving the apartment building when I arrived, but I figured not.

"The night nurse?" I said.

"The night nurse," Ivar said with a comfortable smile.

"Time to go, Ed," Faria said. Our conversation had tired her. Dark bags spread below her eyes.

I felt relieved to be leaving, to have done my duty, to have gleaned the message to take back to Shelby: Go see her, you do not have much time. Or, rather, she does not have much time.

Ivar led me back to the door after permitting me to kiss Faria on both cheeks. It was like brushing your lips over parchment.

"Remember what I said," she whispered. "Do not tell Shelby I asked for him. He must come without prompting."

Her head slipped forward, and her straw hat fell from her head so that you could see what it was supposed to hide: livid scar tissue across her right temple and into her scalp, pink as a vulture's neck, the kind that comes after third-degree burns have destroyed too many layers of skin for recovery. I was too shocked to do anything but stare at her. More than any words, the panicked, desperate look in her eyes said: Do not tell him what you have seen; do not judge me like this.

As I reached the door, Ivar the Swede took my hand in a bone-crushing grip.

"She is looked after. Twenty-four hours a day. She is in no pain. And she will be in no pain when the moment comes. I will make sure of that."

I wondered how.

"How long has she got?"

"Not long. Tell this to the heartless Joe Shelby. Tell him to come see her. He is all she is staying alive for."

His eyes watered with the humiliation of a confession dictated by a terrible honesty.

"Does she forgive him?"

"She forgave him a long time ago. Did he tell you about the fire?"

"What fire?"

"The fire in Beirut. Ask him. Ask the great Joe Shelby."

"You are a good man, Ivar," I said.

"She is a good woman."

He handed me a scrap of paper with a single sentence written on it.

"It was in a letter addressed to Shelby. The last thing she wrote while she could still hold a pen and move her fingers."

The handwriting was spidery, labored. The words formed jagged parabolas, barely legible, like some kind of weird spiky graph.

"I would rather be alone than hurt by the people around me," it said.

"Tell him," Ivar Bild said. "Take the message—perhaps he will remember it. After all, he once said the same words to her."

CHAPTER TEN

BEFORE THE START OF OUR SHIFT, BEFORE WE FIRED UP OUR COMPUT-ers (the Mighty Wurlitzers, as we called them), before we switched on the TV news and began calling around to correspondents from Soweto to Shanghai, we had taken to meeting at Le Primerose, a café-bar in the Parisian style where the waiters sport long aprons and supercilious demeanors. The owner, known only as Madame, had curly brown hair and eyeglasses and never missed a centime as she guarded the till like a revolutionary *tricoteuse*. Over time—in the right light and in the broad, soft focus of the true romantic— she became if not exactly lovable then less hostile, almost alluring. From the moment he first met her on his assignment to the *Star* newsroom, Shelby began a reflexive courtship, smiling, inclining his head in a suitor's bow to request the honor of a croissant and a *double allongé*—as if he were about to kiss her hand and sweep her off her feet.

I imagine he thought himself a Don Juan, but he reminded me more of Don Quixote—which made me Sancho Panza, so I discarded the metaphor.

We saw her in the very early hours, when her staff lugged wicker chairs onto the sidewalks and her mysterious, polished chrome machines hissed and rumbled with the first of the day's caffeine injections and her own cook appeared from the subterranean kitchen with trays of hot, fresh *viennoiseries*, glistening from the oven.

Outside, the street cleaners sprayed the sidewalks and the traffic began to build. Within, as the lights flickered in cautious greeting of a new day, we felt warm and welcomed. Madame smiled. She deliv-ered our coffees and tartines with grace and sometimes a coy hint of wiggly haunches. The morning's edition of the *Paris Star*, its spine clamped in a wooden rod, was laid before us, and we took turns in deconstructing it in the way journalists know best.

Jeez, who writes this garbage?

Oops, we do.

The rest of the world came to know this particular day as the day of the Great Crash, but at that hour in Paris, the bubble of delusion, deceit and denial still enfolded the financiers of Tokyo and London and New York. It was the day I finally planned to transmit Faria's message from her loft to Shelby, but I did not know how to bring the conversation around to it. I had prevaricated for a long time, trying to work out how to tell him, how to demand his presence after work at her apartment. A weekend had gone by, and I had tried to call him, but his cell phone rang continuously without inviting me to leave a message. I wasn't sure how to broach the Swede's question about a fire, either, so to my enduring regret, I left it for another time. Whether we like to admit it to ourselves or not, inaction can be just as devastating as dynamism. History isn't made exclusively from grand gestures: neglect unravels empires; when small talk replaces decisions, you have to look out for what you're ignoring. Easy to say now, I know.

That morning, I was recounting the latest episode in a long-running story about an infestation of what I believed to be weasels in one of my barns. I even showed Shelby a leaflet advertising various brands of poison for rodents and bearing the ink stamp of my local feed store. For his part, Shelby was reminiscing about an incident in Africa—a memory triggered, I suspected, by the combination of a warm beverage and some more recent encounter. I was only half listening, halfheartedly trying to summon the courage to tell him I had been with his dying lover just days before while he tarried elsewhere.

"So we were stuck in this conference center, see, and the organizers couldn't give a stuff about the welfare of the old hacks. Only security: no one comes in; no one goes out. No facilities—no bar, no tea shop, no john, nothing. And no air-con. So we're all waiting for a press conference by some honcho who was going to tell us it was peace in our time for the Namibians, or some such. I was sitting next to this Brit correspondent called Michael Stanley. Old-school. Eton, Oxford. Always wore pink socks. A bit Graham Greene–ish: tropical-weight suits, shirts in Egyptian cotton from Turnbull and Asser. Could have been the high commissioner of Khartoum or the viceroy of Zanzibar. You know the type: looks like Mr. Respectable till the boudoir beckons and then it's all whambo-zambo and don't spare the horses. So the temperature is about a zillion and we are sitting round expiring and suddenly someone—think she worked for one of those liberal papers in Zim—blurts out, 'Christ, it's hot in here. A kiss and a cuddle for the first man to bring me a cup of tea.' I guess it was her idea of a joke. But quick as a flash, old Michael Stanley pipes up and says, 'Well, if I'd known, I'd have brought my thermos.'"

Then my cell phone rang. It was the Asia desk.

Tokyo. Nikkei down.

"So it's down. So what?"

"Brought my thermos." Shelby was still chortling. "Bloody thermos and we'd all have got—"

"Eleven percent?"

Shelby stopped laughing. He probably had stock in Mitsubishi.

"And the others? How much down? Christ."

"Plummet?" Shelby inquired. "Corrective adjustment? Slide? Spiral? Swoon? Fell sharply?"

"Crash," I muttered.

"Crash and burn. Zippo-zombo." He seemed almost exultant. I paid Madame in a hurry, almost forgetting the courtesies of "*bonne journée*" and "*à bientôt*" that accompanied our partings. I was vaguely aware of Shelby picking up something that fell from my pocket. But I was still thinking of my encounter with Faria Duclos and how I could persuade Shelby to go visit.

Back at the office of the *Paris Star*, at that hour, we were the only hands on deck. Bereft of its crew, the place looked especially mournful—you had to wonder how many cups of coffee, nuked soup, flat cola, sneaky vodka, or surreptitious Sancerre had gone into creating the particular mottled patina of dark stains on the faded, once-pink carpet. Why pink? You had to wonder about that, too. Who would ever expect news hounds to respect the sanctity of pink?

Shelby was already fizzing, writing straight into an editing program—Clefstik—with direct access to the mysterious procedures that somehow led to posting on the home page of Graphic.com. Normally, I urged him to write in the personal, eyes-only box—Homepatch—that no one else could access. Then it was a simple operation to transfer the finished article into Clefstik, which I could access from my terminal to edit and send to our breathlessly waiting public. Clefstik was open to every signed-on *Star* or *Graphic* editor on either paper's system. It was no place for jokes, errors, cock-ups. So I coached him on the protocols.

"We don't use 'crash' until it's 1929," I said.

"It is 1929."

"Eleven percent is 'plummet.' Not 'crash.'"

"Depends whose pension fund you are talking about."

He was already writing, pulling together pronouncements by alarmed television news readers and good old-fashioned wire reports. As he wrote, he had the phone on speaker, autodialing stringers in Singapore and Hong Kong, Frankfurt and London and New Delhi, telling them he didn't care what time it was where they were or whether they were eating muesli for breakfast or masala for lunch, they needed to haul ass and call the dealers and fund managers and all-purpose economic analysts and harvest the quotes and the wisdom that would make the story shine like bling on a stripper's G-string.

Bylines for all, he promised.

Free lunch next time you're in Paris.

But get me the quotes and keep them coming. Vox pops. Color. Full-court press. Dealers hurling themselves from windows. Grandmothers marching on banks. Families heading West through the Dust Bowl. Whatever. It was hard to tell whether he was hack, conductor, or general marshaling the troops. Maybe a little of all three—in his own mind at least.

Asian shares plummeted Wednesday as investors abandoned banking stocks after reports that leading Wall Street institutions had run out of cash to cover their trading commitments.

The contagion spread rapidly from the Nikkei in Tokyo, which fell 11 percent, before the Hang Seng index fell back by nine percent in heavy trading.

"This is beginning to look like a panic," said Tom Rafferty, a fund manager in Frankfurt.

European stock futures—a market device to forecast likely opening prices—were indicated sharply lower.

"Okay. Hand it over." I took over the first few hasty paragraphs. It reminded me of the days when you would grab paper stories from typewriters, take by take, and pencil them on deadline.

One of Shelby's lingering habits from the newspaper era was to write the word "endit" after the closing period of every story, but "endit" had no place on the web: the web consumed and moved on, never pausing or ending for a minute or a second. So the first thing you did with Shelby's stuff was to update it: with one stroke of the backspace, "endit" became ~~endit~~

Shelby was clicking frantically through opposition websites. Like Graphic.com, our competitors—nytimes.com, wsj.com, ft.com— were still using the early wire service bulletins. No one had a bylined piece from one of the paper's own correspondents. As the corporate strategists put it, our four original grafs would provide value added—from two guys minutes away from coffee, croissants, and speculative glances toward the emollient Madame.

"Post it. Post the damn thing," Shelby said.

I flipped through it, cursor flying, composed a headline: "Asian markets plummet, Europe set to follow."

I hit the controls that cleared up the text and made Shelby laugh: clean up quotes, clean up dummy tags.

I put his byline in bold.

Paris dateline.

The coveted Paris dateline.

"Post it for Chrissakes."

I hit the command that said "Copy to Graphic.com." I pinged the web producer. We waited. Looked at our watches. Scanned the opposition—still abed, we prayed. Why did it always take so long?

The site flickered. High on the homepage, the headline crystallized into view.

"Asian markets plummet, Europe set to follow. By Joe Shelby. One minute ago."

"Bingo," he said.

The phone rang.

Marcel Duffie was calling in from home, obviously seeing Graphic.com being fed onto the *Star*'s own website.

Shelby still had the phone on speaker. Duffie was fuming and his voice echoed through the empty newsroom.

"How come you guys suddenly get to cherry-pick the markets story? I have reporters ready to go on that."

"I don't see them, Marcel," Shelby said.

"They're on their way in."

"On the way isn't good enough. We need to move fast. To the victor, the spoils. As in love and war. Big story and all that. This newsroom looks like the *Mary Celeste*."

"That's my newsroom you're insulting."

"It's the *Star*'s newsroom, owned by the *Graphic*, which pays my salary to do this stuff, Marcel, so please take it easy."

I broke in. It was one thing for Shelby to do fifteen rounds without the Queensberry Rules with the executive editor of the *Paris Star*. He was independent of Marcel's command, run from the *Graphic* in New York. But I was on Duffie's payroll, and I was on the *Star*'s masthead. The last thing I wanted was disgrace by association with the flammable Shelby.

"Marcel, hi. Ed. Look. Crossed wires. We tried to reach your guys. Really. But it's getting pretty competitive out there. And the *Star* is really looking pretty good. Way ahead of the *FT*, the *Journal*. They still don't have bylines. We are just getting in a crop of quotes for the next go-round. And your guys will look amazing in print. Trust me. We'll just do the grunt stuff. We'll build the stage for them. You can tell them how to pirouette."

"Blarney! Bullshit, Clancy," he said. But he was mollified. "Well, next time you call me first. Right?"

"Sorry, Marcel. Are you on a cell? Just lost the signal for a moment."

"Fuck you, Clancy."

"Marcel, you still there?"

"Build the stage," Shelby was muttering. "What are we? Carpenters?"

Carpenters, I felt like telling him, should be so lucky. We were on the cusp of the meltdown, pennants flying, riding forth against the heathens of Mammon. But he did not always see it the way I did. There were times when our day would start with screaming messages from far-flung correspondents demanding that cuts in their sacred prose be reinstated, insisting that their oeuvre must on no account be tweaked lest their readers be robbed of the benefit of their wisdom.

"What do they think the web is?" Shelby liked to say. "The garbage can of the vanities?"

He had the story back on his screen. Stringer copy was flowing in, borne on torrents of gloom: Sydney down nine points, Seoul down seven, and the Hang Seng in a tailspin. Analysts in Shanghai and Singapore forecast a protracted decline, a big bear market if it turned out that the reports were true and American banks had gambled the farm on income from shaky mortgages just as the housing market began to retreat. But it would not end there. If American banks had clambered onto the subprime bandwagon, London and Zurich must have, too. Once the bubble burst, the whole world would feel the impact. All those fancy bankers and hedge fund managers in their Gieves and Hawkes suits and Hermès ties, driving their Bentley coupes from their mansions bought from ill-gotten bonuses, would be naked emperors running for cover—at least if people like Shelby and me had anything to do with it.

Across Europe, the markets were about to open—Paris, Frankfurt, Zurich, London. They would take their lead from Asia, anticipating a flight from stocks. Gold would surge. Investors would be scrambling, talking down short-sold stocks so that smart investors got rich by destroying the paper wealth of companies while the rest of us perished. I was beginning to think like Shelby.

"Greed," he was saying. "Every time—the dot-com crash, Russia, Asia—it's greed. Change and decay in all around I see! It's arrogant sons of bitches crooking the rest of us and figuring you can fool all the people all the time. Markets just got back to where they were six years ago, and now they're down the pan again."

Listening to him, I figured I had better keep a close watch on his stories: the web might offer him the biggest bully pulpit he had ever had. I asked him to start subsequent versions of his story in Homepatch before he transferred them to Clefstik.

By this time, the urgents were beginning to pile up and Shelby ran me through them: Russia announces the suspension of share trading on both Moscow exchanges; Icelanders begin queuing in sub-zero temperatures outside Reykjavik banks, demanding their deposits; gold prices surge; civil aviation authorities in the Cayman Islands report runways overwhelmed by private jets as Mafia dons withdraw cash from secret accounts.

"That true? About the Cayman Islands?"

"Nope. But it sounded good."

"You didn't post it?"

"No. It was just in Homepatch. A doodle. Wishful thinking. Film scripts."

"You shouldn't do that."

"No one would see it unless it was in Clefstik."

"True."

"But it makes you think."

"What?"

"Well. It makes you think," he said slowly, as if an idea was forming that amazed him with the brilliance of its simplicity. "We are influencing this story. We are telling people markets are down. So they pull their portfolios. Sell! Sell! So the markets go down further. They believe us. We can make it come true. We can make events happen by saying that they already have."

"And your point is?"

"Never mind. I'm just saying that if some unscrupulous person were to put out a ringer that influenced the markets, that unscrupulous person might know a broker . . ."

"Don't go there, Joe. Please. Don't ever, ever go there."

I can't recall how many versions we went through that day in the hours New York was dark. In the end it was all a blur of code words and labels—Fannie Mae, Freddie Mac, CAC 40, FTSE 100, DAX, Euro Stoxx, ECB and BoE, LIBOR and prime rate, swaps and shorts and spread betters and something called the Baltic Dry, which I might once have imagined to denote a Swedish ship's captain in rehab or a cheap brand of Latvian gin but turned out to be a way of measuring how much merchandise was being shipped around the world. In any event, it was way down. By midday in Paris, we had a pretty definitive story, a saga whose iterations were defined in the rainbow markings of edit-trace, showing where Shelby had written and I had honed.

Asian and European shares plummeted Wednesday as investors abandoned banking stocks after reports that leading Wall Street institutions had run out of cash to cover their trading commitments. Stock market futures forecast that the leading American indexes would decline sharply.

The retreat was the worst in decades, possibly since the Great Depression, President Nicolas Sarkozy told an emergency session of Parliament here.

From Sydney, Australia, to Leeds, England, depositors besieged banks to demand their deposits, some of them bringing small tents and folding cots to camp out on sidewalks. Trading was suspended at stock markets in Moscow, Milan and Reykjavik.

"I am ruined," said Ilsa Sigurdardottir, a 67-year-old Icelandic writer who said her savings portfolio worth $600,000 had been wiped out. In London, witnesses said they saw top bankers at their Canary Wharf headquarters loading boxes of files into parked Range Rovers. Home owners in Turin barricaded villas to preempt seizure by bailiffs. Prices of gold, silver, paintings and sculptures rose as investors looked for safe havens. Works depicting dead rodents suspended in formaldehyde sold at auction for $10 million each, a spokesman for Sotheby's said.

A leading Wall Street banker was seen in television footage boarding his 57-foot sailing yacht, "Derivative," refusing to specify his destination. Another attempted to flee in a luxury 75-foot motorboat called "The Shorted Stock." A Coast Guard cutter was reported to have set out to locate the vessels.

Yet another banker was filmed as he balanced on the 27th floor balcony of the head offices of a leading financial institution in Canary Wharf, England, threatening to leap before a police negotiator persuaded him to step down. On the sidewalk below police used tear gas to disperse angry account holders, ruined investors and junior staff chanting, "Jump! Jump!"

"This is really only the beginning," said Alfred Tannhauser, a broker at Migros cie, a private bank in Geneva. "We are looking at a global crisis, a meltdown."

Led down by banking stocks, the CAC 40 in Paris was off 12 percent and the DAX in Frankfurt fell 15 percent. The FTSE in London plummeted by 13 percent.

Spread betting agencies forecast a massive decline on Wall Street when American markets opened. Under American market rules, trading in premarket options was suspended when the contracts exceeded their maximum forecast fall of 550 points in the Dow Jones Industrial Average of leading stocks.

Our version went on to include quotes from press conferences and professors explaining the crisis and the contribution of hedge funds and investment banks to the creation of a huge market that, in the end, was built on the frailest of supports: the ability of poor people to finance debts they were encouraged to run up by bankers and their own politicians and never stood a chance of repaying. But such had been the profits from drilling into this last, large tundra of human hope, folly, and deceit that no one escaped contagion. We were beginning to hear unconfirmed reports of suicides.

It was midway through this maelstrom that a messenger arrived in the newsroom of the *Paris Star*, laden with arguably the most ostentatious bunch of red roses ever seen outside those markets in Antwerp where the world's florists buy flowers flown in overnight from Africa, harvested and packed by dollar-a-day laborers to feed the demand for ten-dollars-a-stem blooms. Keyboards fell silent. Screens went into saver mode. Eyes followed the roses' procession across the stained carpet. The messenger stopped once or twice, reading a name from a card attached to the mega-bouquet and inquiring as to the identity of that person. Gradually, it became clear who the lucky recipient was to be, and people fell back in a semicircle around Gloria Beeching's desk.

Maybe it was my slight insider knowledge of the preliminary events, but I thought I detected a smudge of tiredness under her eyes, a hint of extra makeup covering part of her neck, but I was not in the business of trying to guess where her meeting with Shelby in Saint-Germain had taken the pair of them later. The roses told their own story of gratification or expectation, hope or thanks, or even apology. She was at least twenty years younger than Shelby, but age differences had never been a deterrent to either of them. As the messenger arrived at her desk, she flushed a deeper crimson than the roses, looked at the card that came with the flowers and shook her head with obvious relief. Some mistake, she seemed to be saying. Wrong address. Wrong name. Return to sender. The messenger remonstrated, then relented. Then retreated.

As he was passing the executive editor's corner office, Duffie himself emerged to inspect the pasteboard card accompanying the roses, his manner suggesting a disinterested readiness to help solve the problem of who the flowers were intended for. But when he read the note, he too flushed red and glowered first at Beeching, then at the glass-walled box that housed Nonstop News. I noticed that he tipped the messenger and kept the card.

When big news broke, the tough part for Shelby was always the handover. He had been brought up to believe that if he started a story he would see it through to the final crossed *t* and dotted *i*, before the very last print deadline, before the presses rolled and ink flowed and delivery trucks rumbled out of plants laden with bundles of the *Graphic*. Even then, he stayed with the story heart and soul as the papers flew to America's front door, muscled into the news kiosks to push aside the girlie mags, fell open on breakfast tables and in railroad cars, nestled in briefcases and purses, before finally lying forgotten, rumpled and abandoned, on the plastic benches of Manhattan diners.

Once, he had told me, early in his newspaper career as a staff reporter, he had been carousing in New York's West Village with a British colleague who had asked him who his favorite imagined reader was.

"As for me," the Brit said, "I always think I am writing for an English country vicar—retired—who gets the paper a day late in the deep countryside when the steam train arrives down the branch line."

That was when Shelby spotted a bearded, frizzy-haired professor-type waiting eagerly for the first sales of the *Sunday Graphic* late on a Saturday night, and he had approached him and said, "You are my country vicar. Wherever I am, I'll write for you!"

The man thought he was insane—and said so—and Shelby was more than a little miffed to have his gesture rebuffed. But still he believed that, somewhere out there, awaiting his *Sunday Graphic*, was that same professor or his descendant. (Once, he told me, he had been driven in from Kennedy by a cab driver of Ghanaian descent and Shelby had told him, "I write for the *Graphic* from Africa." And the driver had replied with a laugh, "So you are one of those guys who write all those stories we all don't want to read about.")

But in the digital era you did your shift; you handed off; you split. You did not wait for the presses to roll because there were no presses. There was no professor to stand in line because he could read the paper on his PC or his cell phone or his tablet. So you stepped aside. Like a relay runner, you passed the baton and left it to someone else to cross the line first, to win the accolades.

Shelby had no idea who read him on the web, except for the people who e-mailed indignant messages protesting errors in punctuation or spelling or accusing him of bias to one side or the other or both, usually in stories from the Middle East. "How much did Hamas pay you for that one?" was one of his favorites. These cyber-correspondents had little shame, much anger, and usually very bad manners. "Call that journalism? It reads more like propaganda from the Tehran playbook," someone would write. "As usual, you *Graphic* whores are Zionists' lickspittle," another opined. Most were anonymous.

It was impossible to know if anyone other than the crazies even noticed who wrote the endless gigabytes of "content" that spewed from the network of servers and hard drives and cables that gave the web its digital spine. As one particularly disgruntled web editor described the process, it ended not with the glory of a page one byline but in a journalist's equivalent of coitus interruptus.

Shelby wanted to own what he wrote—if only for a news cycle. His stories were his creations. He had launched them into the world, and he needed to see them crawl and toddle and walk to their readers.

Handing over was bad enough. Worse still was handing over to Gibson Dullar.

The two men had similar careers, both traveling widely to hell-holes, both filing prize-winning dispatches (I had worked on both and knew which one I thought more skillful, more fluid, more rooted in truth), both achieving an after-hours reputation that others might envy. But their similarities ended with their résumés.

Dullar, Shelby liked to say, had a knack for claiming he had been in the right place at the right time, especially when no one was around to disprove it. Now, in this digital era, you never even knew where Dullar was when he took the handover. Sometimes you would glimpse an unusual number on the digital readout of your office phone and figure he was in this country or that. But he kept his whereabouts close, and the bosses seemed to treat that as his foible— a quirk of genius.

Gibson Dullar had limpid, pool-like brown eyes that begged mothering, set in features reminiscent of the deities of heavy metal. Somehow he had preserved jet-black locks swept back, Elvis-style, from his forehead. His slender frame had resisted the bumps and swells of other well-past-forty-years-olds. He functioned with ratlike cunning, sensing, rather than knowing, which way the wind was blowing and how he should trim his sails in response. There were plenty of people left in his wake who rued the day they had entrusted confidences to Dullar only to find their secrets betrayed or manipulated.

Every day at the close of our shift, Dullar would call up in his precious way—at the beginning of his workday wherever he was, six hours behind us or four hours ahead—and we would bring him up to speed on our activities and he would say with a faux-reluctant sigh, "You guys have done everything, real worker bees, so I guess I'll just take it from here and tidy up the scraps."

And then, if you looked in Clefstik, you would see the edit-trace with his initials, spilling over your story like a rash of tiny veins, or a gossamer web enfolding and suffocating your creation. You could almost hear him saying to his bosses, "Well, I just gave it a little tweak here and there"—which translated as "Christ, these guys in Paris would be nowhere without me."

But the thing about Dullar—"The Dullard," as Shelby misnamed him—was that he was very smart. He knew when to seem to give credit, when to take it. He had a reputation for somehow going that extra mile of reporting that yielded the moment of illumination. He was, much as I hated to admit it, a pro on the keyboard and a formidable player in the politics of the *Graphic* newsroom. He knew his way around the complexities of Clefstik and Homepatch like no one else. He was the guru who retrieved stories that had disappeared into the Bermuda Triangle of a suddenly and mysteriously blank screen; he knew how to put acute accents on words in French and umlauts in German and weird strokes through the letter *o* in Scandinavian tongues. (It crossed my mind—maybe uncharitably—that the Argentine soy vote imbroglio might well have his gumshoe footprints beneath it, if only we knew how to look for them.)

Even at this stage in his career, he still planned to go further still, and anyone who crossed him would not be invited along for the ride to glory. So you played a careful hand with Dullar. I noticed that Shelby himself refrained from talking to Dullar to his face in the same way as he talked about him to me. When I asked him what he thought made his rival tick, Shelby told a story he claimed to have heard from Dullar himself.

Someplace in Africa, he said, a guide had told Dullar that the lion prevailed over all other beasts because it stands at the head of the food chain: no one else wants to eat lion meat, but the king ate everything that moved.

"He wants to be king of the jungle," Shelby said. "Simple as that."

So, on the day of the meltdown, it was with some pain that we handed over the story, knowing that we had no control over how the quotes, stringers, and color from correspondents and contributors we had conjured forth after that first call over coffee in Le Primerose would be applauded, or warped, or misrepresented, or simply woven into the building symphony of the Dullard's triumph.

He had called in with his usual chummy congratulations, and I could see from my phone that he was not in New York. The number looked surprisingly familiar, but I was too distracted by the technicalities and maneuvers of the handoff to pay too much attention.

On the *Graphic* website, I could see Dullar's byline creeping into a lowly slot at the end of story—normally reserved for mere contributors rather than masters of the scribbled universe. But I knew his tactics. His byline was viral. Once unleashed, it conquered all. Like a coiled leopard, it was poised for the hungry leap to the top of the story and the easy, greedy swallowing-up of its predecessors, notably the line that proclaimed "By Joe Shelby."

We were about to close down our systems when Marcel Duffie dropped by. His face was contorted and pink with the effort to suppress white rage. While we had been batting out the ledes and new tops and writethrus, he had been to lunch, signaling his approach to us now with a rich, odorous bow wave of wine and garlic.

He tossed two pieces of paper onto Shelby's desk. One was the card that had accompanied the bouquet of roses. The other was the poison ad from my local feed store.

"You might at least have got her name right, Shelby, you snake in the grass. What the fuck is this "Mon Aurélia"? Her name is Gloria. Or don't you inquire? And as for you, Clancy. That's your locality, isn't it?"

He pointed at the inky stamp of my local feed store.

"So you want to poison me, eh, Clancy? Like a ferret, stoat, weasel, or rat? Well, let me tell you, you toxic shit, that if anyone is going to get poisoned around here . . . I gave you a month. Make that weeks."

"Mea culpa," Shelby broke in. "Just a joke, Marcel. All my doing. Nothing to do with Clancy."

"If you didn't spend so much time joking," Duffie said with a sneer, "and spent more time working like Gibson Dullar, you wouldn't miss so many angles. How you two hotshots missed that Mafia line beats me."

"What was that about a month?" Shelby asked as Duffie stamped his way across the newsroom floor, his footfalls sounding like receding thunder.

I went back into Clefstik and looked up the latest iteration of the meltdown story. As I had suspected, Dullar's byline was now up top with a jumble of names at the bottom including "Joe Shelby contributed."

But Shelby was not rising to that particular bait. He scanned the story and began to read out loud.

"'Civil aviation authorities in the Cayman Islands reported runways overwhelmed by private jets as Mafia dons withdrew cash from their secret bank accounts . . .' Now where the hell did that come from?"

"More to the point, how in hell did he get his hands on it?"

As we wound up for the day—"the day I lost my 401(k) and my byline and didn't know which hurt the most," as Shelby put it—I noticed that he had slotted a USB stick into his computer and was busy copying over files, then deleting the originals from the PC on his desk. Then he deactivated the virus shield and spyware protection and left the machine online. With any luck, he muttered, the desktop would be so infected by the next morning that the techs would have to scrap and replace it. And anyone hacking in would go down with a severe case of contagion.

I was closing down my own computer when the news alert device monitoring the French wires brought up a two-line item marked "Urgent."

The headline declared: "Renowned War Photographer Dies."

The brief story below it said:

PARIS—Faria Duclos, one of the first female photographers from France to cover the Vietnam War, died suddenly after a long battle with a neurological illness. Police are investigating. Obituary follows.

I looked for Shelby to break this terrible news to him, but he had left the building. So, too, I noted, had Gloria Beeching.

CHAPTER ELEVEN

SHELBY HAD TAKEN A PLACE ON THE RUE DU CHERCHE-MIDI—"ON personal, historical grounds," as he put it—but he also claimed visiting rights at a fishing shack an old buddy maintained on a pristine stretch of the River Avre near Nonancourt. It was there that we repaired to prepare and brace ourselves on the eve of the funeral of Faria Duclos.

"I kept meaning to go see her," Shelby said as we drove out to Normandy with the Jaguar's roof folded down. He was wearing the old retro pilot's helmet with its flaps and buckles and had somehow acquired a set of matching goggles since Faria Duclos presented him with the gift all those years ago. The outfit drew a lot of second glances from startled motorists catching sight of this latter-day Red Baron in their rearview mirrors, suddenly on their tail, coming out of the sun, and so forth. I couldn't make my mind up whether he looked midlife goofy or just plain silly.

"But I didn't. I wanted to keep it like it had been—not two old crips getting their sticks and zimmers and wheelchairs all caught up in an emotional train crash. What kind of metaphor is that? I wanted it like it was when we could both run for our lives. Which we did quite a lot, as I recall. And now I can't go see her again. Ever. So there's not much point in being pissed at her, is there? Or myself. If there's a moral, Clancy, it's to never put yourself in a position where you end up saying 'if only.' 'If only' are the two worst words in the English language."

It wasn't the whole truth.

Piecing together the little I could glean from the archives and conversations with HR types in a position to know, I had begun to feel fairly sure that there was a significant gap in Shelby's CV between Beirut and Paris. His last report from Lebanon was a lengthy magazine article—"Farewell to the Orient" by Joe Shelby. Given the lead time for such self-indulgent pieces, it must have been written several weeks earlier, to be published around the time he left. Then, if Ivar Bild was to be believed, there was the question of a fire. And then, months later, Shelby had arrived in Paris. Between those markers, there were only questions.

"Wasn't there something about a fire? In Beirut?"

He made as if the wind had whipped away my words and he had heard nothing.

With a nonchalant indifference to each one of the variable speed limits, he drove the Jaguar along the N12 leading out of Paris toward Normandy, slotting between the gears in the automatic six-speed box and flooring the throttle to get the thump in the lower back from V8 acceleration and the Le Mans rumble and roar from the twin exhaust pipes. In the passenger seat, I huddled down against the beige leather and reached for my hip flask rather than watch the roadside trees and the Paris-bound cars rush toward us like a movie on very fast rewind.

"What happened after Beirut?"

"Did you ever fish, Clancy?"

"Not even for compliments."

"Fishing 101. Starts tonight."

"Beirut?"

"History."

No wind to steal his words that time.

"How come we are fishing when we are supposed to be mourning?"

"Sentimentalism is to be avoided at all costs," he said. "Faria never did approve of mawkishness."

Or denial. I thought.

The fishing shack had a fairy-tale feel to it, with exposed external beams, brown against cream stone, and a small terrace. It was a tranquil spot, a two-bedroom cottage on its own grounds, including eight hundred yards of river, dimpled with rising trout below the low boughs of trees that cast deep shadows and shielded the fish from terrestrial predators. Shelby flung open the locked doors and shuttered windows. With some awkwardness, he shook charcoal into a barbeque, poured a liberal splash of lighter fluid, and tossed in a match.

"Trout on the barbie good enough for you?"

"Where's the trout?"

"Right in there," he said, pointing at the river. Beyond the stream, a flock of plump sheep grazed on the evening meadows—as round and white as those you see in classroom drawings by city children imagining rural life. Looking at them, then looking at Shelby as he struggled into a set of thigh waders, I had the feeling that there was about as much likelihood of *carré d'agneau* with all the trimmings as there was of grilled trout for supper.

He pointed toward a well-stocked drinks cabinet that looked as if it had been provisioned for an alcoholic siege, with at least a dozen bottles of scotch, bourbon, cognac, vodka, and gin.

"Don't worry about running out," he said. "There's resupply in the car."

I poured us both a jolt of Johnnie Walker Black on the rocks.

"See this?" Shelby said. He was waving a tuft of feathers wrapped around a small hook attached to the end of a thin nylon leader, which, in turn, was bonded to the heavier strand of his fly-casting line. Before I could reply, he was deep into an explanation.

"Ordinarily, this would be called a Gray Wulff. It's what Italian fishers call a *cacciatore*, a hunter. You cast it on the waters and old tommy trout can't resist. Whatever other bugs may be flying around, he'll go for this one. Out of curiosity, anger—who knows? Now, I've tied this one myself and it's a slightly different pattern and I call it the Homepatch Hunter and I'll explain the principle. You float this by a trout's nose and the trout knows it shouldn't but it can't stop itself so it snaffles it and it's hooked."

"So why name it after a *Graphic* editing program?"

"You'll see, old sport. You'll see. Now tend the barbie while I hit the water. And one other thing: swans."

"Swans?"

"Don't piss off the swans around here. They say they can kill a man with a single strike from their wings. Probably some kind of old wives' tale. Rural myth. But they don't like intruders."

With that he cranked himself almost upright and headed for the water, an old built cane fishing pole in one hand and a worn leather-seated shooting stick in the other. The light was still good, but you could feel the stealth of sundown on the air. The trout were into their evening rise, like gourmands nibbling at canapés to limber up the taste buds and flex the stomach for *la grande bouffe*.

Shelby's illness had left him with an awkward weakness, mainly on the left side of his body, complicating what should have been a routine amphibious transition. He clung to a stout, overhanging branch with one hand, his fishing rod clenched between his teeth and his other hand steadying the whole operation with his shooting stick. He achieved this operation with a series of grunts and obscenities, but surprisingly little disruption to the smooth flow of the water.

Sitting on the patio area outside the cottage, nursing my scotch, I had a slightly uneasy feeling about the Homepatch Hunter but suppressed it. Just a joke. Just a Shelby joke, I thought, though a small inner voice kept on saying, Shelby jokes are the kind that cost careers. If he is comparing this trout fly to a plot hatched in the newsroom, it could only mean trouble. Swallowing another jolt, I tried to distract myself with the spectacle in the Avre ahead of me.

Once submerged to his thighs, Shelby began a laborious, crabbing maneuver with his shooting stick to gain a midstream position. Just below the opposite bank, I could see supper rising underneath a patch of nettles that provided a canopy of shade and cover, making Shelby's looping casts of the fly line more challenging. Every few seconds, or so it seemed, the water would dimple as the trout rose to suck in a passing bit of winged insect or fallen bug or about-to-hatch nymph in the surface film of the water.

It had a hypnotic effect on both of us, and I quite forgot about the swans.

Shelby had begun to cast with an easy, gentle rhythm, feeding a little more line out every time he flicked his antique rod back and forth, building a curve into the line so that, as it landed on the water, the thin nylon leader bearing the Homepatch Hunter unfolded in a deft parabola designed to ensure that the fish saw only the tuft of feathers, not the line it was attached to or the unsportingly and—on this stretch of water—illegally barbed hook among them.

I had to admire the tactics. In this quiet corner of Normandy, Shelby was the silent hunter, infinitely patient. He had reached a midstream position and had lowered himself onto the seat of his shooting stick to take the strain off his bad leg. Twice the trout rose to the Homepatch Hunter. Twice it either turned away at the last moment or Shelby struck a fraction too early or too late. He gathered in his line, paused, fumbled in his fishing vest for a cigarette, and lit it. The light was beginning to fade, and I stirred the coals in the barbecue as they began to take on the grayish tinge that signals the perfect temperature for cooking.

Several hundred yards upstream, a swan was feeding on the abundant Ranunculus weed that unfurled in the river in long, dark mermaid strands. Several hundred yards downstream, another swan was looking back upstream, maintaining eye contact—I assumed—with its mate, like a couple at a party signaling across a crowded room that it's time to go. Shelby was relocating himself, moving a little farther into midstream to gain a better casting stance on his shooting stick. Idly, as I poured a second—or was it third?—Black Label, I wondered if there was some kind of riverine code that said not to interpose yourself between raunchy swans. I racked my general knowledge data banks. I had heard, from Shelby himself, not to get in the way of a hippo and its calf, a lion and its cub. In fact, I thought of the times at crowded parties when I had become distressed when I lost sight of Marie-Claire across a chandeliered salon because some oaf had come between us. It seemed swans weren't that different, after all.

Shelby was rapt now, in communion with his piscine target, close to the hunter's perfect Hemingway moment when the prey's foibles have been sussed and there is only the technical matter of the means of capture still to be achieved. I had watched him fiddling with a new fly tied to his leader—a Beeching Blunderbuss maybe, I thought, sniggering as I recalled an article I had once edited about the way the estrogen of the human female attracted certain other species so that women held records on mighty Scottish rivers for capturing enormous salmon. Whatever. It was only a matter of time before the plump, bloodily gutted trout would lie briefly above the hot coals to provide the first, last, and only course for supper: Shelby had not, as far as I knew, stocked up with any non-liquid provisions.

He began to cast.

The swans began to move.

The upstream bird turned downstream to look for its partner, or spouse, or whatever the parlance is for the conjugality of swans. Downstream, as if by some secret, arcane signal, its mate turned upstream.

Swans are always reckoned to look stately, and most times they do. They glide with their perfect downy white necks set in a haughty curve. They traverse smooth waters in silent, stately procession. But these swans were making bow waves.

"Shelby!"

"Shhh."

I had gotten up from my folding director's chair on the patio and tiptoed toward the water, still clutching my tumbler of Black Label. Shelby was making abrupt, impatient gestures with his hand, indicating that I should retreat.

"Shelby."

"Back off."

He was casting again now. The moment had come when the hunt and the timing and the waiting all coalesced into the perfect moment. It was inevitable that the trout would be hooked, the hunter would return with the prey, the supper would cook on the coals. The evening light had turned just a shade darker, and Shelby had taken off his UV fishing glasses, allowing them to swing from a cord around his neck.

He cast.

"The swans!" I hissed.

"The what?"

He swung his neck around.

The trout rose.

The swans stepped up the pace to attack speed.

The trout impaled itself on the hook of the Beeching Blunderbuss.

Shelby looked quickly up- and downstream. I had a feeling that it was like one of those moments he had shared with Duclos, when you hear the mortars landing that little bit closer, and the snappy whine of gunfire gets too intimate for comfort, and you figure that even your most faithful readers cannot demand the ultimate sacrifice of you—it's time to split.

From both sides, the swans were closing in fast, paddling so furiously that they seemed to be rising up on their downy breasts, extending their Boeing-like wings for takeoff.

Shelby turned clumsily in the water, grabbing his shooting stick for support. The swans were getting much closer now—speeding through their own element where Shelby was an alien, ungainly intruder—their wings jutting like medieval weapons. What had Shelby said about swans killing a man with one strike of those bony leading edges? And now he was caught between two of them.

The effort of pushing through the thigh-deep stream was giving him trouble.

"Jesus, Clancy. Gimme a hand."

It was no time to tell Shelby that I had never learned to swim and had a deep-rooted fear of water.

Shelby was pushing toward the bank, his shooting stick in one hand, his fancy cane pole in the other. The hooked trout was still hooked, indifferent to the drama of the swans and the fisherman and the whiskey drinker on the bank. Desperate for release from the barbed hook embedded in the hard corner of its jaws, it was performing pirouettes and leaps like a ballerina, skittering across the darkening surface of the water. For their part, the swans did not look like the kind of dancers that take their part in the Tchaikovsky opus related to their species on some Russian lake. They seemed to be making aggressive, hissing noises. They seemed to be very close.

Close to the bank, Shelby stumbled.

"Get the net," he said, nodding toward a long-handled landing net he had left on the bank. I grabbed it, thinking he wanted to pull himself out of the river with it. I extended the handle toward him, trying hard to balance on the slippery bank, do my bit to help, and not spill my whiskey all at the same time.

"No, for Chrissakes. Net the trout."

He had taken his angling pole back between his teeth and was pulling in the line hand over hand with the suddenly submissive trout on the end. I slid the net underneath it and raised it up, feeling a solid weight.

Shelby tossed his rod to me.

"Run, Clancy. Run for your life."

I wondered if I should say something like "I won't leave you, Sarge," but running seemed the better option.

The swans were now only a few yards away, their fearsome wings extended and beating with intimations of extremely prejudicial intent.

Shelby turned toward them and waved his shooting stick at them as I retreated to the paved terrace area with the rod and the net and the exhausted trout. He backed out of the water, grasping at branches and undergrowth, making an awesome crashing noise like a rhinoceros lost in bushlands. Even the reunited swans seemed somewhat nonplussed.

"Get indoors," he shouted to me as he slithered and slipped his way up the bank, then limped and hobbled with improbable alacrity across the lawn. Then he saw the other invaders.

"What's that?" he cried, pointing at the cottage, where dark objects inside hurtled around a rustic wooden chandelier in a crazed frenzy.

The swans had come ashore, waddling and hissing toward him. But our safe haven had been overrun behind our backs by flying black rags, filling the air, flapping, squeaking.

"Bats," I said.

"Bats? Did you say bats?"

The swans were crossing the lawn. One had its wings outstretched as if practicing some kind of a karate chop.

"You must have left the door open."

"Me," I said. "Why me?"

Even at that moment, the question took on a kind of metaphysical significance. Why me? Why me hooked up to this mad trout fisherman? Why me pursued by pissed-off swans? Why me locked in harness with an aging, limping hero who blamed me for everything that went wrong? It was like a bad marriage.

"Get them out," he barked.

"Why me?"

"Oh, for fuck's sake, Clancy." Shelby pulled his wide-brimmed fishing hat down over his forehead and wrenched open the double doors of the main room leading from the cottage onto the terrace. "You hold off the swans. I'll tackle the bats."

Tackle?

He plunged forward, waving and flailing with clenched fists, bellowing a stream of obscenities that challenged the bats' provenance, species, parentage, procreative abilities, and many existential points about their presence on the planet.

Facing the hissing swans, the bats and Shelby at my rear, I prodded toward the big white birds with the landing net.

"Shoo," I said.

"The net!" Shelby bellowed. "Gimme the net."

I became aware of small black things hurtling past my ears, whirling and twirling upward and over the still, darkening river.

I figured maybe fifty of them came by, like tossed gloves, ragged, venomous, sharp-toothed. Bats. Protected by law. Endangered species. Bats by the score. Vampires. Rabid. Every single mental association brought up rapid-fire images of Dracula, sinking teeth, pale flesh, rivulets of coveted blood. The bats swooping and circling until the swans themselves retreated toward their familiar element.

Thinking more of supper than of Shelby, I turned the net inside out and the trout flopped onto the patio, its gills quivering. Its body curled halfheartedly in a final attempt to flap its way back a habitat it understood. Then it became motionless, though it was unclear whether that was a result of a lack of waterborne oxygen or bewilderment at the turn of events around it or simple exhaustion—it had been a busy afternoon for all of us.

I turned back toward Shelby, offering him the net. He grasped it and, with the long handle fully extended, blundered and crashed around the living room, flailing at the dark, vile creatures that the French call *chauves-souris*—bald mice. One of the bats, particularly dogged or dumb, tried to hang upside down from the chandelier, like a dictator run down by the mob. Shelby netted it with the skill of a lepidopterist snaring a Red Admiral, then deftly turned the knotless mesh inside out to free the nasty little creature. Immediately, as if preprogrammed, it joined the crowd that jiggled and dived over the river until some lemming instinct among them carried them away toward a deserted barn that was soon to be colonized by their uninvited presence.

"All clear," Shelby called out, and with some relief I turned and fled into the shelter of the cottage.

"Now I remember it, my buddy did say something about bats," he said. "Something about not leaving the doors open."

"So you knew! You asshole! You prick! Jesus. I can't stand bats." I shuddered. I did hate bats. My whole body shook with rage and loathing.

But Shelby turned to me with just the beginning of a smile, lost in the triggered memory of some greater battle fought and lost on foreign fields, and said: "Did I ever tell you about the time I covered the Romanian revolution and actually got to Dracula's castle? In Transylvania. Not a bat in sight!"

Unsung, the last of the day slid effortlessly into night, and I had to acknowledge that, after the adrenaline that had substituted for the hors d'oeuvres, grilled river trout washed down with whiskey seemed a pretty good idea. It was not the most delicately cooked of fish, or even the most cooked of fish. The coals were still too hot, and the skin of the trout charred black around pale, tepid flesh not too far removed from sushi. It was a plump, tasty fish—three pounds, Shelby reckoned, so I knew it had to weigh considerably less. But it did not seem appropriate to challenge his estimate. And the scotch—by now we had located a fiery, peaty single malt from the Isle of Skye—promised preemptive purgation of any potential toxins, along with accelerated anesthesia.

So, with several immodest toasts to our valor and chuckles over the less glorious moments of the encounter, we celebrated a victory that had called forth the full gamut of our military skills—waterborne warfare followed by battle on land against swans that called in air strikes. Von Clausewitz would have been proud of us—though, as any real military strategist might divine, it was no more than a skirmish, a diversionary moment, a prelude distracting from the business that had brought us to this corner of Normandy.

"All your life you look for perfection," Shelby was saying, refilling our glasses without bothering with ice or soda. "And while you look, you construct a version of life that will do for now, a humdrum shadow of what you know it could be but never is."

"And it was yours for the taking."

I assigned myself the role of sounding-board-cum-therapist, venturing into the private depths of Shelby's soul, where I trod warily. I was not even sure I wanted to be there. He was somewhere way back, in Rwanda or Cape Town or Nairobi, long before illness overtook the both of them and they washed up in Paris, like separate items of flotsam far apart on a long and cluttered beach.

"I had perfection within my grasp. All I had to do was trust her. All I had to do was to have faith."

"But you couldn't do that, I guess."

"As the Brits say, I bottled it. You see, with Faria, you were on the roller coaster, and if you said to yourself, okay, this is the ride and I'll be fine, then you would be. But if you doubted, if you asked yourself where the ride was leading, if you asked for proof, then it would lead to disaster. And I couldn't make that leap, any more than she could just be something she wasn't. So, yes, in essence, we were perfect for each other. We brought each other joy. But we neither of us could take that step to make it permanent. If we had, we would have been together to the end, whichever one of us went first. You know, when I headed out with Eva, Faria waited. In all that time, I don't think there was anyone else."

"But you never went to see her when she got sick."

"And she never came to see me," he snapped back, but the anger soon fled.

"Look at this." He reached for one of his leather-bound travel companions from his library of Nervalia. The paper was thin, frail; the binding scuffed. The gilt title, barely legible, said this was *Aurélia*—considered by many to be Nerval's masterpiece in prose. The subtitle was *The Dream of Life*. When the poet died, the final pages of his manuscript were found in his pocket. I never figured why Nerval chose that moment to go, but his shrink was said to have observed, "Gérard de Nerval hung himself because he looked his madness in the face."

I figured I did that every time I shaved—or met up for joe with Shelby.

Careful not to sully the page with charcoal-smeared fingers, Shelby directed me to a passage marked lightly in pencil.

"Read that."

The French was a bit florid—I'd have cut it back pretty easily without losing meaning—but I followed it well enough. As I scanned it, Shelby leaned back, like a professor awaiting enlightenment to befall a slow student.

"At first I only heard that she was ill," it said. "Owing to my state of mind I only felt a vague unhappiness mixed with hope. I believed that I myself had only a short while longer to live, and I was now assured of the existence of a world in which hearts in love meet again. Besides, she belonged to me much more in her death than in her life . . ."

"See what I mean?" he said, his eyes shining.

It occurred to me then that he had never imagined she would die first. And I was sure he never expected her to die the way she had, in a wheelchair, even less capable of determining life's twists and turns than he was.

The way she had lived, the abandon with which she greeted danger, and her passionate embrace of risk all seemed to point one way—toward obituaries recording her final moment in some fire fight or air raid or land mine blast when her luck and trade-craft both expired in the enveloping red wetness of combat-zone departures.

"You're right, Clancy," he said. "I didn't go see her. I guess I bottled that, too."

The moon over the Avre caught a splinter of a tear in his eye. I still had not told him that I had visited her, that I was the bearer of her last message to him on this earth. And that I knew their story was nowhere near as simple as the legend he was trying to build.

CHAPTER TWELVE

SHELBY BREWED A STRONG BLACK LIQUID THAT TASTED OF CHARCOAL and burned Arabica. There were no trimmings such as croissants, milk, sugar. I cleared up the detritus of the Battle of the Avre, shaking the cold barbecue tray into the fabled stream, as if spreading crematory ash according to the final instructions of a departed angler.

The morning mist had burned off the river and sunlight gilded its surface. Across the way, sheep still munched, unperturbed. Normandy stirred.

As if part of a Viking burial rite, a languid current bore away the gray smear of cinders and fish bone surrounding the charred head of Shelby's quarry with its querulous, gaping eye sockets. I savored an early cigarette, tobacco fumes rising around me—the smell of victory?

Dust to dust.

Ashes to ashes.

Upstream, the swans hovered on sentry duty, watching the despoilment of their domain with disapproval. I bared my teeth at them, and they ruffled their feathers back at me.

Round two to us, I figured, making it a points draw over all.

The plan was to stop by the railroad station in Dreux to pick up Elvire Récamier.

The police had, at least, released the body of Faria Duclos for burial. But I had seen nothing to indicate that they had closed the file on their investigation into her death.

As he drove, I thought I heard Shelby muttering disjointed phrases in French as if they were an incantation of some kind.

"*Je suis le Ténébreux . . .*" I translated the words as "I am the dark one" and figured he was referring to his mood after the combined assault on his equilibrium of swans, bats, and single malt. I caught the word "*veuf*"—it means "widower"—but I thought no more of it. Another clue missed, as it turned out.

We pulled up in the station forecourt underneath a sign that said "No Parking at Any Time." Shelby ordered me to fold myself into the jump seats in the rear of the car so that Elvire could slide her svelte, starved frame into the front.

She was immaculately groomed, with fringed black hair that combined the looks of Man Ray's models and Coco Chanel, draped in a black silk pantsuit over a red silk blouse, the whole outfit wrapped in a loose-fitting, belted overcoat of fine cashmere, also black. Her makeup was unambiguous: red lips, black arching eyebrows, eyelashes cemented by mascara into a shocked curl. She smoked old-fashioned unfiltered Gauloises, picking loose strands of tobacco from lips as bright as stoplights.

"*Alors*, Shelby. The old warhorse. Gone lame."

"The *animaux de la guerre* all grow old, Elvire," he shot back. "*Même les chiennes*—even the bitches."

"You know, you always were a shit. I told Faria so, but she would not listen."

"It's so good to see you have not changed one single bit," Shelby said, smiling toward her, leaning across the Jaguar's high transmission tunnel to kiss her pale and proffered cheek. "*La belle dame sans merci.*"

They were still fighting old battles, as people do when they bid the last farewell to special friends, folding their hurts and unredeemable slights into the shroud. The sparring reminded me of the evening Elvire Récamier told me the story of Shelby's wild motorcycle ride to the arms of another woman. Elvire had said that, in this opera, the lady had not yet sung, so I wondered whether she was rehearsing the first lines of her libretto. At first blush, it sounded like her arias would be more Wagner than Mozart or Puccini.

As we drove off, Elvire launched into a catalog of Duclos stories, each one designed to needle Shelby a little bit more than the last.

"So this one time, her boss from the picture *agence* in Paris arrived in Phnom Penh and started looking for Faria," Récamier was saying. "And he went up to old Mr. Liu at the reception desk of the Royal and says, 'Which room is Mlle Duclos staying in?' And he replies, '124, 337, 428, 507.'"

She chortled but Shelby did not. I intercepted a look between them—she mischievous, he enraged. I had heard the story before, or variants of it, told about any number of women photographers and writers who had become the object of professional jealousy. I wondered how often derivatives of the same anecdote were recounted about those swashbuckling male reporters who, in the ethos of the times, actually felt obliged to share their favors—and their boudoirs—without restraint.

"And of course she was the first to discover the opium in Cambodia, and the naked swimming in the pool at Le Royal."

"No reason men should have all the fun," I said. "I mean, in this day and age. It would be sexist to think otherwise."

"Why don't you just shut the fuck up, Clancy?" Shelby growled.

Shelby pulled over for gas and Elvire turned back to me, speaking in a stage whisper that could not have been much louder if it had been amplified by rock-concert sound systems.

"I remember once at the Commodore in Beirut, she came up to me and said, 'If Shelby asks where I am, tell him I am in the camps with the Palestinians.'"

"And wasn't she?"

"Of course not. She never liked to be tied down, pinned, like some beautiful butterfly in a collection."

"But I thought she and Shelby were a big number."

She looked at me with scorn.

"Of course they were," she said, "the biggest ever. He was the love of her life. But she had demons"—she pronounced it "*de-moons*"—"and she believed that if she stopped running she would be boring and men would find her boring. But if she kept running, she would run away from the people who loved her the most. Catch-22."

She shrugged.

"And you, Elvire?"

"That is for me to know—and nobody to find out," she said. "I never kiss on television!"

"But she didn't stick with him. After the other woman left."

"She did not want to be Shelby's nurse."

"And in the end she needed nursing herself."

"But not by Shelby." Récamier rolled her big eyes that had absorbed so much but that betrayed nothing.

We drove on through the apple orchards of the Eure, across valleys latticed with chalk streams whose trout population was at least one less than the day before, through woodlands that would be either mysterious or menacing, depending on your mood. Shelby insisted that he knew the route to the Duclos ancestral home, where Faria was to be buried, but he took some wrong turn at a complex traffic circle and slowed the car to a halt on loose roadside gravel bordering a mowed wheat field to scan his Michelin map, curse, and throw the Jaguar into a tire-squealing one-eighty, ignoring an oncoming truck that blared its Klaxon and began to weave as the driver slammed on the air brakes.

Shelby pushed the car to maximum power, heading back the way we came, passing a rental car coming in the opposite direction laden with fellow mourners who, seeing Shelby's Jaguar with its telltale Lebanese license plate, spun their modest Citroën into the path of the same truck and lit off after us.

The wrong turn would delay us beyond the official starting time of the service.

Our Keystone Kops chase made us ridiculous.

If Faria had been among us, Shelby said with a guffaw, she would be hooting with laughter: the old hands, veterans of the battlefields, navigators of the human condition, chroniclers of hidden wars, lost in the apple groves of Normandy, late for a funeral, but chasing one another, hell-for-leather, as if they still ran scared of rivals who might get there first, take the pictures before the bodies were removed, bribe the telex operator to block the lines, dismantle the public call boxes so no competitor could call in a story first or ever. How often had they done that, he wondered—laid false trails, slipped out of town at dawn, driven like the possessed to escape the hack pack in pursuit.

"She'd love it," Shelby was chuckling.

"But she is not here. She cannot be here." Elvire Récamier said without a hint of sadness or sentimentality. "And you did not even go visit her on her deathbed. But I tell you who did: Dullar came. Dullar always loved her. Way back when. Dullar came to see her in Paris when she was dying. And you did not."

Now I realized who I had seen slipping away into the shadows as I approached the Duclos apartment, the man who brought roses but left no calling card.

"Dullar? Gibson Dullar?"

Shelby reached over to the glove compartment and pulled out his leather flier's hat, ramming it on his head so that the flaps covered his ears.

The onward drive got a bit strained after that.

The village was as remote from Saigon or Beirut as you could imagine—"not just in distance but in the life of a woman laid to rest here the other day, the final halt on a journey from the breathless theaters of twentieth-century warfare to the bathos of death by accident," as one of her overblown obituaries recorded.

We parked on a grass verge and scrambled up a narrow lane to the church, Shelby propelling himself with his stick as if he were some gigantic crane striving for vertical takeoff. Reaching the church, Shelby pulled off his leather cap and held it in both hands, like a schoolkid late for roll call. The service was already underway, conducted by a woman lay preacher in the absence of a priest to conduct a mass for this woman who believed only in what she saw through the range finder and recorded on celluloid and published in magazines. She had died broke, supported by fellow photographers who auctioned their work to finance her apartment and her medication and her day nurse from Vietnam and her night nurse from

Sweden. Her colleagues had paid for the funeral, too, and they gathered now in a wooden-roofed village church whose gracious, curved beams gave it the air of an upturned Noah's Ark, bearing souls in ones and twos back to the memories of the good times. Her coffin lay between the hard wooden benches that did for pews, draped in the kaffiyeh headdresses of the underdogs and terrorists and fighters who had scrambled for position in her world of smoke and flame and spilled blood.

As an outsider, contemplating the graying men clutching unfamiliar prayer sheets, I wondered how many of these hobbled warriors had paraded before her in hotel bars and combat zones, questing for her favors, and for some sign from her that they meant more than the fleeting fly-by-night couplings so common to their kind. I took up position in a shadowed corner at the rear of the church and watched.

Shelby's eyes locked on the shiny wooden coffin, garlanded with roses, as if trying to peer through its lid to something long past. I scanned the other mourners. All of them, maybe, wanted to turn back the pages. And as at most funerals, all of them wanted to behold the dead to reconfirm their status on this side of mortality's divide and say, one more time, as they did when they trudged back from the fray, eyes glowing with relief and adrenaline, that they had made it, that they had survived when others did not.

There but for the grace of God . . .

Was that what they all thought as they filed past the coffin, laying a flower on it, clumsy with their unwonted, unfamiliar gestures of the cross, touching the burnished casket as if reaching out through time to reconjure a kiss, an embrace, a sudden glimpse into her hidden soul across tangled sheets and storm-tossed pillows?

I scanned the church and saw Ivar Bild. His blue eyes brimmed. I would have liked to ask him, So what did you tell the cops, Mr. Night Nurse? When he felt my eyes on him, he turned his head toward me, then looked sharply away.

Shelby was not listed among the eulogists, among those who would read a line of Palestinian poetry, a Buddhist incantation, a

simple biography of a complex life, offering the editing and censor-
ship, the gentle recasting of history that decorum dictates for the
dead. But plenty of the mourners cast surreptitious, sidelong glances
his way, trying to guess whether, finally in her death, he would
acknowledge the loss he had experienced far earlier than her physical death when she had left him to his illness and returned to the war
zones.

When his turn came to lay a rose and offer a prayer, he paused
at the head of the casket, leaning on his walking pole, canted at a
spindly angle. His stance reminded me of one of those heraldic
images of the knight leaning on his sword over the body of the
damsel that destiny has taken from him. Shelby scanned the mourners, looked down at the coffin again, then took a deep breath and
began to speak, his gaze ranging over all of them. No one seemed to
want to make eye contact.

"You all know me," he began with a smile, sounding for all the
world like Quint, the shark-hunting ship's captain in Jaws. "And I
know you. And we all knew her."

He looked down at the casket again and fell silent.

You could tell in that pause—when men, alone or with their
wives and partners beside them, peered up toward some indeterminate point of suddenly overwhelming interest in the rafters or looked
down at their feet—that he had the audience in the palm of his hand.

No one knew what Shelby would say. Everyone feared what he
might.

"We all loved her," he said finally. "In our different ways. We
loved her in the best ways we knew how, and she loved us according
to her own way of loving. We loved her and now she has gone. Some
of you helped her, the way she deserved to be helped. Some of us
failed. I did. I failed and I should say so. She failed me, of course, but
that was her way. And I never knew the full extent of it until
today"—he cast a savage glance toward the heat-resistant shields of
Récamier's Christian Dior sunglasses—"but I could never act in
vengeance toward Faria Duclos. How do you avenge pure love, transcending the ownership of the body, transcending earthly gestures?"

There was another long silence. Someone coughed. A cell phone began a chirrup and was smothered. Outside, a blackbird called out and a wood pigeon answered.

"Yes, we all loved her. I see you out there. Jean-Pierre, how's Baghdad? Jonno, still chasing the Kurds? Hirsch flew in from Beirut, of course. Récamier. Well, Elvire. What can I say that you don't already know? You are here and she is not. You dodged this particular bullet. She didn't. She would have mourned you with as many tears if the situation was reversed. And me?"

His voice rose suddenly, and he spoke clearly to make every word audible and understandable to all the assembled gathering.

"Faria, my dear lost Faria Duclos, whom I neglected and betrayed and who was never what anyone expected. And who was capable of neglect and hurtfulness, too. I wish it was me in there and her out here, making you all want her again. But it's not like that."

He paused. You could hear a murmuring, a muttering of discontent among the congregants. His words were not going down well. I could not figure out whether it was embarrassment or annoyance. If Shelby was confronting his demons, this was not the place for it. Some things were best left unsaid, even among these truth-tellers, these chroniclers of other people's woes who so jealously guarded their own. From a dark corner of the church, a man in a fancy leather jacket—I had not noticed him initially—slipped out of the building and I heard a car engine start up. There was a squeal of tires on tarmac—it sounded angry—and then the sound faded away.

"I am saying the things you are not supposed to say at funerals, aren't I? I apologize. I don't know how else to honor her except with the truth. My truth. My truth with her. She taught me a poem, you know, by someone called Gérard de Nerval. It's called "El Desdichado" and I won't bore you with all of it, but there's a line that says this:

"'*Dans la nuit du Tombeau, Toi qui m'as consolé, / Rends-moi le Pausillipe et la mer d'Italie . . .*' Give me back the sea of Italy. Give me back the days of innocence, really, before desolation took hold. In the night of the tomb, when everything is dark, give me back the light.

"And then there's a bit that says: '*Mon front est rouge encor du baiser de la Reine . . .*' I guess you all know what I mean: My brow is still red from the kiss of the queen . . . red and bleeding."

I thought of her brow, scarred and unhealing, and wondered if he would have used those words if he had seen it, too.

Shelby delved into the pocket of his worn and crumpled linen jacket and withdrew the copy of *Aurélia* he had showed me the night before. He turned to a different passage from the one he had shown me, as if he had cherry-picked the great poet for echoes of his own grief. He read first in French, then English for any of those present who did not quite get the message.

"She is lost," I cried out to myself. "And why? . . . I understand. She has made a last effort to save me; I missed the supreme moment when pardon was still possible.

"The abyss has claimed its prey. She is lost to me and lost to us all."

With extreme awkwardness, he knelt and rested his head on the gleaming coffin, supporting himself in what seemed to be prayer on its trestle. Then he raised his eyes to the ceiling and blinked furiously, but it was too late to hide the tears. He laid his beloved old edition of *Aurélia* among the roses laid on the casket lid.

Shelby drew himself upright and walked down the nave, holding his cane under his arm like a general's baton to show he needed no aid or assistance, gesturing for me to follow him out of the church, as if I were some attendant, or maybe his consigliere. But I hung back to show I was neither of these things.

We clambered into the Jaguar— just the two of us. Elvire had arranged another ride back to the city, which came as something of a relief after the journey to the funeral. I ventured to tell Shelby he should not blame himself. Faria had suffered but among colleagues. She had known the stakes.

"Look, Clancy," he said. "She went quick in the end. Some go slow. But we all go."

He slapped his bad left leg with his good right hand.

"Do you think this will ever just go away? One day it'll wing in, accelerate. The limp will get worse. The rest will go with it and I'll be done for. Like her. Whambo-zambo."

Even at her funeral, I thought, maybe uncharitably, his thoughts had gravitated back to their solipsistic default setting.

On the drive back to Paris, he smashed his hands against the wooden steering wheel so fiercely I thought it would splinter. Tears came and we did not speak.

But just before we reached the city, as he powered the Jaguar out of a tunnel and onto a curve of highway with a fine view of the Eiffel Tower, he seemed to pull himself together.

"Gibson Dullar," he said. "Old Faria sure knew how to hurt a guy. Never by halves. She never did things by halves, I'll say that for her."

"Did she know you knew Dullar?"

"Did she know I knew him? I introduced them."

We bowled over the Seine, crossing the Pont de Sèvres.

"There are so many things you can't undo," he was saying. "Could've, should've, would've, didn't. Okay, so you can't turn the clock back. But you can't stop it ticking, either. And all you hear in it is everything you didn't do. Every person you hurt, neglected, treated badly. All those people who lived their lives in a mess because of something you did or didn't do. Parents. Lovers. Name it. All ticking away in there, somewhere, in the back of your mind, buried under your memories. Then it explodes. All your life you deny that you damaged people. And then one day, the shutters fall away and you see what you did and what you can't undo. You wonder how you could have done the things you did: Was that really you? Did you really walk away from the people you left scarred? Did you really deny them and pretend they never existed? And when that light dawns, it's too much to take, Clancy. Too much."

"Look. There's something I have to tell you," I finally said when my patience with his monologue snapped. "I saw her."

He stamped on the brake pedal and the car squealed to a halt.

"When? Where?"

"Before she died. In her apartment. I saw her. I saw the scar tissue. Something about a fire? What the fuck was that, Joe? What are you hiding? Or hiding from?"

"Get out," he said. "You Judas, Clancy. You rat. You snake in the grass. You and Gibson Dullar. What a pair. *Et tu, Brute!* Get out."

I was relieved he decided to eject me within sight of a Métro station. With the car stationary.

The twin exhausts rumbled to a howl as he drove off.

On the passenger seat, folded into his leather hat, I had left her scrawled epitaph: "I would rather be alone than hurt by the people around me."

Part Two

CHAPTER THIRTEEN

NOT LONG AFTER SHELBY ARRIVED IN PARIS, MARIE-CLAIRE, MY beloved wife, decided we should have some kind of place of our own in the capital. If I was going to spend time there with Shelby, she said with what I took to be humor, she would need to be on hand to keep an eye on me, post bail, call the medics, and so forth. Maybe I should have pressed her more closely about her reasons, but I trusted her. Perhaps more accurately, I *wanted* to trust her, even though I worried that she might be preparing an escape route from what we had built together, what she had built for us. Don't worry, she said. It's bricks and mortar, an investment, a pied-à-terre for us both to use as we wished—a retreat from the farm now that it no longer required the constant tending it had seemed to demand under my exclusive stewardship.

She had a point. The stud farm was doing well. She had brought in professionals to maximize profit, and local muscle to cope with the straw-baling and mucking-out I had once done myself. My old Ferguson tractor from the 1950s had been pensioned off, replaced with several much larger and newer models. (I insisted that it be reconditioned and parked near the stud entrance in its original sparkling red livery, its yellow wheels as bright and unsullied as my heart told me I still was.)

The goats I had kept as a sideline had been sent away, she said with all apparent sincerity, to one of those farms where children get to feed or be bitten by truculent critters. My old ledger books had given way to encrypted accounting systems on her computer. Accountants kept us honest. Managers managed. With a lurch in my guts, I realized she had created wealth. Big time. A hideaway in Paris was no great stretch.

I tried not to dwell on what she had said when we first met—that the country life was the life for her and she never wanted to return to the big city. I was reminded of the old vaudeville song: *How you gonna keep 'em down on the farm after they've seen Paree?* I was not too enthused, either, about her choice of neighborhood. Personally, I might have gone for the old favorites around the Rue du Bac in the chichi Seventh or even the Latin Quarter in the Fifth around Saint-Michel, within reach of the Île de la Cité and the *bouquinistes* along the Seine. But, maybe in a nod to her father's ambitions for her, she chose the Sixteenth, the old *haut-bourgeois* neighborhood beloved of foreign envoys and missions, where, on some streets, you would never find a cup of coffee or a croissant with the early-morning street sweepers, or a place to buy milk at midnight among the sober-fronted apartments staring silently into the blind, curlicued facades across the street, like mirrors.

The Sixteenth was a place for discretion, anonymity, far from the sidewalk theater that most visitors associate with the capital.

But in a way, it was thanks to our location in the Sixteenth that I began to understand what I came to call Shelby's Great Disappearances.

Not that he ever missed his shift, or went AWOL when he should have been batting out his ledes and new tops or calling stringers in Kandahar or Dire Dawa to inquire about obscure and bloody events on their turf.

Professionally, he was impeccable.

But somehow it seemed there were ever fewer of those afternoons when we would head out after closing down our computers (Shelby had a new one by this time, his previous machine having succumbed—mysteriously, the techies thought—to legions of assailants: trojans and viruses and spybot invaders) and locking our offices.

Our aperitifs in Saint-Germain dwindled, and there were ever-fewer occasions when he prevailed upon me to stay over and destroy a few brain cells at Le Dôme or La Coupole.

At first I thought it all had to do with Gloria Beeching. Duffie had moved her onto permanent night shifts as a punishment for the abandon he believed she must have displayed to earn her roses. In fact, though, I had my doubts about whether Gloria had been as wayward a lady with Shelby as Duffie imagined. Perhaps there had been some fumbled quest for mutual gratification, perhaps not. But whatever this newsroom peccadillo entailed, it was not a *grand amour*. There really had been just one of those in Shelby's life, and his vanishing acts only began after he buried her.

Marie-Claire and I had decided to celebrate the new apartment down from the Étoile off the Avenue d'Iéna by spending a weekend together. There was something illicit about the idea, like borrowing a friend's apartment, where you did not know quite which way to turn the faucets, or where to switch on the hot water supply, or how to find a way to the bathroom at night without stumbling into a Louis XV sofa.

After a sometimes uproarious evening with friends—movies at Odéon followed by dinner around the corner at l'Alycastre—we repaired to our new love nest.

Marie-Claire disappeared into the bathroom, telling me to fix myself a nightcap and put some music on the sound system. I concurred on both fronts, pouring a scotch and sliding a CD of Dire Straits into the wall-mounted Bang and Olufsen sound system she'd had installed. When she reemerged, she had shed her party clothes down to a sheer, silky slip that hugged her curves. She was dancing in a way that made me think back to my first sighting of her. She writhed and shimmied and pushed me back into a newly acquired armchair, still in its plastic wrap, sashaying back and forth, her eyes closed. Then she moved closer, spreading her legs to sit athwart me and take my drink from my hand and begin unfastening my shirt. Our lovemaking had been regular and—I thought—exciting out at the farm, but some other factor seemed to have gotten tangled up with it at this apartment in this most sober arrondissement.

If I hadn't been married to her, I'd have said she wanted a dirty fuck.

And if I had not been so preoccupied with eagerly following her instructions, I might have started wondering what I should make of this journey into the explicit.

By the time the morning came, I was bleary and hungry, drained and mystified. And that was when, hastily dressed, pungent and unshaven, I began the quest for croissants, combing the empty Sunday-morning streets of the Sixteenth.

The low-slung silver Jaguar was parked at an odd angle with its roof down on the Rue Auguste Vacquerie. Something about the way its tires scuffed the sidewalk and its rear wing protruded into the street suggested an uncharacteristic negligence. The coachwork that had been so pristine when the car rolled down the ramps outside the offices of the *Star* now bore the scars of urban warfare—paint scratches, minor dings that sullied the perfect lines.

I glanced around surreptitiously, a caricature of a car thief, then checked the glove box: the Nerval volumes were in their place. Shelby could not be far away if he had left the car to guard the Michelin Guide to his dark-starred soul.

I was about to close the glove compartment when I caught sight of a stapled sheaf of paperwork. Surreptitiously I fished it out. The letterhead proclaimed it to be from a company called Saad & Trad s.a.l., Corniche El Nahr, in Beirut. In the old days you'd have called it Christian East Beirut, but I wasn't sure those labels were still observed as meticulously as they were when Shelby and Duclos haunted the Commodore but never told anyone where they were heading out.

Saad & Trad s.a.l., it seemed from the letterhead, was the place to go in the new, post-war Lebanon for Bentleys, Lamborghinis, and Jaguars. The document seemed to be an innocuous enough bill of sale for a secondhand Jaguar XKR. Silver. Super-charged 400 bhp model. The price tag looked as if it might just have been in the range of some middle-aged guy splurging on his crisis. The buyer was identified as one Joseph Shelby. The previous owner was listed as the company itself, as if it had been a display model or a vehicle that had suddenly made its way into Lebanon with no previous documentation. There was no mention of a shooting gallery in the Bekaa Valley, or a warlord, or an Israeli drone. Was the document just a cover, a piece of paper to persuade customs officers in Lebanon and France to approve the shipment of a car? Or was it exactly what it seemed to be: evidence of a humdrum transaction at a car dealership, a midlife trade of dollars for delusion?

I replaced the document in the glove compartment with the Nerval, fitting it snugly alongside the leather helmet, which, I noticed, no longer contained the scribbled note I had folded into it as we returned from the funeral of Faria Duclos. Quite the Hercule Poirot or Sherlock Holmes, I turned my attention to working out where Shelby might be. I did not need to look further than a kind of origami depiction of a knight and a dragon in red metal, bolted to a sign indicating that here was the Church of St. George.

It did not look much like a church, though I confess that I have little expertise beyond the familiar images of thatch and steeple that I had observed at the Duclos funeral. After my literally bare-knuck- led introduction to it as a kid, organized religion had not really been part of my adult life. It wasn't only the corporal punishment meted out by the Brothers that put me off. I found it difficult to spend my days chronicling human cruelty, folly, and hatred for the pages of the *Paris Star* and then to accept, after hours, that it was all part of some grand divine plan directing the world's havoc to the greater good of redemption. My skepticism only deepened with the wave of sexual abuse scandals that washed over the Vatican and all its subsidiaries soon after we set up Nonstop News–Paris Outpost. I channeled the avalanche of articles about priestly perversion onto the website with a mixture of rage and relief: rage at what these depraved custodians of young souls had been capable of and relief that they had not inflicted anything beyond overzealous beatings on *me*.

I also had a kind of fear of clerics, as if, once they spotted you hov- ering in the rear pews, they could somehow cast a spell over you and your cash flow, enslaving your soul and your bank account forever.

St. George's Anglican Church was in a basement with stripped walls of reddish-brown brick, approached—counterintuitively, I thought as I entered—by steps leading downward, as if to the diabol- ical depths of eternal pain rather than to the celestial heights prom- ised to those who truly believed and behaved without blemish. (I wondered if I could lay claim to that status after my night of magic, stretching the limits of blue movie inventiveness, albeit within the lawful embrace of holy matrimony.)

There were no windows. So how would anyone see the light?

The church itself was, I guess, no more than a couple of decades old, built at a time when people figured modern architecture would draw in the recruits to the heavenly divisions more efficiently than dusty beams and chilly benches. Above a slab-like altar, a boxy lighting device descending from the ceiling suggested a "beam me up, Scotty" pathway to heaven. In a corner, a choir intoned the Agnus Dei, the Lamb of God. "Have mercy on me," they chanted, and I could not fault that particular request. I approached cautiously, checking my watch to work out whether Marie-Claire would have started wondering where I had gotten to. I could hardly say I had been at church with Shelby, as if that trumped the prospect of returning to her svelte body enfolded in rumpled sheets of the finest, if stained, cotton percale. Like a latter-day Quasimodo, I took up position behind a metal grille that allowed me to observe without being noticed and dragged before the congregation for all to witness the agnostic deformity of my spirit—or, worse still, forced into public confession.

It was that time in the service when the faithful form a line to go up to the altar and kneel before the cross to receive the body and the blood of Christ. Most were dressed in a way that would define the term "Sunday best"—stout women in stout shoes; men in fawn slacks, navy blue blazers, and knotted ties.

Not Shelby.

His faded blue jeans seemed to be hanging from his frame, and crumpled shirttails peeked out below an old sand-colored suede jacket. He mingled, nonetheless, with a blue-rinsed set you might not have suspected to be his first choice of fellow travelers on the highway to eternity. He shuffled forward and knelt, his hands outstretched to receive the holy wafer—the body of Christ—from a priest in heavy green robes. He took the chalice eagerly, and I thought there was a brief tussle over how deeply he might quaff from the blood. Shelby remained on his knees for slightly longer than anyone else, then rose and joined the line of congregants returning to their places, reaffirmed in their faith by their solemn encounter with the Almighty.

I left quickly and silently, but not before observing Shelby's tired, craggy features fixed in a beatific expression, as if, with that evocation of the Last Supper, he had truly communed with a power that passed all understanding, illuminating the benighted recesses of his being.

"Goddamn Sixteenth," I complained to Marie-Claire when I got back. "Can't find a croissant or a pint of milk for love or money."

I might have hoped for a reprise of the previous night, but she already had showered, dressed, done her makeup, brewed espresso, and changed the sheets.

"Time to go back to the farm, big boy," she said. I thought there was a note of regret in her voice, and her mood seemed brittle. I put it down to fatigue after our exertions.

Shelby's next mystery tour was rather more dramatic and not nearly so spiritual.

The call came on a Monday morning as I pulled out of the stud gates, past my shiny restored Ferguson.

The sky was lightening in the east, toward Paris, and white mist floated over the still dark paddocks and gallops like luminous chiffon or ectoplasm. The early staff was on duty, and before clambering into the car, I paused to sniff the familiar, ripe air and listen to the intimate snuffles, snorts, and whinnies of a horse farm. Stable lads carrying riding helmets nodded respectfully toward me (respectful, of course, because of my association with their boss, my wife) and headed for their tasks, armed with brushes and bridles, saddles and blankets for the early ride out atop their frisky charges.

As usual, at that hour, I had snuck from the conjugal bed to shower and dress on the lower floor. Marie-Claire slumbered on. Our weekend in the Sixteenth had rekindled the physical aspects of our relationship to such an extent that these early starts for the office had become an effort. I brewed coffee and poured a generous measure into a thermos flask for Marie-Claire whenever she rose. The flask reminded me of one Shelby's stories and that, in turn, reminded me of our weekend in the Sixteenth and that, in turn, made me wonder who would notice if I goofed off and went back to bed, seeking to redeem the promise of the thermos.

But I resisted. My routines held the line: rise, shower, cuppa joe, drive. The car radio was tuned to a scratchy version of the BBC on AM, offering me my first infusion of news.

The day seemed quiet enough. The suicide bombers had not yet detonated their explosive vests, the F-16 pilots had not yet unleashed their missiles, the CIA drones had not yet splattered some mud hut in Waziristan, the politicians had not yet taken their bullhorns to bend the truth—at least not so far as was known to the armies of stringers and correspondents and editors who formed the chain that ended in those time-honored words ". . . and this news just in."

Sometimes you had to ask yourself why news was always so noisy: bombs/blasts/explosions that ripped/tore/shattered mosques/minibuses/markets. The crude language was a code for mayhem, its familiarity easing the pain of actually visualizing and confronting the participants' true trauma—disconnected limbs, blood on baby shawls, blank eyes with the life snuffed out as quickly as you or I might flick a light switch; futures that should have been measured in decades destroyed in a high-decibel nanosecond.

It was no time to be thinking such things and I settled in for a quiet drive.

Then the call came. Unusually, my cell was switched on.

It was Shelby inquiring in his most exaggerated, anglicized accent—"old sport"—if I might vary my route to drop by a police precinct in the Eighth to stand bail or otherwise extricate him from incarceration so that he might start his shift on time.

"Bail?"

I was juggling the phone to switch it to hands-free as I rolled along the highway toward Paris. I figured at first it might be about the Duclos inquiry. There had been rumors that Ivar Bild, the night nurse, had returned to Sweden shortly after the funeral. There was some muttering among her surviving colleagues and friends that her death just seemed to come too quickly. She had died at home, in her top-floor apartment. There had been no suggestion that she had been hospitalized and there were plenty of questions about why an autopsy had been ordered—was there a suspicion here of euthanasia, aka murder? Were the investigators looking for toxins or evidence of an overdose? And, if they were, who was suspected of administering it? Faria Duclos had never struck me as a likely suicide but Ivar Bild had assured me she would feel no pain at the end. What on earth could that mean? Was Shelby somehow implicated? In the absence of news, I often suspected, my colleagues fell all too easily into the recycling of gossip and rumor, conspiracy, even. But the cops were saying nothing beyond the boilerplate: our inquiries are ongoing. So I kept the rumors about her death to myself.

Shelby's case was rather less mysterious.

"Slight misunderstanding, nothing more," he said over the phone. "Not sure, in fact, if it's bail or they just want someone to ease me quietly off the premises."

"What the . . . ?"

"Can't talk right now. Only one call permitted and all that . . ."

I drove faster than usual. Shelby had given me an address off the Champs-Élysées—not too far, in fact, from the Church of Saint George and the love nest of Clancy, but in a different, almost-as-snooty arrondissement. The fact that he was in detention—or somehow deprived of liberty—at least helped explain why I had been unable to reach him all weekend.

I had been trying intermittently to call Shelby ever since an informant at the *Star* passed on an item of news—not for repeating, mum's the word, *entre nous*, hush-hush, deepest background, etc.— which I immediately planned to transmit to Shelby on much the same ground rules of confidentiality.

The story was this: a delegation from the top echelons of Big Brother *Graphic* in New York was planning to visit Little Sister *Star* in Paris.

There was a time when the arrival of the head office luminaries could be turned to advantage, when the pooh-bahs could be lured into situations of such embarrassment (usually involving a literal cocktail of booze and sex) that they would never again threaten to sack you without risking full disclosure of behavior that neither their wives nor their own uber-bosses would approve.

Shelby himself had told me of an occasion when he still worked on the wires and some high-up from the executive committee had rolled into town while he was covering an uprising in the Congo, then known as Zaire. In those days, Mobutu Sese Seko ran his enormous country from Kinshasa, with his juju motifs of a leopard-skin hat and a stick carved with representations of intertwined naked women. (No story from Kinshasa, in that era, was regarded as complete without reference to Mobutu's full name—Mobutu Sese Seko Nkuku Ngbendu wa Za Banga—which translated variously in hackspeak, if not in any known language, as "the warrior who goes from conquest to conquest, leaving fire in his wake" or, alternatively, "the cock who goes from hen to hen, showing no fatigue.")

The senior wire service executive, technically Shelby's superior by many rungs on the bureaucratic ladder, went by the name of Whitecroft, and he tracked down Shelby to his room at the Intercon to inquire with a nudge and a wink where he might locate what he called "Congolese music."

"Try the radio," Shelby said.

"No, no," the executive said. "You don't understand. Congolese music. *Live* music."

Shelby understood exactly what the executive meant. "Congolese music" denoted merchandise of a type that Kinshasa specialized in, purveyed in the kind of place that throbbed darkly to the rhythms of West African boogie and the transmission of HIV. Elsewhere I had heard a story about American television executives mulling how to bill their head offices for such moments of abandon in the tropics and coming up with the term "Zulu translators."

Congolese music. Zulu translators. Receipt lost!

"I took him down to the Jambo Jambo, which, I guess, meant 'Hello Hello' if you translated it direct from the Swahili," Shelby began. "It meant a lot more than that to every lonely expat roaming the bushlands looking for solace. It was an awful spot. Sweaty. Steamy. Great music—I mean real music—but the most awful hook- ers, the kind who take out a glass eye, shake off a wig, and park a wooden leg on the bedpost before they get down to business. But Whitecroft had a weakness. A passion. Some guys do. An itch that needed scratching. Off we went to the Jambo Jambo, with him insist- ing all the time that he really only wanted to listen to what he called "the old boomlay-boom," and so once I'd gotten him in there he'd be fine on his own. But I saw him exiting out back with a particular- ly lurid example of 'Congolese music' on his arm, and he saw me watching him. So he knew that I knew, and I knew that he knew that I knew—et cetera, et cetera—and he could never put the squeeze on me again. Friend for life, you might say. All I had to do was ask, 'How's the Congolese music?'"

I could match the story, too, with uproarious yarns told and retold since Reynolds Packard's day of hungry news executives land- ing in Paris and demanding a guided tour of Pigalle, saying all they really wanted to do was research the influences that had produced Toulouse-Lautrec's distinctive backdrops at the Folies Bergère.

For "Toulouse-Lautrec," read "Congolese music."

But this latest sortie by the brass was unlikely to offer either of us opportunities for self-advancement or blackmail.

This was a different, more earnest era, clouded by the prospect of financial ruin as newspapers saw their income eaten away by treacherous readers decamping to the web, taking the advertisers and their home delivery subscriptions with them, forcing economies that would once have been considered a poor show, or even bad form.

"With each cut," one of New York's finest and bravest editors had once observed, "it becomes harder to keep the scalpel away from vital organs." (The metaphors of parsimony are always those of the blade.)

The delegation coming our way—and this was what I had wanted to tell Shelby—was led by Curtis, the top executive on the business side, accompanied by acolytes such as Green, the foreign editor, and Potts, the head of NND. I knew them all.

I compared their coming mission to the *Star* to the work of a

mortician coming to settle the dentures of a cadaver in a solemn rictus and apply a touch of rouge to the lips and tweak the shroud
before the final voyage to the altar and the sanctimonious eulogy as
the doors slid closed and the furnace roared.

Potts, in particular, had always made me think of the unctuous
attendant at a funeral parlor, showing guests into a lilac-draped
Chapel of Memory to the strains of Muzak, as if burdened by a grief
too immense for any solution other than the transfer of assets from
the deceased's family to his bank account.

When the downsizing begins, you always wonder whether you
will be the first to be called in for the terminal interview when they
summon security to relieve you of your door pass, and your e-mail
address starts bouncing back messages. I did not want to become
that kind of relic in the debris of the digital train wreck. Partly it was
pride, partly sheer terror at what I imagined would be the look of
horror on Marie-Claire Risen's face when I rolled home, drunk and
unkempt, with my old metal spike and my potted ficus tree and all
the world's self-pity in a straining box courteously supplied by a
solicitous colleague.

What would I tell her? *I failed, honey.*

I failed you.

But the real news, for Shelby, lay in the identity of the fourth
rider of this apocalypse: none other than Gibson Dullar, who was
rumored to have been dropping hints to the New York elite about his
fluency in French and his experience in those parts of the world that
fell under the purview of the NND outpost in Paris. It was not immediately clear whether Dullar had joined the visitors as bag carrier or
hit man. Either way, it did not look good for Shelby.

There had been suggestions that whispers of the Argentine Soy
Vote Affair had gotten back to New York.

I could imagine Dullar spreading the furtive word, even as he
imagined himself replacing Shelby in the boulevards and boudoirs of
Paris, not to mention the newsroom of the *Star*. If word got back to
Dullar that his rival had languished for a weekend in a French slam-
mer, the consequences were too awful to contemplate.

I took Shelby's call, thus, with an unsettling mix of feelings—

relief that he had checked in, foreboding about our shared future, and, most of all, a towering pissed-off-ness at the stupidity of his behavior.

If I'm to be brutally honest with myself, there was another ingredient in the emotional stew. Before Marie-Claire took the apartment in the Sixteenth, my worries about our future together had been receding. Although I had once figured she might abandon our cozy domesticity, I had started to believe that she had finally found her niche, come to terms with her restlessness, resolved the quest for some kind of modus vivendi that roughly corresponded to her needs.

But after she took the apartment, I began to wonder—with nothing by way of evidence—whether I had displayed the classic complacency (C for Charlie, C for Cuckold!) that catches out life's rubes just as they imagine they've got things taped.

Of course, there was no obvious correlation between Shelby's disappearances and her stays at the apartment. But I took to making a turn around the Sixteenth on my way from the office to the farm, just to see if I could spy vehicular evidence of undeclared residence—either in the form of her SUV or in the torpedo phallus of a Jaguar XKR.

The green-eyed monster is a sickening beast.

Your stomach lurches when you see yourself as outsiders would see you—mistrustful, paranoid, a snoop, a voyeur. You hate yourself for the sin of mistrusting your life partner. You start to wonder whether your fear at what you might discover is just a cover for actually wanting to find out the worst.

But you can't stop yourself.

Sometimes I would find a parking spot and take the old cage-elevator up to the apartment, opening the door quickly like some Stasi operative on the hunt for dissidents. I'd check out the place, sniffing at the air—even, for God's sake, inspecting the bed linen for signs . . . of what?

Then I'd snap back to my senses and flee, riding home to the stud farm posthaste, wanting to monopolize my spouse in those magical, notorious hours between 5 and 7 before anyone else did.

If she still wished to. If she was home. If it was not too late.

One of my secret visits did, however, turn up a clue.

Exhibit A.

Normally no mail was delivered to the apartment, but this time, there was a large opened envelope addressed to my wife that had contained a shiny brochure for the latest Alfa Romeo Spider sports car. A salesman's note to Marie-Claire thanked her for her interest and invited her for a consultation on the color, engine size, and optional extras.

My guts squirmed. When had she been here to open the letter? Who had been with her? Most of all, was she preparing to reenter the fast lane she had abandoned when we met? What other telltale signs had I missed? Was her happiness with me too forced, a legend to disguise her preparations?

I looked again through the brochure. The technology had certainly advanced since my old Spider. The performance figures were in a different league, too. But there was the same spirit of freedom, the same zest. As I put the brochure back exactly where I had found it on the coffee table, the light from one of the tall windows fell across the front cover and I thought I detected a slight powdery dusting. I raised the brochure again and sniffed at it. Still not sure, I ran my forefinger over the glossy cover and tasted what I thought was a trace of what I feared.

Exhibit B, your honor.

CHAPTER FOURTEEN

I DREW TO A HALT ON A SIDE STREET IN THE EIGHTH—TAKING CARE
to park legally in light of the number of blue-uniformed cops hanging around the precinct. Inside, an end-of-shift officer gave me the
stink eye from behind a counter kept clear of debris. Even indoors,
he was fully kitted out with Kevlar vest, cuffs, service pistol, night-
stick, and tear gas canisters. If this was how they dressed in the bour-
geois reaches of the Eighth, I wondered what they wore in the far-
flung reaches of the Nineteenth or the grim redoubts of the *ban-
lieues*—chain mail?

"Monsieur Shelby?" I said inquiringly to explain my presence.

"And you would be?"

"A friend."

"You speak French?"

"Certainly."

"You understand this form?"

He slid a legal document toward me. The gist was that I would
take responsibility for Shelby, Joseph Gerard, pending further
inquiries into an alleged incident in the late hours of Sunday when
citizens had complained that a man had exited Le Drugstore on the
Champs-Élysées and begun disrobing in public. The cops got to him,
the officer said, just before he could bare all. It seemed he had been
pretty much down to his skivvies and a leather helmet of a type once
worn by aviators.

"He was drunk?"

"*Fou,*" the officer said. Crazy. Mad.

"How crazy?"

"Crazy enough that he told us he was following his star."

"Anything else?" I asked casually, disguising my relief that this seemed to have nothing to do directly with the Duclos case – just a routine, collegial, public breakdown.

"He gave his name as Gérard de Nerval. Fortunately, we recovered his wallet where it fell from his clothes and discovered the name Joseph Gerard Shelby on a visiting card. Eventually, he accepted that name as his own."

It was the first I had heard of Shelby having a middle name, and I wondered when he had acquired it. I signed the form. Maybe the fact that he was being held under a potentially false identity would help if the police decided later to take action—or have him committed to an asylum.

Shelby emerged from some back room, disheveled and unshaven. He signed for his watch, wallet, belt, cane, laces from his battered suede shoes, and helmet. He might have been any old drunk emerging from the cooler into the hard light of temporary sobriety, blinking in the brightness and toying with thoughts of vodka.

How could I have begun to explain to the cops who he really was? How could I tell them this was Shelby of Sarajevo, Pulitzer winner, warrior of the fourth estate?

Was he still, in fact, that same person?

There was no way that he could make an appearance in the *Star* newsroom looking like a clochard from under the bridges of Paris.

He looked at me sheepishly, then tried a grin.

"Don't ask me to explain," he said.

"Never explain, Joe," I said.

"Never explain. Or apologize," he said. "That's the motto, isn't it?"

"You should know. Old sport. Let's go."

"Your call, chief," he said, handing me the keys to his apartment with the docility of a chastened child.

I bundled him into my car and drove back toward the Rue du Cherche-Midi, hurrying to get there before the odor of unwashed human and stale booze overpowered the Jeep's ambient fragrance of horse and tobacco. Blessedly he had left the Jag parked there—if he had been prepared to disrobe on the Champs-Élysées, who could say what he might have contrived with backup from a 400-horsepower V8 engine?

From the first time I had seen it soon after his arrival in Paris, the apartment surprised me with its neatness, almost fastidiousness—as if Shelby was expecting a notable guest or keeping it in an appropriate condition for some kind of second coming known only to him and, maybe, the ghost of Gérard de Nerval. Maybe I had been expecting a squat, one of those old bachelor pads with noisome mounds of discarded boxers marking the territory in much the same way as a rhinoceros uses its midden, but this was almost *House & Garden*.

It was on the sixth floor, one below the maids' level to which Faria Duclos had been consigned in her far less salubrious part of town. A complex set of security codes propelled a carpeted elevator that opened directly into the hallway of his apartment. In the main salon, with its corniced, stuccoed ceiling and burnished floor, lined drapes of dark wine-colored velour were still drawn.

Shelby threw a wall switch that controlled the sound and light systems, filling the place with sensual glows and low-volume, schmoozy tones of Astrud Gilberto. I guessed that, at some stage of his Sunday evening, he had been expecting company, perhaps from Gloria Beeching or an out-of-office equivalent.

He had transferred most of his stuff from its initial entrepôt in the newsroom and had arranged it with a degree of taste that, to my jaded eye, looked feminine—the lamps positioned just so, casting pools of peach-colored light over deep burgundy rugs from the Orient, the spots illuminating the supposedly fake Monet I had seen unloaded in his early days at the *Star*. There were even vases of flowers, for Chrissakes. It had that feel of good taste I would happily associate with Marie-Claire, for instance, but not with a partner in the crime of news-gathering. I wondered if he ever got around to placing a bloom in the barrel of the decommissioned AK-47, now hanging in a display frame with a discreet brass plaque that declared, "*Ceci n'est pas un Kalashnikov.*"

"Gotta shower," Shelby said, waving me toward a kitchenette.

"Amen," I replied, but he did not seem to hear.

"Joe," he said. "Fix joe. Joe for Joe."

I placed a large hexagonal Italian coffeemaker on a low light and listened for the shower. The hiss of hot water fused uneasily with a sound it took me some time to recognize as singing.

From the depths of his humiliation in the police precinct, Shelby was rebuilding, like one of those molten silver pools in the *Terminator* movies that re-forms into humanoid shape even after an express train has careened through its previous form. His voice gathered strength and confidence. He worked his way through an off-key rendering of "The Man Who Broke the Bank at Monte Carlo." The choice of ditty made you wonder whether Shelby really saw himself strolling "along the Bois de Boulogne with an independent air," as the song put it, with the girls all sighing and dying to draw his attention.

His apartment opened onto a modest outdoor deck that looked across a large inner courtyard, most of the time in complete privacy. Shelby had installed a small outdoor refrigerator with ice-making facilities and a generous stock of his favored Menetou-Salon dry white. He kept hard liquor and crystal glasses in an old, weather-beaten cupboard made of some African timber called yellowwood. Looking out from the wicker armchairs, you usually saw only the closed and shuttered windows of other apartments across a wide courtyard. But one evening—one of those close summer evenings when you strain for any breath of cooler air across the hot roofs of the city—I was distracted to see a young woman in a summery top and shorts, perched on a windowsill with a guardrail at half height. At one point she stepped down and, with a casual indifference to our presence, began to undress.

"Some neighbor," I said.

Shelby contemplated her with a look of painful regret and near bemusement.

"Lorelei, I call her. That's her room. At the back of the hotel where she works. I had dinner there one night and she waited my table. I recognized her and I guess she recognized me. I smiled. We chatted."

I peered judiciously into the large Jameson he had poured me.

"So. Anyhow. The next time I'm out here, it's late. I just have a candle burning. I'm on my own and I pour a jolt. It's pretty dark and there's a bedside light in her apartment. But she comes to her window and peels off. Silhouetted. Naked as the day she was born. And I know she's looking at me."

"So you went back to the restaurant?"

"Never."

"Why not?"

"What for, Clancy? What the hell for?"

That evening, as we sat over late drinks, she returned and stood in silhouette, her back arched and her head flung back. I could not tell whether she was clothed. But she held the posture as if we did not exist. Shelby peered across at her.

"'And should I then presume? And how should I begin?'" he said.

"'Should I, after tea and cakes and ices, Have the strength to force the moment to its crisis?'"

"I never had you down as a Prufrock," he said with an uncharacteristic hint of admiration.

"Nerval wasn't the only wordsmith, you know."

"Careful there, Clancy! Heresy is a punishable offense."

Soon he would emerge from the shower refreshed, drink his coffee and mentally consign the night's adventure to the growing catalog of episodes about which he preferred to be in denial. I would be expected to ignore it, too. Truth was becoming elastic.

With little time to snoop, I made a beeline for the study across the central high-ceilinged hallway. The workroom was more what I would have expected from a onetime alpha male, the walls hung with trophies and souvenir photographs of Shelby and his buddies posing in their familiar hellholes. Here they all were, at the bar of the Commodore in pre-jihad West Beirut; under a sun-filtered bamboo awning at some hotel in Africa, looking solemn and smug; in wooden pirogues, poled across the Chari River from Chad to Cameroon.

There were the individual, post-interview shots, too: Shelby with the King and Queen of Jordan in Amman, Nelson Mandela in Johannesburg, Boris Yeltsin in Moscow; in the ruins of Grozny with some wild Chechen in an astrakhan hat; alongside an Afghan warlord in his Pashtun headgear, swathed in cartridge belts. I couldn't help thinking it was like one of those shrines that stalkers build to worship the targets of their obsession—except that Shelby's altar was dedicated to himself.

In a mess of file folders and old-fashioned postal correspondence on his writing desk, I noticed a paper wrapper smeared with white powder. I ran my finger over it and touched it against my upper gum, which turned instantly numb. The sensation, the chemical purity of the smell, transported me back to my discovery at our apartment in the Sixteenth. Shelby's powdery trail across his desk offered one more reason to keep him away from my bride.

Next to the wrapper, a Visa Carte Bleue from his French bank had been tossed aside, still bearing a rime of the same white powder. I ran it across my nostril, then licked at it gingerly, wondering what exalted sensation she drew from it yet, like a cautious swimmer unwilling to take the plunge in wild waters, a toe half in the water. I thought I felt something, a buzz, a shift of focus, an edge. Was that it? Was that all there was?

In full Holmes-and-Watson mode while Shelby showered, I continued my search, turning up an overnight courier pouch containing an official-looking envelope made of brown recycled paper. I shook its contents onto the old partner's desk that Shelby once told me he liberated from the *Graphic*'s bureau in Cairo. There was a cover letter in bureaucratese: *pursuant to your letter of, etc., etc.; under the Freedom of Information Act of blah-blah*. There were redactions highlighted in thick black slabs to blot out the names of other people who had seen the documents, faded stamps with the words "classified" and "not for unauthorized transmission" and "NOFORN." Some of the pages were typed on the personal letterhead of the American consul general in Paris. A scribbled note on a separate, unmarked sheet of notepaper said: "Guess this evens the score, Joe. This time, we really are quits!"

I recognized the name below the signature as that of a high-ranking State Department official notorious for indiscreet liaisons and mischievous behavior in the tropics.

In the shower, Shelby had abandoned the man who broke the bank at Monte Carlo to become Marlene Dietrich, falling in love again, never wanting to . . .

The documents were in chronological order. A certificate, issued by the French authorities in the down-at-heel Clichy district of Paris, listed the birth of a child called Shelby. The given names were Joseph Donald Gérard. A handwritten scrawl described the father as "*inconnu.*" The mother was identified as Jenny Colon. A scribbled annotation in the same handwriting suggested that the maternal moniker could be "an alias or stage name." Issued only a matter of days later, a formal certificate attested to the child's adoption by a couple called Labrunie, he American, she French, residents of Paris, living at a smart address on the Avenue de Suffren, near the Eiffel Tower, in the Seventh. The mother's only stipulation on giving away her child was that the infant should retain the surname she wished for it: Shelby. Finally, a naturalization document confirmed the child as one of Uncle Sam's own.

In the shower, Shelby had switched to German—"*und sonst gar nichts*"—but in the documents he was a mix-up of French and American, a transatlantic chimera.

I shoved the documents back into the envelope and tried to figure how Shelby might have felt discovering these crude building blocks of an autobiography that had been projected quite differently in public. From his study, the high windows looked out beyond the courtyard over rooftops leading across the chimney pots of Paris with their little covers known as *chinois* (they looked like the traditional shallow hats of Chinese peasants in the rice paddies) toward the Eiffel Tower in whose shadow Shelby had been raised. In all the time I knew him, he had not even hinted at a Parisian childhood. I should have guessed from his faultless accent in his long conversations with Faria Duclos that he had a special affinity, but I had not inquired closely, the way guys don't. I had just believed his myth, and maybe, in the end, he had been tempted to believe it, too.

Had he suspected all along that he had been abandoned at birth, a mother's reject, father unknown? Maybe he had not even known those details himself until the batch of documents from some dusty archive in the American consulate had arrived in his postbox. Or maybe he had known it and preferred not to acknowledge those roots, until curiosity—or an intimation of mortality—got the better of him and forced him to confront his history. I glanced again at the FedEx pouch. It had been couriered to a mail drop in Beirut—a common enough ploy in the kind of place where the postman might run off to join a militia or get shot on his rounds by someone from the rival gang. The date stamping was smudged, but it looked to me like it had been marked for delivery well before Shelby's arrival in Paris. Were the contents the magnet that had drawn him to my city? Or was there something else in those dark months between his documented departure from Lebanon and his known arrival in France?

My snooping put me in a delicate position. It was always a professional and personal courtesy among people like Shelby and me to allow other people their legends, their cardboard-cutout personae. We lived for the present, the next bar, the next adventure. We indulged each other's Peter Pan pretensions. We didn't pry.

Another scrap of documentation caught my eye. It was a page torn from the Beirut newspaper *L'Orient–Le Jour*, carefully preserved in a sealed plastic folder like some kind of evidence bag. At first I couldn't fathom it. Then I noticed a faint pencil mark next to one of the items in the run-of-the-mill Faits Divers catalog of petty crimes and minor stuff. A headline proclaimed (why do headlines never just *say* things?) "Incendie à l'Hotel Commodore." Fire at the Commodore. It told how a blaze consumed a corridor of the hotel just off Hamra Street in West Beirut. Three journalists escaped, two of them unharmed, one suffering from burns. It did not identify them by name, but I had an awful feeling I had seen some of the damage during my clandestine visit with the woman in the wheelchair.

So who were the other two?

More to the point, did I really want to know?

I looked again at the tear sheet. The date at the top of the page predated Shelby's departure from Beirut by a matter of days.

"Bang-bang, you're dead," Shelby said.

I turned from the window. Across the desk, he was standing in the doorway with a faded African kikoyi wrapped around his waist, his wet hair plastered on his head, the AK-47 removed from its moorings and pointed toward me.

"Is that thing loaded?"

"I'm not that glad to see you, Clancy."

"You know, that damn rifle may be dangerous. You should ditch it."

The coffeemaker in the kitchenette hissed and gurgled, demanding immediate attention.

Shelby tore open a consignment of laundry, packaged with ribbons and heavy tissue paper, from a particularly high-end establishment in the neighborhood. He pulled out a crisp white shirt and pressed, faded Levi's in the old-fashioned heavy, high-waisted cut with a button fly that you hardly ever see anymore, and repaired to his boudoir.

I took another opportunity to snoop. On his desk, a leather-bound, original-looking copy of Nerval's *Voyage en Orient* was open at a page where, as far as I could gather from a very quick scan, a guy called Hakim had reentered his own palace on the banks of the Nile in disguise and found a party underway at which a mystery man was sitting with the woman of his dreams: his sister Setalmulc! I wasn't sure who Shelby was most likely to imagine himself to be. I flicked a few pages backward and forward—Hakim sulks, Cairo burns, Hakim dies. Not pleasant reading.

Another guy got a mention, Yousouf. In the denouement he turned out to be Hakim's half-brother, but you only found out after a mortal fight over the same woman.

And fire. Again.

Always fire in the Orient—Cairo for Hakim; Beirut, it seemed, for Faria Duclos.

If I had one thing to thank my parents for—and that was a big if—it was that, after their initial experiment with procreation, they never tried again to give me a brother or sister. In my childhood, I sometimes felt peeved about that. But the story of Hakim and Yousouf and Setalmulc convinced me that, really, one was enough.

Shelby's choice of reading made me feel unaccountably anxious. But that may just have been because Marie-Claire had begun to talk about maybe having a few old friends over for a fiesta of some kind. A big party with lights and candles and music—just the same as Nerval described in his Oriental phantasmagoria.

Next to the book, there was another volume, a more recent version of the collected works from the Pléiade series by Gallimard. Its green bookmark ribbon had been left at a section of *Aurélia* where Nerval began to describe an episode in which he resolved "to search the skies for a star that I thought I knew, as if it had some influence on my destiny."

Here began, for me, what I will call the dream pouring out into real life. Finding myself alone, I rose with some effort and resumed my journey towards the star, never taking my eyes from it. As I walked I sang a mysterious hymn which I thought I remembered from some other existence and which filled me with ineffable joy. At the same time, I abandoned my earthly clothing and spread it around me . . .

I wondered if the cops who arrested Shelby on the Champs-Élysées had figured that it was just his dream pouring out into real life.

As I read on, a slip of paper in Shelby's own handwriting fluttered from the pages.

I broke my own heart
When I broke yours.
Isn't that what the faithless plead?
Isn't that their spell to stem the guilt
That crushes them anyhow?

I just had time to scan the title—"For F.D."—before he reappeared.

"Reading the master?" He was kitted out in pressed denim, scuffed but expensive Italian suede loafers, and a buckskin jacket slung over his shoulder. He took the book from me and folded it closed.

"Fancy laundry," I replied, gesturing to his stash of clean clothes.

"Let me give you a tip, Clancy, about traveling, especially for a full-blooded man like yourself." His voice had slipped into an accent resembling a faint Irish brogue, as it often did when he pronounced my surname. He lit a cigarette and inhaled.

"There are two things a man should never, ever bring home to his beloved from a spell on the road. One of them is a bag full of dirty laundry. Hence that." He gestured to the neat rows of folded shirts and ironed boxers, then fell silent.

"And the other?"

"The other what?"

"The other thing a man should never bring home after a spell on the road, along with a bag of unwashed clothes."

"Come on, Clancy. Use your imagination. Work it out!"

There was no hint of an explanation or an apology for the mess he had gotten himself into—or thanks to me for getting him out of it.

CHAPTER FIFTEEN

BY THE TIME WE GOT TO LE PRIMEROSE, WE WERE RUNNING LATE but not as late as we might have been. Shelby piloted the silver bullet around l'Étoile with the vigor of a Le Mans veteran, while I clung on in the white-knuckle slipstream at the wheel of my protesting SUV. We ordered our usual start-of-the-day pick-me-ups of caffeine, sugar, and starch. I added a fried egg, and it came with a double yolk, a good omen.

"Parallel," Shelby said.

I looked at him sharply—what now?

"Parallel destinies. Two yolks, same old hen—which one came first? One mirrors the other. Maybe one's real, and the other is an illusion, a shadow."

"It's a fucking egg, Shelby."

"You'll see."

My cell phone had begun to purr and wriggle. News was happening. We needed to be on it. Journalism needed to be committed. The screen on the cell phone told me Hong Kong was calling. There was a missed call from New York. We were the hinge between the two time zones, Asia and America, keeping the light burning, crafting the news in Nonstop News–Paris Outpost.

Whambo-zambo.

This morning, the hinge was a bit creaky.

Even with our late start, the newsroom was still becalmed and we had the place more or less to ourselves. I scanned the wires for the familiar crop of destruction.

In my more cynical moments—that is, most of the time—I wondered whether there was some grisly poker played among the self-immolators and suicide squads in the badlands: *I see your five dead cops, and I raise to ten teenage schoolgirls. I see you and raise thirty police cadets and ten women at a mosque.* But in this game, there was a twist: no one survived to collect the winnings.

Shelby was working away feverishly in Homepatch, and I deployed the time-honored water cooler gambit to reconnoiter, bringing him a comradely white plastic cup so as to spy over his shoulder.

Then I wished I hadn't.

Pirates based in a remote corner of Somalia's breakaway region of Puntland vowed Monday to launch a campaign against America-bound crude oil and cargo shipping as what they termed their contribution to global jihad.

"First I heard of it," I muttered.

"A game," he replied. "Like casting for trout. Homepatch Hunter."

A pirate leader who identified himself only as Siad Barre told local reporters the campaign would begin soon, adding new perils to the shipping lanes leading from the Persian Gulf through the Gulf of Aden and on to the Suez Canal.

"Where are you getting this from? The Nairobi guy? The stringer in Mog? Hargeisa? Berbera, for Chrissakes?

"Patience, dear boy."

He returned to his keyboard.

An upsurge in the hijacking of merchant shipping has inspired growing international concern that the price of oil and other cargo could soar—augmenting the woes of American and other consumers at a time of financial crisis—if vessels are forced to divert onto the much longer and costlier route around the Cape of Good Hope.

"No American vessel or vessels under the flag of Washington's puppets will be safe until prisoners persecuted for their faith are released from Guantanamo Bay and other concentration camps," Mr. Barre said in a telephone interview from his coastal headquarters in the pirate den of Bossaso.

Mr. Barre has claimed to be the mastermind behind several high-profile seizures of oil tankers and other vessels, whose owners have paid ransom worth millions of dollars. But, apparently fearing retribution from the U.S. Navy's powerful fleet in the Indian Ocean, he has avoided previous attacks on American shipping and has insisted that his motives are purely financial.

Recent news reports say he has used some of his illicit earnings to buy sophisticated weapons, including ship-to-ship and antiaircraft missiles as well as high-powered night-vision and satellite-tracking technology and long-range fast attack vessels.

"Our war against the infidel can now move to a higher plane," he said in the interview.

endit

"What shift is the Dullard working?" Shelby asked as he punched Ctrl-S to save his story in Homepatch.

I saw no byline or dateline on the piece. Neither was there any evidence of note-taking or recording equipment to indicate that a telephone interview had taken place at all.

"Early, I guess."

"Good," said Shelby, sitting back in his chair with a satisfied half-smile on his face.

"By the way, a limp dick," he said as I turned back toward to my own workspace.

"What?"

"A limp dick."

"What are you talking about?"

He rolled his eyes with theatrical exaggeration.

"The second part of the famous hack adage. The two things a hack should never bring home from his travels: a limp dick and bag full of dirty washing. Sound advice, I believe. Especially the former. The lady might forgive the occasional sweaty T-shirt, but you can never explain the flaccidity. Or so I'm told."

* * *

After his piratical fantasies in Homepatch, Shelby had written an undeniably poignant story about 237 would-be migrants from Africa whose leaky vessel had overturned in the Mediterranean Sea somewhere between Libya and the Italian island of Lampedusa—the gateway to a fantasy Europe where jobs grew on trees, insults were unknown, and social safety nets scooped up the stragglers in webs of unquestioning benevolence. There was something about Shelby's language that stirred memories of an earlier time.

> Their own lands were broken, and so they resolved to embark on a journey to salvation. But they had not reckoned with the desert winds that howled offshore and churned an unfamiliar sea into a maelstrom . . .

My first reaction was to edit without mercy—"The dead were largely economic migrants aboard a leaky ship . . ."—but the style of his writing reminded me of the way Shelby had gone about his trade for most of his working life.

I remembered one of his stories from someplace in Burkina Faso where the Sahara had begun to encroach on the green lands to the desert's south.

The small plane he chartered from Ouagadougou to reach his far-flung interviewees had been engulfed in a sandstorm that blotted out the sky, the land, the airstrip. He had asked himself whether he had perhaps terminally miscalculated the equation that balanced exclusive news against the risk of reporting it. But what he saw convinced him that the journey was worthwhile.

> They came across the emptiness that hooves had turned to dust, the women of a distant tribe, without men but with children, astride donkeys, 30 or 40 of them.
>
> From afar they might have seemed to be warriors, adrift from medieval times, robed in darkness and menace. But, no, they told an outsider, they had not come with hostile intent to this village in the north of a poor country. Neither did they wish to beg or intrude. That day, they said, they had covered 30 miles in their flowing black robes and had now arrived, seeking water lilies from a swamp to take as food . . .

Reading it later, a diplomat, steeped in the cynicism of the trade, asked him why he felt the urge to be the "avenging sword" when his job was to report the news. And Shelby had replied that, as far as he was concerned, the news alone could never provide the whole story without a peppering of outrage and passion, without a powerful, irresistible urge to tilt against injustice and oppression and the unfairness of a planet that rewarded greed and trampled on suffering.

In his time, Shelby himself had been jailed in far-flung places, expelled by unsavory regimes, praised in the citations for human rights prizes that he preferred not to accept, not so much out of modesty as embarrassment.

But in the persona he adopted for general public consumption, there was no room for compassion. He insisted, for instance, that he had dashed off the Burkina Faso article perched on a gilt chair at an antique desk in the Crillon in Paris on his way back from his Saharan assignment before handing in his sheaf of typescript at the Reuters bureau to be sent to New York—and then repairing to La Coupole for dinner.

Yet his record showed that he had never balked when the truly oppressed and irredeemably downtrodden chose him as the chronicler of their desperation, the balladeer of their woes.

For all that, I edited his piece about the sunken migrant vessel without mercy and figured he was in a rage about my slash-and-burn revisions when he walked into my office and slammed the door behind him.

"Seen the site?"

I clicked onto the screen that always displayed the *Graphic* website. I got a shock.

High on the home page—the main display—was a familiar byline above an eerily familiar story.

Pirates Threaten Jihad

By Gibson Dullar

Pirates based in a remote corner of Somalia's breakaway region of Puntland vowed Monday to launch a campaign against America-bound crude oil and cargo shipping as what they termed their contribution to global jihad . . .

"Scroll down," Shelby barked.

I checked out the bottom of the story. A tiny line in blue italics read: "Joe Shelby contributed reporting from Paris."

"Jesus H. Christ."

"I mean, he's gone too far, for Chrissakes."

I was about to offer agreement in equally blasphemous terms when the news wires began to put out breathless one-line bulletins on another screen that I kept open to view urgent, breaking news.

"URGENT—American cargo vessel captured off Somalia."

"NEWS ALERT—Maersk line vessel with 18 American crew seized by pirates"

"BULLETIN—Maersk Alabama nabbed with skipper and crew."

"Oh boy," I said.

My office door opened again, and Marcel Duffie strode in.

"If you guys spent less time gossiping and more time reporting, you'd score the kind of scoop that Gibson Dullar just did with the pirate interview, don't you think?" he said. "I mean, he actually forecast this. And what were you doing?"

"As a matter of fact . . ." Shelby began, but Duffie had already bustled on to spread the word of our abject failure.

CHAPTER SIXTEEN

As Shelby's personal disappearances grew into a habit, his Jaguar seemed to be absent, too, from the *Star*'s underground parking lot. Suddenly, on the occasions when we did manage to meet for coffee and aperitifs, he was full of stories about the Métro told with the peculiar ardor of an explorer who does not realize that his new frontiers are in fact quite familiar to most of the people around him. One time, he recounted how he fled one car because a woman wore a bulky overcoat on a hot day and it reminded him of a suicide bomber. But when he reboarded at the next car, he found himself trapped between two accordion players busking in stereo.

I had not traveled on the Paris Métro in years. I remembered it without nostalgia or any great desire to return to those packed cars, those bug-eyed trumpeters playing Fellini music, the passengers' fixed gaze locked onto some indeterminate piece of the coachwork as a crazed zealot demanded that they repent their sins. I enjoyed Springsteen on the car radio and, at home, the operatic selections chosen by Marie-Claire as part of her mission to educate me in the finer things of life. But the buskers on the Métro—the guitarists, the accordionists, the songsters, and the off-key flutists—left me cold. Once I had caught myself thinking that if there were a sudden, loud single shot and then silence, the shooter would have done humanity a service.

"What's better: blown up or deafened?" Shelby wanted to know after his near miss with imagined jihad.

"Did the train explode?"

"Nope."

"So your point was?"

"My point was just this: you see all these people with their tiny white plugs in their ears and you think they are listening to their own music. But that's not the point—what they're really doing is drowning out the appalling musicians."

Another time he asked me—in the hope of raising a smile—if people who flirted on the subway qualified as Métro-sexuals, or would they have to achieve some kind of advanced physical contact to reach that status?

"'The apparition of these faces in the crowd,'" I murmured. "'Petals on a wet, black bough.'"

He looked at me blankly for a long second.

"Pound!" He finally exclaimed. "The goddamned haiku about getting off the Métro. At Concorde! Ezra Pound! Shelby, you old dog, hiding your light under a bushel."

"Not quite a haiku," I said. "Just haiku-like."

There was no point in explaining to him that we didn't all validate ourselves through flashy cars and serial bylines. We didn't all need to wear our Eng. Lit. 101 on our linen sleeves. We didn't all need to boast of our familiarity with the 1 to La Défense or the 6 to Trocadéro and the 10 to trendy Mabillon.

Every Métro station had its story, its destination, its history, and its chronicler—from Clichy and Henry Miller's quiet days there, to Bastille and the rolling heads of the revolution, to Pigalle and the ghost of Toulouse-Lautrec. The tunnels chronicled grand battles—Solférino and Austerlitz (no mention of Waterloo, a station name beloved of the victorious British, or the Somme or Dien Bien Phu)—and honored the literary lions prowling the city's dark belly—Avenue Émile Zola and Anatole France, Victor Hugo and Alexandre Dumas (no Gérard de Nerval, thankfully).

Somehow I did not see Shelby as a Métro man. He always said that he took public transport only if it offered a setting for a story: a bus on the same route as a bus bomb in Tel Aviv, a London tube ride on the same explosive principal. More usually, he said, he had taken cabs in far-flung places where public transport was a minibus that might wait hours or days until sufficient passengers filled its cracked and splintered seats to persuade the

driver to embark on his designated mad dash to the next halt in
Kenya or Kazakhstan. Third World cab rides were not like brief,
First World rides from the East Village to Central Park or from
the Groucho Club to Hampstead. Once launched on the subject,
Shelby liked to explain that Third World cab rides were bone-
breakers, ball-busters, in worn-out, clapped-out Peugeots and
Renaults, from vintages forgotten in the rest of the world, held
together with gum and prayer, hope and copper wire. Their fuel
lines clogged like old arteries. Rust perforated floors. Watered-
down gas froze en route to the carburetors. Suspension clanged.
Steering strayed. Gearshifts groaned. Throttles jammed—closed
or open—or hovered in some uncertain zone between motion and
immobility. You took rides that lasted hours. You negotiated the
price up front for the day. You prayed you'd still be alive at the
end of it. One time, Shelby said, they—he and Faria and a translator—had taken a cab across eastern Turkey, from Van to
Hakkâri, from Hakkâri to Çukurca, from Çukurca to Cizre, from
Cizre to Diyarbakir. The road was so bad that it almost disappeared, and they tumbled out to push the cab up the sides of
ravines. The driver got so tired he fell asleep and Shelby took
over. The track led through the no-man's-land along the border
between Turkey and Iraq, between Ottoman and Arab, a line
sketched presumably by some diplomat in some remote conference hall in Lausanne or Geneva, and they bumped into a bunch
of members of the Iraqi Republican Guard, notorious for "shoot
first, ask questions later" peremptoriness and brutality. But at
this time, in unfamiliar retreat, with the destiny of their dictatorial leader in doubt and the source of future protection unknown,
all they wanted were Marlboros. At the roadblocks, Joe and
Faria got so used to their translator saying where they were going
that they could recite it themselves: "*Gazeteciyiz. Çukurca'dan
geliyoruz. Cizre'ye gideceğiz.*" We are journalists, going from
Çukurca to Cizre.

   "I know I'm going to die in a Third World taxi," Faria had said
laughingly as the Murat, an old locally made version of a Fiat, stag-
gered into Cizre, its driver once more at the wheel, its tires bald and

its brake shoes shot. But, of course, that particular prophecy of hers—so often made—was not borne out by events.

The riddle of the disappearing Jaguar resolved itself one morning when I saw Shelby's assigned parking bay reoccupied, recolonized by an almost identical XKR, with the same Lebanese export license plates, but painted jet-black. On inspection, I could see it was indeed the original car with a remarkable professional paint job that obliterated its previous incarnation in silver. Picked out in gold lettering on the driver's side of the long, sleek front wing of the car was the new name: "Le Soleil Noir." The Black Sun. Straight out of Nerval: "*Ma seule Étoile est morte, – et mon luth constellé / Porte le Soleil noir de la Mélancolie.*" My only star is dead, and my spangled lute bears the black sun of melancholy.

Or some such.

It was part of the same poem, "El Desdichado," that Shelby had recited at the Duclos funeral.

Since then, Shelby had spoken very little about what he was doing outside the office, but I could see from the state of him—the weight loss, the red eyes, the appearance of someone with a chronic sinus problem—that he was burning up, or even burning out. If he had come to Paris looking for release from his ghosts, it looked to me as though the ghosts had won and he had been dragged into their netherworld.

Then I had something of an insight, an inspiration. It was the first time that I had realized that the name of the newspaper where we both worked—the *Star*—bore such immense significance for the Nervalistas. Stars bore mythic significance. They exerted deep, irresistible pulls on the soul. They drew you to your destiny. In the poem, the star was dead, replaced by a black sun. (In life, the *Star* was broke, not replaced at all.)

As I went over the words in my mind, translating back and forth, jumbling them up, another connection emerged: black sun, lone star, black star—Black Star! The name of Duclos's picture agency that sold her work around the world and kept track of her assignments.

Black Star, Black Sun. I was beginning to get psyched by the same riddles as Shelby. The car, maybe, had become his memorial to her, a rolling V8 sarcophagus of memory.

It did not augur well.

. I had to admit, though, that when he pitched up for our weekend party at the stud farm—"just a select few," Marie-Claire had promised—the Black Sun fit right in with the array of dark-windowed Citroëns and Mercedes, even a single Bentley Continental, belonging to some of the other guests.

Marie-Claire had chosen a summer weekend and could not have known beforehand that the *Graphic*'s top team would move up its visit to begin soon afterward—a rescheduling interpreted by the staff of the *Star* with much fearful speculation as to their purpose: Were they coming with axes to lop off the head count, or was their intention much more sinister? Would there be pep talks or eulogies, commitments or commiserations? In a way I was very grateful to Marie-Claire for offering a diversion from the febrile gossip and rumormongering so prevalent within the community of scribes, hacks, impostors, and poets who had provided my lifelong habitat.

She had closed down the stud's business for the event, freeing up the guest cottages she had built for the visiting owners of our more prized charges. She had hired live bands and legions of caterers whose trucks arrived laden with silver platters and ice sculptures of swans, which I found unsettling. Throughout the day, vehicles of varying dimensions pulled in, bearing the aluminum skeletons and billowing white fabric of a marquee big enough for a three-ring circus. Like roadies preparing a rock band gig, laborers unloaded and assembled wooden decks, erecting enormous industrial-strength air conditioners at strategic points within the tent, while, outside, our lawns offered accommodation to portable lavatory facilities and gigantic barbecues with rotating spits. As the setting took shape, the interior of the tent became an enormous, upscale restaurant with trestle tables for bars, circular tables for guests, flowers from Africa, napkins, knives, forks, spoons, coasters, flutes, beakers, saltshakers, pepper mills, cups, saucers. Forget the parties of youth with their paper cups and boxes of wine. The tableware was all bone china or crystal. Delivery trucks disgorged case upon case of liquors, beers, wines, and champagnes. Armies of waiters, chefs, and sundry attendants arrived under the command of their own generals and lieutenants, who fussed and barked orders and paid profound homage to my wife as the undisputed field marshal and pay-mistress of the whole shebang.

When I quizzed Marie-Claire about the outlays, she smiled and assured me that the party actually saved us money as a tax write-off. And additionally, she reminded me with the tones of a schoolmarm addressing a student caught napping at his desk, one of our fabled stabled animals, Sunset Strip, had just won the Prix du Jockey Club at Chantilly and the party was a way of rewarding the owner for keeping his steeds with us, recycling the side-bet profits through the official books, and encouraging *les autres* to entrust their fillies and stallions to us for safekeeping, training, and procreation.

Shelby arrived in style, the roof down in the XKR and a Vuitton suitcase (so scuffed it had to be genuine) lodged casually in the jump seat. He nudged the Black Sun cautiously over the speed bumps, between the whitewashed fences that kept the verdant gallops and paddocks safe from contamination by anything other than the best-shod hooves. The plane trees lining the driveway were hung with lanterns the color of emeralds and rubies, and I watched as Shelby drew briefly to a halt, consulted one of his volumes, and looked back at the lanterns as if to confirm something. Then, frowning, he drove on.

He wore a ruffled dress shirt and hand-knotted black bow tie with a tuxedo jacket at the ready. Marie-Claire had not mentioned a dress code, but Shelby seemed to have assumed that, if you were invited to an overnight party at a fancy stud farm outside Paris, you should dress the part, even if, for him, that seemed to include a leather helmet and goggles on the drive in. I would not have been surprised to find that he had brought a set of matched Purdey shotguns in the trunk for a spot of rough shooting.

Instead, he had brought the AK-47.

"What the hell is that thing for?" I said when I saw its barrel with the distinctive front sight poking from a black tote bag.

"You never know."

"Never know what?"

"You told me I should dump it."

"But not in my backyard."

"Ah, *le fameux Joseph*," Marie-Claire exclaimed.

As on the evening in Saint-Germain when I introduced them, he took her hand in that formal way beloved of European nobility, raising it to his lips without making contact. For a moment, I thought she might offer a mocking curtsy.

I looked at the two of them—my best buddy in his tailored (but by no means new) tux and my wife in her couture (and definitely new) dark satin gown from her favorite designer in the Rue du Faubourg Saint-Honoré. She had modeled it for me earlier, showing me, tantalizingly, how its various layers hid the most outrageous lingerie. ("For your eyes only," she said.) The dress was cut with an artful, and relatively modest, décolleté neckline. It hugged her waist and swelled modestly over her sculpted, equestrian hips. A double string of pearls that had almost broken the piggy-bank glowed on the smooth expanse between neck and breast. The deep jungly tones of her dress accentuated the green of her eyes.

If she was out to make an impression, she had succeeded.

Personally, I thought she looked spectacular however she dressed—in her riding boots and Barbour coats, her white toweling gown over the first coffee, or her jeans-and-baggy-T-shirt "welcome home" mode. But that evening, she looked utterly magnificent. I could not believe she had chosen me as her spouse. Neither, I suspect, could Shelby. In the spirit of things, I had decided on my most recent dark suit, a pressed white shirt from Sulka, and a birthday gift Ferragamo tie with a horsey motif. In the bedroom mirror, I thought I looked pretty nifty. But seeing Shelby and Marie-Claire, I had the feeling that, if an outsider had to guess the most likely couple among the three of us, the choice would fall on the two of them—with their looks and manners that made my understated James Cagney mien seem distinctly second feature.

I thought back to the Alfa Romeo brochure I had found in the apartment in the Sixteenth. She had not mentioned it to me. There was no sign, indeed, of an Alfa Romeo in our garage. So was she leading some kind of double life—a sports car, open-top, two-seater clandestine existence?

But then, I told myself, the marriage certificate binding Marie-Claire to earth named me, not Shelby, as the spouse. And that counted for everything.

The marquee was lined in a navy blue fabric picked out with golden stars—those damned stars again—and the menu was full of Middle Eastern delicacies: spit-roast lamb with radishes for eyes, kebabs, roast pigeon, tabbouleh, hummus, falafel, Turkish burek and baklava, baba ghanoush from Egypt. Some of the serving staff wore purple sashes over white shirts, dark vests, and pantaloons with a faintly Ottoman look to them. Who needed Nerval's *Voyage en Orient* when its culinary equivalent was set out on your own lawns? But, then, who would want to, considering its fables of fire and betrayal and assassination?

The guest list included quite a lot of the intermingled equestrian-political set, people I knew only faintly—some from passing acquaintance, others from the society pages. But others were well known to me—The Duke, Marie-Claire's aristocrat from our first meeting, and a sprinkling of journos from the big papers and networks, bureau chiefs clinging forlornly to the life rafts of their expense accounts.

We all called ourselves buddies, old-school. But I detected a hint of bitter reproach directed toward me and Shelby: we, after all, were working our shifts on the footplate of the digital express, holding on to our hats as it hurtled onward at unconscionable speeds; we were the chain saws in the primordial forest, stripping away the camouflage of the pterodactyls and brontosauruses. We sucked the news out of the day like a thirsty kid draining an orange slice, leaving only the peel in the gutter for "old media" to chew on. But in the process— and this worried all of us—our judgments had to be quick, sometimes too quick. We made calls on stories simply because something somewhere went bang; we stretched thin the sanctity of citing multiple sources for every nugget of information, resorting to bits of unconfirmed chitchat attributed to "people said" or "a local official said on the condition of anonymity" or, worst of all, "analysts said"—we had started to quote ourselves. We were not only building the new tribune of the Internet era; we were hollowing out the ground beneath it.

The other thing that colored my relationship with the old crew was the thinly disguised envy among some of them of my marital status. In the pre-Marie-Claire era we had all been on pretty much the same level. If anything, I was the poor relative, ponying up for rounds I could ill afford on a *Star* salary. But now my drinking buddies figured that I had landed with my feet under the table, bum in the butter, laughing all the way to the bank. Why did I even bother to work, they asked, when I could retire to the stud farm and sip mimosas for breakfast for the rest of my life? And presumably invite them for a free noggin, too.

But I couldn't.

My place at the *Star*, my slot on the masthead, had become more important than ever when I met Marie-Claire. The *Star* was my badge of office, my shield, my sole claim to equality. If I lost that, what would I be? The kept man? The houseboy? The poodle? So, sure, it was cool being a rich woman's husband—but not some kind of lackey. If I lost my job to some buyout deal, some cost-cutting sidewinder of a head count maneuver, I would not be able to look myself in the eye.

More important, I would not be able to look her in the eye, either.

So, yes, I was married to a rich woman. And, yes, under French law, I would not starve whatever happened: even if she left, the alimony would keep me immune from hardship. But, no, that did not mean I could ever abandon my one claim to a kind of success in a world outside her orbit, to independence of action and means.

Marrying rich tied me forever to the Sisyphean rock on the slippery slope of Nonstop News.

"Who'd like a drink?"

Shelby strolled into the main marquee with a band of kindred spirits. He was on his relatively best behavior. I had been watching him as he worked the crowd, stopping to nod to some cabinet minister ("knew him in Chad when he was just a spook") or some ambassador ("remember him as first secretary in KL—loved the bar girls!"). Surprisingly, he had that party lizard's way of interposing himself into other people's conversations, then extricating himself—having jogged some memory, renewed some bond, recalled some unpaid debt—to move on, like a sleek bee in a garden of honeysuckle. Reassuringly, he did not seem to be drinking heavily. Occasionally, I would lose sight of him, as if he had slipped below the radar in some social Bermuda Triangle, but then he reappeared, smiling, energetic, almost—it occurred to me—acting as if he were the host of this magnificent party.

But there was one episode that gave him pause.

Elvire Récamier arrived in her own car—one of those retro Fiat 500s—bouncing over the speed bumps with crashing disdain. As she pulled up, the passenger door of her car flew open and out stepped Gibson Dullar in slender blue jeans and a supple brown leather jacket, sweeping back long locks and looking around like a leopard set down in unfamiliar bushlands, eyeing the cover, sniffing the breeze.

"Look who I found lurking along the boulevards," Elvire said in a voice that could not disguise its mischief. "Is this okay, Ed," she said—it sounded like "*Ez zeez hokay?*" I had no quick answer. Across the parking area, in a knot of dignitaries, I spotted Shelby. An expression I could not fathom crossed his face like a cloud across the sun. Then just as quickly dissipated.

"I don't believe we've met?" Marie-Claire said.

"Dullar. Gibson Dullar. Friend of Ed's. And Joe's," he said. "Elvire insisted. Gate-crasher, I'm afraid."

I thought the description evoked more of a state of being than an explanation for his specific presence among us. But I said nothing.

"Of course. You are most welcome. Ed has told me all about you."

"Not all, I hope, Ed?" His winning smile rivaled Shelby's.

"How very mysterious," Marie-Claire said. Her voice seemed to have shifted into a slightly lower register. During one of the Iraq wars, Dullar had acquired something of a reputation for refusing to take to the bunkers when Saddam Hussein's missiles rained on Tel Aviv. But that was not the only reason they called him the Scud-muffin.

"Jesus. Gib Dullar!"

"Hey, Joe. Old buddy."

"What brings you to town?"

"I guess I'm on this junket with the masthead? Visiting the *Star*? Boosting morale. Inspecting the troops. So I figured I'd get in early to stake out gay Paree."

The handshake reminded me of the touch of gloves before the opening bell of a prizefight. Marie-Claire glanced between the two of them speculatively, as if the hostile, one-bull-in-the-kraal spark that crackled between them ignited something that had been dormant, buried in our tranquility.

One aging Lothario was enough for the party. Two was downright dangerous.

Elvire's operatic lady had begun to trill. And we all had prime seats in the orchestra stalls, if not parts in the chorus.

"Maybe I should take your car keys, Joe," I said, thinking of the assault rifle in the trunk.

"No worries, old sport," he said. "Best behavior. Promise."

Elvire Récamier spent part of the evening in a frenzy of understated networking, nailing down editors and publishers for promises of work and contracts, extracting pledges of access and photo shoots from wealthy racehorse owners and government ministers who held the keys to other doors. She fussed around Gibson Dullar until, like some latter-day pirate, he seemed to have brought himself up to boarding speed alongside a renowned chanteuse whose bedding would represent a significant trophy, made all the more thrilling by the reputedly ferocious jealousy of an absent, Mafia-linked husband. I watched him operate—the smile, the chat, the practiced flick and gentle light of a Cartier gold lighter engraved with some kind of conversation piece inscription. ("To Gib: Who Dares Wins.")

I had been half expecting Marie-Claire to offer a repeat of that first-sighting dance with The Duke, so I contrived to take it in my stride when the familiar strains of an old Stones number, played by an enthusiastic and halfway competent band, drew them together onto the dance floor. But what surprised me was the spectacle of Elvire Récamier and Gibson Dullar joining them in a kind of writhing foursome. Other partygoers formed a circle around them, half bemused, half encouraging, like at some kind of '60s-type happening. Someone clapped his hands in time to the music. Others joined in the dancing. Then the medley shifted into a different register—the quarter tones of the Middle East flowed across the dance area, as if transplanted from a Lebanese wedding or a Turkish belly dance or the radio in any of Shelby's cabs on the night run from Aleppo to Amman. The sound seemed to lift the dancers higher, to ever more improbable displays of serpentine agility. The four of them shimmied and glittered, spinning and whirling in pagan abandon. The Duke proved to still be surprisingly lithe. Marie-Claire shivered and wriggled so that the disco globe overhead drew deep, sensuous tones from the pearls around her neck. When the couples switched partners so that Dullar was making snake-hipped gyrations with Marie-Claire, I caught sight of Shelby watching me across the crowd, narrowing his eyes as if in solidarity, as if to say, This will not stand.

Then he moved into the circle himself, seizing the chanteuse wooed earlier by Dullar, breaking the spell of the magic four, throwing down a challenge. He danced relatively well—like an arthritic Jagger unrestrained by any suspicion that he might not look to others as he imagined himself to look. Another couple joined in. Then another. Dullar was swept away by his potential conquest. Shelby danced briefly with Marie-Claire and said something that made her look shocked, then smile. Then he gestured to me and I danced with my wife—"how it should be," Shelby said.

There were toasts and mini speeches—nothing too serious to distract from excellent food and drink, served by waiters and waitresses at tables arranged around centerpieces of chrysanthemums and dahlias in tricolor shades of red, white, and blue that honored our host country as much as my own. A small handwritten card at every setting of cutlery and crystal marked every guest's allocated position in Marie-Claire's placement, ensuring that no one felt snubbed or bored or dissed. At her table she positioned herself between a cabinet minister and the well-heeled owner of the champion Sunset Strip, leaning over to exchange light, humorous chitchat with her aristocrat buddy, an old-fashioned crooner, and a movie star who had made a second career out of saving the descendants of the same exotic animals whose pelts had once adorned her now-reconstructed frame. I was interposed between a ministerial spouse encrusted in equal parts of jewelry and malice and an ambassadorial trophy wife, a gold digger who had a knack for pricing everyone she met and allotting them a place in her firmament of future consorts. Without hesitation, and to my relief, she assigned me to an outer galaxy.

At his table, Shelby was telling his old hack tales to a receptive audience, among whom I recognized the stud's personal banker and a top editor of *Le Monde* who had once had a reputation as something of a Don Juan among the Middle East press pack—the Camel Corps, as they liked to call themselves. A waft of conversation carried the words "Argentine soy vote," and I thought Shelby was being much too loose-lipped while so close to Gibson Dullar.

Where had I come from? I found myself asking. What was I doing here, for fuck's sake—a kid from Queens with a career that started on the sports desk and police beat and for a time looked like it wouldn't go anyplace else, a chance vacation job way down the copydesk of the old *Star*, a few maneuvers as the generations changed, a liking for horses. If you had asked me a few years back where it all would have ended, I'd have said the die was cast for good: I had my job and my few trusty steeds, and that was it. Then Marie-Claire Risen had hijacked my life and I had ended up like Cinderella at the ball, never knowing when midnight would toll. I looked across and caught her eye. She smiled and offered an almost imperceptible, gamine flutter of an eye that sealed our tryst and said, Midnight is a long way off, buddy boy; enjoy the golden carriage; we are in this together. For the long haul.

As the set piece speeches came and went, I noticed Shelby rattling a silver spoon against a crystal wineglass until the imperious tinkle silenced the other guests.

The idea that he might offer this assembly a repeat of his Nervalian outburst at the Duclos funeral was nerve-racking.

Elvire Récamier looked across at me from a table of bankers and diplomats all hanging on her anecdotes of understated but immense valor in Lebanon and Cambodia.

Now she rolled her eyes toward me in self-mocking Gallic trepidation.

But Shelby surprised us both.

"Most of you here know and work with Marie-Claire, which makes you the envy of Paris. I work with this man here, Ed Clancy. That does not make Ed the envy of Paris, I can assure you. Or me either, in fact." Even I laughed at that one. "But looking at them here tonight, among friends and well-wishers, it occurred to me that maybe we should raise a toast to the pair of them to wish them long life and happiness together. To Marie-Claire and Ed." As he raised his glass, he was looking directly at Gibson Dullar.

And in front of all of them, Marie-Claire stood up, maneuvered her way between the guests to my table, and pressed her lips firmly against mine.

CHAPTER SEVENTEEN

ELVIRE RÉCAMIER WAS IN A RUMINATIVE, POST-PARTY, SMALL-hours mood. She had kicked off her scarlet Jimmy Choo shoes and was smoking a home-rolled cigarette that smelled as if its tobacco content was minimal. The dancing was done. The band was packing away its instruments. The waiters had circulated with flutes of Bollinger. The guests had been served many courses of hors d'oeuvres and entrées from the Orient and closer to home, lubricated with the appropriate produce of noble vineyards.

At the prearranged hour, with the midsummer sky dark and building with moist heat, they had made a line to offer their adieux and their thanks. The words "super" and "impeccable" seemed to float on updrafts of flattery. Now, as the chauffeurs nudged the Mercedes and the big Citroëns down the driveway, you could see the roadies who had put the whole set together begin to dismantle tables and chairs, stacking vertiginous piles of soiled china and half-empty crystal glasses into their vans to be taken off to some distant scullery for restoration to a pristine sparkle. Bulging, black, heavy-duty garbage bags were spirited away at the wave of a caterer's wand. All that would remain to be cleared in the light of day was the marquee—too big and cumbersome to be moved so late at night—and the barbecue pits, whose coals still glowed, fanned by an uneasy night wind that had begun to discomfit the plane trees. Elvire and I sat companionably on a sofa the caterers had somehow managed to forget, alone in a dark and conspiratorial corner of the big tent as its walls and roof rustled like the sails of a great vessel seeking wind and forward motion.

"So what I am really saying, Ed Clancy, is beware of Gibson Dullar. If you are smart, you will not get in between him and Shelby.

In Africa they say that when the elephants fight, the grass is trampled. No one will do you any favors."

"You're the one with the grass, Elvire," I said, somewhat testily.

"I am serious, Clancy. I know many things about them both." She paused, allowing any number of inferences to creep into her silence. "But there is something new, something I don't understand."

"New since when?"

"Maybe since Shelby was in Beirut. You know, when he was leaving, the *Graphic* sent in Dullar to cover some stories."

Shelby had never told me that. In all the times we had worked together on Nonstop News–Paris Outpost, he had been generous with all his stories—except, I realized, for anything related to his departure from Beirut and the long, unexplained gap in his personal chronology until he pitched up in the newsroom of the *Paris Star.*

"So they worked together?"

She shrugged to suggest depths of insider knowledge to which I would never be privy.

"By the way, where is Marie-Claire?" she said, out of the blue. "Come to think of it, where is Joe Shelby?"

She stretched out on the sofa and, quite abruptly, closed her eyes and dozed off, exhausted by so much networking and reminiscing and champagne and other substances. Her shoes lay on the wooden deck like discarded playthings in a child's nursery.

Outside the wind had gotten up a little more boisterously, and there was that hot smell in the air, almost sulfurous, that comes before a lightning storm. I wove a slightly inebriated way along the pathways in between our guest cottages, guided by ground-level electric lights designed to act as navigational beacons. I remember thinking that, while Marie-Claire seemed to have been everywhere at once during the party, never allowing a single guest to feel slighted or neglected, I had not seen her for a while. And, as Elvire Récamier evidently had wanted me to, I realized that I had not seen Joe Shelby for a while either.

"Cuckold" is a terrible word, a double-edged sword, a fine example of the moral relativism of the male: cuckolding a man is an act of chest-beating primeval assertion, perpetuating the gene; being cuckolded negates your life, denies your dreams, whatever Reynolds Packard might have said. Marie-Claire had given me no reason for real suspicion that she had betrayed me, but imagined betrayal is the child of uncertainty and I had never been one to assume good fortune. If you balanced things out, weighed up the pros and cons, why would someone of Marie-Claire's caliber undo the life she had created for the sake of a chimera like Shelby? And why should a guy like Shelby, a friend through life's manifold vicissitudes, resolve to do the dirty on his old buddy? The answer came in two words: human nature. At that point in my rumination, I rounded a corner between two of our cottages and came upon one of those sights that haunt you as much as they throw all your calculations out of kilter, leaving you unable to match what you are thinking to what you are seeing.

Each guest cottage had a divided, stable-type door with the upper half made of four glass panes. There was a low light in just one of them and, positioned at the window of the door so that he could not be seen from within, Gibson Dullar was peering inside, utterly still, concentrating on whatever was unfolding before his Judas eyes like some kind of bush tracker in the presence of a rare and exquisite animal. I came to a halt, with much more stealth and silence than I would have thought myself capable of, working out how I could take up a position to see what he was seeing. I had not seen Joe Shelby or my wife for some time, I realized, and I had no way of knowing how long Gibson Dullar had been absent while Elvire Récamier told her tales and wove her spells.

If anyone had shot a video of the moment, I guess there would have been a pantomime appearance to it, like the sketches in those British children's comedies when the good guy on the stage turns to the youngsters with their parents in the audience and asks them whether they have seen the bad guy: Dullar standing stock-still; me creeping up on exaggerated tiptoes—*Where's the ogre, children? Behind you!*

Surreptitiously, Dullar moved his hands and at first I thought he was fiddling with his fly like some monstrous voyeur. Then I realized he was changing the dials and settings on a slim digital camera, probably to switch off the flash and the illuminated viewing screen that would betray his presence to the people inside. He did not hear me approach.

Clearly visible through the windows of the stable door, Joe Shelby and my wife were at either end of a chaise longue upholstered in deep crimson, unaware of their audience. Shelby had taken off his tuxedo jacket and loosened his bow tie so that it hung like untied bootlaces. He was reading aloud from one of his leather volumes. Marie-Claire was bowed over a glass-topped coffee table chopping white powder into generous lines, a rolled-up bank note at her side. On the floor beside her was her evening purse, lying open, the kind they design to look good and carry little more than minimal cosmetic or narcotic reinforcement. Or had Shelby been the supplier? In my house? Was he the one who had brought it into my home? To deliver to my wife?

"I'll take the camera, Dullar. Or I can call Shelby. Your choice."

He spun around, looking at me with unalloyed scorn.

"Poor sap," he hissed. "Your wife's playing the field and your buddy is working up to the old rumpy-pumpy, and you defend them."

"The camera. Now."

He drew back into the shadows. Neither of us spoke beyond venomous whispers.

"Can't you see what's happening? Don't you want evidence?"

"Nothing's happening that's going any further than the two of us, Dullar. Nothing's happening, period."

He was a good few inches taller than I was, obviously in shape, buffed. But workout muscles don't mean all that much in a street fight. What counts is fast movement—the first strike and the readiness to make it.

Marie-Claire had folded a tab of paper, a wrapper, around the dwindling remains of her stash and slipped it into one of those nickel wallets people use for their visiting cards. She wiped clean the surface of the table around the lines she had drawn, as if to remove all trace of the drug, or maybe just to give herself a little extra by licking her fingers. I wondered what Shelby made of that and the thought made me very angry. Red-mist angry.

"The camera, Dullar. Now."

He drew himself up in the shadows. I advanced, my fists curled, my body bunched to reduce the target area. I felt light on my feet now that I had committed myself.

Most people don't suspect me of violence—passive-aggressive rage, maybe—but when I am truly incensed, I have been told, there is an air of menace that suggests I will feel no pain as I inflict it.

Over Dullar's shoulder, I saw Shelby lower the Nerval onto the chaise longue between him and Marie-Claire. Like what? A marker? An invitation? She was straightening the white lines with a credit card—there is a kind of narco-fastidiousness to the coke ritual. When she had gotten the lines straight, she ran the credit card across her lips, then replaced it in her purse. Shelby reached down to his tuxedo jacket and withdrew a slender silver tube. He said something I could not hear. She laughed and waved the curled-up bank note.

"Give me the camera, Dullar. Or I swear I'll beat you to a pulp."

For the first time, he looked uncertain. I caught a flicker in his eye, the narcissist's fear of disfigurement, the coward's fear of pain. Dullar had written plenty from the war zones, but I wondered how often he had fought for his life, how often he had ducked out of that final step into the Death Zone that Shelby and Duclos had owned as their prime habitat.

I knew then—and so did he—that if it came to fisticuffs, I would prevail. And there would be noise—the sound of knuckle on nasal gristle, for instance—that would bring Shelby and my wife out of their Nervalesque cocoon, their chemical tryst.

Shelby had crossed from the chaise longue to a music player. He made to turn down the lights, but Marie-Claire gestured for him not to. She looked at her watch as if impatient.

I advanced closer to Dullar and grasped him by his fancy jacket. My face was very close to his—so close that, beneath his all-year tan, I could see a fine latticework of facial surgery. No wonder he didn't want his features rearranged. Again. I had the collar of his leather jacket scrunched in my fist and pulled him toward me so that he was close enough to head-butt—the favored tactic of the smaller guy to bring the big guys down a peg or two. The thought exhilarated me, as if one blow would expunge years of slights and put-downs from arrogant shits like Dullar, wipe out the images of my wife and Shelby, level the score. I felt my neck muscles steeling, like a cobra preparing to strike. He sagged like a rag doll, but I held him up by his jacket to keep his pretty face in range. You could see the panic in his eyes. Fear. The sudden knowledge that I would do exactly what I was threatening to do, like a poker player urging you on to raise so that he can clean you out. He made as if to strike.

"Try it, Dullar. Just try it."

His first uncurled. His arm fell back.

"Take the fucking thing. When this gets out—and I'll make sure it does—no one's going to take the word of a coke-snorting two-timer against mine."

I was sorry he folded so quickly. I had truly wanted to do harm. To him. To anybody.

I reached for the camera. He dropped it to the ground, grinding it onto the stonework of the path with his heel so that it splintered and cracked into shrapnel shards. He pushed past me and I braced my shoulder for the impact. But he slid by like a wraith, melting into the darkness along the path. There was something in the way the shadows enfolded him that recalled my visit with Faria Duclos and the mystery man who mistakenly thought that many roses, bought from a store in Paris, could ever eclipse a single stem in 'Nam.

I bent to retrieve the pieces of Dullar's camera, stuffing them into a pocket. I leaned back against a wall and the whiskey wooziness came back, reinforced by a vomit-flavored cocktail of adrenaline and rage.

How the fuck could they do this? Cocaine behind my back, and then what else on the menu? And the humiliation: Every time Gibson Dullar looked at me henceforth his eyes would say, I saw them, Clancy, Joe Shelby and Marie-Claire playing footsie; I saw them whether it's on camera or not, and I can tell who I like, when I like.

I shoved open the door.

"Okay, kids. Party's over. Home time. Goody bags. *Finito*."

Joe looked up at me. If he was surprised at my intrusion, he did not show it.

"Hey, Ed. A line? Feel like a line?"

Marie-Claire had vacuumed one strip of white powder and was holding out the rolled bank note to me.

"Sure, Ed. Here. Join the party," she said. But she knew me better than to think I would accept.

"Party, some goddamn party."

I was roaring and slurring all at once. It's true what they say about the color of anger, except with me it seemed more of a rainbow burst across the spectrum. I had left the door open, and outside I could feel the wind rising, hotter. A distant artillery clap of thunder shuddered across the sky.

"There was one thing, Marie-Claire. Just one. And look at this shit. And as for you, Shelby, this is my wife. This is my life. This is what I have and want to keep, and you want to drag it all into your fucking drug-crazed netherworld."

The speech surprised even me.

"Edward, there was nothing. Only this." She gestured to the chemical trace.

"Only this? Only? Snorting coke with this prick? After everything . . ." My oratory had forsaken me.

"Ed, Ed. Please," Shelby pitched in. "It's not what you think. It's not how you think. Honestly. I would never . . ."

"Do you know who saw you? Do you?"

There was never time for them answer to that.

The mist around my eyes was painting the sitting room of the guest cottage a kind of orange and pink that flickered and cast exaggerated shadows. On the paving outside the cottage, I heard the first spatter of rain spitting and hissing like oil in an overheated skillet. Nearby, in the closest stables to the cottages, a fretful whinnying superimposed itself onto the sounds of the storm.

Alarms began to clang. A siren howled. Someone shouted: "Fire!"

Shelby levered himself upright with his cane, spilling the last vestiges of the cocaine. Marie-Claire rose with him. I spun around. Beyond the cottages, flames were running up the guy-lines of the marquee and its side walls had caught light.

The whinnying was building into a crescendo of fear.

"Sunset Strip!"

Marie-Claire tore off her high heels and began to run, clutching her shoes in one hand and her purse in the other, her stockinged feet flying over the gravel.

The way the marquee had been erected, it stood well clear of the stables where the champion horses were pampered and quartered. But the tent had caught fire in the stormy wind that sent a choking wall of sparks and dark smoke reeking of burned chemicals toward the horses, spreading panic among them.

We had given most of the staff the night off. Only a handful of stable lads came stumbling from their dormitory block. The storm was building, with the rain howling in gusts through the trees of the estate. The festive lamps in the trees of the driveway swung crazily, caught in the tortured branches. From the marquee, the sparks had begun to swirl upward, as if caught in a *Wizard of Oz* twister, flying toward the stables where all I could immediately think of was the dry hay in the stalls that housed not just Sunset Strip but also many other winners and one or two also-rans, as well. Marie-Claire propelled herself through the rain, wind, smoke, and cinders. How could the fire have started? An ember, maybe, from the dwindling barbecues, fanned into life by the quickening wind on the skirts of the storm. Did that matter? If the fire spread to the stables, the horses would not stand a chance. Suffering aside, everything Marie-Claire had worked for would go up, quite literally, in smoke. But it would be the lurid, gruesome death of Sunset Strip that would seize the headlines: the top French racehorse grilled in an accident redolent of negligence. Marie-Claire was not just a businesswoman; the loss of her charges would destroy her, body and soul.

In the distance, above the storm, I heard the first sirens of the *sapeurs-pompiers* and wondered in this slow-motion moment of random impressions and random events beyond all control whether the gates had been closed and padlocked after the last guests, whether the fire service could get through.

Then we found our savior. Gibson Dullar was leading the skittish, prancing Sunset Strip from the stables out into the fresher air as

Marie-Claire sprinted toward them through the gathering downpour and the stable staff began evacuating the loose-boxes.

"This what you're looking for?" he said with casual gallantry, smirking toward Shelby and me.

But there was no time for smart-aleck ripostes. The rain made no apparent impact on the blaze of the marquee. Flames had spread from the walls to the roof, probing into every dark, secret corner where the bars and dance floor and musicians' stages had been.

Where I had left Elvire Récamier, sleeping the death sleep of marijuana.

I turned quickly. There was no hint now of the whiskey stumbles. Vaguely I heard Shelby's voice calling to me. But no one else knew what I knew about the somnolent Elvire. The entrance to the marquee was an archway of flame, but there was no other way into the choking smoke-filled cavern that had been our party venue.

I shouted to Shelby.

"Elvire—she's in there."

He made to move toward me, then came to a halt. Stock-still. Frozen.

"Elvire. We've got to help her."

But he seemed not to hear me, as if something much more important had just occurred to him and he wished to give it his full attention.

I threw off my jacket and ran into the inferno. Above my head flames crackled along the crossbars of the steel frame that provided the marquee's skeleton. Everything burned: the bunting hanging from the ceiling, the dark silk of the lining, its golden stars eaten by fire. Sheets of silk detached themselves and fell from the roof. Part of the dance floor seemed to be smoldering. A trestle table stacked so recently with champagne had become a blazing altar. I tried to remember where I had left Elvire and turned toward the corner where I thought she was resting. I hoped it was not her final resting place. Above the sofa, I saw a section of the marquee lining caught in a frame of fire. If it fell, it would be too late. But the smoke was catching my throat. My eyes were stinging, running with tears. The heat was on my skin. I smelled something that reminded me of burning hair, then realized it was probably my burning hair.

I plunged forward to the sofa. Elvire was just waking, woozy and confused, as if the nightmare incineration around her were some crazy dope dream and if she blinked often enough she would wake from it. She rose, then fell back, coughing, reaching distractedly for her fancy shoes.

"Gotta go, Elvire. For fuck's sake."

"The shoes. Jimmy Choo."

"Fuck the shoes!"

"Choos. Not shoes."

She fell back again, unconscious from the smoke. I tried to lift her, but unconscious, she was deadweight and I would struggle to drag her to safety. I tried to revive her, slapping her cheeks but getting no response. I cursed Shelby—why had he not ridden to the rescue like he did in his war stories? Maybe because his tired yarns were all talk, myths, figments. *Les Chimères.* Maybe his self-invention had limits when it crashed up against the buffers of reality. I felt my knees buckle. I tried again to lift Elvire, sling her over my shoulder in some kind of fireman's lift, but that didn't work either.

If I left her, she would die.

If I stayed with her, so would I. And who would look after Marie-Claire then? That, at least, was a no-brainer: the line of suitors would stretch around a city block. Twice. And I would be charcoal. Like the fish in the Avre. Or Hakim's Cairo.

But I knew that I could not leave a fellow human being to burn even if I burned with her. I had to stay with her, in the hope that salvation would arrive from somewhere—the fire brigade, God, Joe Shelby.

Joe Shelby. Delirium had come with the inhalation of toxic fumes. An imaginary Joe Shelby was at my side, mouthing soundless words, his hair fringed with a halo of fire. The avenging sword. This would be my last vision: a pretend friend sending a pretend double to help while I was alone.

Until the pretend friend started to bellow. And Elvire miraculously became lighter, raised aloft on some heavenly trajectory. My strength had doubled, trebled. She was vertical now. Unconscious but no longer deadweight. My dream friend began to move and I with him, Elvire between us.

We each took an arm over our shoulders on either side of her, lifting her off the ground. From the roof, spars of the framework, red with heat, fell through the smoke, remnants of blazing fabric clinging to them like phantom pennants. The smoke was thicker and the archway at the entrance was now only fire. Off to one side, there was a gap, a hint of a place where the flames seemed less impenetrable. I looked across Elvire's lolling head to my imaginary friend. We had died, clearly, and this was the final challenge, to brave the wall of fire that blocked the route to Paradise. If we failed, the flames would be eternal, infernal. This was the tipping point between heaven and hell, and we were lighter because we were no more than spirit beings, straying in the flames, seeking a home for lost souls.

"Now, you assholes. Now. Run," Elvire said, sounding anything but spiritual. I felt heat like a steel plate bolted onto my face. Distractedly, I watched the hair on my arm turned into spirals of brittle charcoal. We ran. Through the smoke. Through the fire. Visions of orange and vermilion demons reaching out to hold us back, enfold us, take us into a final embrace of incineration. We ran, stumbled, zigzagged, lurched. Almost dropped Elvire. In a flare-up of satanic light, I saw Shelby's features locked into a fixed rictus as if he was laughing hugely. A final arc of fire rose before us but it was too late to change course and we ran through it. Into clean air.

Rain in sheets.

The worried faces of Marie-Claire and Gibson Dullar, hair flattened by the downpour.

Her makeup had run, but the pearls still glowed. There were ambulance crews. Paramedics. Fire crews had hitched up their hoses and were training great jets onto what was left of the blazing marquee. The water arched and fell onto the flaming hulk in clouds of sudden steam. I coughed and spluttered. Elvire vomited, then turned on me accusingly.

A paramedic made to hook her into an oxygen mask and set a drip in her arm, but she struggled free.

"My shoes. Where the fuck are my Choos?" It sounded like "*Where ze fook are ma chuz?*"

Then she focused on Shelby.

"Joe, You saved me. From Charlie. At last."

The lady had sung, but not quite the aria she had been planning. She looked at Shelby with glowing eyes. I almost forgot to be pissed with her for leaving me out of the hero-grams. "That was close, Ed." Shelby's face was black. "You're the hero. You led the charge."

I didn't mention my earlier act of unsuspected courage, facing down Dullar.

The front of his fancy evening shirt had turned into a crisp of burned fabric. His armpits ran with sweat. Someone had recovered his tuxedo jacket, and he hung it over his shoulders, fumbling for a pack of cigarettes.

"Guess it was easy after 'Nam." I was trying to joke, and he cracked a lopsided smile.

"So now you know what it's like under fire, Clancy, you desk-bound warrior," he said.

"Under fire? That was *in* the fire."

"Like the fire in Cairo, Ed. Hakim's fire. Never forget that."

Before I had time to offer some Nervalian response, Dullar spoke up.

"Must have been something, a spark, from the barbecue pits," he said.

Shelby and I looked at one another, then at Dullar. In all the drama, he seemed to have remained collected, his pressed jeans and buckskin jacket barely sullied by his adventure in the horse trade. When he spoke to us, he seemed to be looking—maybe staring—at a far-distant point over our shoulders. It made me think of the expression they used to use for shell-shocked vets—the thousand-mile stare that comes with having seen too much.

Marie-Claire moved toward me and took my hand and smiled.

"I'd kiss you but you look like"—she struggled for a comparison that would work in English—"like a coal cellar."

"Cigarette me, Joe," I said.

Shelby flipped a Marlboro from his pack and I took one. Dullar was in quick-draw mode with his fancy gold lighter. I noticed that it was set to issue a long jet of flame, not the usual demure flicker.

Then my guts heaved and I passed out.

* * *

I came around in time to stop an overenthusiastic ambulance
crew from taking me to some hospital or another. I said I would be
fine. I said all I would need was a shower and some deep breaths.
Someone talked about the perils of smoke inhalation but we all
ignored him. Marie-Claire had taken control. You would never have
guessed where she had been—or what she had been doing—a little
while earlier. But then, on that night, little whiles stretched into life-
times. One of the stable lads had brought a quilted jacket, and it was
draped over her shoulders. She said a firm good-night to Gibson
Dullar, thanking him for rescuing her prize racer but making clear
his services were no longer required, save as a chauffeur for the still
queasy Elvire Récamier. I guess most people would have welcomed a
little hospital treatment after what she had been through, but Elvire
had survived worse in the battlegrounds of Baghdad and Beirut. I
kissed her on the cheek and heard her say, sotto voce, "Merci, Ed."
With Dullar at the wheel, her crazy little car bounced down the
driveway and was gone before anyone could ask him too many questions about the chronology of his evening.

Once in my own bedroom, I took a long hot shower and
scrubbed smoke and debris from my body. Afterward I tried to comb
my hair as I would normally have done, but part of it had disappeared, leaving my head looking kind of patchy. I wrapped a towel
around my waist. Marie-Claire was peeling off her fancy evening
wear, now stained with rain—ruined, probably. Her eyes were still a
bit starey. Her hair was wild, unkempt from the frenzy of rescuing
the horses and the drenching rain. The pearls still glowed around her
neck. The choker I had gone broke to give her had not broken.

I wanted her back as she had been. For me only. Exclusive rights
for both of us.

I advanced and caressed her shoulders. I was not much taller
than her, so I could look into her eyes, the pupils slightly smaller
than they should have been. I leaned forward to kiss her.

I had survived. She had survived. Somewhere I had read about
the irresistible urge of trauma survivors to reassert their hold on life

when they have looked death in the face. Now I understood that it was no myth for either of us. She pushed me back onto a silk rug on our marital bedroom floor and straddled me, her hands on my shoulders, her legs looped around mine so that she could move back and forth as if on one of her mounts. But I wanted fulfillment, too. I had waited. Saved a life. Risked my own. Seen her snorting coke with Shelby, saving horses with Dullar. There was a whiff of other men on her that I needed to expunge, banish, obliterate. I pulled back from her and she looked surprised, aggrieved. Then I laid her back. She made to remove the pearl choker, but I stopped her, pinning her arms.

"Look at me," I said when her eyes closed again. "Look at me." She obeyed.

"Who are you looking at? Say my name."

"Ed, Ed Clancy. My love."

"For how long?"

"Forever. Look at me, Ed. Tell me who you belong to."

"To you."

"Who am I? Say my name. Say you belong to me as I belong to you."

"Marie-Claire Risen, I belong to you."

"Then show me," she said.

After the dawn peeked over the charred skeleton of the marquee and the staff readied the horses for their exercise, we finally could inspect the damage properly. I had allowed Shelby to stay on in one of the cottages and his Jaguar, presumably with the AK-47 in the trunk, was still where he had left it in the parking lot, but there was no other sign of him. Marie-Claire and I stood in our robes, our arms around each other, looking out at the treasure we had come so close to losing. If the fire had leaped to the other buildings—our home, the stalls, the fencing of the paddocks—we might not even have been able to survive it together as a twosome. Instead we had hung on to something, reclaimed and recovered ourselves.

"That asshole Shelby."

"He's your best friend. He's the only one who ran into that fire after you."

I did not tell her that he had hesitated, had let me go on alone.

"Brought coke here, for Chrissakes."

"He didn't bring the coke, Ed," she said gently.

"I guess I knew that. I just wanted to hear you say it. So now?"

"Now that particular party is over."

I hoped she meant for good, but she didn't say it in so many words. I wanted to ask her a lot of questions, about our apartment in the Sixteenth, about the brochure for a sports car, about the company she kept, but I was no interrogator, more passive cynic than active inquisitor. Her assurances seemed enough. If you cannot trust the person you love, then maybe you do not really love her at all.

But I could not quite let it go.

"And the Alfa?"

"Alfa?" she said with an expression I could not quite fathom. In retrospect, I guess you would say there was something of a sparkle in her eye.

We dressed and lingered over coffee. It was time to reassure our workers and inspect the horses as they returned from reestablishing the routine of their exercise. Soon enough, there would be insurance inspectors and police officers and specialist fire service investigators arriving to ask questions, harvest forensic evidence. There had already been calls from the sporting newspaper *L'Équipe*. A clutch of camera crews made camp at the main gate. As a journalist, I knew that a fire at a stable full of champion horses was a story. A big story. It would affect the betting, lengthen odds, sow doubt about runners and riders.

In my early days on sport, I had covered the saga of a rabid dog reported to be prowling Louisville on the eve of the Kentucky Derby. Any amount of high-end bloodstock was imperiled by the threatened snap of canine jaws. I kept up with the news for days, feasting on the byline vanity that grips the practitioners of my trade until the last of the final editions, the end of the print run when their personal press-room goes dark forever.

It was my story. I owned it. Every development came to me first. Then a veterinarian let slip that a sample of the dog's saliva, collected after a failed attempt to track it down, had shown it to have something called dumb rabies—the kind that locks an animal's jaw before it can infect another. The race horses, in other words, were safe. The dog would die before it could harm anyone. The panic was over. Technically, the story died the minute the veterinarian broke the news to me. But writing the story would mean the end of the bylines, the glamour, the congratulatory slaps on the back from editors craving exclusives, the extra dollars in my bank account.

I had a choice: break the news and end the run, or maintain my silence so the story might linger a day or two longer with my name all over the sports pages and my wealth increasing exponentially. The decision I made will haunt me to the grave—and remain my secret until then.

I mean, it was only a goddamn dog, for Chrissakes.

Now, as an owner of bloodstock, I was not relishing facing my professional colleagues, the mask of their friendship stripped away to reveal the merciless fangs of the newshound, and I kind of hoped that Marie-Claire would take it upon herself to bamboozle them, feeding the beast without betraying the questions that remained from the awful blaze.

There was a knock at the kitchen door. One of the cleaners had found a leather-bound volume along one of the pathways: an early edition of Nerval's *Voyage en Orient*.

I leafed through the pages, looking for the references to Hakim and Cairo that Shelby had made just after we emerged from our own conflagration. There was a line that Shelby had underscored in pencil: "That terrible night, when the sovereign power took the trappings of revolt, when the vengeance of heaven used the weapons of hell."

Shelby had said "Hakim's fire." And in this old work by Nerval, it was Caliph Hakim who ordered the fire that consumed his capital: "Fire, fire everywhere in this city . . ."

Cairo was burned by arson, and I had a memory of Dullar's lighter set to produce a flame, not a flicker.

* * *

I went through my jacket pockets in preparation for dropping it at the dry cleaner on the way to work the following morning. In the wreckage of Dullar's camera, I found the bent shape of a high-capacity SD card. A film camera would never have survived the impact of being smashed under Dullar's heel and the exposure of its innards to even a hint of light. But I wondered, in these digital days, how robust the digital successor to Kodak Tri-X or Ilford HP5 would be, and how long it would keep its secrets.

CHAPTER EIGHTEEN

WE KEPT AND WERE KEPT BUSY, MEETING, AS BEST WE COULD, THE demands for information from insurers, the staff, camera crews. Racehorse owners called in for reassurance and were reassured that, even now, their investments were out on the gallops, gulping pure air. Marie-Claire gave television interviews that won sympathy but left the whodunit question unanswered, partly because we had plenty of suspicions but nothing that approached evidence. The mystery of how the marquee caught fire remained just that—a mystery. The forensic teams from the fire service and the police took away any amount of evidence and photographed charred debris from any number of angles. Anonymous investigators in white suits picked through the wreckage. Some of the metal framework had survived, blackened and skeletal. Miraculously, you could still make out the shape of the sofa that had almost become Elvire Récamier's funeral pyre. The investigators wanted it preserved as a potential crime scene. But, in all honesty, we wanted it dismantled. It was an eyesore, a reminder of how close we had come to disaster.

We wanted every trace of the nightmare obliterated.

In the late afternoon, there was another knock on the kitchen door. It sounded timid and I nearly missed it. When I saw Shelby, his hair singed and patchy, I almost laughed.

"Look at yourself," he said in response, and I ran my hand over my head, finding rough, uneven patches where they had once been smooth expanses of hair.

"Touché. Come in."

"Just came to say goodbye. Till tomorrow at any rate."

"You wanna drink?"

"Tea?

"Tea?"

"Did I hear tea? What a good idea," Marie-Claire said.

I handed Shelby his copy of Nerval.

"I guess I owe you guys an explanation," he said.

"Of what?"

"Of what I may have gotten you into."

"Why don't you start from the beginning?" Marie-Claire said. "Or should I leave you boys to it? Men's talk! No place for the ladies!" She spoke in mischievous tones. I was sure she had no intention of missing Shelby's confession.

"No. Stay, please. If that's okay with you, Ed? Marie-Claire? No secrets, okay? Maybe surprises, but no secrets."

Shelby and Marie-Claire settled in around the big sofas in the living room. You could still smell the fire on the air that wafted in through the open doors leading out onto the lawns. I stayed in the kitchen to brew a pot of Earl Grey. When I entered the living room, I had a feeling that a conversation had been suspended at my approach.

"Joe was just asking whether you wanted the full unexpurgated version."

"Well, maybe Joe could ask *me* that." The anger from the previous night stirred and they both looked at me in some alarm.

"Hey, buddy. Sorry. I just didn't want to lay a big trip."

"Oh, sure. There's no big trip. We have a fire that nearly burns the place down. Horses and all. Christ! We nearly lose Elvire in the flames. I find you snorting coke with my wife, and there are no big trips? Did I understand that right?"

"Maybe I should leave," he said, pushing himself up from the deep sofa with his cane so that he almost lurched into the low table where I had deposited the tea.

"No, you don't, Shelby. You've got a story to tell? Fine. But you've got questions to answer, too. Old buddy. Old sport. And I'm going to do the asking."

I glanced at Marie-Claire. I swear to God that, in that moment, she actually admired me.

"Fire away, man," Shelby said, then smiled. "So to speak."

We laughed and things got a bit easier.

Now that my role as inquisitor was established, I didn't know where to start. Should I mention his parentage, the letters I had seen while snooping in his study? Did that matter? After all, I knew as much as Shelby did about the official documentation. But my real interest lay in the gap in his CV between Beirut and Paris, the missing months that might explain what happened between him and Faria Duclos. Elvire Récamier had hinted, too, that Dullar had an influence, a bearing, a presence in those secret months. There was a big, messy blank, a black hole in my knowledge, and now Shelby was saying he had gotten us into something that he wanted to confess. Did that make us his priests? If we listened to him, would we be drawn in further? Or was he offering a way out? Was he saying, I might be foundering on my own personal bridge, but you can make for the lifeboats?

Above all, was there something in Shelby's murky past that would somehow explain the events of the past few hours?

"Beirut," I said finally. "What happened in Beirut?"

"Just that?"

"That and after. Why do you keep clippings about a fire in Beirut? Why is there so much fire in all this?"

Marie-Claire looked at me more sharply now.

"There was another fire?" she said.

"And afterward, Joe? What happened when you dropped out of sight before you came here? What happened with Faria Duclos? Was that to do with a fire? And Dullar, where does he fit in all this?"

Shelby eased himself back onto the sofa, his cane propped beside him like a bishop's crook.

"I wish I had all the answers."

"Then just tell us what you know, Joe," my wife said, very gently. "It seems to me you owe Ed that. And you owe yourself."

For a moment, I thought he was choking up, but he coughed and suggested that, perhaps, we might brace ourselves with something a

little stronger than Earl Grey tea. I told him we could wait a while
for a sundowner. He sulked, then stretched his arms above his head
and looked up at the ceiling. If we'd had a grandfather clock, you'd
have heard its heavy ticktock. The evening quiet was settling in, the
kind of Sunday quiet that is so much deeper than on any other day,
as if the world is pausing to draw breath.

Finally, he started.

"Well. They were re-assigning me. Again. New post. *Ma'salaam*,
Beirut. Hello, Web."

He fell silent, as if marshaling his memories, weaving a timeline
through the scattered remnants of events.

"So where'd you go?"

Marie-Claire gave me a disapproving look for breaking the
charmed circle, but I knew Shelby liked to spin things out, and I was
losing patience. For once, we were on my home ground. I set the
rules.

"Nairobi," he said. "I went to Nairobi to see Eva Kimberly."

"I'll be damned!"

Marie-Claire looked a little confused. She was not as familiar as
I—or the entire press corps for that matter—with the story of Joe
Shelby's betrayal of Faria Duclos to take up with Eva Kimberly. Before
Duclos walked away from him, of course. Some people said Joe led a
complicated life. But that was something of an understatement.

"Why?"

"We are getting out of sequence here," Marie-Claire said. "Go
back to Beirut. Before Nairobi. Something happens, right? What
is it?"

"Well. A few things happen. Good question, by the way.
Sometimes you don't really know why. In my line of work—well, the
way it used to be in the old print days—there were plenty of times
when you'd finish up in someplace on a whim or an editor's whim
or for some nefarious reason. And you'd check in at the hotel and
check out the phone lines and make a few calls. But there always
seemed to be someone or other from the traveling circus around."

"Circus?" Marie-Claire said.

"The press corps, he means the press corps."

"True enough," Shelby said. "We were always just circling one another. So you got used to the idea that you'd be in some place and people would drift in and out and you'd bump into them at the Commodore or the Sheraton in Damascus or the Intercon in Kinshasa. You didn't really ask, I guess. Trade secrets. Whatever."

"But you lived in Beirut," I interjected.

"Sure, I did. But I was moving. Packing up. You saw all the stuff I had to crate and ship when it arrived in Paris. Where does it all come from over the years? Souks? Flea markets? The power of accumulation. Show me an oil painting of the Battle of Adwa and I'll show you a hack who's been to Addis. We all have the same mementos—Pashtun hats, Iraqi Air Force watches, masks from the Congo, wooden giraffes from Zimbabwe. Anyhow. I packed up my apartment out near the lighthouse in West Beirut and moved into the Commodore for the last few days. Not what it was, of course. Not like the old days. With the boom-boom. And the parrot that did an imitation of incoming—the kind you least want to hear. Makes a whistling noise then—ka-boom! I remember once, in south Lebanon—"

"Okay, Joe. Back on message. You can tell your war stories another time."

"Sure. Sure, Ed. So I move into the Commodore. Old time's sake. Sentimental journey. First thing, when I plug in the laptop, the *Graphic* tells me they've sent Dullar to stand in till my permanent replacement arrives. Dullar! Then, I'm heading down to the bar and who do I see walking in—well, limping would be a better description? Faria. Dear, dear Faria Duclos. We spotted each other at exactly the same moment. She was on a zimmer. I was just on the cane. We stopped in the lobby and looked at each other. Stunned, really. Turned out she'd been given a retrospective show by some group in Beirut, showing all her great photos. So there she was. And there I was. Both wobbly. I went across to her and put my arms around her. Kind of like a crazy waltz because I was not standing too steady and without her frame she was as weak as a rag doll. It felt like years since I'd seen her. Wasted years. Wasted muscles! So much to catch up on. She laughed. You know that laugh she had. I was supposed to be mad with her after she walked out after the Gaza thing . . .”

"Gaza thing?"

"Gaza. We'd split up. Me and Faria. Then we got back together after I got sick. Then she left again. So I was pissed. Then *she* got sick. But I hadn't seen how sick she was till that day in the hotel lobby. Back in the Commodore. Back in Beirut. Walking wounded. Then, of course—surprise, surprise—in walks Gibson Dullar holding a catalogue from her show. 'Fantastic, Faria,' he's saying. 'Great stuff! Genius!' And then he sees me. 'I didn't know you were here already, Gib.' 'No worries,' he says, 'got in early. You know me. Don't like to miss the show.' 'So how'd you hear about the exhibit,' I asked him. 'Didn't you know,' he says. 'Didn't they tell you? The *Graphic* was a sponsor. I'm here as part of the committee. More to the point,' he says, 'aren't you supposed to be shipping out?' So there we all were again. Back where we were in 'Nam. Circling. Again."

I made to head for the drinks tray, but Marie-Claire beat me to it. She splashed single malt into crystal tumblers and poured herself a glass from a leftover bottle of Chassagne-Montrachet that had escaped the caterers' cleanup.

"I'm sorry, Ed. I should've given you a heads-up. But I guess I was too embarrassed."

I peered into the peaty depths of Talisker.

"So that's why you went to Nairobi? Because of Dullar?"

"It kind of gets worse," he said. "Quite a lot worse, as a matter of fact."

The evening had begun to ease toward the gloaming. I moved around the lounge switching on the big, fabric lamps that Marie-Claire had installed. It made the place look cozy.

She and I had instinctively positioned ourselves on one of the super-stuffed sofas and Shelby had gotten up to stretch his legs, then settled back in a maroon leather wing chair with a small, spindly table next to it to support his drink. He raised his glass and held it to the lamplight, then lowered it without drinking.

"The fire, Joe. Tell us about the fire. The fire in Beirut."

This time he took a decent slug and a deep breath.

"Back up a bit. The problem was," he said, "that I couldn't love her anymore. Not in the way I had. Not in that fiery, passionate, consuming way. I always thought I would love her whatever happened, but when I saw her like that with her shriveled legs . . ."

"Maybe I should leave?" Marie-Claire said.

"No. Stay." I don't know who said it first—me or Shelby.

"It was too much. What she was, I was going to be. Sooner or later. The nerves would give out. The muscles would fade. Maybe it was something in the water in 'Nam or Rwanda or someplace. Maybe it wasn't even the same thing with us both. The same illness."

It was almost too intimate. You can know a guy for years without getting too personal. Then, when they start really talking, it get's a bit squirmy. I just wanted to keep the narrative on track, without all the emotional meanderings.

"So you split?"

"No, Ed. I didn't. Not then. Not right away."

"And the fire?"

"I'm getting there. Jeez. You've been on Nonstop News too long—cut to the chase, the boom-boom, the death toll! NND rules! What happened to storytelling, Ed? Sorry. But you know what I mean. Just the context with me and Faria for Marie-Claire. The history. That's what I remember most. But there was still something. Something really big. Not passion like there had been, all physical and the heart will follow. Something deeper. A spark. Possibilities. But when you have been through everything we had been through together, and when you've been through separations when all you thought about was her, you don't just draw a line. The passion of the body isn't everything."

He paused and glanced speculatively from Marie-Claire to me and then back to her.

"Well. Maybe that doesn't apply to you love-birds," he laughed, making a joke of the blushes he brought to her cheeks. "Not yet."

"Go on," Marie-Claire said.

"It was different. Maybe for the first time I wanted to protect her, to just be there, to read poems for her—she was the one with the thing about Nerval, by the way. I was not sure if she wanted me like that. She didn't want me doing the nurse stuff, for sure. But if I was just kind of there to hand her a glass of wine, or make sure we had a table booking for dinner, or to listen to her and talk to her about what had happened in all those places, or to hold her—just hold her in my arms—she seemed sort of happy with that. And I was happy, too, now I think of it. We didn't have to be up all the time. We didn't have to be scanning the wires for some crazy bang-bang someplace to head out to. We just enjoyed being together and we knew that we were where we were meant to be. If that isn't a hopeless cliché."

"You know what I think, Joe?" Marie-Claire said. "I think what you are talking about is a kind of love that people yearn for and never achieve."

"Like Darby and Joan?" I interjected. Maybe sneered would be a better word.

"No, Ed. Not like Darby and Joan. Like us. Like we'll be."

Now it was my turn to blush, but Shelby seemed to have missed our little exchange and was plowing ahead, determined to get confession over and seek his absolution. Or another jolt. Or maybe he was not even with us at that point, cruising a parallel world, trying to work out why he had missed so many chances.

"But of course there were still stories to do and if I didn't do them, Dullar would do them and that would annoy me. Dullar hated what was happening with Faria and me. I mean really hated it. You could see it in his eyes. But I still went out now and again to do stuff in south Lebanon. I was doing a big series on militias—old-style leftists, jihadis, whatever. Crazies with guns. Like the one they gave me, Ed. You know, the AK." Marie-Claire looked questioningly at me, but I just shrugged. "And that was how the tragedy happened. Hubris. That's what causes tragedy. Right? Hubris? Tragic error. You make a mistake, and at the time you can't tell it's a mistake because you can't really see. You act in a way that maybe you know you shouldn't. And it changes your life. Act A leads to Acts B and C and D. A chain of inevitabilities all leading in one direction. To disaster. To tragedy. And when that moment comes—I mean, this is where

Aristotle and all those theory-mongers get it wrong—you are supposed to be purged. Catharsis! But it's not like that. The bodies are
left on the stage but you are still standing to take the rap. It's all your
fault. And you look back at that moment, that tragic error. And what
you get is guilt. Because suddenly, looking back, you can finally see
clearly, you can see how your behavior triggered the whole thing.
And you can't understand why you behaved the way you did. Except
that you *did*, and it started this chain of events and at the end of it,
the bodies are on the stage and you can't breathe them back to life
and it's all your fault."

He spiraled awkwardly out of his chair, unsteady on his feet but
nimble enough to turn away from us. His shoulders heaved a couple
of times.

We waited in silence until he was ready to continue. He returned
to his chair, drained his glass. Without being asked, I refreshed it.
Night had fallen, but we never closed the drapes so you could see our
little tableau reflected back to us in the big windows.

"I'd taken a suite, of course, just like the old days. Two bedrooms.
Sitting room. Two baths. All mod cons. Second floor. I hadn't told
anybody when she moved up from the single room on the first she'd
been given for the exhibit, so no one knew she was there. Our little
secret. Well, one day I'm coming back from Tyre or Sidon or somewhere, and as I get into the lobby, Dullar is stepping from the elevator door looking kind of smug. But when he sees me, he looks surprised. Actually, shocked. Now I think of it, he looked stunned.
'Didn't know you were out,' he says. 'Why would you?' I replied. 'No
reason,' he says. He goes his way. I start to go mine. Then the elevator doors slam shut. Fire alarms ringing. Waiters and bellhops scurrying around. Fire. 'Where?' I say? 'Second floor. At least Faria's safe,'
Dullar says, but I'm hobbling and limping for all I'm worth for the
stairwell. Second floor! The fire's on the second floor. And that's
where I've left Faria. With a bad leg you don't cover too much
ground, but when you have to, you dig deep and I was digging hard.
So I get to the first-floor landing and Dullar's behind me and scuttles
off to the room where Faria had been. But I kept on going and he
shouts, 'Don't be a fool, Shelby, the whole floor's on fire.' And I

shouted back, 'But Faria's there, for Chrissakes.' He says, 'No, no. She's on the first!' But I knew better. By the time I got to the second-floor landing the walls are on fire but it looks like you can get through so I figure I have to go on. The idea that she was trapped in that inferno. My God. It was too much. And that's what I remember."

"What happened?"

"I don't know. I knew I had to get to her. I didn't care if I fried. I had to be with her. At the end. I had to save her. It was my fault she was there, goddamn it."

He made no attempt now to hide the tears. His face had dissolved. All of those craggy, wrinkled lines went loose. Thin rivulets trickled down his cheeks. A teardrop fell from his chin and landed in the dregs of his whiskey glass.

"I keep trying to figure it out. It's like, you know, one of those cop movies where someone has stolen the surveillance tape. Or put it on a loop. So you keep seeing the same thing and you can't figure out what's been cut out. What's missing. One minute I was trying to get down the corridor. Flames everywhere. Clothes alight. The next I'm looking up into the face of some Lebanese paramedic in the hotel lobby through an oxygen mask and he's patching up some big wound on the back of my head. And the next thing I'm in an ambulance en route for the ER."

"And Faria?"

He was silent, rummaging through his pockets for something to wipe away the tears. He looked at us both with Labrador eyes and Marie-Claire fumbled in her purse for a pack of tissues.

"Faria? What happened to Faria, Joe?" she said.

He didn't reply immediately, drawing breath in deep gulps like someone coming up from a dive.

"Faria burned," he said. "She burned. When the fire guys got to her she had swathed herself in wet towels somehow and was trying to make it down the corridor on her Zimmer frame when a chunk of ceiling landed on her. That's what they told me. By the time I found out what had happened, she was already patched up and medevacked to Paris, courtesy of Gibson Dullar and the *Graphic*. I got out of hospital after they finished stitching me up, checking for internal bleeding, concussion. I even bought a ticket for Paris, but when I landed at Charles de Gaulle, I chickened out. I couldn't face her. I couldn't face what I had done to her. As if there hadn't been enough. There was a flight to Nairobi so I hopped on that. Cowardice! That's what it was. Pure cowardice. The great two-fisted war correspondent and I had failed her so badly. I couldn't face the way I had let her down. I should have protected her. It was my fault she was in that room. The fire was intended for me, not her. But I failed her. And I knew that so I just ran. When I saw the fire in the marquee last night, that's why I couldn't go with you right away, Ed. It all came back. The fear. The smell of fire. Jesus, that stink."

"But the fire. How did it start?"

"There was evidence of arson of some kind. They put it down to some crazy leftist group I'd been writing about. The *Graphic* sent Dullar and a team of reporters to do our own investigation. And that's what they came up with, too. Arson by loonies."

"I don't remember seeing that story."

"Internal. They kept it internal. At Dullar's request. To avoid embarrassment for the *Graphic*. That was his reason. Apparently."

"And did they say who commissioned it?"

"Commissioned it?"

"Who ordered up the hit?"

"No."

"Wasn't that weird? I mean in a place like Beirut where there's always some worse guy to rat on the bad guys?"

"Strange. You know, you're right. No one ever got fingered."

"But you ran."

"All the way to Nairobi, where, of course, Eva Kimberly refused to see me. Naturally enough. But I was out. It didn't matter. Nothing mattered. I did some traveling on the old routes, down to the Cape. Figured I'd write some pieces on the way but never did. For the first time in my life, the stories didn't seem to matter the way they used to. I heard some stuff from Paris on the grapevine. About the burns. The only thing that made sense was the Nerval books they salvaged from the suite after the fire. She kept them in one of those aluminum suitcases that hard-core hacks and photogs used to schlep around.

Fireproof. Waterproof. That's why the books inside didn't burn. She'd already been medevacked so they brought them to me when I got back to the Commodore and I threw them into the suitcase when I left Beirut. Figured I'd give them to her in Paris. But of course, I never got there to see her, so they stayed with me and I started reading. Like Nerval would explain how to get back to her. It was as if the poems salvaged part of her, started explaining things. About loss. About that terrible feeling when you know you will never get back what you had. '*Rends-moi le Pausillipe et la mer d'Italie.*' You know, in *Voyage en Orient* there are two guys who meet as buddies and get up to all kinds of mischief—Hakim and Yousouf. And then they become rivals over the same woman. But it turns out they are brothers and they still end up destroying one another. So it all made some kind of sense. And the poems made me think of her. She was in them. Sometimes, on the road, I got so steeped in them that I couldn't think of anything else for days."

"Sounds like a breakdown to me," I whispered, but Marie-Claire scowled at me and turned to Joe.

"On maybe a prosaic note, Joe, you said that after the fire, there was a wound on the back of your head. But if you had fallen forward, how could that happen?"

"I've been thinking that myself. I mean, it was a bad wound. Concussion. Scans for brain damage. The works. And when I ran into the fire after Ed put me to shame last night, I had a sudden memory that I wasn't alone when I got to that corridor in Beirut. Someone else was there. Or something. Some ghost."

"Ghosts don't do head wounds," Marie-Claire said. "Ghosts don't give you concussions."

He stayed for dinner and we talked some afterward, just the two of us after Marie-Claire pleaded an early start and reminded us we both needed to be on the road at a reasonably respectable hour to drive in to the office.

He probed about Ivar Bild. Was he some crazy Swedish euthanasiast or what? What was that about an autopsy? What was all that supposed to mean? Had she died of natural causes or what? Was he to blame? "Guilt, Ed. Guilt kills. I killed her by not going. I could have saved her."

"Come on, man. Her death was a medical thing."

"What did she say? Was she expecting me to be there?"

Should I tell him what Bild had told me—that he was forgiven, absolved—or was it too late for that to make a difference?

"She loved you, Joe. What the hell do you think she was expecting?"

CHAPTER NINETEEN

THAT WEEK—THAT ENDLESS, CRAZY WEEK THAT STARTED WITH A blazing marquee and ended the way it did—was never going to be easy. It was as if all the elements had conspired to ensure that it would be climactic and definitive in ways that no one could have foreseen or even wanted to foresee.

At the *Star*, the newsroom was buzzing with rumor, gossip, speculation, and downright falsehoods about the impending visit of the bosses from New York along with their newly anointed acolyte, Gibson Dullar. Word had come down that the quartet would want to cut to the chase, get straight down to business. A town hall meeting had been called. Announcements would be made. Costs would be cut. In the newsroom, neighbor began to contemplate neighbor: Who would survive? Who would inherit the spoils? Who would be cast adrift in this Darwinian lottery?

There had been a time—and I was enough of a veteran to recall and rue it—when voyaging executives, untethered from spousal control, made no secret of their expectations of amusement, some European variant on the Congolese music Shelby had once been pressed to provide in Africa. Those who lived in the city were assumed to be denizens of an older, raunchier Paris in the streets around Pigalle, at the Folies Bergère—the Paris of the post-liberation libations in 1945, the Paris that predated it all, stretching back to the crazy, absinthe-fueled poets of the nineteenth century (though people preferred to forget the ravages of STDs that claimed such geniuses as Baudelaire himself). Long before Sweden stole the mantle of permissiveness, Paris was its capital, inventor of the French letter (although the French called it *la capote anglaise*, which tells you something about reciprocal cross-channel perceptions), French kiss, French knickers, *ménage à trois*, *cinq-à-sept*, *soixante-neuf*, for heaven's sake—lust by numeric code. This was the Paris that was gay before the word assumed another meaning. This was the Paris that was somehow naughtier than anywhere else, the Paris of the cancan and the glimpse of lacy frills that preceded the offer of thrills, the Paris of saucy postcards and garter belts and pale thighs. Of hard-nosed transactions: cash for relief.

Once, it was easy to keep the head office types happy with reservations at the George Cinq and dinner at Taillevent. In the days before cost-cutting, the rule of thumb was to arrange accommodation for the visitors on the assumption that they would never object to a five-star suite even if they knew that perfectly adequate single-occupancy rooms were available. Joe Shelby once told me of a top boss— a *capo di tutti capi* in the newspaper business—who, when visiting a strange city with an executive or two and a correspondent in tow, would visit their rooms in turn to ensure that no one had a bigger or fancier suite than he did. I knew of a Jerusalem correspondent who routinely lodged her visitors in the Presidential Suite at the King David, where Anwar Sadat of Egypt had been accommodated during the peace talks with Menachem Begin, just to see how her bosses gauged their own importance in the scheme of things. (Only the most honest objected to their sumptuous lodgings and insisted on a simple double.) But the recession and the cost-cutters had put paid to such pricey ruses. These days, we maintained short leases on cramped apartments that visitors were expected to use as crash pads, whatever their rank (within reason, of course). You worried not so much about lining them up with illicit company as ensuring they didn't forget the door codes and get themselves locked out when the numbers changed, marooned on the same perilous streets of after-hours Paris that their predecessors had explored with such reckless enthusiasm.

On the Monday after the fire, Shelby and I were not thinking, in any event, about the visitors from the *Graphic*. We had not been invited to the earnest meetings and clipboard brainstorming organized by the *Star*'s upper echelons to formulate strategy with their transatlantic counterparts.

We were worker bees.

We droned, literally: drone attacks in Waziristan, elections in Iran. A war in Afghanistan. Riots in Urumqi. News never stopped. When you least wanted them, bombs went bang, missiles streaked across the sky, blood spattered on dusty byways. Dictators seized power (though it would really have been news to be able to write, as we did eventually, "Dictator relinquishes power"). Earthquakes shook. Tsunamis rolled. Politicians pronounced. Diplomats dithered. Popes pontificated. Or died. Riots erupted. We took them all in our stride, assigning to each its appropriate cliché, filling in the pointillist canvas of history's first stirrings, the paint-by-numbers assembling of the daily news.

We had stringers and staffers out there to beg and cajole, to provide the grand themes and the snippets, the warp to our weft, to create the frail, transient skein of events. So ephemeral! Even the mayfly on the Avre could count on a twenty-four-hour life cycle—three times our allotted span!

On the web, the life of news was counted in nanoseconds before the urge to update trilled along the cyber-conduits that transmitted the commands of distant bosses to the keyboard-tapping fingertips of faraway underlings like Shelby and me.

Post. Update. Post. Update.

The rapid-fire rhythm of Nonstop News–Paris Outpost. Locked and loaded. Rock and roll. Take no prisoners.

It was technology's fault, of course. Shelby loved to turn back the clock to the time it took half an hour of telex time (hey, old-timer, what's a telex?) to send a thousand-word dispatch from some remote station as the perforated tape chattered through those huge, rattling machines that were the correspondents' lifeline to the outside world—a role now usurped by satellite phones and WiFi-broadband-ethernet-whambo-zambo-zippo technology that sends a thousand words before you can blink without the intercession of an operator or technician or clerk or censor. A telex machine, Shelby liked to tell anyone who would listen, was part of a ritual, a liturgy that could not be rushed as it led you from inspiration to execution to deadline and the blessed fulfillment, the release of communion with distant, unseen editors. Like some esoteric rite, the telex machine developed its own codes and language, tracing its origins to the penny-pinching abbreviations of an earlier tongue—cablese—from a time when every single word in a telegram to the head office cost real money, paring English to a brevity that verged on gibberish, a clear advantage in lands where censors scrutinized every dispatch.

Willy-nilly, in the late hours when no one could restrain him, Shelby liked to recite the time-hallowed and possibly apocryphal haikus of the cablese-telexese era.

"Why you unswim sharkinfested waters query," a Fleet Street editor asked in a cable to a reporter whose rival had begun a report with an account of swimming into Zanzibar through such waters to cover a coup.

Another editor sought to establish the age of an emperor. "How old Selassie query," his cable read. "He fine stop how you query," came the reply.

The history of the craft was littered with tales of reporters frontwarding warwise, striving to write fullest colorfullest copy soonest, seeking the urgentest replenishment of their expense funds. And offering multitks in adv for the pleasure of a reply.

"Pls ack" stood for "please acknowledge," as in pls ack the request for a wire transfer of dollars.

"Pls ack asap" meant penury approached.

You wrote your story on your portable typewriter—Olivetti Lettera 32s were a big favorite, but Shelby always had a hankering for the original Swiss-built Hermes Baby, before the factory was shipped to Brazil and the company expired on the altar of progress. You wrote on the reverse side of hotel letterhead if you had no paper of your own—paper!—and you made your corrections in pen or pencil in a legible enough way for a telex operator to read, if necessary. Then you converted the written word on sheets of paper into perforations on a long, looping tape, also made of paper, either using the telex machine itself or, for the more advanced, a blind puncher. The latter machine was little more than a mechanical keyboard designed to punch holes in the paper tape that the telex machine read as text to send to its counterpart in a distant newsroom, like some kind of chattering mating call between antediluvian behemoths.

The slickest practitioners—and Shelby counted himself among them—could write an article straight from notes onto a blind puncher with the telex line open on an adjacent machine and the tape rattling through at fifty baud. If you stopped composing but the machine kept on transmitting, the tape snapped—so there was no greater discipline for the fast-writing, two-fingered, whambo-zambo merchant than an open line and a blind puncher. If you got it right, the first you ever saw in print of what you had written was in the newspaper clippings that arrived by pouch weeks after the event. Sometimes, though, you had to give your composition to an operator, who made the tape for you at her or his own pace, and you stood in line with the rest of them in some dingy PTT office in some hot, humid city to hand over your article packaged in dollar bills to ensure its speedy transmission.

Standing in a line in Kinshasa, at the big, grimy old post office on the Boulevard du Trente Juin in the days when it was still paved with asphalt, before the jungle reclaimed the sidewalks, Shelby had heard an old-stager ahead of him—Wilkinson of Interpress—remark, "My God, those cobwebs were here in the sixties," and he prayed he would never grow so old himself as to acquire such wisdom.

Telex rooms were generally public spaces. Usually outgoing stories were printed on a double roll with a carbon copy (Granddad, what's a carbon copy?) that remained on the machine when the sender had left the building. Shelby once told me of a trick he had developed called the Wireroom Switcheroo when he began to suspect that a colleague (not Dullar this time) was reading his carbons to steal his exclusives after Shelby had taken his turn on the telex and moved on. He devised a way of leaving bogus stories on the telex roll to see who picked them up. And sure enough, the maneuver worked. It took only one story killed and retracted in utter humiliation—"Mobutu Hands Fortune to Mother Teresa"—to prove the efficacy of the switch.

There were censors to deal with, too. In N'Djamena, they insisted you produce your punched tape so they could run it through a disconnected telex machine and read what you had written before you were permitted to hand it in—with dollars or Central African francs—for transmission. So you punched two tapes, two versions of the same story, one unctuously cleaving to the official line, the other spiked with the acerbic observations of a cynical correspondent. You handed the innocuous one to the censor and the unedited one from behind your back to the operator. Then you waited for the answer back that told you the article had been received. And you typed in the hallowed words that functioned pretty much as the Nunc Dimittis: O Lord of News, now lettest thou thy servant depart in peace.

"Pls ack all rcvd ok"

"Rcvd ok"

"Tks"

"Bibi"

"Bibi"

Thus concluded the duet of sender and receiver, ending this tenuous tryst across continents.

Your article had been transmitted and received. In the parlance of reporterdom, you had filed—meaning you had sent your story, not filed it away in some manila folder in a cupboard. You had fulfilled your pact with your bosses, earned your crust. You were free. The night was yours. In those days, no BlackBerry or sat phone or cell phone would hunt you down.

Shelby liked to recount a story from the old Congo days.

As representatives of supposedly competing wire services, he and a colleague had attended a news conference in a room lined with dainty, gilt chairs that also contained the only two live telexes for a thousand miles. A government flack dressed in the uniform of a general was explaining in a mixture of French and English how rebels in the southern province of Shaba were being repulsed by the deployment of what he called "elite pygmy bowmen." No matter that the pygmies stood less than four feet tall, while the elephant grass of Shaba reached three times that height. No matter that the rebels had left of their own accord and were, at that moment, rolling back to their base in a convoy of looted family sedans, pillaging and raping as they went. Pygmy bowmen, the general insisted, had turned the tide.

"You mean pygmies, really? I mean, like pygmies. Elite pygmies?" Shelby said, rising from his chair and backing toward the telex machines at the back of room.

"The little men?" his colleague asked, rising too and heading for the telexes. "*Les petits hommes?*"

"*Oui, les petits hommes,*" the general said with magisterial forbearance.

"*Avec les arcs et les flèches?*"—with bows and arrows?—Shelby asked, backing up more rapidly now.

"*Les flèches empoisonnées?*"—poisoned arrows?—the colleague from Reuters inquired.

"*Oui, avec les flèches empoisonnées.*"

That final detail was too much. Deadlines were looming. The poisoned arrows were the clincher. But by the time the rest of the hacks reached the telex machines, Shelby and his competitor from Reuters were already on open lines to head office, monopolizing the communications, typing frantically, neck-and-neck, graf-by-graf, in a high-stakes derby: "Elite pygmy bowmen armed with poisoned arrows routed rebels in the war-torn southern province of Shaba Tuesday . . ."

These days, there were no deadlines. The web was infinite. Every second offered an opportunity to tweak, transmit, recast, relede, revamp. The formal, single deadline was replaced by an infinite deadline. Ergo, you were never free, the night was never yours. As with multiple orgasms, there was always the technical possibility of another judder, another release.

The end began with such odd, old machines as Portabubbles and Tandys and Zeniths—the forgotten tools of a dying trade, Shelby used to say. For my part, I hated this correspondent chat about means of communication—one of those themes that they used to think was mesmerizing. How many times had I stifled a yawn when they started talking about their road warrior kits and the time so-and-so got his alligator clips inexplicably clamped on his most tender parts?

I had heard friends offer one another cryptic guidance about the correct color combination of the hidden hotel room wires that would produce a connection: "Athens, Grande Bretagne, green and yellow" or "Diyarbakir, Kervansaray, *le rouge et le noir*."

And I had heard them tell rivals: "Athens, GB, red and black, old chap. Never fails."

Sometimes, as an editor awaiting their stories' arrival in Paris, I imagined them with their early dial-up communications, setting ur-laptops to pulse- or tone-dialing, inserting 9s or 0s to bypass hotel internal loops (who wanted to send the story to laundry or room service?), then crouching over acoustic cups to listen for the faint screech of a carrier signal calling out across the ether for an answering mew from within the simple circuits of 1980s technology, cursing and swearing when the transmission failed and they had to crawl anew behind the nightstand to reconnect on different shades of old wire.

Then, later in the bar: "Filed?" "Brown and blue, my dear. Nothing to it."

I had nothing against the old-timers eking out their remaining years with tales of derring-do. For some of them, that was pretty much all they had left. But these early tales from the barely discerned front lines of technology showed just how easily those veterans had been seduced by the first siren calls of their own demise. Innocents, they had jettisoned their typewriters, embraced their laptops, and come to realize only too late that, with every hookup and download, they renewed their Faustian pact with a future that did not include them.

Give me Shelby's pigeon story anytime.

As we worked that day, Shelby seemed to have forgotten about fire, guilt, failure. He was spruce, cleaned up, Stakhanovite. When he caught me looking at him ruminatively, he gave me a thumbs-up, then hit the keyboard again like a concerto pianist working up to a tricky bit of Beethoven. But I wasn't thinking of music. I was thinking of the look in Dullar's eyes after the fire at my spread. I was beginning to wonder if there had been some dark spell in Kolwezi or

'Nam or Beirut or someplace that had ensnared Dullar and maybe Shelby, too.

Too much bang-bang.

Too much boom-boom.

Too much gazing into the sightless eyes of bodies "frozen in the unseemly abandon of sudden death" (Shelby, circa 1980).

Too many questions without answers "when the senselessness was simply overwhelming" (Dullar, circa 1990).

Long after their exposure to human barbarity, even old-timers who had seen it all snapped awake with sweating, quivering flash-backs or smelled the sickly sweet rot of cadavers in the odorless air-con of sanitized hotel rooms. The skyscrapers of New York and Frankfurt became sniper nests, and they ducked for cover in door-ways among strolling shoppers and bonus-laden bankers.

When a car backfired close by and he jumped involuntarily, one of the old Africa hands excused himself by saying to me, "Sorry, old boy. Still jittery from Matabeleland."

Some of them were still jittery from everywhere.

These days they called it post-traumatic stress disorder. But those words had yet to achieve currency in the times that bred Shelby and Dullar. If their jangled nerves played tricks on them for a while, it was the price they paid for the adrenaline of strangers' wars, for the joy of serial survival. It was the price of bearing witness so that the horror would not go unchronicled and people far away would learn a passable truth and would not be able to say nobody told them that the human race was so flawed. It was a price worth paying if you thought you were the avenging sword.

Some, like Shelby and Dullar, thought they could hack it forever, ignoring the press of memory building behind the barrages of denial, imagining they would never succumb to their ghosts and nightmares. As if they could play Russian roulette forever and never draw the loaded chamber.

The smart ones, I figured, hung up their notebooks and their Kevlar and their cameras before it was too late.

Bibi

Bibi

CHAPTER TWENTY

SHELBY WAS WORKING AFRICA. I WAS WORKING GIGABYTES.

I had persuaded one of the tech guys to help me unscramble and download the contents of the SD card from Dullar's digital camera onto my computer. As I had figured—and secretly hoped—the card was not nearly as sensitive as film might have been. The problem was more one of encryption—spy stuff, really, the kind of thing in movie scenes where the frazzled tech-wizard spins multiple codes through his laptop as the clock ticks down and guys with guns come running down a neon-lit corridor outside until—bingo!—the screen says: DOWNLOAD COMPLETE. This one came without the gunslingers.

At first Dullar's SD card proclaimed itself to be unreadable, but the tech guy stroked a few keys to overcome its reticence, then ran a bit of pirated software that slipped by the crude protective barriers.

Jean-Louis Devreux had always been friendly enough to me, but I knew he had a hard, cynical streak. He claimed to have driven a Paris taxicab for a decade before becoming an all-purpose I.T. wizard. Somehow his knowledge of the cobbled backstreets and tangled alleys of Montmartre had morphed easily into an instinctive understanding of convoluted programs and the instructions that made them navigable. His cab-driving days and nights had also given him a scorn for people who feigned *noblesse* but showed him disrespect, usually in the form of parsimony with their tips and demands to know why he was taking them on such roundabout routes to reach their destinations.

Prefixing my requests with many *monsieurs* and frequent use of *s'il vous plaît*, I was always careful to avoid inclusion on his voluminous list of bosses who, at some time and in some way or another, unknown to them, had behaved in a manner that Jean-Louis considered demeaning. Early in his post-cab-driving career, a secretarial mistype had engraved the name on his laminated ID as Jena Louis and he refused to have it altered, preferring to maintain the moniker as a symbol of a managerial slight that would one day be avenged.

In his desire to gather ammunition for this final showdown with authority, Jean-Louis also had a natural curiosity verging on nosiness. Politely but firmly, I had to shoo him out of my office—*s'il vous plaît, monsieur; merci beaucoup, monsieur*—before I began the download of Dullar's SD card. But I noticed that Jean-Louis had slipped a USB storage device into my PC before he began working. When he left, the USB left with him. I guess I should have stopped him. But at that stage he was the last person I wanted to confront or alienate. How was I to know, at that particular moment, on that particular day, that Jean-Louis was preparing to blast open a box beyond even Pandora's dreams?

I surveyed the results of the download. It contained 197 images with time stamps dating back a year or so. I locked my office door and drew the blinds on the windows before I opened the directory.

It was just as well that I did.

The screen lit up with rows and rows of postage stamp–size JPEG images that could be enlarged to full screen with a click of the mouse.

One after another, they depicted Dullar in the company of another person, sometimes more than one. Some of his companions looked to be dazed or asleep or otherwise unconscious. Some were clad. Many were not. Most were strangers to me, but I recognized some of them with that particular frisson that emanates from the familiar seen in an utterly new and improbable context.

One, in particular, closely resembled the spouse of one of *Graphic*'s most senior executives. Another resembled one of the *Graphic*'s senior executives herself. And she was not alone.

With a start, I noticed that, in the photos where Dullar posed half clad with some equally insouciant partner, you could see a curiosity of his anatomy that seemed to confirm Elvire Récamier's anecdote about his and Shelby's fiery pursuit of Faria Duclos in

Vietnam. At first it looked as though he had been born with only one nipple. Then, if you looked more closely, you could see that half his chest was a patchwork of skin grafts, a landscape of restorative surgery. What was most striking was the contrast between Dullar's angelic looks and this ugliness, usually hidden, now suddenly exposed.

Only one of Dullar's compositions had no obvious claim to inclusion in this gallery of fun and frolics. It showed a hotel room door—you could clearly see the number 207—but I figured that was just one of those false starts, like photos you take of your shoe when you are finding your way around a new camera.

Among the most recent was one I could barely bring myself to contemplate (although I did, of course) and I wondered how it could be erased. I recognized the backdrop as Faria Duclos' apartment. She was in her wheelchair. Dullar was crouched beside her, smiling affably, an arm draped over the steel framework. She was looking pensive—no big smile—and leaning away from her guest. There was no suggestion, though, that Dullar had been holding the camera to take the picture himself, like those happy snaps that people much younger than I post on social sites to show themselves partying with their faces pressed together in grimaces and tongue-pulling, party-hat merriment. Either it had been taken on a timer or by a third party— my suspicions fell on Ivar Bild, the inscrutable night nurse, acting in Nordic innocence, thinking it was just a happy snap and not a digital stiletto that Dullar would one day slide between Shelby's psychic shoulder blades. But Faria understood Dullar's motives. And when I saw the image, so did I. Once again, I caught sight of that distant gaze in Dullar's eyes, as if only his body was living in the present and the rest of him was someplace else where unspeakable things happened to other people.

The snap of Duclos and Dullar was not the last one on the SD card, but I had no time or inclination to open the final few. I guessed, though, that I would find them sickeningly familiar, given that they were taken in the minutes before I surprised Dullar at his nefarious business only days earlier. So much had happened since that moment that it seemed like ancient history.

If I had been writing headlines about the whole selection of photographs, I would have come up with expressions like "Blackmail Bonanza" or "Serial Seducer" or, knowing the creative uses to which he put his camera during his trysts, "Lens Hood Lothario."

But I was not writing headlines. I was too stunned to do anything beyond save the whole file to a USB stick of my own and purge it from the computer lest anyone else on the system stumble across it.

This was dynamite, Semtex. HEU, Little Boy and Fat Man rolled into one. Mutually assured destruction writ small.

And like all explosives, it required careful handling to prevent it from blowing up in your face.

I slipped the USB stick into a padded, unmarked Jiffy bag with a hasty note to the addressee then dropped it into the mail room out-tray outside my office door. There was just time for a smoke-break and I drew deeply on my cigarette, the way condemned criminals are supposed to just before they head for the gallows. Then I made my way back to the newsroom, wondering how long it would be before the trap-door opened beneath all of us if those pictures ever saw the light of day. Shelby was crafting one of his fanciful pieces in Homepatch—the kind no one was supposed to be able to see or steal.

By Joe Shelby

CAIRO—Defying Egypt's emergency laws, tens of thousands of protesters poured onto the streets of Cairo, flooding the central Tahrir Square and confronting police who used tear gas and water cannons against them.

"Mubarak out," many of them chanted, expressing the profound discontent that has arisen across a whole generation of young people in the Arab world with their autocratic and unbending rulers.

"We have had enough," one protester, Ahmed Mahmoud Moussa, 23, declared as he and others sent messages using Facebook and Twitter to urge friends and like-minded Egyptians to join them in their effort to end almost three decades of Mr. Mubarak's increasingly ironfisted rule.

"Enough is enough is enough," he said.

It was not clear who—if anybody—had led the protesters onto the streets. Their appearance followed the creation of a Facebook page that drew more than 70,000 posts from Mr. Mubarak's adversaries.

Police sought to deploy in a thin line with batons drawn to protect the Egyptian Museum, which houses the nation's vast trove of priceless antiquities dating to the time of the pharaohs.

As clashes with the police spread to other locations, news reports said Mr. Mubarak had unleashed groups of thuggish supporters from the secret police and his ruling party, urging them to crush the demonstration.

The unrest, which protesters called a revolution or uprising, followed similar clashes in Tunisia that led to the precipitate flight of the strongman ruler, Zine el-Abidine Ben Ali.

In Cairo, the protest seemed to have been ignited after Friday noon prayers, a sacred moment in the Islamic week. Demonstrators marched from mosques across the city, converging on the Nile-side locations that stand as emblems of Mr. Mubarak's control.

At the headquarters of the ruling party, there were initial reports of fires in the lower floors of the building. And functionaries were seen in television footage gathering up bundles of files before the protesters could get their hands on them.

At one point, pro-government demonstrators took to the roofs of apartment houses overlooking Tahrir Square, lofting chunks of masonry and even satellite dishes onto the president's foes 10 stories below . . .

endit

"Christ, Shelby. Where did that come from? What the hell have you been smoking?"

"Only in Homepatch, old boy," he said. "Just in case. Got a call from an old stringer. Old buddy, actually. Did I ever tell you about that old trick called the Wireroom Switcheroo . . ."

Now he was going through his mock-up article again, showing unsuspected skills in the new task we had been given: the insertion of hyperlinks into the text so that readers could click on marked words or phrases on the website to be sent automatically to background material.

If the piece was ever published—and heaven forbid that it should go beyond the confines of Homepatch without some kind of serious confirmation—a reader would be offered profiles and clippings on everything from the course of the Nile to the origins of the pyramids and the story of Mubarak's rise to power as a lynchpin of American foreign policy in the Middle East following the assassination of Anwar Sadat in 1981.

"Close it. Store it. Forget it. Better still, spike it, kill it, erase it till it's real. And do it now before the meeting starts."

"Remember the Cayman Islands Mafia story?" Shelby said. "Or the Somali smugglers? Well, let's just call this the Wireroom Switch-eroo. Version Two."

CHAPTER TWENTY-ONE

AWAITING THE START OF THE TOWN HALL MEETING CALLED BY OUR superiors, we ambled over to Le Primerose for an infusion of caffeine.

"Big day coming up," I said.

"What are you hearing?"

The urge to share the contents of Dullar's SD card was almost overpowering. But not with Shelby. Dullar's victory parade among his female conquests would enrage him, for certain. Every single image in his rival's gallery was a trophy, a notch carved at someone else's expense. The inclusion of Faria Duclos would be intolerable.

"It's looking bad for some of the guys," I said, weighing my words. "Kind of weird that Dullar will be up there on the podium."

"Listen, Clancy," Shelby said. "Listen to an old-stager. Guys like Dullar are their own worst enemies. We're untouchable."

I peered into the grounds of my *noisette*, hoping I looked as inscrutable as they did. I did not share his belief in our invulnerability. With Marie-Claire Risen waiting for me at home, I had more reason than most to cling to my job, my passport to her esteem.

"Just do one thing for me, Joe. Get rid of the AK. I can stick it in the back of a barn or something. Or in a pond."

"Hey, Ed. Don't worry. Office ornamentation, remember? That thing couldn't fire a round if you begged it to."

"For sure?"

"Sure as the Argentine soy vote," he said.

In the conference room, they had organized the gathering around the huge, horseshoe-shaped table that had been installed in

the *Star*'s heyday. Reporters, copyeditors, interns, layout types, and
photo people clustered around it on all sides. Most of them had
come straight from their desks, a sartorial display of shirt-sleeves,
blue jeans, RSI splints, and unraveling cardigans. Some brandished
clipboards and notebooks. I spotted a surreptitious voice recorder
or two—you could smell litigation in the air: no one would be
downsized without a threat of lawsuits and a clamor for compensation. The gathering spilled from the wooden seats around the big
table onto rows of plastic chairs arrayed against walls covered with
framed representations of great front pages, hung in no particular
order, as if the decorators had forgotten their history lessons that
day: Men on Moon, Mandela Free, 9/11, 7/7, Nixon Quits, Kennedy
Shot, Vietnam War, Vietnam Peace, Israelis Take Jerusalem, Israelis
Overrun Beirut, Bhutto Shot, Lazarus Lives (not really), Coup in
Tehran, Soweto Explodes, Pope Dies, New Pope Chosen, New Pope
Dies, Pope Lives.

On several of them, the big front-page bylines were Shelby's: he
had seen Mandela walk free, roamed the genocidal villages of
Rwanda, been on hand for the Tet Offensive, chronicled the after-
math of the London bombings in July 2005. He had seen the Israelis
storm into south Lebanon (again) in 2006. My name was not there,
but my ghostly presence was: on nearly all the major stories for
decades, my edits and tweaks and corrected errors, straightened-out
sentences, judgment calls and last-minute fixes (wasn't the King
assassination in *April*?) provided the invisible frame around the can-
vases of correspondents' art. But editors didn't get bylines; it was just
assumed that they would blow their own trumpets.

On an opposite wall, an enormous plasma screen showed the
real-time up-to-the-minute splendor of Graphic.net, headlines and
photographs, stories distinguished with little red time stamps to
denote when they had been published—the ephemeral crop of our
digital harvest. Every stamp proclaiming "three minutes ago" or
"five minutes ago" carried the seed of its own obsolescence. If a
story had particular value because it was three minutes old, then it
followed that its value diminished when it was four or five or six
minutes old. Contemplating my own personal time stamp at the *Star*,

measured in decades, I felt a chill of apprehension. How many years earlier had my sell-by date expired? At least, though, on this day, Shelby and I had contrived to sound our bugles for the encounter with the bosses: the website's lead story, about a vituperative sermon by one of the elite in Iran, carried Shelby's byline, and if you looked through the edit-trace, you'd find the specter of my craft haunting the punctuation and spelling and syntax, like some craftsman too humble to claim credit in any but the most servile, if undeniable, manner. Of course, the key word in that sentence was "if"—*if* you looked.

Nobody did.

I scanned the familiar faces, each one recorded in my personal *Domesday*.

There was Robinson, fast with his hands on the keyboards, a pleasant enough guy on most occasions, now seized with intimations of revolution, ready to play Robespierre should any "restructuring" seek to unravel the sacred scrolls of French labor law. I caught sight of Gloria Beeching, her eyes fixed on Marcel Duffie as he leafed through his speaking notes, avoiding her searchlight gaze. I spotted the East Europe expert, Coughlin, a bearded single man in crumpled jeans and a too-baggy, Oxford cloth shirt, fresh in from Pristina or Cluj or someplace, full of unlikely yarns and improbable expense accounts. I nodded gravely to Black, the headline sage, and Bancroft, the mistress of first paragraphs, and Courtney, the institutional memory bank of all things Sino. My mien, I hoped, suggested some profound advance knowledge of what was about to be said.

The Star Chamber of masthead editors formed a tribunal at a separate table at the open end of the horseshoe. Curtis, Green, and Potts—the distillation of second-tier *Graphic* power—sat off to one side, while Marcel Duffie took center stage. Always prone to perspiration, he looked pretty clammy. Standing in a corner of the conference room, Gibson Dullar displayed the manner of someone who knows that crucial chunk more than has been made available to the grunts, as if he had been invested with some kind advance, insider bragging rights.

The microphone hissed and whistled as Duffie tapped it.

"Thanks for coming, all of you," Duffie began. He paused and looked around at his suspicious underlings. I wondered what the world looked like from his vantage point. An image came to mind of a hog farmer surveying his charges and figuring how many of them would soon be sides of bacon. But unlike the farmer, he was nervous, and when Marcel Duffie was nervous, you knew it from the way he got his words mixed up in a way that would have made Mrs. Malaprop sound as smooth as Barack Obama delivering a stump speech.

"As you all know—indeed as many of you have written about with great incision and precisiveness—our industry is in crisis. Our ad revenue is down. Readers are moving to the Wild World Web in ever-greater numbers, but the web can't deliver the revenues we need. News is expensive and news is our stocking trade. But what I want to say, what we want to say"—he gestured to the glum triumvirate from head office—"is that in these uncharted waters, there is no better boat for the *Star* to be in than with the *Graphic* at the helm. And the *Graphic* has no intention of switching horses in midstream. Indeed, you might almost say, we should not be looking such a gift horse in the mouth."

As scores of questioning eyes turned to them, seeking some token of the *Graphic*'s benevolence, Curtis, Green, and Potts considered their briefing notes, their pencils, and their fingernails with intense interest. One or two people sniggered. Someone muttered, "Hear, hear." But the more earnest among the assembled employees shushed them into silence.

Duffie plowed on.

"It has been said by some that we have reached the end of the cul-de-sac, that our number is up and with it our jig. But that is not our vision. Our journalism is our premier recourse and our greatest resource. In our branding, its quality is paramour and unexcelled. We have survived crises in the past and will do so again."

Potts, the head of Nonstop News–Headquarters, seemed to have found something of special interest to peer at outside the window, though I could see nothing beyond the pale facade of an apartment building across the street. Curtis, the head of the *Graphic*'s take-no-prisoners financial division, peered up at Duffie, her rather full lips pursed in what might have begun as a smile, then lost its bearings. For a fleeting moment, I had seen her as she might see herself, not as a hatchet-wielding cost-saver but as a woman of warmth and passion. Green, the foreign editor, by contrast, reminded me of his famed counterpart Salter in Evelyn Waugh's *Scoop*.

I half-expected him to say, "Well, up to a point, Lord Duffie."

"But we do face the need to reduce costs," Duffie continued.

He had everyone's full attention now. Costs meant only one thing: jobs.

"As you all know, and thanks to the many creative suggestions from Stephanie Curtis and her staff, we have trimmed here and there to reduce the base cost without impairing our ability to deliver the news-gathering paradigm on which our brand is erected. That, indeed, is our holy grail. We have tried, too, to improve revenues, in big ways and small. Even our company outlet at head office, I am told, has turned a profit on selling scale models in wood of famous vessels, including, I am assured, the *Titanic*. That, perhaps, should tell us a lesson. We, too, are standing on the bridge of our destiny, peering ahead into our own icy seas from the crow's nest of history. We must face our challenge, skirt the iceberg, and cross our Rubicon. There is no point in saying we will cross that bridge when we come to it. We have already gone the extra mile. We stand on the bridge full-square."

He paused to allow his message to sink in. Many of the staff—particularly those unfamiliar with colloquial English—looked utterly baffled.

"And there is no circumnavigating the fact that we need to be more creative on the issue of head count."

Looking back at that moment, I swear people drew in their collective breath so quickly that the entire room suffered a brief bout of oxygen starvation. I looked at Shelby, who made a play of contemplating his fingernails and polishing them on his shirt. Across the room Gibson Dullar hovered like a malevolent knight in a medieval drama, sent to deal with some troublesome priest.

Head count was untouchable. Head count was what French labor law was all about—jobs for life, benefits forever.

"Now I know some of you see head count as some kind of sacred bull. Sorry, cow. Holy cow!"

Curtis winced. Dullar offered her a fleeting, flashing smile of reassurance and she seemed to draw comfort from that.

Duffie looked again at his briefing notes. Perhaps at that moment he realized that he had been chosen as the messenger and, once he had played his role in this cruel charade, the blade could easily sever the frail gristle and tendons and spinal cord of his own neck.

No more lunches.

No more Gloria Beeching.

No more job.

Duffie looked up from his notes to extemporize.

"Most of you will have seen the numbers from our latest quarter. Unfortunately they seem to represent the camel that broke its back. But it need not be. If we build a house of straw, it is one thing. But we can rebuild in stone, as the three little . . ."

He paused, contemplating where that metaphorical trail might lead him in the presence of the head office trio. Quickly, he shuffled his papers. Some fell to the ground. He knelt to pick them up, banged his head on the desk, rose anew, rubbed his gleaming forehead, found his place on the page, and hurried on.

"So in the next few hours and days, some of you will be receiving invitations to discuss with us"—he gestured to the visitors— "ways of achieving this goal with as little pain as possible. I am not just talking about editorial. Support staff, technical staff, administrative staff, all of us have a part to play—even a walk-off part, so to speak—in this restructuring. If we are to chart a way out of this impasse, we must all put our shoulders to the stone and leave no wheel unturned to pull together, setting our sights on a better future and a bright tomorrow. Maybe, you may say, these are gloomy times, but they can be illuminated with a new dawn and they need not last forever for all of us. Some of you will be leaving, it is true, and we will attempt to anaesthetize the pain for those of you who volunteer to walk that line to the maximum of our realistic possibilities. It might well be on the basis of last-in, first-out— the early worm getting the bird, in fact. But all that can be discussed. I think it was Winston Churchill who said: 'Never will so much be done by so many for so few.' And for those of you chosen to stay aboard our valiant ship, sinking though some Cassandras may try to depict it to be, I need only quote from Shakespeare at the battle of Hastings: 'Once more unto the breach, dear friends, once more.'

"Well, I think that should keep the wolves from the hearth," he said as he sat down before he realized that the microphone had not been switched off.

Now it was time for Stephanie Curtis. She rose and smoothed down a houndstooth skirt over what I had to admit was an alluring frame, not that you publicized such thoughts in these blessedly gender-equal days that had brought me a wife who outpaced any man in business savvy and smarts. Curtis had rolled up the sleeves of a plum-colored silk blouse, and I thought I discerned a narrow band of white on a tanned, tennis-club arm where some fancy accoutrement from Rolex or Tiffany had been removed for the purposes of her just-one-of-the-gals appearance.

"Thank you, Marcel. I think that was most succinct."

Duffie puffed up like a pigeon.

"None of us has any doubt now about the dire straits in which we find ourselves."

As an editor, I would have written, No more nautical metaphors, puh-lease! But bosses trump editor drones by a long way. I noticed that Jean-Louis, the tech guy, had quietly slipped away.

Gibson Dullar glanced at his buzzing BlackBerry, his face registering alarm.

"Marcel put it clearly," Curtis continued. "We at the *Graphic* fully support the *Star* and its staff in their daily successful effort to produce first-rate international journalism for a high-quality audience. Already, many of you have taken on extra assignments and made the extra, professional effort to maintain our high standards during the downturn and at a time when advertisers no longer beat a path to our doors. Unfortunately, we will be asking you to do

more. There is no way around that. There will be fewer resources
for the same tasks. In the process, there will be structural changes.
We wish to discuss with you, for instance, the merger of two won-
derful websites—Graphic.net and Star.com—into a single entity
doubling its strength from the pooling of talent while contributing
to the bottom line by bringing new efficiencies to those resources
and talents."

In other words, sacking people. Management-speak never ceased
to amaze me with its use of language to say the opposite of what
words were designed to mean. If you don't agree, try feeding a family and paying the rent and the school fees with efficiencies and syn-
ergies once you have been laid off.

She lowered her notes and looked around the room, seeking out
eye contact. When her gaze settled on me, it seemed almost seductive
and I had to remind myself that I might just as well have been peering into the soul of Lady Macbeth.

"But there is some good news. To help us through these hard
times, at a moment when your executive editor, Marcel Duffie, is
making such Herculean efforts"—I caught a look of puzzlement
from Gloria Beeching—"we have been fortunate indeed that one of
our best and brightest from the *Graphic* has agreed to join you all in
Paris for a temporary assignment to offer support where you need it
and to bring his own great journalistic talents to bear on this great
project."

Marcel Duffie looked up sharply, glanced around the room, and
peered briefly at Shelby, then at Stephanie Curtis.

He was not the only one who seemed bemused.

"There will be plenty of time for all of you to meet up with him,
to enjoy one-on-ones, both in the editorial process and in the downsizing venture outlined so ably by Marcel Duffie. We agonized for a
while about a suitable title for this new person, who will oversee not
just our print operations but also those of NND Global and all other
platforms."

Now it was my time to be stared at and to pretend I had known
all along what was coming.

"What the fuck." Shelby muttered. "Don't tell me . . ."

"So, colleagues and friends, please welcome our new Global Editor of News, Gibson Dullar."

You could have heard a needle drop into a haystack.

In the silence, Dullar stepped forward and whispered something into Curtis's ear, placing a hand casually on her Hermès-clad shoulder. She did not, I noticed, resist. I caught the words ". . . better handle it myself."

Then he took the microphone.

"Well, thank you for that introduction, Stephanie, and thank you to all for coming here. I know you must all have a lot of questions to ask and I will be very glad to answer them. Let me just say, though, that I plan to lead from the front. I will not ask anyone to do anything I am not prepared to do myself. And in that vein"—he held aloft his BlackBerry—"we are starting to get news alerts out of Cairo that look as if something pretty serious is going down there that we ought to get started on. So I will step out while you put your questions to our colleagues from New York. And when you are through with that, let's all get with the message. We have a newspaper to produce. The best in Europe. And we have a website to make ever more into the world-beater that it is! Let's do it."

With that—and to a level of appreciative applause drawn from depths of sycophancy even I would not have suspected—Dullar swept out.

Shelby was scanning his own BlackBerry.

"What is it?"

"You couldn't make it up."

"What?"

"Some kind of riot in Cairo," he said.

"But didn't you just . . . ?"

"Didn't I just!"

"You don't think?"

"I most certainly do think."

Marcel Duffie sidled over to us after signaling for a welcome break as waiters from Le Primerose delivered an unusually generous order of croissants, pains au chocolat, and vacuum flasks of coffee. The condemned man/woman made a hearty breakfast, etc. . . .

"So what do you think of that, Clancy, Shelby?" Duffie said, less gloating than usual since his own stellar fortunes now seemed to have fallen within the Dullar orbit.

"Well, Marcel," Shelby said. "Shoulders to the grindstone, noses to the wheel and all that."

"Can't you guys ever get serious?" Duffie said, but you could tell something in Shelby's reply worried him. "Shouldn't that be . . . ?" he began to say. "Oh, forget it."

CHAPTER TWENTY-TWO

The gathering lost some of its enthusiasm after our new Great Leader absented himself in the name of breaking news, leaving the staff to ingest its last free feed—a takeout *cenacolo*—and forcing his superiors to field any questions with well-practiced obfuscation. Fancy footwork, indeed. Only the muscular corps of hard-line Bolsheviks among the staff kept up the insistent drumbeat of vain demands for more detail on the downsizing, its aims in financial terms, its impact on EBITDA and net going forward, its opportunity cost and bottom-line ramifications, and its implications under paragraph this, subsection that, of some Napoleonic code. It was all part of a game I had seen often enough. The staff played the part of hard-bitten reporters tracking down iniquitous malpractice. The bosses just wished it could all be over. The rest sat glumly, heads downcast, fiddling with BlackBerrys and iPhones, probably e-mailing labor lawyers, or tweeting their availability to rival newspapers, glancing occasionally at the giant Graphic.net screen behind the bosses to see what all the fuss had been about to draw Gibson Dullar away from his moment of triumph.

I noticed that Jean-Louis, my tech buddy, had reentered the assembly with a slight smile—all the more terrifying for its rarity—etched on his impassive, dark features. He scanned the room until his eyes fell on mine. He winked and touched the side of his nose with his forefinger. My heart sank.

Then the screen changed.

I saw the headline first: "Crowds Demand Mubarak Ouster."

Then the byline: Gibson Dullar.

Then the text.

CAIRO—Defying Egypt's emergency laws, tens of thousands of protesters poured onto the streets of Cairo, flooding the central Tahrir Square and confronting police who used tear gas and water cannons against them.

"Mubarak out," many of them chanted, expressing the profound discontent that has arisen across a whole generation of young people in the Arab world with their autocratic and unbending rulers.

"We have had enough," one protester, Ahmed Mahmoud Moussa, 23, declared as he and others sent messages using Facebook and Twitter to urge friends and like-minded Egyptians to join them in their effort to end almost three decades of Mr. Mubarak's increasingly ironfisted rule.

"Enough is enough is enough," he said . . .

"Well, fuck you, Gib," Shelby said, almost admiringly.

"And the horse you rode in on," I added in support.

As one, the three bosses heading up the meeting swiveled in their chairs to follow the massed gaze of their soon-to-be-depleted work-force.

The piece was well displayed, clamoring for attention below a large headline. A file picture of Mubarak accompanied it. There were wire service images of protesters pouring from mosques, doing battle with police on Cairo's bridges. Clouds of tear gas, white and cobalt blue, engulfed young men hurling rocks. Panoramic views from high buildings showed people like ants, teeming in Tahrir Square. Smoke rose from an official-looking edifice on the banks of the Nile, flowing placidly by as it had during the reigns of kings and pharaohs, viceroys and pashas; as it had when Hakim's fire con-sumed the city. Lesser headlines from agency reports spoke of White House concern, but no talk of a Security Council meeting. I noticed that many sections of the text were faintly highlighted to indicate links to related articles and websites. Gibson Dullar had been busy indeed. And Jena, too.

"Now this is the sort of thing we are talking about," Stephanie Curtis said enthusiastically, turning back to the staff. "It's that get-up-and-go we expect from someone like Gibson Dullar, leading—as he put it, I think—from the front. What's the term you journalists have for it? Whippy-whamby? Whatever. It's the kind of example I know we all want to follow going forward. It's the sort of fine international journalism that will distinguish us from our competitors with its speed, grace, and accuracy."

"It's theft," Shelby said under his breath. "It's sheer plagiarism." His voice was rising but his remonstrations didn't reach the ears of Stephanie Curtis.

"This is the kind of page that will beat the competition's pants— sorry, beat them hands down," she proclaimed.

Jean-Louis moved toward her, the soul of helpfulness, linking her laptop to a control box so that she could move the cursor around the big screen.

"Thank you, er, Jena," she said, glancing at his laminated ID tag with the practiced double vision of a longtime conference schmoozer, looking interlocutors in the eye while absorbing their ID info from badges around their necks.

"*Je vous en prie,*" he said.

"Speak of the devil."

Gibson Dullar sauntered back into the room. He was just concluding a conversation on his cell phone, winding up some exchange with thanks and farewells in Arabic. "*Shukran, Gamal habibi. Ma'salaam.*"

"My stringer!" Shelby choked. "Gamal! He even stole my stringer!" I held him back physically, like I was used to doing on the ranch with some over-frisky colt. Thanks to his illness, it was easier than it had once been, but still not without challenges.

"We were just saying, Gib, er, Gibson," Stephanie resumed, "that this has been an example of what we are hoping to achieve on Star.com once it has merged with Graphic.net. Maybe you could talk us through it."

"Well, the credit isn't all mine," Dullar said, leaning over Stephanie Curtis to take control of her laptop's trackpad. He scrolled the cursor down the big screen, looking casually across at Shelby. Maybe a peace offering, a contributor line, I thought. Maybe just some small thing to head off a volcanic outburst from Shelby. But no: "Gamal Nakhoul contributed reporting from Cairo." That was it. Nothing else. No Shelby. No credit. Only the challenge: accuse me of plagiarism and let's see who wins. But how the hell had he gotten it out of Shelby's private Homepatch?

"Well, that is generous of you, indeed, Gibson. To a fault. The kind of collegiality we would all like to see when our two websites merge as one," Stephanie Curtis said, glancing pointedly toward me and Shelby. "Maybe you could explain the links."

At her side, Green and Potts nodded and glowed. The meeting could have had no better outcome than this display of uber-journalism by their chosen one.

Dullar swiveled the cursor around the page in concentric circles of ever-decreasing size, as if he were some Svengali hypnotizing the assembled staffers who followed the digital arrow with rapt attention.

"Now this is a new thing," he said as the cursor came to rest on his own byline. "This is the kind of thing we can all aspire to: a link to our own biog pages so that the reader gets a sense of who is telling the story. My name won't always be here, I can assure you of that. Quite the opposite, in fact. There'll be lots of room for new blood on the merged website"—I glanced at Shelby, but his rage had left him staring furiously ahead—"so this is just an example of the way we can all of us cement our professional reputation and add value to the report. So let's get liftoff."

With a flourish he clicked on his byline. But instead of his biography, the huge screen instantly filled with a single image of Gibson Dullar grinning up at the camera he seemed to be holding in his hand from the rumpled pillows of some boudoir, and next to him, asleep on his scarred chest, the tousled half-profile of a partner.

I noticed Jean-Louis fiddling with his BlackBerry, trying to look as if he wasn't.

Around the world, wherever people were logged on to us—and there were millions of them, every minute, every hour, every day— they would be seeing the same images.

Gibson Dullar tried to move the cursor to the top-right corner of the screen to close the page, but it refused to obey him, zigzagging in ever-crazier patterns, alighting on highlighted sections of text, clicking them open, then closing them.

Every image showed Gibson Dullar in the company of a partner, usually at some advanced stage of the romantic pursuit. With an almost physical lurching of the gut, I recognized the photos on the SD card taken from the camera he had sought to destroy at the ranch. So did Dullar, and he looked for me among his assembled staff. Almost too quickly to see, he ran a finger across his neck and pointed to me. The beginnings of a grin spread across Shelby's face, but there was nothing to smile about: he did not know what was coming. Somewhere in that great mess of vulgar gigabyte obscenity was an image showing Gibson Dullar visiting with Faria Duclos in her wheelchair. Somewhere there were snapshots of Shelby and my own wife bowed over lines of cocaine.

"Let's get out of here," I whispered.

"Wouldn't miss this for all the tea in China, old sport."

I looked across the room at Jean-Louis. His face was lit with a tight, maniacal grin as he spun the click-ball on his BlackBerry like a kid overdosing on PlayStation. No one said anything. The huge screen held everyone in that room in its thrall—a hybrid of Tarantino and backstreet Hamburg. Whatever people had expected from this encounter with the new reality, the ultimate digital peep show was not part of it.

The images flickered one after another. Dullar and this starlet, that model. Dullar and two or three persons unknown (hard to tell from the tangle of legs and bosoms) in a hotel room with a distant view of Saint Basil's on Red Square. How long would it take before the slide show flipped to Dullar with Faria Duclos? Here, always with a different partner, was Dullar in a cornfield, brandishing a cob to cover his overtaxed virility; Dullar on the back of a truck in the African bush, recognizable, if blurred, underneath a tarp covering boxes of ammunition but not the modesty of a female guerrilla fighter; Dullar in bed with the wife of—

"Take it down!" Green shrieked. "Take this whole fucking obscene tissue of fabrication and falsification down. Take it down globally. Now. *Take. It. Down. Now.*"

Technicians scurried, made phone calls, tapped urgent commands into laptops. Every time they sent their digital orders, some higher power seemed to countermand them. Surreptitiously, Jean-Louis worked the omnipotent BlackBerry. The screen was frozen on an image of Dullar and a woman whose face was not shown but who seemed to be   intimately recognizable to at least one of our visitors.

"Take it down," Potts barked now.

Bit by bit the screen dissolved into black, until only a single lurid grimace remained in the space that had displayed Graphic.net. Then, finally, across the globe, the site went dark. Just before it was able to offer up its secrets from the apartment of Faria Duclos. Or from my stud farm.

Dullar strode over to us.

"I will crucify you for this," he said.

"Nothing to do with me," I said.

"Whambo-zambo," said Shelby. "Zambo-zippo!"

Hours later, when Graphic.net had finally been purged of the hidden links to a mysterious phantom site hosted on a server somewhere in Germany, it reopened with an editor's note proclaiming that a malicious cyber-attack using falsified, computer-generated images had been thwarted by the fast work of Graphic.net editors and technicians under the command of Stephanie Curtis. The note referred to what it called the first-known example of a virus-driven porno-prank and suggested darkly that the culprits might be professional rivals.

The note was signed by Gibson Dullar, Global Editor of News, Graphic.net/Star.com.

Getting out of the building was tricky that day. The management called in cyber experts   from the French secret police and the American embassy's FBI staff. Every single employee was physically searched for incriminating materials. We stood in line, awaiting our turn to be frisked for tell-tale USB sticks or data cards, like we were boarding flights after some global terrorist scare. I looked at Jean-Louis and he looked at me as the mail guy with his sack of letters and packages strolled casually by the checkpoint at the newspaper's rear entrance, tossed it into his little yellow van, and drove off. I don't know where Jean-Louis had been sending his version of the incriminating USB stick, but I knew where mine was headed: if it made it across the Atlantic, it would land at the home of a very senior figure at the *Graphic* who would be very interested indeed to learn—and act on—the truth. I had even signed a note offering to testify in any internal inquiry.

Across the newsroom, tech-sleuths scoured hard drives for traces of the images and I prayed that my efforts to delete the full file had been successful. From the *Graphic*'s point of view, it was much too late to put the evil cyber-genie back into the bottle. Word of Jean-Louis's jape had sped around the world with such remarkable speed that he must have had accomplices in the hacking community just waiting to harvest the images. The whole sequence had found its way onto YouTube, and the bosses back in New York were seeking an injunction to block it, but it broke all records for individual views. In polite circles, the images became known as the Dullar Dossier, but there were plenty of other less demure monikers: Willygate, Beater Version, and so forth. The only thing that could slow its spread was the massive pressure to see it. Collectively, the *Graphic* management was trying its damnedest to brazen out the fiasco. Company spin doctors hinted at Mafia involvement, at maneuvers by rivals to depress the company's stock in advance of a hostile takeover of the *Graphic* by the *Wall Street Journal* or the *New York Times*. The tabloids and the media-watching websites were having a field day, pointing out that the *Graphic*'s own high-minded editorials had long defended pornographers' protection under the First Amendment, so the paper could hardly complain that its website had become, however briefly, a celebration of those same rights. "Graphic Graphics at *Graphic*!"

"Oops!"

"Graphic Gotcha!"

"News Hound Bares All!"

"Nonstop Nudes at Nonstop News."

"*Graphic* Exposé—And How!"

Some attacks were distinctly personal. Every editor Dullar had ever trashed scrambled for payback.

"Scud-muffin or Teeny Weeny?"

I guessed it would be that kind of jibe that left Dullar smarting the most—and made his vengeance all the more inevitable.

His partners, mostly, were exonerated as victims of a cruel and perverted power play to humiliate womankind. A post-feminist blogger called Dullar a throwback to days best forgotten when women were scorned as mere objects of sexual gratification.

"Sneaky Snapper: Castration Not Enough."

And the heavyweight websites found a way of linking to YouTube under the guise of pondering serious moral matters.

"'Graphic' Attack Raises Many Questions of Cyber-Security," the *Washington Post* ruminated.

"Web Security Industry Foresees Boom," said the *Wall Street Journal.* "Stocks Rise in Cyber-Sleuth Companies."

I thought Shelby would be in a chipper mood as we finally exited the security lines under the baleful gaze of Marcel Duffie, whose moment of managerial triumph had been transformed into a fiasco for which he knew he would have to pay whether the fault was his or not.

But Shelby seemed distracted. He said something about having some unfinished business to attend to and turned down my offer of a celebratory drink.

"Don't want to be too late twice over, old sport," he said, but did not stick around long enough for me to ask him what on earth he meant.

CHAPTER TWENTY-THREE

IT WAS ONLY A MATTER OF TIME BEFORE IT ALL CAME TO A SHOW-down and I like to think that in some far-flung bar, among the very few who know it, the tale of the Cairo Crackdown is still told with the requisite degree of awe for its leading players.

The day started with the routine coffee and bitching at Le Primerose.

"I don't know how long I can take this, Dullar strutting around like goddamn Hitler." Shelby was particularly bitter that, after Dullar's slide show, the masthead had introduced a new set of security rules for publishing articles on the web. Up until now, it had been enough for me and Shelby to sign off on each other's work before it was posted, guaranteeing a measure of collegial oversight. But after the unauthorized streaming of the rogue's gallery, the regulations changed. Like some kind of triple-key, cold war arrangement to arm nuclear weapons, no item would henceforth be posted on the site without the story being read and approved by three figures of a certain rank. In practical terms, that meant that every time Joe and I wanted to post an item, we had to seek a sign-off from Duffie or Dullar. As if the whole mess were our fault. Or we were not to be trusted.

"I mean, why do we have to ask Dullar or Duffie for permission to do our job? We never had to before. What do they know? What if it was the other way round and they wanted to post and we held up their stuff?"

"Well, maybe that will happen one day and they'll see how dumb their rules are."

"Sooner or later there'll be the O.K. Corral moment, Ed. You know it. I know it."

"And you'll lose—*we'll* lose—if you let it get to you."

I had seen it before – the buildup to cataclysmic newsroom bat-tles that left no room for truces or prisoners. If you were associat-ed with one side or another, you went up with the winner, or down with the loser. I had a lot at stake. I was too closely associated with Shelby now to avoid sharing whatever destiny awaited him. All I could do was try to warn him that, right now, we were not exactly on the firmest ground.

"Look, Joe. About those Dullar photos . . ."

He paused with his coffee cup half raised and a smile began to form.

"You? Ed Clancy? You did that?"

"Well, not exactly, Joe. Let's just say I would not confirm or deny."

"I'll be damned. At least we went down fighting, Ed, me bucko, you old Irish son-of-a-gun."

"Just so you wouldn't say I never told you."

"Hell, no. I'm proud of you, Ed. Never knew you had it in you."

I could hardly confess that it was all Jean-Louis' doing. And I still did not tell him about the photos Jean-Louis had not quite suc-ceeded in publishing. There was no point in reminding him that Gibson Dullar had been visiting where he had not with Faria Duclos. Or photographing Shelby snorting coke with his best friend's wife.

I left the bar before Shelby and headed on to the *Star* to get the Wurlitzer whirring for another day at the coalface. (Metaphors, Clancy, rein in those runaway metaphors!)

I punched in the entry code on the numeric pad to enter the newsroom. At that hour, it was my fief, my exclusive terrain, unchal-lenged. There is a special feel to an empty space, a deep stillness as if, overnight, everything that could expand or contract or crackle or rustle has done what it has to do. The air is still, undisturbed by movement, or whispers, or breathing. Hard drives do not hum. There is no faint tap of a copyeditor's nips and tucks. No hoots of bonhomie. No whispers of conspiracy.

It wasn't like that today.

From the corner office that Gibson Dullar had taken over, rele-gating Marcel Duffie to a space next door with a lower ranking along the corridor of power, I heard voices in a low register, the way people talk in a cathedral or a museum. Or a plotter's dark corner.

Dullar. Duffie. In too early for a routine day.

I sidled to within earshot.

"They want something big, Gib."

"I got it."

"What?"

"Marcel. It's a biggie. Exclusive of the decade. This'll knock their socks off."

"And it's kosher?"

"One hundred percent, Marcel. How could you imagine other-wise?"

"And you'll write it? Your byline? Paris dateline?"

"The Paris dateline dot com!"

"So all we need to do is to get those klutzes to post it."

"After the Argentine soy vote debacle, they'll do as they're told. We only need one of them, after all. Three sign-offs can't be that dif-ficult on a story like this."

"What's it about?"

"Egypt. We'll scoop the world."

"Now that is a biggie."

"Never been done before, Marcel. No one has ever—but ever—gotten wind of what we have. But *I* have."

"Wow," Duffie said. I thought I detected a hint of queasiness in his voice: scoops can be dangerous things, like the Argentine soy vote.

Behind my vantage point, the door burst open and Shelby marched into the newsroom, carrying a black canvas tote bag that banged against the furnishings with a metallic clang. I recognized it from the trunk of his car. I beckoned him to be silent, but it was too late to prevent Dullar and Duffie from overhearing his approach.

"What's in the bag, Joe?" I asked him, warily.

"Office ornamentation."

"Oh, shit. Not the AK-47?"

"You were right, Ed. I don't need it. You take it. You stash it. Dump it. Whatever. Really. I wiped it. No prints. Clean as a whistle."

Any day but today, Joe, I was thinking.

"Sure thing, old buddy," I said.

Shelby laid the black tote bag on his desk. The zip was not completely closed and I could see, quite clearly, the distinctive front sight of the AK-47 peeking from within.

"Promise me one thing, Joe."

"What's that?"

"If someone files bad news, don't shoot the messenger."

He laughed.

"Whambo-zambo, Ed. Right?"

"Sure, Joe. Zippo-zambo."

Today was supposed to be one of our big days—a set piece exercise carrying forward important breaking news into a new day and escorting its progression from incremental, overnight updates to its final iteration as a rounded, crafted piece embracing the facts, the analysis, the color from correspondents and stringers fanning out in Tahrir Square and Mohandeseen and Zamalek. We would point out that this was the umpteenth day of protest; that the president, besieged in his palace, had shown no readiness to leave; that the army's position remained ambiguous.

Shelby was fretting. From Beirut he had ranged across the Middle East. He spoke a measure of what he called "roadblock Arabic"—key phrases such as "don't shoot," "no, I am Canadian, not American," and "which way to the airport?" (He once told me that, during the civil war Lebanon, he had worked out how to say, "What's a nice thirteen-year-old like you doing with a Kalashnikov like that?" But he had never dared deploy this linguistic gambit.)

He wanted to be there now, on the barricades, among the chanting masses who raised their shoes aloft to signal their scorn and hatred of their leader, and who did heroic battle with the regime's goons seeking to dislodge them from Tahrir Square. He wanted to be there at this moment when history teetered on its fulcrum, when the greatest change affecting an entire region was in the air. And he wanted to be there alongside his old buddies, on yet another gallop along the final furlong and across the finishing line. He wanted to see and breathe and smell the truth among the ragged masses who swelled to seek the ouster of their leader, among the soldiers atop their tanks, fingering automatic weapons. He wanted to be on hand when the worst came to the worst. He wanted to preface a paragraph with the phrase "Not since the Arab revolt in the time of T. E. Lawrence . . ."

But this was one war they would have to fight without the presence of his avenging sword.

"All we can do," he said that morning, "is make sure we don't screw up."

At the time, it sounded like an existential statement. With some resignation, he stowed his traveling Nerval collection on a shelf above his head, within easy reach in case of need, the old favorites—*Les Chimères*, *Aurélia*, and *Voyage en Orient*—and settled at his computer.

Usually we worked with a stringer in Cairo—Gamal Nakhoul—but this time we had an army of our own, including some of the *Graphic*'s most gifted correspondents. I didn't like to point out that they were the new generation, that this was their time, just as it had once been Shelby's turn to nudge aside his elders in Saigon or Beirut. I didn't like to ask, either, how he would have managed with the cane and the limp if the mob turned or the army opened fire and he had to run for safety across the Nile bridges. Who would avenge the avenging sword then?

He was keeping an eye on a couple of Arabic satellite channels. One of them flashed a bulletin: "President to speak to nation." We worked it quickly into a revised version of the story. Hit keys. I called Duffie to give us the third sign-off. Then watched our handicraft emerge in the digital perfection of the web.

"Wonder what he'll say?"

"Crackdown." I hadn't heard Gibson Dullar's approach but he was standing in the doorway.

"He's going to announce a crackdown," Dullar pronounced. "He's going to say he won't leave. He's going to order the army to open fire if anyone disagrees. I got it from a source. Copper-bottomed. We can go with it."

I looked at Shelby. He looked at me. We both looked at the Dullard. "Crackdown?"

"Check Clefstik. It's in there. I wrote it. It's ready to go. Like now. We'll look so cool. Fifteen minutes ahead of the TV broadcast."

Shelby clicked on the story in his Clefstik box—one step away from publication to the edification of 18 million potential web visitors. On the newsroom wall, the bank of never-quite-synchronized clocks ticked their way toward the TV broadcast in global time.

Western Europe, 10.45

London, 09.46

New York, 04.44

Hong Kong, 17.48.

In a matter of minutes, the president's pronouncement would be known across the world. But in the digital age—as in the old wire service days—scoops were measured in split seconds. A full minute spanned the gulf between victory and defeat. Fifteen minutes constituted triumph on the scale of the D-Day landings, the liberation of Berlin, twice over.

True enough, Dullar had composed his breathless scoop. Under the Paris dateline. Dot-com version.

By Gibson Dullar

PARIS—The president of Egypt has resolved to remain in office, defying days of protests on the streets of his capital, telling pro-democracy demonstrators that he has ordered the military to use force, including live ammunition, against them.

He will make his announcement this morning in a radio and television broadcast at 11:00 local time, 5:00 in New York, in Cairo, the Egyptian capital, sources said.

"Sources?" Shelby said. "What kind of sources?"

"My sources."

I looked at Shelby. After everything he had said about the slicing and dicing of truth on the web from the Argentine soy vote onward, I was fairly sure that he would assent—it was not his byline that would appear on the story if it was wrong, and Dullar's suspicions about his pirated SD card hardly left us in a position of great political strength. Posting the article—the great scoop—would offer a truce, a complicity. And if it was wrong, Dullar would be to blame and we could invoke the Nuremberg Defense: Only following orders, m'lud.

But if you looked carefully into the entrails of the editing system, the digital trail would leave no doubt that, even if Dullar wrote it, Shelby published it.

"We can't post this," Shelby said.

"What do you mean *can't*? Don't forget I'm in charge around here, Shelby. What I say goes. And I say post this."

"And I say no." Shelby had drawn himself upright, canting toward his desk in the clumsy struggle of the neurologically damaged for dignity and verticality.

"How many sign-offs do you have?"

"Me and Marcel. So we just need one of you. Ed?"

"Lemme look at that again." The showdown had come sooner than I thought.

"We have fifteen minutes," Dullar was saying. "You guys screw this and you lose us the scoop of the century."

"We can't use sources like that," Shelby said. "We need better sources. We couldn't use unidentified sources like this in print. We can't on the site. Forget the three sign-offs. I smell a phony here."

"These are confidential sources."

"Sources where?"

The question made sense. I had long suspected that Dullar was close—too close—to some intelligence services in the Middle East who did not exactly have Arab well-being as their top priority.

"That's for me to know, Shelby. Now post."

"You to know? What is this? Some kind of reading the bones, the Ides of March?"

"Intel," Dullar said.

"Whose intel?"

"Work it out, for Chrissakes."

"No," said Shelby. "It's too iffy. We'll look stupid if it's wrong."

"And we'll be heroes if it's right. I can't believe I'm hearing this from the famous Shelby of Saigon. I am giving you a direct order. Post it."

"No."

Dullar's face had reddened and his fists were clenching and unclenching.

"Listen, Shelby. One day I'll nail you and Clancy's sad asses for that shit with the photos on the website. But before then—like today— I will fucking crucify you with New York if you do not post this story. On my direct orders. If you do not post this, you will be damaging the very reputation we are trying to restore after that fiasco with the photos. Fast, fluent, fact. And we are only going to get that if we cut the mustard on breaking news. There's no other kind. Breaking news is gold dust. Anything else is gravel, secondhand. You either soar with the eagles or go peck shit with the chickens. So publish."

"And be damned," I murmured.

"We can hardly do a recount on martial law, Gib." Shelby was trying to be reasonable, but reason was not working that morning. "I mean, think about it. "

The clocks had crawled onward: 10.48 in Western Europe, 17.51 in Hong Kong. Only twelve, or nine, minutes to go.

"I said publish."

"I said no. What if this is a plant? We announce there's going to be a crackdown. It hits the web. The protesters see it and go nuts. And there *is* a crackdown. How do we know we're not being manipulated?"

Dullar lurched across a corner of Shelby's desk to grab him by the lapel of his jacket. In the process, he knocked the black tote bag to the floor. The gun sight poked its snout farther out of the bag. Outside the glass cubicle, I could see that Duffie, Gloria Beeching, and one or two other early birds had gathered, jaws dropping, to witness the two bulls locking horns in the kraal.

"Listen, you prick, Shelby. Lemme tell you. If you screw this scoop, I will be straight on the phone to the masthead in New York. Curtis. Potts. Green. I will spell out every last detail of the Argentine soy vote imbroglio. I will explain just how you invented facts to cover up a mistake and distorted history in the most reprehensible of ways. Then I will leak the story to the *Post* and the *Journal* and I will ensure that you are out on your ass. Ruined. No lunch in this town or any town. Whatever rep you once had you can forget. You'll be unemployable. Even hicksville J-schools won't touch you."

"What about Clancy?"

"What *about* Clancy?"

"He had nothing to do with that."

"He doesn't count. He's *Star*. This is *Graphic* business."

I have to admit, that hurt.

Dullar had started to roar.

"Do you admit it, Shelby?"

"Admit what?"

"The soy vote fiasco."

"Sure, I admit it. I admit that once—just once and in a way that did not harm anyone—I cheated. I played the old Interpress game, just like Clay Brewster: whambo-zambo. I don't even care to go into the number of ways you have cheated over the years, Dullard, you double-dealing phony."

"What did you call me?"

"I called you what you are."

The Scoop was shrinking. The clocks had advanced further. We had only nine, or six, minutes to go. Dullar's foot caught against the tote bag lying on the floor between them. The AK-47 slid onto the floor in all its lightly oiled malevolence. Both men went for the weapon, but the less-challenged Dullar got there first. Shelby stumbled back, landing abruptly in his swivel chair.

"So this is great, Shelby! You bring firearms into the office. Wait till they hear about this in New York: 'Former Warhorse Goes Insane; Plans Shooting Spree.'"

Whatever else Dullar had learned over the years, he certainly was no slouch with the English of headlines, nor with the working of the world's favorite assault rifle. He snapped out the clip, which we always describe as banana-shaped, to reveal a full load of 7.62 mm (intermediate) shells, some of them tipped in red to denote tracer. He cleared the breech with a slick move of the slide. The metallic clicking sound—so often the prelude to executions and shootouts in distant places—made my stomach lurch. This was much too close for comfort. Then he slotted the clip back into the rifle, pulled the slide back to load a round into the chamber, and began flicking the safety between its three positions—safe, single-fire, and rock-and-roll.

"Locked and loaded, Shelby. So who wants to play Charlie?"

"It's decommissioned," I heard myself shouting. "It can't fire. It's useless. Tell him, Joe. For Chrissakes, tell him it can't fire."

Shelby looked toward me and slowly shook his head.

Across the newsroom, beyond the glass cubicle, a lone TV screen tuned to a twenty-four-hour news channel was running through a weather report. I noticed that it was overcast in Cairo. Sunny in Paris.

Even in my own ears, my voice sounded whiny.

"But you told me it was decommissioned, Shelby. You told me it wouldn't fire."

"See, Clancy. He lies to you. His best buddy. His protector."

Shelby shrugged and raised his eyebrows.

"Sorry, Ed. I guess I should have told you. Time you left. Let him go, Dullar. This is between you and me."

"Is this some kind of sick game?" I thought vividly of Marie-Claire, of her embrace, of how very much I wanted not to leave her widowed, how much I wanted—right now—to skedaddle and head home and put my arms around her and hide us both under the king-size down comforter until it was all over. But I knew that if I did that, I would never be able to admit to her that I had cut and run. And, if he survived, I would never be able to look Shelby in the eye.

"No game, Clancy. This is big boy's stuff. Go."

Dullar traversed the rifle so that it was pointing right at my navel. I thought of how quickly the pink zip of tracer fire would cross the few inches between me and the snout of the barrel, rending the flesh, beginning to tumble before it blew out my spine. Would I hear it? See it? Or would I just be dead and know nothing? And when I was dead, would Dullar turn the AK-47 on Shelby and open fire so that bullets ricocheted around the newsroom, bouncing off battered file cabinets, steel desks, tacky computer screens, exposed air-con ducting, photocopiers, printers, people. Outside the glass cubicle, our small audience had begun to retreat. I noticed Duffie raising his cell phone to take a surreptitious photograph. I didn't want him taking a snap of me abandoning Joe Shelby. We had survived the Argentine Soy Vote Affair and the Great Crash. Together we had charted bombs and bangs and bloodshed across the globe. I had been with Shelby in the heat of the fire to rescue Elvire Récamier. If I had not shied from that escapade, why should I duck out now? And if I scuttled out now, how would I ever live up to what Marie-Claire expected of her men?

"I'll stay."

My voice sounded as if it was coming from the bottom of a deep, dry, dark well.

"Then you're a fool, Clancy. Put the gun down, Gib." Shelby had risen again from his desk, very slowly. "This isn't about Cairo, is it, Gib? I know what it's about. You know what it's about. It's about Faria."

"Publish."

"No."

Six, or three, minutes remained until the president appeared on television. And the winner is . . .

Post-traumatic stress disorder.

Russian roulette.

The loaded chamber.

The TV in the newsroom had switched to live coverage, the cameras showing a podium with a single microphone but no one there to use it.

A banner line under the screen said: "Cairo. Live. Presidential Address."

"Sure, you can tell them about the Argentine thing," Shelby was saying. "So what? I made a mistake. I'll pay for it. But it was one mistake and I relearned a lesson I should never have forgotten. What we do—online, in print, you name it—is fact, the plain unadorned fact, as much as we can demonstrate it to be fact. To be true. That's the only thing that keeps us honest. And if we're not honest, we have nothing to justify what we do. We have no right to ask our readers to trust us. Trust is what it comes down to. It takes years to build it. Seconds to destroy. And sources don't qualify. Mysterious unnamed informants? A single dubious source? Some Mossad guy whispering in your ear doesn't cut it. There's too much at stake. On the ground. For our people in the square. For what you might call the truth. You know that, Gib. So do I. If we let this monster of the web push us into untruths, then we've lost. If we cut the corners, there'll be nothing left. Print'll go down and digital with it. The only commodity we have is honesty."

"That's right, Dullar," I heard myself saying. "We can't play games. Our readers are too smart. They know too much. The web has put us all inside one big glass house with the world peering in, and if we don't live up to those standards, the rocks are going to start crashing in."

"Quit the philosophy and post the fucking story. Both of you." Dullar had stopped fidgeting with the safety. I guessed it was on single shot. Outside the glass cubicle, Duffie had led his platoon of spectators out of harm's way.

I could see them crouching low behind a desk.

Five, or two, minutes. A man was approaching the microphone in Cairo, tapping it.

"Is it worth it, Gib? Two minutes."

"Two minutes for a world exclusive. Paris dateline."

"Two minutes to destroy everything we are trying to build up. Your own career."

"Don't talk to me about careers, Shelby, you conniving snake in the grass. All your career you've looked down your nose at me, sneered. All the time you tried to ace me. With Faria. Well. Did you know I went to see her before she died? But you didn't, did you? You didn't go to her even when she was quite literally dying to see you. And do you know what she said, Shelby? Thanks, Gib, but no thanks. Even then when you were ignoring her and she was dying, she still wanted to hear about you. She was still waiting. And now you have the nerve to come between me and a story."

A man had walked up to the microphone in Cairo. He looked

pale, spectral, with dark bags under his hooded eyes, his thinning hair swept back from his forehead. Even at this distance from the TV set, you could see it was not the president.

Two minutes, or none.

"In the name of God the merciful, the compassionate," the man began in Arabic. A voiceover offered simultaneous translation.

"Post it. There's still time," Dullar shrieked. But Shelby held up a hand to silence him.

"Citizens," the man was saying, "during these very difficult circumstances Egypt is going through, President Hosni Mubarak has decided to step down from the office of President of the Republic and has charged the high council of the armed forces to administer the affairs of the country."

"What?" Dullar said

"May God help everybody," the man on the television said.

"Amen," I said.

"But it was supposed to be martial law," Dullar said, sounding puzzled. "They told me. In Jerusalem. Just for you, Gib. A scoop. The big one."

He stepped back a pace, his fingers uncurling from the unsafe AK-47 so that it dropped to the ground, firing off a single round with a deafening blast and a whoosh of muzzle flash. The wall of Shelby's glassed-in cubicle dissolved in a starburst, spreading instantly from the small hole that marked the exit route of the bullet. Then the entire fractured window slid to the floor with an amplified crackling noise that reminded me of parents collecting kids' discarded birthday wrapping paper.

Ricochets generally move too fast to be visible in an enclosed space, but this was a tracer round that left a sudden comet impression of zigzagging pink light, like a migraine, zipping around the newsroom. It whizzed into an exposed air-con duct and bounced off of it: ping!—and not just from the computer messaging system. It flew very briefly along a metal desk, plowing a quick furrow through a pile of back copies like some phantom editor underscoring felicitous headlines and atrocious bloopers. I noticed Duffie and his acolytes hitting the deck in terror and wondered why their reactions were considerably quicker than ours.

The bullet, tumbling on its way, tracing its trail of bright color, pierced a water cooler that became a horizontal fountain, careened with a dull clang into a metal file cabinet, and continued on to the plasma screen of a distant TV set, piercing it through the heart and abruptly ending the moment of news and history from Cairo. Then you knew what was happening but could do nothing about it because it was all too quick. Like a homing pigeon—that damn pigeon again—the bullet turned back on itself, zingo-zambo. Its power was beginning to wane as it headed back roughly to whence it came, as if it espied three adult males transfixed, rabbitlike, in its headlight gaze. In retrospect—and this impression may be as reliable as our account of the Argentine soy vote saga—you could see it but not move. You knew where it was heading but could not run or hide. One of us, surely, would take it. It would all end in tears with that rending of flesh and spurting of arterial blood that spelled the final moment. Heart shot. Head shot. Flesh wound. You could run through the options but not escape, as if your mind was in supercharged high-octane overdrive while your arms and legs had stalled.

"Shit," Shelby said as the bullet flew back into his office through the space where the glass partition had once been. "Where the fuck did that go?"

The answer came from the shelf above his head.

The collection of Nerval's writings shuddered, then fell onto Shelby's desk, the rear of the bullet just visible in the O of *Voyage en Orient* and its tip peeking out of *Les Chimères*. In the silence, Dullar snickered. I thought of a large Jameson on the rocks somewhere far away. Shelby gazed at his old and faithful volumes as if he understood their purpose for the first time.

"*Merci, Gérard*," Shelby said. "*Tu m'as sauvé la vie.*" You saved my life.

Things got a little crazy after that. And not just in Egypt.

"You told me that thing wouldn't fire," I shouted at Shelby.

"That's what the guy who gave it to me said."

"Which guy?"

"Does it matter?"

He had the telephone jammed to his ear, taking notes from Cairo.

"Crackdown," Dullar moaned and slipped to the floor. "How was I to know . . ."

Shelby was calling the web producers.

"Post an Alert! Mubarak quits! What? Sure we got three sign-offs. Me and Clancy and Dullar. Right, Gib?"

Dullar replied with something between a snigger and a groan.

"Joe." My mouth was dry, my voice a choked whisper. "Wakey-wakey. I mean, shit, man, we have something of a crisis here. Gunfire. Newsroom. End of career. That kind of thing. You know?"

"News comes first, old sport. Zippo-zambo-whambo-AK-ambo."

He was banging furiously on his keyboard. To an outsider he might have seemed to be embarked on a passable imitation of those apocryphal chimpanzees working hard to conjure *Hamlet* from a million typewriters. But considering the circumstances, the product was fluent enough.

"Nothing like a spot of gunfire to focus the mind, Ed. Wouldn't you say?"

After 18 days of building protest by hundreds of thousands of Egyptians, President Hosni Mubarak stepped down, ending almost three decades of dictatorial rule.

An announcement by Vice President Omar Suleiman on state television drew a huge roar of approval from crowds massed in Tahrir Square who had made his ouster their central demand in the Arab world's first example of popular revolution.

The President's announcement was a clear victory for an uprising that had no clear leaders and relied on online social networking tools to spread its message of dissent.

"He has gone. He has gone," cried one protester. "God be praised."

The revolution's triumph provoked deep concern in Israel. But the United States welcomed it.

"Dateline, Joe? What dateline?"

"Paris. The Paris dateline. Dot com. First take. Here it comes. Get the third sign-off from Duffie."

"Byline?"

"What do you think, Ed?"

"By Joe Shelby."

Then Shelby was barking down the phone again to the web producers. He had acquired a sudden, impressive fluency with all the gizmos of the production process—dummy tags, phantom pings. "More follows. But let's get this up now!"

He turned to me after hanging up. He put a finger to his lips. He had a theory that someone may have developed surveillance techniques that kept phone lines open for ten seconds after callers thought the connection was closed. Imagine, if that were true, the number of times ostensibly courteous conversations would be followed by inadvertent epithets: asshole, dodo, etc. If everyone found out what other people really thought of them, the world would not be a happier place for it. Without hypocrisy, after all, where would the human interrelationship be?

"Cover. We had to have cover. That story will hold them. I've got the Cairo crew scrambling for updates. It's their story, after all. I guess I finally have to admit it."

"But at least on the first go-round you are the Paris correspondent."

"You know what, Ed? You're right. I am the Paris correspondent—for the next ten minutes. Now, let's get this crap sorted."

He gestured to Dullar.

My political antennae told me that this ought to be the final settling of scores, the ultimate disgracing of Dullar.

All it needed was one call from Shelby to some super-boss: Dullar insisting at gunpoint on a wrong story; Dullar opening fire with a supposedly decommissioned weapon that was about to be handed over to the authorities. The details would be lost in the artful telling. The story that would linger would be a crazed Dullar abusing his authority to insist on an erroneous post—and Shelby, the white knight, standing his ground for the forces of honor, justice, light. Truth.

And when Dullar went down, so would the tormentor Duffie.

But Shelby surprised me.

Duffie was in his glass-walled office, his head in his hands. Gloria Beeching was nearby, looking pensive. Shelby called his extension.

"Duffie, get Dullar out of here. Into some clinic. Rehab. Whatever. Strain of work. Post-traumatic stress disorder. Too much boom-boom. Too much bang-bang. Right to the finish. Bang-bang in the newsroom. Get Gloria to help. Mum's the word. Okay?"

Then he turned to me.

"Marie-Claire still got those weirdo spooky contacts?"

"What has my wife got to do with this, Shelby?"

"Covering your ass, that's all. We need to dispose of a recently fired weapon. Dump it. Okay?"

I rang her cell. There must have been something in my voice that communicated the urgency of my request for someone—anyone—to head over and pick up a certain item for delivery to the River Seine before the cops got wind of recent events.

Watching all this, Gloria Beeching must have figured her moment had come, for she sidled over to Marcel Duffie, entwined her arm in his, and whispered to him what I imagined was an offer he could not refuse, something along the lines of promotion, or death.

From the floor of Shelby's office, Dullar peered down that long, thousand-mile tunnel that had no light. I had not figured that he would deflate so quickly. Maybe it was the gunfire—the final round that broke the camel's neck, as Marcel might have said in one of his speeches. But there was a shifty look to him that made me think he saw the outcome as a decisive artful ploy: Who could argue with a nervous breakdown after the combat he had seen in his time? Who would not be sympathetic to the great warrior brought low?

We worked. Duffie worked. He issued a blanket three sign-off edict for all our stories. He made calls. He summonsed an ambulance. Shelby wrapped his hands in printer paper and lifted the AK-47, securing the safety catch and clearing the breech. Then he removed the clip and laid it next to his computer so that it rattled as he pounded the keyboards. I noticed that, with even greater reverence than before, he gathered up his Nervalia, complete with one exhausted round of 7.62 mm (intermediate) ammunition firmly embedded in it, enfolded it in the latest edition of the *Paris Star* and stuffed the package into his black tote bag The phones were going crazy with calls from our heroic staff in Cairo. My cell rang and Marie told me to expect a visitor, to have the package ready. The courier would bring the required shipping materials. She did not ask what the hell was going on and I was very proud of her for that.

With a blare of sirens and flashing lights, the ambulance arrived.

As the nurses surrounded Dullar, Shelby asked for a moment with him.

"Who torched Clancy's marquee, Gib?"

Dullar looked him in the eye. He handed over his gold lighter: "Who Dares Wins." I started toward him, determined to punch him out, as I should have done at the stud farm, but Shelby restrained me.

"Exhibit A, if it ever comes to it, Ed," he said, handing me the Cartier lighter, then turned back to Dullar. "I only wish Faria could have seen you for the shit you truly are."

"I at least went to visit. Or didn't your buddy here show you the photographs?"

Suddenly I had a question I wanted to ask. Urgently.

"Joe. When you told me about that suite at the Commodore in Beirut, what was the room number?"

"207," he said, quick as a flash. Joe never forgot a place of happy memories.

"Yeah, I got the photos, Gib," I said. "All of them. Especially the one of a hotel room door. 207, if I recall. Was that the one you gave to the torchers so they'd know where to play with fire?"

"Sweet Jesus," Shelby said and slumped back in his chair. "You, Gib. You bastard. And you slugged me, too. From behind."

"You are really so slow on the uptake, Joe," Dullar said. "No wonder you never quite made the big time."

Then they led him away.

Soon afterward a man whose face was hidden by the peak of a baseball cap and a pair of shades, a scarf wrapped high around the collar of his leather jacket, arrived with a shoulder bag full of bubble wrap, gaffer tape, and brown paper.

"Marie-Claire called. The name's Franjola, not that it matters."

"Can you dust for prints?" Shelby said.

"Sure."

"So dust it. Get me copies."

"You're Franjola? Nick Franjola?"

"The same. The ex. So it's all in the family. Kind of." He went about wrapping the rifle.

"Yeah, kind of."

I did not even want to begin contemplating the magnitude of the debt Marie-Claire had called in to secure his secret services.

Franjola left the newsroom, carrying with him the shattered plasma screen of the television set and a bag full of Kalashnikov.

"I'll kind of miss the old AK," Shelby said.

"You know this was a cover-up, Joe."

"I guess. But a cover-up in the name of the truth. The best kind."

After that we settled down to the normal routines of covering an Arab dictator hounded out of office by his own population.

Shelby and I rode down together in the elevator leading to the underground parking garage.

"What was that about photographs of Faria?"

"Just a happy snap, Joe, and she didn't look too happy."

"Should I have worried?"

"Not on the basis of the photograph," I said cautiously.

"Then on what basis?"

"That's something you'll have to work out for yourself."

Shelby had been tugged many ways since Faria's death. The police autopsy had found that she died after a stroke as her weakened systems and the prolonged inactivity caused by her neurological condition left her bloodstream prone to thrombosis. But then Ivar Bild had written an article in *Dagens Nyheter*, the Swedish newspaper, chronicling her final days and confessing both his readiness to offer her a lethal injection and her stubborn rejection of any outside intervention. He did not mention Gibson Dullar's visit. But he did quote her final words: "I broke my own heart when I broke yours."

"You know when I wrote that, Ed?"

"Tell me."

"It was two days before the fire in Beirut."

Shelby fell silent as the elevator lumbered and shuddered into the concrete netherworld of the parking garage. It was hard to figure where we'd go next. We'd create a legend, a myth, excluding the AK-47 but including Dullar's mental collapse: strain of work, fallen hero, etc.

Then we'd set about initiating the cops in Beirut and Paris into the mysteries of his pyromaniac proclivities.

We'd floated the idea with Marcel Duffie that the time for him to seek a buyout might be imminent. A foreign posting for Gloria—somewhere restful like Baghdad or Kabul would do just fine. With no witnesses left, the narrative would be ours to mold.

Just like the Argentine soy vote story.

"I need a favor, Ed" Shelby said as the elevated came to a halt.

"Don't we all, Joe."

"No, seriously. I need you to come with me for an hour or two to meet somebody and tell me what you think. Nothing dangerous. Nothing dodgy. Just a visit to an old lady who hasn't got much time left."

How could I refuse?

We walked past the Black Sun toward the Red Menace—the Alfa Romeo two-seater that had been delivered to the stud farm shortly after the marquee blaze. Over breakfast, Marie-Claire had handed me a set of keys.

"It always was for you," she said. "Whatever you thought."

I lowered the hood, declined Shelby's offer of the leather aviator's helmet, and nudged my new wheels up the corrugated ramp into the daylight. Shelby instructed me to turn toward the Porte de Clignancourt.

CHAPTER TWENTY-FOUR

THE APARTMENT WAS IN ONE OF THOSE NONDESCRIPT SIX-STORY buildings faced in a kind of yellow-brown brick that looks faintly lavatorial to non-French eyes, and maybe to French eyes, too. There was a numeric pad on the door and Shelby seemed familiar with the four-digit entry code. We rode up together in a narrow *ascenseur* with the customary proportions of a vertical casket.

"I took me a while to find her," Shelby said. "When you went through the papers on my desk, I almost got pissed with you. But it was kind of easier for you to discover the story that way rather than for me to have to tell it."

"Is this what you were looking for in Paris?"

"Partly, I guess. Mostly. Apart from Faria. And the job."

I remembered the documents tracing his parentage back to an anonymous father and an actress mother called Jenny Colon—the name that I now saw on the bell push of an apartment door when the elevator bounced to an approximate halt, leaving a sizeable step between it and the landing.

"I had a name and a D.O.B. from the paperwork, so I guess it wasn't too difficult. There was some old stuff—flyers, a couple of theater critics who'd do anything for a free feed, archives, an agent who figured she was eking it out someplace up here. Then just the routine gumshoeing. Pre-Google. Old-school. Asking around. Checking names on doors. I guess it was different for you, Ed. Good old solid Irish American stock. Folks you could rely on."

"You'd better believe it."

He slid a key into the lock and opened the door. A uniformed nurse peered into the half-lit vestibule, hung with old and faded

posters from productions at the Comédie-Française and small theaters in backwater neighborhoods and provincial towns. Her
name—Jenny Colon—never rose much above the level of the supporting players.

"She's expecting you."

"*Merci, madame,*" Shelby said. Then in English he added:
"Found her at one of those nursing agencies. Otherwise Jenny would
be in some kind of institution and she didn't want that. She thinks
the woman's her maid."

From the vestibule, we were shown into an equally dark bedroom furnished in French 1950s one-star style: high bed with brass
bedstead; enormous, dark wardrobe; yellowing wallpaper and lace
drapes that had turned the same color. There was a faint odor of
urine and I noticed a slender line snaking from the covers. Another
tube led from an oxygen tank to her nostrils. A cannula clung to the
string of vein in her arm. A monitor recorded a whispery pulse. On
the nightstand, medication jars and bottles of pills jostled for place
with pots of theatrical makeup that she seemed to have applied herself without the intervention of either the nurse or a mirror. The
result was strangely jaunty—a brightly rouged spot on each cheek
highlighting skin stretched to gossamer, a matching slash of red lip-
stick. Her silver hair had thinned but she had tied it back with a
length of pink silk.

"She thinks it's the Queen of Sheba's waistband," Shelby said,
shaking his head slowly.

Jenny Colon's eyes had once been blue but the color was leeched
and pale, almost white. The bedspread was stained and her hands lay
on it like lifeless claws attached to stick-figure arms blotched with
liver spots. Her breathing came in short gasps.

"The doctor thinks it will be today," the nurse said, as if Jenny
Colon was not there. "He is on the way. And the priest."

"No priest!" She suddenly snapped alive. "You may leave us
now, Fatima. I will ring for you when it is time to bathe and dress
for dinner. Return to your quarters." The nurse rolled her heavy
brown eyes and left, muttering in a language I could not immediately place.

I saw no sign of a bell to ring.

"*Alors, Donald, tu es revenu.* You have returned. Your French was never good," she said. Her residual facial muscles strained in what I thought might have been intended as a smile.

"We go through this every time," Shelby whispered to me. He smiled back.

She looked at me for the first time, the pale disks of her pupils fixing on me almost dismissively.

"*Qui est là, Donald? C'est Monsieur Brewster, n'est-ce pas? Le méchant! Avec son chapeau à deux trous que tu as volé.*"

"*Clay Brewster est mort, Jenny,*" Shelby said.

"*Commes tous les autres. Sauf nous.*"

"*Sauf nous.*"

"Come closer, Donald," she said, still speaking in French. "There is something you must know."

Shelby approached her and sat warily on the bed. She was propped up by some kind of hand-cranked metal frame. Below the worn pastel covers, her emaciated body was so thin it might not have been there. How many stage door Romeos had yearned to share her boudoir with her? How many dreams had there been—never to come true—of standing ovations, roses in the dressing room, romance? Now there was nothing left beyond the illusions, the last curtain call. I found myself welling up and looked away, wondering if I should break with habit and look up my own parents. I realized I no longer knew where they lived. Or *if* they lived. Then I looked at the pain smeared on Shelby's face and figured I would give it a day or two before I resolved to track down the Clancys of Queens, if I ever did. No point rushing things.

Shelby took her hand and looked down at her. For a moment, a shaft of light broke through the curtains, reflected from a mirror in another apartment across a ventilation well, catching them both in profile—the same hawk nose, the same prominent jaw.

"You know, Donald, after you left, I had a son. Did you know?"

Shelby did not reply. Sometimes it is better to be silent and listen if you wish to hear more.

"You say nothing. So you knew, Donald. You knew. What happened? Did some new woman not allow you to look for me? For your son? Donald, I was bad. I was evil."

"*Jamais.*" Never, he said.

"Boys need fathers, too."

"I know, *maman*. I know."

"Why do you call me *maman*?"

Now his eyes had filled with tears and I made to leave the room, but he gestured for me to stay.

"Bear witness, old buddy, bear witness," he said, turning to me. I had never seen his face like that before. I thought to myself that he looked like he had seen a ghost. Then I realized that he was raising his ghosts and laying them all at the same time.

"Yes, I was a bad mother, Donald. I gave him away. Our son. I called him Joseph and Gérard for that silly poet you always loved. What was he called?"

"Gérard de Nerval."

"Joseph Gérard Shelby. And I lost him, Donald."

"No, *maman*, you did not."

"Do not call me *maman*, Donald. I do not deserve the term."

Her eyes closed and her breathing seemed to pause, then restart. The monitor hiccupped and the nurse peered around the door from where she had been listening, I assumed, to every intimate word.

"Donald. I missed you. I missed you and our son. I always wanted to find the little boy. Joseph Gérard. You know I gave him your name: Shelby. Not mine. But I lost him."

"No, you didn't, *maman*. You didn't. You found him."

But she had slipped away. The monitor barely stirred, registering a heartbeat so faint it seemed like a forlorn call intercepted from a distant galaxy. Maybe it already was.

From the vestibule, I heard the nurse murmuring into a cell phone with low urgency.

"No priest," Shelby called out. "My mother did not wish for a priest. She had made her peace."

"So did you, Joe," I said. "So did you."

AFTER JENNY COLON'S FUNERAL, WE FOLLOWED THE TWISTING paths at the Père-Lachaise cemetery that led from her burial site, past the tombs of the prominent people she would once have cast as her natural counterparts elsewhere in the artistic pantheon—Oscar Wilde, Marcel Proust and all the others. We skirted the crematorium whose soaring chimneys flanking the dome reminded me uncannily of a mosque somewhere in Turkey or Egypt—another one-way voyage to the Orient. Inevitably, our path led to the shaded bowers where—opposite the grave of Honoré de Balzac with its imposing bust of the novelist—a slender column, a sort of obelisk crowned by what might be an overflowing urn, is inscribed: "À Gérard de Nerval."

Nerval was born in 1808 and died in 1855, but these bookends of a life are not inscribed on the gray stone. Indeed it has always been far from clear to me whether this place was a tomb, complete with remains, DNA, etc., or simply a memorial, placed there by his admirers after his tragic death in the Rue de la Vieille-Lanterne, suspended from the Queen of Sheba's waistband. So much of what I know of the poet's life is hearsay, gossip, hand-me-down myth. But that has not been important. What has guided me has been the work, the canon, the oeuvre. The dark loss and longing of "El Desdichado" was my loss. His yearning for the unattainable star was my quest, too. He lived in a world that became mine, where the lines blur, between dream and reality, where love is something lost and never refound, where there are fires and betrayal. Of course, you can follow his biography—in and out of asylums, to and fro between sanity and madness—and conclude that his work is no more than a mirror of that clinical trail. But it is much more. Nerval turned words into magic spells, waves of a literary wand, hocus-pocus constructions that conjured feeling from souls thought doomed and barren. If he was the Prince of Aquitaine, so was I. The black sun doused my heart, too, in its icy light. On his last outing, on that January night in Paris, he told his aunt, with whom he had been living, not to wait up for him "for the night will be black and white." My life, too, has veered between chromatic and other extremes.

Elvire Récamier took my hand as we approached Nerval's monument along the gravel path. I had not trusted myself to visit the memorial before, and it was easy to stray off course among the homes of the dead in their neat, ordered rows, like macabre bathing huts for the changes of attire required on the banks of the Styx.

I had asked Ed Clancy and his wife, Marie-Claire Risen, to join us, because he had been dragged through so much at my side. Since he took over the executive editorship of the *Paris Star*, he had become if anything, more dyspeptic. But he had kept me on as a columnist with a generous traveling budget "for as long as you want it, old buddy."

Elvire disentangled her hand from mine, prancing back and forth with her battered Leica, the brass showing through the black paint. She snapped me and Clancy and Marie-Claire and the tombs and Balzac and the columns. And she caught forever—on celluloid black-and-white Tri-X Pan 400 ASA film, for God's sake—the moment when I wrapped my old volumes of Nerval in weapons-grade waxed paper (all except for a flimsy paper copy of *Les Chimères*,) dug a shallow trench amid the deeper graves, and left the almost-complete works with their terminal bullet as close as I could to the imagined feet of the certain master, murmuring, by way of incantation, "'*Je suis le Ténébreux, – le Veuf, – l'Inconsolé—* '"

The hallowed words. Now redeemed.

"I sure could use a drink," Ed Clancy said.

endit

Paris, May 2011.

ACKNOWLEDGMENTS

I WROTE THIS BOOK IN PARIS AND I WOULD NOT HAVE BEEN ABLE TO explore the city if it had not been for Bill Keller, the Executive Editor of *The New York Times*, who sent me here, and Alison Smale and Marty Gottlieb from *The International Herald Tribune* who put a professional roof over my head. My thanks to all of them.

I owe a huge debt of gratitude to my friend Richard Berry, a masthead editor at the *Herald Tribune*, who spotted stories I did not, deftly erased errors before they could do harm and kept our operation honest. He gave wise advice, made funny jokes, took time to read the manuscript of this book out of hours and, in the office, remained *il miglior fabbro.*

Yet again, my wife, Sue Cullinan, showed patience and forbearance for my mental absences as I worked on the book, as did my daughters. I am perennially grateful to them for indulging me.

At Inkwell Management in New York, Michael Carlisle was agent, friend and advisor, and I am grateful to Peter Mayer and The Overlook Press in New York for his trust and counsel and to Stephanie Gorton for shepherding the project to fruition.

—ALAN COWELL
Paris, May 2011.